THE GREATEST GIFT

Danny Leigh was born in 1972, *The Greatest Gift* is his first novel.

The Greatest Gift

DANNY LEIGH

faber and faber

First published in 2004
by Faber and Faber Limited
3 Queen Square London WC1N 3AU
This paperback edition first published in 2005

Typeset by Faber and Faber Limited
Printed in England by Mackays of Chatham, plc

The right of Danny Leigh to be identified as author of this work
has been asserted in accordance with Section 77 of the Copyright,
Designs and Patents Act 1988

A CIP record for this book
is available from the British Library

ISBN 0–571–21506–8

2 4 6 8 10 9 7 5 3 1

To Lucy

The Beat of a Hummingbird's Wing

This is how it ends.

Nine floors up and looking down. Nine floors up and looking down, and feeling weak, and asking whether this is really where you want to be.

Step one.

And then you ask some more.

How long's this going to take? You know, the whole process. The whole transaction. From roof to ground.

From start to finish.

Now I'm dancing.

Waltzing toward.

One. Two. Three.

Shimmy to the side.

There's a cinderblock kerb around and ahead. Twelve, fourteen inches tops. And this underfoot, like rubber, asphalt, carpet, all at once. Gives like a new trampoline.

Next, up.

Twelve, fourteen inches tops.

I let myself teeter, just a little, let my weight take me further, just a touch, then deliver me back on to my heels.

When you've lost two pints of blood in a morning, it's easy to go with the flow. Even the breeze makes it an adventure.

Eyes rolling in my head. Whisper in my ear and I'm gone.

I say lost.

But lost – to have parted with through theft, accident or negligence – isn't what it was.

It wasn't theft. Wasn't an accident.

Certainly wasn't negligence.

There's blood on my sleeve. Just a drop, soaking through:

a pinprick on a gauze of cream cotton. Too small to even see the scab.

That's what happens.

Straighten my back, look down again. This time it's right there, up close and personal. I move from the left, across all the places I can recognise:

Bethune Street and Scala. DeKalb Ave. Praça de República. Michurnisky Prospekt. Beverly Boulevard. Shinjuku-ku. Goodge Street. Viale Castro Pretorio.

All mine.

The people in a huddle on the pavement, I take their pain, their joy, their absolute indifference, and I plug right in. Let them course through me, and me through them. One big happy family.

And I still don't know how long this is going to take.

Shuffle to my mark. It's almost imperceptible, the way I'm moving.

I'm still moving.

The arch of my left foot floats in nothing, nine floors up. Then the rest. My right's solid. That's quality of grip. The handiwork of children. These soles were made for anything, and used for nothing.

Til now.

A pirouette? Just a small one. Nothing vulgar. A quick three-sixty.

To business.

I'm Harry Truman, 6 August 1945, setting loose Fat Man and Little Boy. I'm Shi Huang, throwing another copy of Confucius on the bonfire. I'm Ben Johnson, Seoul '88, waiting for the starter's gun, scleras yellow from the steroids.

I'm Matthew Viss, and I'm here to wipe the lot. Beauty, hope and honesty: erase, delete, destroy.

You know, right this moment there's hospitals itching to claim your lungs.

You can help the sick to breathe.

It's 12.15. My right foot's on tip-toes.

4

How long's this going to take?

I close my eyes and throw my shoulders forward. Leave this city rooftop and with it all I've ever known, or ever will.

A simple incline of the body. Then it's done.

It's strange. For the longest time, I'm just not falling. I'm hanging. Undecided. Unresolved. Head slanted to the sky, feet so close to the edge I could limber out my calves and find myself back on something solid. Rewind. As if I never left. And this goes on for what seems like hours.

Of course, strictly speaking, it barely goes on at all. The beat of a hummingbird's wing. One frame in a movie that never ends.

Til the point at which I am falling, a vision of grace and economy, gently fluttering to earth, tissue paper thrown from a moving car.

Right now, I'm focused past my shoulder, over to the loft on the ninth floor of the building, the desert of blonde pine you pass through on your way to the roof. Right now, there's nothing in it apart from trunks and boxes. I have a key. I pay to keep my stuff there.

Sometimes, on my way through, I'll run into Carl. I don't remember his surname. I don't remember asking. Carl is – and this makes me laugh, hard – our concierge. Mine and the other tenants'. For the title, and whatever meagre, by-the-hour salary he gets, Carl attends our every need. Within reason.

Within reason is important here. Within reason is what means nothing beyond sorting our mail and maintaining a log of visitors. Within reason is why Carl spends his after-noons watching daytime TV while pipes clank and hallways go unlit. That is, when he's not in the loft.

I honestly have no idea what he does there. I know he sits a lot. That's what he's doing whenever I see him. Obviously, he doesn't stick around. The moment I walk in he's out the door, fast, giving me the same blank, embittered glower he gives me when he looks up from the TV and says, Hello, Mr Viss, or Goodnight, Mr Viss. Like I'm the one responsible. Who made his life what it is, or isn't.

And then he's gone, a stooping blur of liver spots and resentment.

You know, it's possible to donate your skin after your death. They use it for grafts. They peel away the very thinnest layer with a dermatome. Usually, it comes from the back, or the leg. Then they give it to burns victims.

When you register as a donor, you get a plastic card featuring two impressionist figures holding hands in front of a grassy knoll. One of them's surrounded by a shimmering white aura. That's you. You're both smiling.

Anyway, when I look over, Carl's not there.

What I'm wondering is if they've got what I sent them. Blood, mine. Whole, AB positive. Red cells, white cells, platelets, plasma. The various products thereof.

I've been giving blood for twelve months. After a while, you start keeping track. Enjoy the sense of oneness.

After a while, you're leaving sweat trails at the gym so the next sculpted young thing on the StairMaster leaves with you all over them. Rubbing the sleep from your eyes right before a handshake. Combing your hair on rush-hour trains. Crying into your co-workers' drinks. That's what happens.

It starts at a clinic with a tube in your arm, thinking of all the good you're doing. Then you're jumping off nine-storey apartment blocks.

This is how it ends.

Usually, by this time of day, I'd be at work. Usually, I'd have dealt with a dozen clients by now. Legs tucked under me in my cream cotton shirt and charcoal ground silk bow tie in a pristine space in a purpose-built complex on the corner of Pearl Street and Creed.

Because I, like Carl, am a concierge.

Of course, neither of us is a concierge in the popular sense of the word. We don't show patrons to tables in exclusive restaurants, or order bellboys to carry bags through the mar-bled lobbies of hotels. And I'm not even a concierge in the definitive sense (*noun.* a caretaker of a block of flats, hostelry, etc., esp. one who lives on the premises). In that sense, Carl is more concierge than I. In a real sense, I'm more of a concierge than that desiccated flunky could ever be.

I work for The Greatest Gift. The greatest gift is time. The Greatest Gift is, therefore, a company hired by other compa-nies to help their employees manage time. On the spectrum of executive perks, you'll find us somewhere between pension plans and in-house shiatsus.

And usually, I'd have dealt with a dozen clients by now.

How may I be of service?

That's me, answering the phone.

The Greatest Gift, Matthew Viss speaking. How may I be of service?

But anyway, that stuff, it's not important. Not now. None of it.

What's important is Alice's birthday.

Alice is my daughter. My only child. Tomorrow is her birthday.

Once, a year ago, I forgot the date. Forgot my daughter. It clean escaped me. And then I lost her.

Lost, as in negligence.

And that is why this had to be. The blood, the jumping. I had to win her back. To put things right. To be her hero.

Tomorrow is her birthday. I got her a card. One day, when she's older, I hope her mother will explain this. And when she does, she does it kindly.

Of the many great holes offered by the Avelden Country Club's prize-winning golf course, the fifth is Jonah Hoffman's favourite. It always has been. A long par three, demanding sturdy handling up a dog-leg fairway, it makes him happy like nothing else. And he stands before the fifth hole now, inspecting the contents of his bag, leather, spotless. It is 12.15 p.m.

Four, he says, and the caddy passes Jonah a club from the handmade set he bought last Christmas. The company that makes them trades under the slogan Because You're Not Like Everyone Else. Jonah agrees. He isn't. He could never go back to the pro stores now, not having experienced the give of the pre-heated carbon steel, perfectly tailored to his grip, or the classic feel of the oversized graphite head, delivered just as he asked.

Jonah loves these clubs, and he loves this course. He loves the framing of the seasoned oaks and the contours of the natural valleys, the bent grass on the greens and the fairways' winter rye, the frequent punctuation of bunkers and water hazards. The course, along with the rest of the Avelden, was built at the start of the 1960s, designed by men with oil-slick hair and a hard-wired terror of distant ideologies. Yet when he reaches the fifth hole, it feels like this was here for ever. And here, the follies of the world are immaterial. Wars could rage and pandemics flourish, but Jonah would be free of it all, insulated, divine.

Settling to his club, he splays his legs. Today, on this crisp spring morning, he can barely contain his vitality. A dedicated golfer should be fit, trim, discreetly in shape. He is. Looking good, Jonah. How old are you again? That's what they say in the bar at the Avelden, with such flimsy bonhomie he can almost touch their envy. When he consults a mirror, however harshly lit, he still likes the results.

The grass on the fairway seems luminous, glimmering. As if poised to take off. So few people will ever see this, he thinks. While they sit picking at their miseries, he's out here, his club a mallet and a scalpel, exercising total control over something half the size of his spleen, in a space as big as most towns. He doesn't care that the caddy will be his only witness. In fact, he prefers it that way. Golf, he believes, is, or should be, a solitary pursuit. He never warmed to team sports and even tennis bores him now, its memory tarnished by too many failed doubles partners.

And this is beautiful. The fifth hole at the Avelden, with the greens aerated and the summer hordes far off. Here, alone with his handmade clubs, Jonah Hoffman truly knows serenity.

8

For just a moment he thinks he tastes salt in the air. But none of that can touch him here. Left arm thrown across his chest, he readies his shot.

The company prospectus gets distributed at business conferences. Right now, there's a copy on my kitchen table.

The first time I met Jonah Hoffman, I pulled it from my bag to show him. He told me he'd already seen it, and we kept on with our business. I think of Jonah now, and it makes me flinch inside.

I know a lot of the prospectus verbatim.

On the first page, there's a picture of an ornate grandfather clock and the question Why Choose The Greatest Gift?

Underneath is text. The text explains the premise of The Greatest Gift.

Near the bottom of the first page, there's a photo of the staff. I'm not in it. It was taken right before I got my job. Everyone's dressed in their cream cotton shirts. The men are wearing their charcoal bow ties. They're all smiling. The caption says:

Meet The Greatest Gift's dedicated team of Guy and Gal Fridays. They'll handle the little details – so your employees can focus on the real challenges.

Usually, the real challenges involve producing reports that no one reads and abusing some temp receptionist. The little details are life. The prospectus doesn't mention that.

Ask me what I do, exactly, and I'll tell you. I do everything. We do anything. I am a fairy godmother in a ground silk dickie bow. We are a management tool made up to look like God.

Anyway, I'm not there now.

Right now I'm somewhere else entirely, somewhere closer to roof than ground, with a single drop of blood soaking through my cream cotton shirt. And if he hasn't done so already, Jonah Hoffman will shortly make a call to The Greatest Gift from the driver's seat of a black BMW, demanding to know where the hell I am.

The Greatest Gift. How may I be of service?

Where the hell is Matthew Viss? Who's going to book my table at Marlowe's? Pick up my favourite shampoo? Take care of my gingko?

This is what kills me.

I should have been a nurse. Only I can't stand hospitals.

When you start doing a job like this, you begin to see the people you're working for as children. You're arranging payment on a CEO's pool-cleaning bill, and all you can picture is a boy with gap teeth, throwing himself into dappled water on a halcyon June morning. You know, like on Super-8.

Or you're organising some marketing guru's dinner function at her townhouse, and all you can think of is a little girl in her favourite party dress, handing cake to her friends on paper plates. And they're all smiling.

Thing is, after a while, you have to stop thinking like that. You keep finding yourself in tears. Great, authentic saline tears.

After that, it's like you're looking through a window at night, except all the lights are on inside. So the harder you look, and the closer you get to the glass, the more the only thing you can possibly see is you, squinting dimly at your own reflection. And all anyone outside can see is you. Squinting dimly at your own reflection.

Right now, I'm falling.

First, if necessary, you cut the paper down to size. Then lay the gift in the centre of the sheet. Next, fold the two outer edges of the sheet across the gift, with an overlap of maybe half an inch. Take a strip of tape, nothing more than you might actually need, and attach it over the join, lengthways.

Eleanor sits cross-legged on the floor, surrounded by paper and presents. Seven gifts, modest but expertly chosen, to be opened tomorrow on her daughter's birthday. One for every year.

Stretching her right leg out in front of her, she stares at the glossy coils of gift wrap. The roll she fixes on is covered with garlands of balloons, each encircling a teddy bear in a conical hat, tugging a cake on a skateboard. With his spare paw, he – because somehow he looks like a he – holds a trumpet up to his lips.

Do bears even have lips? This, beyond the skateboard and hat and appropriation of opposable thumbs, troubles her. Lips? Surely they couldn't have lips? Eleanor sighs, a deep, prolonged encapsulation. She holds a good degree, is the head of an infants' school that ambitious parents clamour over, and these are the questions that play on her mind.

The largest of the gifts is an art activity centre. Inside its elaborate packaging lies a spectrum of felt pens, with a colouring book full of albino rainbows. She takes the paper with the bear, turns it print side down, lays the box in the middle.

To Eleanor, the absence of ponies from the wrapping is a source of continued relief. Ponies, she feels, are the beginning. The start of the road that leads to clothes, ever more trying in cost and design, and then to cosmetics, til finally you don't know the names of their friends or what they do in the evenings. The death of childhood, ritually mapped in displays of parental affection.

The card from Matthew to Alice is in her bedroom. Torn from having been jammed through the door. His car remains outside, skewed at the most unlikely of angles. She wonders who to call to have it moved. All she asks is that he doesn't show up for the party. Doesn't burst inside with the house full of Alice's classmates. She can deal with his fatherhood by proxy. Just doesn't want it in person.

Last week she saw him, for the first time in a year. Afterward, she called her lawyer. Now there are divorce forms in her bedside drawer, out of sight of Alice along with the leaflets that accompanied them. Dry How To's with functional titles: Parenting And Divorce, Fair Spousal Alimony. Their presence in the house makes her feel jittery. Why they should is a mystery. Twelve months on, this is just loose ends. A belated closure. She could, with one calm stretch of the imagination, already be widowed.

To her family, colleagues, the other mothers at her daughter's school, she is, exclusively, Eleanor Carlin. No one, bar junk-mail databases and possibly her husband, thinks of her as Eleanor Viss. Viss is gone. Viss is past.

She folds the edges of the paper across, joins them with a strip of tape. Takes the first two corners, folds them into a triangle. Then folds that triangle down.

The doorbell hasn't rung yet. She's been expecting it all day. The doorbell will ring, and a courier will be outside with a sack, stepping impatiently from foot to foot. And she'll go to the door, and the courier will peer at his or her clipboard and look up at Eleanor, and say in a tone of massive, cosmic indifference:

Miss Viss? Miss Alice Viss?

And inside the sack will be presents, lavish, grandiose, thoughtless, inappropriate. Products of guilt and abandonment.

Turning the box, she takes the remaining two corners of the paper and folds them into another triangle.

It's better, she feels, that she does this now. Came home in her lunch break to prepare things. If she waits til evening then Alice will see her, will find a way to glimpse the surprises designed for tomorrow. This is the custom of girls her age. Six, so very nearly seven, brazenly conscious of some of what a birthday means – gift wrap and ice cream – yet still unknowing of the way in which one will lead on to another, coolly transporting her through now unimaginable numbers, ages, experience. And that, at a certain point in this process, she will, as Eleanor has, begin to measure time not in her own birthdays – which will slowly have ceased to be noteworthy – but in her children's. And then will come ponies, and clothes, and cosmetics.

It's a quarter past twelve already. She stares at the wrapping, the bear with the trumpet, and tries not to dwell on the infinite sadness about to engulf her.

In the Spring of Last Year

Falling slow. But still falling.

Obviously, I know enough basic physics to expect some kind of exponential quickening, somewhere between here and there. It's just not made itself apparent yet. In the meanwhile, there's always giving blood.

I first gave blood last spring.

I was watching TV in the apartment I'd moved into four weeks previously, a sunlit one-bedroom in a portered block on Bethune and Scala. The area, the agent said, was coming up. I was lucky to get in here. Now there were young artists and scurrying professionals among the single mothers and first generation immigrants, gyms and coffee shops amid the unfranchised burger bars and cut-price supermarkets.

Eight weeks after moving in, I still double-took when I walked in the door. Like I had no recollection of what this place was, or why I might be here. Although the view from my living room gave me a local panorama, I truly felt there was nothing beyond these walls. That if I should leave here, only rubble and space would be waiting. As if some terrible apocalypse had swept it all away, and I was the last man on earth, bunkered. The curator, with his totems.

For hours, I'd been crouched on the floor, pretending I was getting things done. Dust collected in the soft pink corners of my eyes. Spry, productive bursts of motion dwindled to inertia. Unpacked boxes everywhere, scattered remnants of former lives spilling out of plastic bags.

I owned too much. That's what happens. And, in that moment, none of it had anything to do with me. So all you want is something known. A dab of reassurance to soothe away the flux.

15

I took a bath, the way I always took a bath. Hot water, too hot to hold your finger under for longer than it takes the nerve endings to register. Scalding, cauterising. Let that run a while, til the whole room fills with steam. Then cold. Arctic, numbing cold, together with the hot. Let the water rise. No foam. No scent. Set a candle by the side, turn out the light. The way I always did.

I never took showers. Somehow, they always seemed too aggressive. A bath left me tranquil. Lying rapt in my own detritus.

The tub here was narrower than I was used to, and at least a foot shorter. My elbows flapped when I reached forward, knees clattered leaning back. But you make the best of what you have. After a few minutes, scrubbing, soaping, waiting to prune, it felt just like old times. Nostalgia dictated I shave.

Rather than step out and do it at the sink, I shave in the tub. Ask me now and I'd be lost as to why. It's just the way it's always been. Work up a lather. Rinse my hands in my bath. Run the hot tap again, just for the razor.

I shave with a Hercules III. A modern classic in grooming design, with a slinky but substantial rubberised handle and three aligned blades that glide and hug where others yank and drag. Eleanor, my wife, used to borrow it to shave her legs. I didn't mind. I was happy to share. In the two years since buying the Hercules, I hadn't cut myself once.

That night, I sliced myself wide open, a fine, deep sliver running square across my jawline.

At first, I didn't notice. That's the way it is with shaving cuts. You never notice til you see the blood. That night, I only saw the blood once I'd finished with the razor and plunged my head into the bathwater, which I know is unhygienic, but like I say, old habits and so on. The sting came immediately. I hauled myself back up, shaking like a dog. Sure enough, when I focused, there was a small red billow in the water.

I checked the Hercules' lubricant strip for a sign the blades had dulled. They were keen as always. It didn't make sense.

Pulling the plug with a reflexive grunt, I clambered out. Sopped on the linoleum in front of the mirror.

Usually, my first instinct when confronted with my own reflection was to grimace and correct my posture, in the fond conviction I would, from now on, always stand like this. That night, all I saw was the thin laceration across my face, the blood oozing from it. A nick, a trickle. Sweet cherry syrup, glooping over vanilla ice cream.

Feet apart, water puddling round them, all I could do was stare. Like I didn't quite recognise the vision in front of me, staring back in mutual bafflement.

Sorry, have we met?

The blood ran down toward my chin. Leaning in, peering ahead, fingers groping, I reached up to the cabinet for a bottle of antiseptic. Then cotton wool. A slop from the bottle onto the swab. Then onto my face. The fibres stuck to my jaw, Christmas white and downy. The blood wouldn't stop.

With my hair still wet, I dried my torso and legs, pulled on the calf-length terry robe my wife once bought me. My initials, sewn into the breast in navy thread. The M was fraying.

Cotton wool pressed to my face, I padded back into the living room. That morning's newspaper sat unread and precarious on the arm of the one chair I'd brought with me. I never got round to buying furniture. Were they to visit my apartment now, people might think it chicly ascetic. Deliberate. They'd be wrong.

Lolling in my chair, I grabbed the paper. Skipped directly to the back. There, tucked neatly in a self-contained subsection, were the personal and small ads. Lovers sought, boot sales announced. The minutiae. Text-heavy squares, idly compiled with out-dated typefaces and blurry portraits, wedged tight together.

I'd flicked through these pages a thousand times before. This was the first time I'd read them.

It was the death notices that grabbed my attention. Little boxes full of dread and wonder. Most were in clusters, multiple boxes for single passings, families and friends united in grief. Their inarticulate stumble clean breaking you apart.

My head swam. What could they mean? Would I even merit this? A halting epitaph on a tiny paper tombstone, paid for by the word and dictated in sobs to a bored telesales assistant with ninety words per minute and their mind on other things.

Can you spell that out for me?

V for Victory, I, double S . . . No, S.

Who would do that for me?

I felt the blood drip, and reached up to my face at the exact moment I realised my fingers were covered in newsprint.

I'd left the TV on the whole time I was in the bathroom. The last time I'd looked, a tanned and chiselled anchorman was presenting the news. Now, there were ads. Toothpaste, chocolate, alcohol, cars. Then something else entirely.

A busy city hospital and a female paramedic calmly steering a patient inside, the camera fixed on her for just a moment longer than you might expect, til she looked straight at the camera as if only just noting its presence. And said, like in passing:

I saved somebody's life today.

Then a lifeguard, strolling bronzed and thick-limbed down clean white sands. And he too glanced into the camera before announcing that:

I saved somebody's life today.

Of course, at this stage, stripped of further context, I had no idea what any of this meant. What these people represented, what they could be selling.

A smartly dressed black woman in her mid-thirties looked up from a desk, and a fiftyish white man at a potter's wheel did the same, and each of them said:

I saved somebody's life today.

As, apparently, had a teenage girl in a college library, a cheerful bus driver, a suited businessman wading through flip charts, a grey-haired woman doing yoga.

Then a brisk reprise through each of their faces as their disembodied voices rang across the soundtrack, flowing into one like a choral round.

I give blood. I give blood. Give I give blood I give give I give blood.

Til the screen dissolved to black again and a single male voice-over explained that thousands of operations both routine and emergency were carried out every day, and none would be possible without the help of blood donors. Their small but vital acts of kindness.

And cut back to the paramedic, who looked up again like she'd only just realised the camera was still there, and she said:

It's up to you.

I sat with my robe wide open and blood running onto my chest, smelling of newsprint and disinfectant amid the hard, defiant proof of transience. Then a phone number came up on screen.

It was that simple. Into the light. I fell asleep with the TV on and when I woke the next day the blood had dried on my face.

One week later, I was bouncing out of the rain and through the automatic doors of a glass-fronted clinic on Mortimer and Upas.

Swish. Swish.

Hello. My name's Matthew Viss. I'm interested in giving blood.

No. Make that I'd *like* to give blood. I *want* to give blood.

And the receptionist with her orange scrunchy buried in her frizz smiled and said:

OK, that's great. I'm Carmen. Can I ask if you've had breakfast?

Ah . . . yes. I have. Definitely . . . had breakfast.

For some reason, I was prevaricating. I'd absolutely had breakfast. There was no call for hesitancy.

OK! Great. So, here's some –

Sorry . . . why do you want to know if I've had breakfast?

She's just this side of condescending.

Because you can't give blood on an empty stomach.

Right.

She turned and produced a pale green form, then turned back, held it out to me.

So, here's the paperwork. If you could just take a seat and fill this in, we can –

(her inflection lurching into that quote unquote cadence people use when they're saying something twee, as if to excuse their not saying something else)

– get right on with the show.

And I thanked her, took the form. Sat adjacent to her desk and five feet back on the scuffed seat of a moulded plastic chair.

That's what happens. The first time you give blood, you fill in the pale green form, scored with cavities of white space in which to give the answers that gauge your suitability as a donor. Right underneath where you write your name and address in blue ink and block capitals, you guarantee that:

No, neither you or your partner are HIV+. No, you have never worked as a prostitute. No, you have never injected drugs (including steroids) or the extract of human pituitary gland. You have never been sexually active in Central or South America, or taken aspirin in the last three days.

There are other criteria. These are the ones I remember. Filling in the form takes three minutes, give or take. Then it's on with the show.

Uh, hi . . . I think I'm finished.

The receptionist smiled again, mechanically this time, and took the form.

Great! So if you want to have a seat, someone'll . . .

And she trailed off, as if she'd said whatever it is she was going to say so many times even a stranger would know how it ends.

I sat back down, the receptionist tagging my form to a transcription stand next to her keyboard. Began typing out everything I'd just written in blue ink and block capitals.

There was nothing on the walls to suggest the function of this place. No enthusiastic posters featuring soulful oncologists or ardent paediatricians to thank you for your small act of kindness. Just the receptionist blankly informing a database that no, Matthew Viss has never injected extract of human pituitary gland, and an MDF coffee table sprinkled with last winter's lifestyle magazines.

Mortimer and Upas, with the rain drumming skittishly outside. Just a waiting room like any other. You could be a dental emergency, your rotten stab more insistent by the second, or poised to take your driving test.

Then a doctor, I think, came buzzing absentmindedly from an office that I hadn't even realised was there. The receptionist stopped typing with a flourish.

All done, she said, removing my form from the stand and handing it to the I think doctor. He thanked her without eye contact.

Mr Viss?

And I followed the doctor past another, smaller MDF table, surrounded by chairs and supporting a faux-wicker basket, past a young brunette woman who stood behind a counter to the side. I moved beyond all this without paying much attention, and on through to the office that I hadn't even realised was there. An ill-lit off-white box with more blank walls.

He began reading every last question on the form again –

Just checking, Mr Viss

– as if I couldn't quite be trusted first time round.

And this took maybe ten minutes. Because whereas before I was simply skim-reading the questions and writing yes or no in blue ink and block capitals, now I was listening to the doctor asking me the questions in his self-consciously ponderous manner, then verbally telling him yes or no. And I was giving my verbal answers more consideration, and therefore time, than I did my written ones – presumably out of some weird, neurotic impulse to appear like a reliable, everyday kind of guy in front of him – and he was then checking my verbal replies against my written ones. So basically the entire process tripled in duration.

Eventually, the doctor asked me to hold out my right-hand index finger. He took a needle – a regular, sewing-kit needle – and pressed into the fleshy pad til it released a single viscous bead.

This is the iron test. To see if I had enough iron in my blood to qualify as a donor.

The doctor held my bleeding fingertip over a test tube full of clear, watery liquid, and waited for a drop to fall.

If the red turns green, and you neither vomit nor faint in the next two minutes, you're in. Welcome to the club.

You might think the first time you give blood they make a fuss of you. Make you feel important. Think again.

Soon I'd seen the last of the doctor. He ushered me outside his disregarded office with a casual smear of antiseptic held in place with a Band-Aid.

Then came the crux. The what we're here for.

A dirty splatter on fine Italian leather. Heavy brown churn over the supple black calf-skin of Jonah Hoffman's right shoe, imported at fearsome cost from a rustic, mountain-top tannery, hand-stained, hung to breathe, now caked in native mud.

Barely audible, strictly to himself, he mutters dark oaths and foul profanities. This, the wide expanse of gravel drive and tended garden, is Jonah's home, or at least its outermost boundary. Where, a moment ago, he slipped in the drizzle, turning one ankle over on its side before, in the attempt to steady himself, his other foot came to rest a yard off the path, landing flat and weighted on the ground beside. His lawn, typically manicured, swiftly turning to marsh.

He feels a soaking in the shoe's bespoke lining. Lifting his leg to correct himself, the arch of his foot contracts, insole filling with seepage, morgue cold against his skin.

It is 8.14 a.m. A peevish squint up at the house, its high, pin-bright windows, their curtains drawn, then back around to the end of the drive, still a dozen sodden steps away. A sombre foreign man in canvas overalls hunches with a spade at the gravel border, forehead damp with rain and sweat.

In theory, Jonah is witnessing the construction of a security fence around his property. It will, in time, bristle with surveillance, pitiless, intractable.

Now, however, an hour since a white mini-van holding five burly personnel pulled up in a screeching flurry, there is simply this one man, toiling in the morning rain. Digging holes for the posts, his workmates huddled toasty in their vehicle. His name escapes Jonah. He suspects he should remember it. This man with the spade is the cousin, or perhaps the brother, of the Hoffman family maid. The security firm hired to build the fence employs the cousin of the maid. It was on her recommendation – or rather because of her ceaseless pleading to Jonah's wife Christina – that the contract was awarded.

They, Christina said, the company that employ the cousin of the maid, have been having a terrible time of it lately. A gesture, Christina said. If you'd just seen her expression when she asked.

So here they are, the cousin or the brother of the Hoffman family maid, glumly digging while Jonah watches, damp and rooted. He stares back at the house, its architects' graces, seamless gutters, pale stone, then at his driveway, gardens, fountain, guest cottage, wedding ring, four round buttons on the cuffs of his suit jacket, the glinting handle of his car's right-side passenger door.

From nowhere, he feels an urge to grab this man, shake him til he sees, make him gape and genuflect. Instead, he curls his toes inside the wet, and scowls, confounded. A single watery clot has penetrated the welt at the back of his shoe, irreparably damaging the coarse thread binding the heel. Jonah does not know this yet. It is 8.16 a.m., and the day yawns out before him.

My orderly, a stringbean white guy with blond hair like a rag doll and shocking parchment eye bags, was called William.

His name was printed on an oblong tag, pinned to the breast pocket of the short-sleeved tunic he wore over a faded sweat-shirt.

Standing in front of me, holding the receptionist's transcript of my pale green form, he vaguely looked me up and down.

Hi, he said, each syllable followed by the softest clicking in his throat. I'm *click* Will *click* Yam *click*. If *click* you'll *click* come *click* with *click* me *click*.

He led with his shoulder through a heavy set of double doors into a smooth-floored barracks full of brown leather examination beds five feet off the ground, where nurses and orderlies of both sexes giggled and whispered in the far corner. The walls were still bare. I headed for the bed nearest to the door.

Sitting upright, I dangled my legs where the ground should have been, madly kicking back and forth like a kid on a swing. William *clicked* behind me.

There was something exotic about his constant palatal gabbling. Not unpleasant. Just alien. Crickets on a balmy night.

Do you want to take off your jacket? he asked.

Uh . . . no. I'm fine.

Well, you'll need to. So we can strap you up.

I pulled off my windcheater and handed it to William. Then I thanked him. He left me in my T-shirt, hung my jacket on one of a row of hooks by the door.

OK . . . So, do you want to lie down?

I did as I was asked.

You always forget how helpless you are when you're prostrate. How vulnerable you are to pretty much everything. In a token display of mobility, I craned my neck away from the door. All I could see was that the brown leather on the far side of the bed had partially worn out, leaving a peekaboo gash of dirty foam. In the corner, one of the nurses, a woman with a holiday-fresh tan and what looked like a friendly disposition, peeled away from the group and out through the double doors.

William stared at my pale green form.

OK, Mr Viss, he said. So, neither you or your partner are HIV+?

(This again?)

No.

And you're not currently using drugs?

(This again.)

No . . . I'm not.

Including steroids?

Yes. No steroids. Do I look that buff?

I tried to make it sound jovial. William looked up, impassive.

We just need to make sure you're not in any high-risk category.

And he stepped away. To have kept him in view, I would have had to sit up, straight-backed and gawping. Somehow, it didn't seem appropriate. Confining myself to a spastic flick of the head back over toward the door, I watched as the friendly nurse returned, William beside her. Now my form was gone and in its place he held a wide, velcro-covered cuff. The kind they use to test your blood pressure.

Which arm would you like to use? he said.

I assessed the relative merits and perils.

The left.

He fixed the velcro tight around my bicep, tying off the circulation like I'd only ever seen in films. Then he handed me the ball. The ball, I wasn't expecting.

It was rubber, about the size of a tangerine. The kind of thing people with dogs keep around the house for games of fetch. I had no idea what to say.

You clench it, William told me. You clench it to raise the veins.

So I took it in the palm of my left hand, closed my fingers round it. Made a fist. Sure enough, a stripe of blue half an inch below the crease of my elbow came pounding vehemently to life. There was pride in my eyes when I looked back up.

OK, Mr Viss, if you want to keep that up, I'll get you . . . organised.

Letting my head loll backward, facing the ceiling, I did as I was asked. Clench. Unclench. Clench. Unclench. Thinking of nothing but the whitening of my knuckles and the pulse in my arm.

By the time William returned, the vein was throbbing. And I felt exhilarated. Set for one durable moment of virtue.

Carrying a clear plastic medical baggie fitted with an IV, he took three loping steps behind the bed where, I assumed, he fixed it to a drip stand.

When you give blood, you can't watch the bag filling up. It's a wholly disassociated process. Lying flat, you'd have to be able to turn your head 180 degrees to see it. You can't even see the blood chugging out of your arm, because they trail the drip line along the side of the bed until it's past your line of vision.

That's exactly what William did. After he got the IV into me.

This might sting, he said, taking the ball from my hand.

I didn't look. There was a scratch, a flea bite, then the briefest pinch of discomfort. I found my lips had pursed. Glancing down, the nozzle of the IV tube was hanging from my arm, across which William had taped a sliver of lint.

They hadn't shown anyone actually giving blood on the commercial.

OK? William said. Comfortable?

Yeah, I said. It's fine.

Which was at least half true. It wasn't not fine in the way I'd expected. There was no searing pain. It just felt stiff. As if someone was taking every capillary in my left arm and carefully starching it. Like if I bent my elbow joint upward, the surrounding muscles would shudder and tear away.

That was how it felt for the next ten minutes. Ten vacant minutes in which a pint of my blood slowly percolated through the IV tube and into the clear plastic baggie, neither of which I could see, for later use in life-saving operations and routine though no less essential surgeries. A small act of kindness. I closed my eyes and focused on the rhythm in my arm. Then William.

How you doing?

It seemed like a genuine question.

I'm OK. I mean, it's a little . . . stiff at the elbow.

Right, he said, pulling off the lint and taking out my IV cord, then swabbing up the excess and sticking a Band-Aid over the puncture. Well, it's nothing to worry about. It's just the pressure. Everyone gets it. Do you want to try sitting up?

In the time it took me to lean down on my right elbow and haul myself vertical, William removed my bag from the drip stand, handed it to another orderly and shared a joke with him. I only caught the punchline.

. . . well, what else would the parachute be for?

When he came back, he was still grazing on a laugh.

What do I do now? I said.

Well, if you're feeling OK, you can –

I was on my feet before he could finish.

OK?

Fine. Maybe a little light-headed.

William narrowed his eyes.

Well, you'll probably feel that for a while. So what I'd suggest is that you go back through to the lounge, ask the waitress for a drink. Take five minutes, sit, have a Coke, a juice, whatever. Just make sure it's sugary. Try and eat some of the snacks. No alcohol this evening. Do you smoke?

No, I don't.

Well, if you do smoke, don't smoke for another two hours.

He ushered me toward the double doors, returned my jacket. Held out his hand. I shook it with my right.

Have a safe journey home, he said. And thank you.

No problem. It was –

He'd already made it halfway to the corner.

My pleasure.

27

I walked straight out through the double doors, keeping my left arm flush by my side, past the doctor's office and back toward the waiting room. The young brunette woman stood behind the counter. The lounge, I realised, was the table, the basket and chairs. As I approached, she dipped out of view.

Hi, what can I get you? she asked, righting herself again and smiling.

A Coke? A juice? . . . You know . . . whatever.

Well, she said, we've got both.

I'll take a juice.

OK.

She bent down beneath the counter again, re-emerging with a two-litre bottle of fluorescent yellow cordial and a multi-grooved plastic cup.

Actually . . . can I have a coffee too?

Sure. A coffee too.

She smiled again, a quizzical crease inching up her cheek. Broke into a grin before we each looked in opposite directions.

I wondered if this was supposed to be some kind of pastiche of a traditional bar. Did I stand here with my plastic cup shooting the breeze and bemoaning my fate, complaining about my team or my tax return, training one eye on the single girls, the other on the TV? Then stagger out of the door, shouting at phantoms, a pint of blood down and swimming with glucose?

She handed me the juice. Poured coffee from a rounded, diner-style pot into another plastic cup.

How do you take it?

Black's fine. Thank you.

I took both cups and sat beside the table. The basket was filled with chocolate bars, potato chips, individual packs of biscuits, single, saran-wrapped slices of fruit cake.

I reached forward for a chocolate bar, and sipped my yellow juice. If I'd been eight years old, this would have been heaven. As it was, I kept gazing at the second-hand of my watch, waiting for William's five minutes to end. The additives in the juice made my tongue feel bloated and synthetic. The chocolate was coating the roof of my mouth. The coffee was tepid, but I drank it anyway. Til the second-hand swooped round to save me.

I got up, smiled at the waitress, who smiled back with a warmth I hadn't felt in months, and left the same way I came in.

With my back to her, Carmen the receptionist called out to me.

Thank you, Mr Viss.

I spun on my heels.

Sure. No problem. I was meaning to ask . . . when can I do this again?

I hadn't meant to put it like that.

Well, you should really see how you feel after today . . . but twelve weeks is the minimum rest period.

Twelve weeks.

That's the minimum.

OK . . . Thanks.

Thank *you*, Mr Viss.

The automatic doors again. Swish. Swish. Entrance, exit. And the rain poured, and the sky hung like gun metal, and it still felt like the whole street and everyone on it had been overexposed. Bleached out.

I hadn't lied when I said I felt dizzy. There was a slapstick note to my stride as I turned off Mortimer and Upas, onto Wells and Maiden Lane. My left arm stung like a bitch. But it was worth it. Some little brilliance was worth it.

This was the spring of last year. Since then, I've thought a lot about what went on that day, and everything that happened after.

In the meanwhile, there's always the falling.

Chumming for Sharks

So, how long's this going to take? Even now, I'm not sure what effect the variables of height and weight are having on my descent. There's no wind to speak of, and I took no form of run-up, so this should be straightforward. A to B. A being me – adult male, 6' 5", 220 lbs – B whatever lies a hundred feet below.

All I know is I'm beyond the loft, drifting past the eighth floor. Two storeys above mine, to the right as I fall, is the apartment belonging to Chris and Helena. They're not at home right now.

Although for a long time I really only knew them through their mail – credit-card circulars, magazine subscriptions, bills – our stilted conversations on the stairs eventually blossomed into something more substantial. Chris, for instance, recently told me they were selling up and looking for a bigger place. On another occasion, he said they were doing so because Helena wanted more room to start a family. When on a third occasion I mentioned this to Helena, she looked at me wearily.

Chris occasionally opens his mouth, she said, without engaging his brain.

Chris is a stylist. Helena works at a record company. Right now, they're not at home. What I'm wondering is, what would they see if they were? An anonymous streak of cream cotton? An angel come to earth in balletic slow-mo?

Except, of course, right now, they're somewhere else entirely. Right now, they're off the coast of South Africa, watching exotic marine life in its natural habitat. Throwing raw meat into the warmth of the ocean. Chumming for sharks. Luring monsters from the water, so they can take each other's photograph with fins looming in the background. Apparently –

You think it's going to stop, it'll pass, it'll fade. But it doesn't. It just comes stronger, deep swoons of nausea, ceaseless, gathering.

Helena grips the starboard rail, each moment a new horror. When the boat first rolled to a tilt, she thought they were sinking. Now she sees they're navigating tight, concentric circles. The tannoy splutters as the guide attempts a commentary. Every crackle makes her sicker. She has to get off. Back to land. Closing her eyes, she pictures the hotel bed, fresh sheets, plumped pillows. Chris' face, grimly contorted as they labour for the child he craves. Her eyes flash open to the chum bucket. Smells as you might think. Like nothing good.

Chris pulls down his sou'wester. Through the babble of the tannoy, whole words become clear. Male, tiger, thirty yards, aft. A firing squad of lenses turns as one, his included, til skin brushes skin. Helena, half bowed overboard, clinging to the rail, fingers touching his.

How many times did he say they could go somewhere else? All he wanted was a week. A week to themselves before the conception of the child she pines for.

The guide hands the bucket to an adolescent boy, who wails and hurls its contents at the water. Downwind, Chris feels viscera spray across his lips. Helena moans, lost and guttural. And he places his hand over hers. A twitch in her knuckle. Acknowledgement. He looks across at her, thinks maybe this kid would be welcome. Pictures himself with a pram and realises he's smiling at the image.

And Helena brings her head up, cautious. Feels the lurch in her stomach recede. Can keep her eyes open for long full seconds. Would it be so rash of them to do this? She knows that no one's ever ready. Maybe you just do it. Maybe that's the only way. They're good together. Could give it security. Wouldn't brand it with hand-me-down agonies.

Fifty yards ahead a shank of light hits the water, slick with chum. Turns it, for a moment, to a rich blaze of colour, a glamorous shoal passing near the surface. They stand at the rail, and the cameras flash around them. They are decided.

chumming trips are all the rage right now. Dolphins are over. Chris and Helena get back tomorrow.

In the meanwhile, there's always the falling.

You know, it's possible to donate your bone after your death. Not your bone marrow. The actual bone. As long as the tissue is intact, they remove your femur, your humerus, or whatever, and use it for reconstructive surgery. They often freeze-dry in lieu of an appropriate recipient. That's what happens.

In the spring of last year, I'd just moved in to Bethune Street and Scala. The Greatest Gift had called to confirm my appointment a month previously, shortly after my interview. Despite my lack of experience, I must have aced it.

There were three interviewers on the panel, sitting across from me with identical expressions of polite curiosity. I'm a people person, I told them, and to me, working as a concierge combines the most satisfying aspects of a career in retail with the opportunity to take the initiative in any number of exciting scenarios, within an environment where resourcefulness and a genuine commitment to customer satisfaction are both valued and rewarded.

Of course, I know now I should suffix that with something glib. An acidic stage whisper to distance my contemporary self from its earlier, artless incarnation. The truth was, I believed it. And the tiny part of me that didn't, I'd long since stopped listening to.

You know the professional smile people at counters and the tip-dependent give you? That strange, docile rictus, all teeth and artifice? That's how I look all the time. Except I mean it.

They asked me why I wanted to leave my current (i.e. previous) position. I told them that when you reach a certain stage in your career, you have to stand back and look at the big picture and that, within the context of my current (i.e. previous) position, I simply felt the time had come for a new challenge. For a role in which I could grow both personally and professionally. To be candid, if I might be candid, it wasn't so much a question of why I wanted to leave my current (i.e. previous) position, as how much I wanted to be a part of The Greatest Gift. I wanted to help people. That's what people people do.

They called a week later. A month after that I moved in here. I moved in on my own. Carl helped me up to the sixth floor with my cases. We traded small talk as we yo-yoed in the elevator. He seemed friendly.

How long have you worked here? I asked him.

Pheuuuu . . . he said, whistling through his teeth . . . Been a while now.

Really?

Oh, yeah . . . *pheuuuu* . . .

Right.

OK. Sixth floor. Let's get these inside.

Even then, I noticed it. What I would later define as a criminal ear, small and protuberant, with a pronounced rolling of the helix. First noted as a distinguishing feature within the underworld by the Harvard anthropologist E. A. Hooton. Without wanting to stare, I glanced over Carl's face as we grunted our way to my door. He also had the low, sloping forehead and thin, petering eyebrows identified by Hooton as potential giveaways. But, like I say, he seemed friendly.

Once the last case was inside, he left me to unpack.

The place was part-furnished, which was good because most of my possessions were still in storage for another week. Chair, couch, stereo, most of my kitchen equipment. There was a bed, standard double, and a wardrobe. After that, I was on my own. The only articles of any real bulk I had with me were my bookshelves, TV, espresso machine, my weights and treadmill – a Pro-Form 585 Pi whose patented Space Saver design didn't stop it taking up at least half my bedroom. Carl looked like he was about to have an aneurysm when we brought it up.

I'd bought the treadmill and the weights right before I came here. I'd always meant to work on my fitness, build up my physique, the shoulders that drooped like cheap wire coat hangers, but time conspired against me. Now, I was able.

I arranged the empty bookshelves against the wall. Positioned my reading light on the floor.

I was always a voracious reader. Most of the packing cases contained my books. After a few minutes of hauling, I sat in the lotus position in the middle of the room, the cases surrounding me. Each had been numbered according to its contents, 1 holding those books whose titles began with the letters A–C, through to 5, T–Z.

The only exceptions were two unmarked cases, one of which held clothes – the staples, T-shirts, so on – the other a range of books bought specifically in readiness for starting work at The Greatest Gift, and my complete works of Eric Handler. I unpacked those first.

Throughout my life with Eleanor, I'd arranged my books by author. Here, to represent the change I was enacting, I would do so by title.

Lifting the dust cover from inside the case and getting to my feet, I began with the shelf farthest from where I would later put the couch. The highest slat was full in less than a minute. From left, I started with *Angels at the Water Cooler: Inspirations for a Kinder Workplace*, by Barbara T. Emmerich. At the end, I just about found room for *Building Bridges: Setting Free the World-Changing Power of Teamwork*, by Michael James Mangold.

I moved fast. The second shelf began with *Coffee Break Moments: Tranquil Visions for the Workaholic*, by Richard Zink. The last book on the fifth was *Strategies for Success*, by Edward D. Gruber.

For the sake of convenience, I filed my Eric Handlers in chronological order. *15 Simple Wisdoms; Reinventing the Soul: How to Become Who and What You Always Dreamed of; Rescuing the Soul: The Big Mistakes We Make and the Lessons We Can Learn from Them*. Then, finally, his latest and I felt most insightful work,

Another Soul Rescue: Thoughts on How to Be. I had two copies of each. One for reading, the other for passing down to Alice.

Eric Handler had been my favourite writer ever since *15 Wisdoms*. I'd been time-killing in a bookstore when I noticed it on a display stand. Intrigued, I leafed through the opening chapter. By the third page, and forever from then on, I was a devotee. For a long time, I kept the receipt from that day in my wallet.

He never disappointed, and I always understood. I loved the way he used his own life as the premise of his writing. With a lot of motivational literature – and I've read a lot – you know deep down, you're just being fed buzz words and platitudes. Not with Eric Handler.

For the longest time, I'd wanted to meet him. Just so I could shake his hand and let him know how much of an impact his work had had on me.

I found myself thumbing through *15 Simple Wisdoms*, greeting its assurances like an old friend come to visit. Put the rest of the shelving on hold.

Later, I hung my clothes in the wardrobe, set out my vitamins and supplements on the breakfast bar. I was out of echinacea.

Fortunately, I'd already located a health-food store just a short walk down from the far end of Bethune Street. On my way over here, in a rickety hire van with cardboard boxes stacked to the roof in the back, I'd made sure to pinpoint significant landmarks. Nearest supermarket, cash machine, pharmacy, dry cleaners, station.

The health-food store was next to a pizza joint, a dank patch of waste ground running beside.

Time was against me. Outside, it was getting dark. I took the elevator down to the ground. Nodded at Carl as I left.

Goodbye, Mr Viss, he said.

I retraced my arrival on foot, hastening as I finally caught sight of the awning, waste ground beyond. The light was still on.

Inside, the place was emptying of customers. Scooting through the aisles, I picked up vitamins B and D, echinacea in both liquid and capsule form, and a 1800 mg bottle of Hyperi-Max. At the check-out, I waited to introduce myself to the sales team.

While the assistant rang up my purchases, I made sure to catch her eye, gave her my widest professional smile.

Hi, I said. I'm Matthew.

Hello, she replied, a name tag identical to those at Mortimer and Upas lopsidedly fixed to her sweater.

You're Sara. No H.

I'm sorry?

And I pointed at her tag.

Right, she said. That's thirty-two ninety-five.

I just moved into the area, I said, giving her the money.

Welcome to the area, she said, taking it from me then handing me my receipt and change.

It's just I'm very into health. Food. Supplements.

Uh-huh.

So I just wanted to . . . meet the team.

Right. Well that, she said, gesturing at a man with fuzzy sideburns and a price gun, is Ed. The guy with him is the manager. Mr –

She made a noise, a brusque sibilance. I must have looked blank, because without trying it again, she grabbed the receipt from my hand, wrote across the back, then laid it out in front of me.

C-E-H, it read.

Ceh, she said. He's from Slovenia. In the former Yugoslavia.

Right, I said. Well, thanks. I'm sure I'll be in again soon.

Don't forget your receipt, she said, flashing her teeth and pushing it toward me.

Right . . . Thanks.

I took it and left.

Returning to the apartment, early evening penumbra descended, I took in the neighbourhood. Skipped over streetlit pools of rainwater, wove through the bodies pulsing to and from the station.

39

On the corner of Bethune and Sheridan, one block from my building, was a toy shop. The window display was a riotous jumble of stuffed animals, glove puppets, pop-ups, wind-ups, magic sets, novelties, trinkets, fancies. A thick wire grill hung over the glass. Looking in, I could only think of Alice. One oversized teddy was the spit of Belinda Griselda, her constant companion since the age of two.

From the street, through the grill, my gaze spun from a green furry crocodile to a miniature farm to an ornate wooden top. All of them would have been enough. Any of them would have sufficed.

The longer I stared, the clearer and more inescapable my recall of the events that led to my standing here.

Coming downstairs on a weekend morning, ambling into the living room, baffled at the sight of Eleanor and Alice kneeling beside each other, a plastic treehouse between them. Standing maybe a foot high, it was occupied by a mischievous chimp and a rotund hippopotamus. Then I saw wrapping paper strewn across the carpet.

Alice and her mother looked up at me, expressions diverted from joy to confusion.

And like a mallet in the chest, it hit me. Today was Alice's birthday. Her sixth. The first on which I'd neglected to shower her with presents. The first, in truth, I'd completely forgotten.

I don't know how. Every year, the date was circled in red in my diary. A day hardly went by without my thinking of it, the weeks beforehand a frenzy of impulse buying and impossible hiding places. And then it just got clean away.

The year before – her fifth – I'd had everything bought and wrapped months ahead of time. So many gifts, such light in her eyes at their opening. The year before had been perfect.

A week later, a fine rash across her stomach proved to be the measles. She lay in her room, cooped and gloomy, before she was parcelled back to school.

Once she was better, I wanted to take her out for the day. I was between jobs. The last had finished the previous week.

The next wasn't starting til the following.

This was a Tuesday. It looked like it would rain, but it never quite did.

I didn't think to call Eleanor. I didn't see the need. She'd looked after Alice while I worked out my notice. She'd had her time.

I was already unhappy with the way the school were treating Alice. At this point I remained convinced she was a prodigy. I had no evidence. I could just see it in her. Eleanor and I had fought about it. I'd called the headmistress and upbraided her for failing to recognise my daughter's precocity. Turned out she was an acquaintance of Eleanor. The incident, she said, caused her a lot of embarrassment.

I picked Alice up mid-morning. Eleanor had the car. I booked a cab. Waited outside her classroom, knocked. The children were finger-painting.

When her teacher came to the door, I said there'd been a death in the family. No one close. All the same, I should probably take my daughter home. And I led Alice out to the cab.

We got to the theme park two hours later. Had a blast. As it was a school day, the place was pretty much deserted. We took in all it had to offer. Rides, burgers, puppet show, petting zoo. I'd never seen her laugh so much in my company. Look at me with such affection.

When it happened, I was over at the hula stall. Trying to win her a stuffed toy. I assumed she was beside me, watching. After the last hoop sailed from my hand, I looked down and realised she wasn't. She was with Mr Deedelus. Mr Deedelus, the cartoon gorilla from the cereal commercial, whose cult appeal among the pre-pubescent had been successfully parlayed into a TV series and a recent spin-off movie to which Eleanor took Alice on four separate occasions.

Now, he was standing on the walkway, handing out candy and vouchers for rides. Whichever unfortunate was inside the costume, his mass of foam and fur left him standing six inches taller than me. A dozen kids thronged around him, jabbering. Alice among them.

41

I saw her stumble to the ground. Mr Deedelus stood over her.

There was the half-second pause that always prefaces a child's reaction to trauma, the deadpan processing of information. Then the wail.

I ran to her. Her knee was gashed. From instinct, I went for the guy in the costume, demanded an explanation. Cursing, I pushed him in the chest. Heard him protest from inside the suit.

She fell, he said. She fell.

And I turned back, and she was gone.

It's odd the way you absorb these moments. The same deadpan process, translated into adulthood. You gaze at the space where the child should be. Think you're just looking at it wrong. Then you look again, and panic.

I don't remember much about what came afterward. The call I made to Eleanor. Her slapping me when she arrived, then breaking down. The female police officer gently asking us if we had any photographs suited for use on a Missing poster. Mostly, I just recall the haywire lurch from moment to moment. Words losing meaning. Time eliding. Everything unfastened.

Five hours after she disappeared, a cleaner discovered her in the bathroom of a mall a hundred and twenty miles away. She was with a middle-aged woman in a wheelchair. The woman was cutting Alice's hair. When the cleaner walked in, the woman jumped from the chair and ran. They never caught her.

The police brought Alice home. She stared at me past Eleanor's sobbing embrace. Scored across her features was everything I had always dreaded seeing there. Disillusion, realisation, loss. A tiny grief. An end to heaven.

And something between us was broken from then. A chasm opened. If I tried to hold her, she'd shy away. She never spoke about the lost five hours. Didn't speak at all for the next two months. To me. To anyone.

Eleanor took her to counsellors, speech therapists, anyone she thought might be able to help. And I prayed alone, my hands clasped together, prostrate before a God I neither worshipped nor trusted. Prayed that everything would be OK. The way it was before. Keeping my distance for fear I would only make things worse.

But while I did, I still hungered to make amends. To prove – to her and to myself – I deserved to be her guardian.

What was needed was a seal. Some just and formal resolution. And while she slept I told her she would witness that.

The failure of the police to find the woman in the wheelchair, her continued liberty, they taunted me. As the months crept past, my unease deepened. I foraged through papers for news of similar incidents. Kept a file to study, learn from. Offered my help to the police however they could use it, but they never took me up on that. I called them once a week, then twice and three times, asking after the investigation, til they said they'd be in touch if there were any developments. I'd sit late into the night, writing explanatory letters to politicians and law enforcement agencies, appealing for their help.

Eleanor pleaded with me to stop. Said none of this was doing Alice any good. I didn't listen. In the week leading up to her sixth birthday, I twice returned to the theme park, distributing leaflets concerning the woman in the wheelchair to passers-by. To request information, warn other parents. The lack of conclusion began to devour me.

I was at home on a Friday afternoon when a TV news show reported a child's abduction at a fairground near Saint Remi, fifteen miles from the theme park. This time, someone had been arrested.

I didn't even switch off the television. Just took the car and drove. Just wanted to be there. To see for myself and know this was over.

It was 7 by the time I got to the police station. 10 once I convinced the goon at the front desk to let me talk with a senior officer.

The senior officer wouldn't tell me anything beyond what had already been on the news. He expressed his sympathy when I told him what I was there for, but would still only say that a suspect was being questioned and there was no real point in me being here. I asked if he could tell me if the suspect was a woman and he said no. But, if I wanted his opinion, the woman in a wheelchair was probably a man in drag. It's usually a man, he said.

So I just sat there waiting as the drunks were rough-housed to the cells. And prayed again, begged that this would be the right person. That they would be charged and tried, then convicted, removed, erased.

It wasn't the right person. Shortly after midnight the senior officer approached me, told me I should have taken his advice and gone. The man they had in custody had been in prison on the day of Alice's abduction. He said he was sorry, but next time I should really just liaise with the local authorities.

It was getting light by the time I got home. And I came downstairs the next morning, ambled into the living room, where I stood baffled at the sight of Eleanor and Alice kneeling beside each other, a plastic treehouse between them. And Alice held my gaze til it almost shattered me.

I know now I should have thought laterally. Affected a wry, paternal smirk, concocted a yarn about picking up an order from the grotto or the birthday factory. A lie fit for a child. Then go directly from the house straight to the nearest toy store, strip the shelves and come back laden.

Only I didn't. I just stood transfixed, til their eyes fell from me and Eleanor threw an arm round our daughter, pulled her in close.

I felt guilt, of course, and shame, but also somehow rage and envy. Neither of which I could justify.

I wished her Happy Birthday.

Thank you, she said, without looking back at me.

Come on, sweetness, Eleanor said. Get your coat. It's cold outside.

Can Belinda Griselda come? she asked her mother.

As long as you're quick. Go and get her while you're putting your coat on.

Alice skipped from the room, and as she passed I squatted, til our faces were level. And scored across her features was everything I always dreaded seeing there. Disillusion, realisation, so on.

Happy birthday, angel, I said.

She smiled at me with what I swear was kindness, and disappeared upstairs. Eleanor followed across the room.

Where are you going? I said.

I'm taking her to the movies. Like we arranged.

And I tried to speak, but Eleanor said:

Don't.

Then Alice returned. And soon they were gone.

I couldn't stand it. Couldn't stand the thought of Eleanor screaming at me later that night, turning Alice yet further against me. Couldn't stand the knowledge she had every right and reason.

While they were out, I packed two bags and checked into a hotel. Wrote them a note, obviously. I didn't want to worry them. Monday morning, I hailed a taxi, waited on the street til the place was empty, then let myself in and moved my stuff into a storage lock-up half a mile away. In total, it took me four trips.

The whole experience seemed unreal. Like none of this was actually happening, or if it were, it was just an exercise. I kept on packing boxes all the same.

You see them disappointed with such crushing regularity, worn down by your deficiencies, til you just can't stand the sight of it. So you go. Absent yourself without thinking of the next day, and then it's the next day and you're in a hotel, and then an apartment on Bethune Street and Scala. And sometimes you remember the point was to go back, to find out what was wrong with you, correct it, but the route to that correction gets lost amid the weeks, and with it the direction home.

All I knew was I could never give Alice cause to look at me again the way she had that morning.

The reproachful glare from Eleanor was less surprising. I'd grown to expect it, the same way I expected her barbed dissections of my failures, limitations. How she gave up her photography for me, the landscapes on our walls a constant rebuke, and the way her friends, our mutual friends, would routinely call her in sympathy.

Although we only felt it in ever-cloudier throbs of memory, what haunted us both was the trace of before. Dancing to the radio, exhausted and hysterical; days at the sea, cotton candy, skimming pebbles; her comically bony feet, pressed to mine in bed on cold mornings; the divine elevation of a mundane shopping trip through the simple ecstasy of the other's company; endless me-too revelations; learning to calibrate the seen and heard by its value in their reaction. The plush, narcotic merger of tastes and aspirations, cravings and identities.

I found myself weepy chancing on her sleeping, came to see time apart as at best irrelevant, at worst a torment. She, in turn, said she loved my quiet. Lying together on idle Sundays, she teased me for my shyness, tickled the conversation out of me.

The clam, she called me. My beautiful clam.

I'd never seen myself as beautiful. By the last months, years, neither did she. Everything falls apart. Everything fell apart. And still, through it all, there was Alice.

At the toy store window, I started crying. The first time since I left. Great, authentic, saline tears.

The walk back to my building seemed to take for ever. Stepping in, red-eyed, I passed Carl and nodded, again.

That evening I ate a take-away, then ran five miles on the Pro-Form. Before bed, I set my clocks, leaving all but two in obscure nooks way out of reach. That night, I slept like a baby. A baby in a coma. The way I always did. It was a problem I'd had for years. Right now, it was raging.

I have hypersomnia. I can't wake up. I sleep more, and deeper. At night, I'm dead. I sleep sixteen hours if I let myself, the grand oblivion of the jet-lagged and shift-worker. I never remember my dreams. Coming to is like swimming through tar. It takes all my strength not to slip back into the mulch. Then, for hours after I'm theoretically awake, I'm somewhere else entirely. My motor functions don't kick in. I can't form words, and my lack of co-ordination has me daubed in bruises. I stumble over greetings and trip over household fixtures. Asleep, it's like I'm under anaesthetic. Awake, it's like I've had a stroke.

As a kid, people just thought I was lazy. I'd fall asleep in the afternoons, humid, insidious freefalls into nothing. I fell asleep in classes and in the detentions I got for falling asleep in classes. My first job, I was sacked for absenteeism. I just kept sleeping in.

Three years ago, my doctor – bested by my sheer persistence – referred me to a neurologist. They told me I had idiopathic hypersomnia. If you're not depressed and you still can't wake up, you've got hypersomnia. Idiopathic means no one knows what causes it. At first, I took various medications, heavy on the side effects. Amphetamine with pretensions. Now I take Provigil. That's just a brand name. But it helps. There's no cure for hypersomnia.

I have seven alarm clocks, the loudest of which I scatter round my bedroom, so I have to physically get up to turn them off. Then I build up my defences.

Usually, by this time of day, I'd have taken two Provigil, washed down with five cups of coffee. Though I've never smoked a cigarette, I get through half a pack of nicotine gum per day. Balance, of course, is everything. Forget my gum and I'm out cold in an hour. One too many espressos and I get palpitations. Moment to moment is a see-saw.

And mostly you just deal with it. I take my medicine. I tell select people what to expect. I avoid scheduling important business early in the morning, I screen my calls before and after certain times, I exercise, I read. I keep mind and body in shape. And, every night, I make a solemn pledge to get up again the next morning.

The night I moved in, I must have dreamt, because when the fifth alarm clock woke me up, I felt worried. Gnawed at. As if there was something essential I'd forgotten, some vital task or directive, and the harder I tried to remember it, the further it sank away from me.

The day after that, I started work at The Greatest Gift.

The orange bulb hangs low from the rear-view mirror. By now, the car should be filled with the scent of Sweet Rosemary air freshener. Delicate fragrance should already be wafting gently through the interior. At the wheel, Eleanor Carlin breathes deep, inhales stale, chlorine-soaked towels, chocolate bars wriggled into seat covers, spilt milk down the back seat.

She turns right, into the main drag, closing on the infants' school where, ten minutes from now, Alice will recite times tables in an otherwise silent classroom as her mother meets the headmistress, Tina Karlsson.

They've known each other for years. A long professional acquaintance, occasionally bordering on friendship. Which only makes this more uncomfortable. They will sit, facing, in Tina Karlsson's office, walls covered with children's paintings. They will, inevitably, drink warm tea from logo-slathered mugs. And with earnest, productive rigour, they will talk about Alice, her aspect and behaviour, the buds of what Tina Karlsson described as anti-social tendencies when she rang, yesterday, to ask Eleanor in for what she called a chat.

Don't worry, she said, Eleanor's mind swimming with playground barbarisms. Really, it's not that serious.

She said this in the same bright, emollient tone Eleanor herself uses with the parents.

Alice just seems a little . . . withdrawn. Do you mind me asking how things are at home?

Something obstructs the gear stick, needing a hand to dislodge it. Belinda Griselda emerges from under the seat. And Eleanor hopes, hopes with a passion, that Alice doesn't have what Matthew has. Anything but that. She thinks of a theme park, hour upon hour with countless speech therapists.

They're . . . difficult, she told Tina Karlsson. Her father's left.

On the passenger seat, her handbag holds keys, diary, a pack of cigarettes. Cellophane torn off, but full. She bought them last week. Hasn't smoked in years. While she blithely told herself the air freshener was for Alice's debris, she knew this might happen, carrying the pack around, ready. Eyes on the road, fingers dip inside the bag, remove a cigarette, lift it to her mouth.

Her lane change is approaching. As she tips the indicator, a black BMW hurtles out of nowhere, baulking her til she's forced to slow and stay in lane. Tight-lipped, she watches as it speeds to the horizon, air freshener swaying in her line of sight.

Moron.

Bitch.

Jonah Hoffman glances at his watch, curses the ferocity of his schedule and opts to switch lane. An ageing maroon people-carrier trundles sluggishly beside him. He needs to get past it. Yet the second he tries to, the cold-looking woman at the wheel jitters and accelerates, leaving him swerving in mid-manoeuvre. The gingko tree and expensive modern art propped beside one another on the back seat slide loudly to the floor.

Jesus Christ. Who lets these people on the road?

It is 10.02 a.m. Sweeping on toward the city, he considers pulling up to reorder the mess. Instead, blindly groping over his shoulder, he wrestles the gingko back upright, his free hand at the wheel. The painting can wait, even with its frame digging into his kidneys.

The painting features geometric black slabs overlaid with some kind of fabric collage. The idiot from Lukas Concierge who picked it out and sent it over told him it was redolent of Robert Motherwell. No, Jonah said, I'm familiar with Robert Motherwell. Robert Motherwell is a genius. His work moves me beyond words.

And this, my friend, he whispered down the phone, is shit.

The joy he took in saying this was so pronounced, you might never guess that he – in fact – despises Robert Motherwell. But you say something like that to someone like that, they draw their own conclusions. You can hear it in their voice, making up the rest – the rich white male, knows nothing of art, spends all day on the golf course, and so on. Like they know the first thing about him.

The painting jabs into his back again. Better that, he reasons, than looking at it. God knows, he could barely watch as his maid took it down from the study wall. Mindful of the plaster beneath, he helped her remove it before she carried it to the car, swapping hellos with her cousin or brother, now graduated from spadework to spending all day in the van with his colleagues.

Of course, when he complained to Lukas, the unctuous middle manager was lavish with his apologies. Bleatings that Jonah would of course incur no charge. This, however, misses the point. Money is not the issue. And now when they call him, they sound like jilted women. But what do you *want*, Mr Hoffman?

What he wants is to find a lush thicket of roadside undergrowth and dump this garbage into it. And then he wants a new concierge. It is 10.05 a.m.

I can honestly say the weeks that followed were among the best of my life.

On my first day at The Greatest Gift, I reached their offices on Pearl Street at eight, having woken at six to allow a decent period in which to come to. As soon as I got there, my senior manager Greg Hopper billeted me in a windowless annex beside what I would later learn was the New Client Liaison Room.

He wore a cream cotton shirt and a charcoal ground silk bow tie. I'd met him before. He'd been on my interview panel. He was easily the least approachable member of the group. When I talked about my being a people person, I'd made sure to catch his eye in the hope of eliciting a response. There was no response.

This time, he shook my hand and, palm pressed into my back, showed me toward his extension. His touch felt clammy. His manner toxic.

Inside was a desk and chair, a phone, headset, computer.

OK, he said, make yourself at home. There's a few things I need to take care of.

Greg reported only to Mike the CEO and Caroline the Head of Personnel. In addition to his role as senior manager of the phone crews, he worked the front desk and dealt with companies interested in opening an account with us.

Sure, I said. By the way, I've actually moved since my interview.

He looked at me, baffled.

So the address on my form . . . it's out of date . . . Shall I give the new one to you?

Ah . . . no. Just drop a note in to Caroline.

I'm a lot closer to the office now.

Great, he said, wholly incurious. One minute, OK?

And he left. Came back an hour later.

Sorry for the hold-up. Wasn't sure you'd still be here.

With a joyless snuffle, he put the phone and headset in front of me.

So, we're starting you off with Home and Family. I've sent a memo flagging you up to the rest of the team. I'll make the introductions later.

He handed me a file of phone numbers listed beneath directory headings.

Our suppliers and contractors, he said. From now on, anyone calls for an airport limo, plumber, locksmith, they're yours. The call comes through here –

He gestured at a button on the phone.

– When it flashes red, you're on. So . . . flash, you're on. OK?

OK.

Good. So, this is how you greet the client. Your client greeting.

He put the headset on and paused. Then:

Good morning, The Greatest Gift, Guy Friday Matthew Viss speaking. How may I be of service?

His voice rose to a sing-song on certain nouns.

Good *morning*, The Greatest *Gift*, Guy Friday Matthew *Viss* speaking.

He did the same with *service*, but somehow it came out thwarted. He took off the headset and gave it to me. Slipping it on, it felt cheap and flimsy.

So . . . want to take a shot?

Good *morning*, I said. The Greatest *Gift*, Guy Friday Matthew *Viss* speaking. How may I be of *service*?

When I said service, it sounded like fresh towels and blue skies. Greg Hopper's lip curled. I assumed it was involuntary.

Very good, he said. Now get their details. Feed them into the system.

He touched return on the keyboard and a programme appeared on-screen, a single white box at its centre.

Here's what you're going to need. Their name. Their company name. Remember these, but don't feed them into the system yet. Now get their account number. A lot of the time they won't remember their account number, but we need their account number, so you wait until they do remember it, or their PA remembers it. Now, enter their account number into the system.

He filled the white box with the word

dummy

Type as you speak, he said. When you enter their account number, their company file will appear on-screen.

Another screen, various white boxes. At the top was

dummy

So, remember their company name. Check you have the right file on-screen. Check their name against the list of employees who have access to the service. Enter their name into the system.

Under the word dummy, the word dummy was repeated several times. Greg Hopper put his finger to the screen.

These are the employees, he said.

Each had a white box beside it, and he filled every one with dummy. Did the same with a single white box at the bottom of the screen.

Their password, he said. Now, occasionally passwords get changed at the company's request. They get changed because if they don't then people who've just been fired call us to book manicures and limo rides. The company still has to pay.

The company is angry. So get their password. Check their password. Never book anything without it. Type as you speak. OK, so –

He stared at me, as if imparting mystic philosophies.

Get their name. Get their company name. Get their account number. Enter their account number. Check their company name. Check their name. Enter their name. Get their password. Enter their password. OK? Make sense?

Absolutely.

Good. Now we move on to the important part. The Greatest Gift's golden W's. The what, the where, the when. What is it that they need? Where do they need it? When do they need it by?

The cursor flashed beside the password. Greg Hopper pressed return and the screen changed to three white boxes.

The golden W's. Type as you speak. OK?

He stared at me again.

What service do you need, sir or madam? *OK*. And *where* will you be needing that? And *when* will you be needing that by? I see. *OK*.

He filled each of the three white boxes.

OK, sir, that's all taken care of. And if you have any problems, or you need any further services, please do let me know. My name is Matthew Viss. Goodbye, sir or madam. *So*, now take your folder, find the relevant entry. They need a balloon trip? Go to Entertainment. Find the entry for Balloon Trips. Call the number. Most of the important ones are on speed dial. Tell them you're from The Greatest Gift, give them our account number. You tell them the where, and the when.

Not the what?

They don't need the what. They are the what. Book it. (He pressed the return key, another screen, a single white box.) Enter the contractor's name.

dummy

These are the basics, he said. And what we're going to do now is a run-through.

He stalked out of the annex, back into the room outside. Sat at a desk, picked up the phone, and dialled. A second later, the button on my phone flashed red.

Good *morning*, The Greatest *Gift*, Guy Friday Matthew *Viss* speaking. How may I be of *service*?

Good morning to you, he said. This is Greg Hopper over at Hopper and Hopper.

He was using an accent so outlandish I couldn't pin it to a town or even region.

Yeah, I'm going to need a locksmith for my PA's apartment.

OK, sir.

Got herself locked out again. Always the same.

OK.

Comes back from who knows where in the middle of the night, loses her keys.

OK, sir.

I mean, Matthew, don't get me wrong . . . It is Matthew, right?

Right.

No, what she does on her own time is strictly her business. But when it infringes on her duties here, that's when I get annoyed.

Of course, sir. OK. Now, what I'm going to need is –

Greg Hopper, standing in front of me.

OK, he said. That was good. But think about the need to know. What beyond the basics do you need to know? Nothing. Because while I'm sitting here telling you about my PA, there's a client standing in six inches of cold water in their executive bathroom who can't get through to Matthew Viss, whose responsibility it is to find him or her a plumber, because Matthew Viss is making chit-chat on the other line. So maybe the next time that client needs a plumber or a locksmith or a balloon trip, maybe they'll remember what happened the last time they used The Greatest Gift, and they'll save themselves the trouble and call Lukas Concierge instead.

Lukas Concierge was a rival service, over on Glendower.

OK?

Absolutely. Sorry.

Remember, you're the client's friend. But you're not their *friend*. OK?

The bland derision in his voice was, for me, an epiphany. I knew then there could never be any real kinship between us. That this would forever taint him.

So, let's try that again.

He stepped back toward his office.

Greg? What should I be typing . . . when I'm taking your call?

Dummy, he said. Just type dummy.

He used the accent again the second time he called. Began detailing the fictitious PA's truancy, but now I'd learned. Secured and entered every number, password. Typed dummy into each white box that presented itself, politely ignoring any attempt to divert me from reaching the final screen.

Very good, he said when he returned. You've got the basics.

Over the next twenty minutes, we went through the procedure maybe a dozen times. Sometimes, he was a lawyer needing an urgent airport pick-up, sometimes, an accountant with troublesome taps. Sometimes, my fingers slipped as I typed.

sdummy

dum my

djummy

And every time he gave a muffled snort, and I felt myself set against him. Til we were through.

OK, he said, rubbing his hands together. Let's hit the nerve centre.

With his palm to my back again, he showed me out of the annex, toward the open-plan snarl of the phone room. A coffee machine outside. I stopped and refilled.

Tired? he said.

I hadn't told him. When he turned his back, I popped a nicotine gum.

The phone room was lit by white strip and gorged with cubicles. Fingers to my spine, Greg Hopper directed me toward a tract of five. The fifth cubicle was empty. The occupants of the other four looked up, all awkward smiles and mute enquiry.

OK, people, Greg Hopper said. Say hello to Matthew Viss. Our new Guy Friday.

He turned to me, no eye contact.

Matthew, say hello to your phone crew. The boys and girls of Home and Family.

Then he turned to a stocky, well-tanned white guy with a careful goatee.

Robert?

Without acknowledging Greg Hopper, the man got up and leaned over his cubicle wall, hand outstretched.

Matthew, hi. Good to meet you. I'm Robert.

Greg Hopper stood back, hands on hips.

Robert's team leader down here at Home and Family. So anything you need to know, he's the man to talk to. Aren't you, Robert?

Greg Hopper nudged me conspiratorially.

Just don't call him Bob. He doesn't like it.

Robert grinned like his head was in a vice, and every time Greg Hopper opened his mouth the jaws were tightening.

So, Matthew knows the basics. I've given him plumbers, locksmiths and airports. OK, Robert?

That's fine, Greg.

OK! he said, and clapped his sopping hands. Robert, if you can introduce Matthew to the rest of the team, that'd be great.

And Greg Hopper left, and Robert made the introductions. He twice forgot my name, but seemed so mortified each time I could hardly hold a grudge.

In theory, every member of Home and Family dealt with the full range of services mentioned in the prospectus, as did every Guy or Gal Friday. We were all supposed to be capable of using our skills across the operation. In practice, everyone had their niche. If you needed something outside their area they'd take your call, but more often than not they'd pass it on afterward.

Robert was household. If you needed a repair job, he got you an estimate, then he booked it. If you had to be out at the time that he booked, he'd sit discreetly on your sofa til the repairman arrived, then supervise their work. Then he'd take care of paying them. If you were single and you needed somewhere warming up, Robert warmed it up. (Warming up an apartment involves visiting the premises an hour before the employee returns for the evening and mussing cushions, over-running baths and realigning *objets*. It's done to create the impression that someone else lives there. This service is not referred to in the prospectus.) If you needed an interior designer, Robert showed them round, booked them, and paid them. If you needed a tailor sent to your house, he sent one to your house, and if you wanted stuff dry cleaned, you called Robert and it would be back with you the next morning, pristine and sweet-smelling.

Robert was slightly older than me. On his desk inside his cubicle was a framed snapshot of another man who looked exactly like him. Robert had been with The Greatest Gift for five years, the last two as team leader. Later, I learned that Robert's partner David was the man in the picture, that David was an investment analyst, they enjoyed walking trips together, and that Robert used to be an investment analyst too, til he turned thirty-five and, he said: *just realised I wanted to do something else with my life*.

I'm not making any kind of joke or generalisation in saying Robert was gay and into interiors. That's just what he did.

Alison took food. If you wanted a pizza and weren't inclined to make the call yourself, she did it for you, and if you needed banquet catering for a traditional Hindu wedding with 400 guests, she did that as well. Her Rolodex heaved with the mobile numbers of freelance chefs.

She was about my age. Her cubicle was decorated with postcards of prints by Kandinsky, Paul Klee, others I didn't recognise. A large photograph of a white stepladder in the middle of a bare room, a magnifying glass hanging from a chain above it. Alison had been with The Greatest Gift three years. Later, I learned that she trained as a painter herself but never followed through on it, could juggle like she grew up in a circus, and wanted to travel in Africa.

When I started, she was wearing a grey cashmere sweater bought for the price of a cab ride from a pair of men on the corner of Monroe and Fleet, standing beside a steel rail full of the following winter's collections, still wrapped in plastic. Warehouse fresh, they said, watching the street, pockets stuffed with thrusted bank notes.

Jon covered children, pets and the elderly. If you wanted to take your nine-year-old paintballing or your Vizsla grouse-hunting, Jon found the numbers and made the calls. If your nine-year-old or your Vizsla was sick, Jon called the doctor or the vet and, if they needed further treatment, Jon took charge of it. Alternatively, if you required a nursing home for a parent or grandparent, he could have them installed within forty-eight hours and, if they then absconded in a furious Alzheimer's haze, he would contact the police. If your parent or grandparent was confined at home and needed a reminder to take their medication, Jon called them up and said to them, gently but insistently:

No, not the green ones, the pink ones. That's right. The pink ones.

Jon was slightly younger than me. His cubicle was studiedly disorganised, with film posters tacked to the wall. He'd been with The Greatest Gift for a year.

Later, I learned that he held a postgraduate diploma in Medieval History, had been single his whole adult life, and frequently attended conventions devoted to old science-fiction programmes. He refused to admit this if you raised the subject.

Although Jon had neither a child or a pet (I knew little of his relationship with his parents and grandparents), he was good at the job. If you told him that, he got defensive and sarcastic.

Naomi assisted Jon and Alison. If you needed a top-class sommelier at an hour's notice or a nylon tie-out leash for your angora rabbit, and Jon was busy and so was Alison, you'd end up speaking to Naomi. Jon and Alison got to have an assistant because, pro rata, Food and Pets/Children were the busiest sections of the Home and Family sub-division. Household got frantic too, but Robert said he worked better alone.

Naomi was the youngest member of the phone crew. Her cubicle was pretty much empty apart from a papier mâché bust of Elvis, roughly the size of a pumpkin, face lime green, lips a racy scarlet. Personally, I found it creepy. Naomi had been with The Greatest Gift for just over six months.

Later, I learned that she passed her driving test first time, enjoyed clubbing, and had recently ended a relationship with a boyfriend her colleagues suspected was beating her up.

It was an eclectic mix, both culturally and socio-economically. I always thought we'd make a great sitcom.

I liked them. I liked them all. In many ways, we had a lot in common. In many ways, we didn't.

Our one devout bond was our shared contempt for Greg Hopper. Within my first month, I grew to loathe his sweating, his tawdry sadisms, his habit of aggressively snapping his fingers to indicate that he was both busy and important on a scale we could barely comprehend, and his constant diminutives in reference to the phone crews. Kids, boys and girls, guys and gals. On at least one occasion, oompa lumpas.

And the way that, when he smiled at you, it was always the preface to giving you an order.

OK, if one of you kids could get on to that, *a-sap*.

Jon called him a martinet. He also described the clients as parasites, and labelled us whores. I liked Jon, but you could feel the tension humming through the cubicles whenever he got started.

Me, I didn't think anything bad about the clients. They were just people who needed our help. And I didn't feel like a whore. That first month, listening to the assistants of vice-presidents with badly blocked sinks and panicky heads of acquisition stranded on rickety charters, I felt like a white knight.

My hero, they'd say, breathless with gratitude. My saviour.

Now and again, Home and Family would socialise together.

We'd head off at night, when the graveyard crew took over. The graveyard crew consisted of four people. Most of their time, I learned, was spent dispatching junk food and pornography to stockbrokers' homes at 3 a.m.

Outside our cubicles, we told stories about Greg Hopper and discussed the previous evening's TV. It was fun, even though Jon was frequently silent and Naomi always drank too much. One big happy family.

Me, I drank within my limits, and then I switched to juice. Usually, after an hour or so, I'd say my goodbyes and head back to Bethune and Scala. Again, the rest of the team thought that was a riot. They called me Party Boy. Mr Life And Soul.

In truth, I just preferred my own company, thoughts, order, drill. I always have. The reflexive solitude of the only child. The older I got, the more pronounced it became. At home, in my apartment, finally unpacked, I felt like I was recovering. Reading, exercising. Not thinking of Alice, Eleanor, anything. As Eric Handler says in *Reinventing the Soul*:

Smiling in the face of Now.

At work every morning I was the model Guy Friday: fast, efficient, courteous, inventive. Half a pack of nicotine gum, and I flew. I sent plumbers to fix drains in blue-chip office blocks and locksmiths to the second homes of executive systems directors. My days were a blur of filled white boxes.

dummy dummy dummy

That's what happens. Then you start helping out.

Henry the Schipperke and Lily the Chow

I helped out Robert, I helped out Alison, I helped out Jon. Then I helped out other sections. If Deborah from Business was drowning in paperwork, I rang round agencies to locate a well-referenced financial administrator. When James from Entertainment phoned in sick, I tracked down the most competitive price on a pirate's costume for a fancy-dress ball.

When the call comes through, there's a hot jab of panic before you pick up, a dumb instant in which you have no idea what it is you're going to be asked to find, book, hire, reserve, dispatch, deliver. I grew to love it.

I learned to figure out which kind of client typically wanted what kind of service, and which contractors could best provide them. I hooked them up like Cupid with a headset. In my lunch break, I'd read passages from Eric Handler, and then I'd hit the white boxes again.

If you needed flowers sent to a spouse or loved one, I got the most appropriate garland from the best possible florist and, if necessary, couriered them to your office first so you could handwrite the card. If you wanted a hairdresser with their own brand of conditioner to visit your hotel and tidy your nape in fifteen minutes flat, I had their number. If you hankered after a puppy, but didn't have the time to look for one yourself, I took down your specifications and talked to breeders til I had the right match. It was always the right match.

If you liked, I could name it for you too. Henry the Schipperke. Lily the Chow.

Jon always came up with self-indulgent names the clients were never happy with. Kierkegaard the Golden Lab, Che the Schnauzer. My names were perfect.

Then I'd have it vaccinated and chewing through your furniture by the time you got home. I don't even like dogs.

This, I realised, was vocation. Whenever my shift was scheduled to start, I was there an hour beforehand, and whenever it notionally came to an end, I was still chasing dry-slope ski trips for weekending professionals. 8 to 4 meant 7 to 5. 11 to 9 kept me there til 10.

I wasn't looking for approbation. I just wanted to be good at what I did. From the moment I took my first real client call, I became a Guy Friday. And that, to me, was a source of pride.

Four weeks after I started, clients were asking for me by name. A week later, they'd hold til I was free. A week beyond that, they'd refuse to deal with anyone else. I honed my phone technique paper-cut keen.

In theory, Greg Hopper was guiding me, monitoring my skills and development. Practically, following my induction, he abandoned me in favour of the front desk, exiting it only to patrol the phone room, loudly snapping his fingers, or to meet with new clients he'd mimic unkindly after they left.

Occasionally, Mike or Caroline would stop by my cubicle.

How we doing? they'd ask. Settling in OK?

I settled in fine. No one says no when you offer to help. Weeks passed and I mastered every job the clients could throw at me. And now, when Mike stopped by my cubicle, he'd say:

Good to see you, Matthew. Keep it up.

By the first long evenings of summer, I was getting through forty, fifty calls a day. Just one was a complainant. The single dismal cloud on my horizon.

And, yes, it was my fault, in that I should never have let Naomi take the job. I knew then I should have supervised the job myself – even if that meant putting the client on hold – or waited for Alison to get back from sourcing Vietnamese restaurants. Because, in truth, as much as I liked Naomi, she was often hung-over and flaky as routine, and the complainant's request for three experienced sushi chefs for a formal dinner that evening would have taxed the very best among us.

I thought it might build her self-confidence. I thought it would be good for her learning curve.

But when she said she had a free morning and was there anything she could do, I should still have said no. So, yes, in that sense, it was my fault when the sushi chefs didn't come. Which was how the complainant saw it too.

I avoided blaming Naomi when talking with the complainant. It was, and remained, my call. As Eric Handler said in *Rescuing the Soul*:

No one gets anywhere pointing their finger. Collective responsibility is the only way that a team will prosper, on the field, at the office, or in the home. It's not about one person dodging a bullet. It's about all of us embracing our interdependence. In the East, they call it karma. Me? I call it common sense.

After the sushi chefs' non-appearance, the complainant rang me twice daily for three days. There were militant demands for reparations, obscene name-calling. I apologised, repeatedly. Then they called Greg Hopper.

Greg Hopper sent the complainant a company cheque and a letter explaining how sincerely he hoped this regrettable incident would not deter them from using The Greatest Gift in the future.

I was distraught. Humiliated. At night, I'd put in long miles on the treadmill and berate myself for my frailties. Afterward I'd look in the mirror and say, actually say, to my reflection:

You're stupid and irresponsible, ugly and lazy. Stupid, irresponsible, ugly, lazy, and selfish, and thoughtless, and useless, and worthless, and you can't even haul your stupid, ugly carcass out of bed in the morning.

Greg Hopper savoured my pain. He glowed with it. In the middle of hectoring Alison or condescending to Robert, he'd arbitrarily bring the complainant into the conversation, talking just loud enough about the need for Home and Family to really start pampering the clients right now, what with that whole sushi chef fiasco.

When I asked Robert for a morning off to give blood for the first time, Greg was at my cubicle in minutes.

Matthew, he said, do you really think this is a good time to be focusing your energies outside the work environment?

Then he lowered his voice.

You're not the senior manager yet.

When I got back from Mortimer and Upas, left arm tender but otherwise glorious, I ploughed through my voicemail til a familiar moisture settled on my shoulder. My aura of well-being, exactness of vision, it all just evaporated.

Matthew, he said, fingers over my cubicle wall. Need to borrow you for a few.

I took off my headset. Caught a wave of commiserative glances from the rest of the team.

Don't worry, kids, Greg Hopper said. Just borrowing Matthew for a few.

I left my cubicle, and followed him to the meeting room.

The meeting room was seldom used. Despite this, it was kept immaculate, its broad mahogany table finished to a high shine, black leather swivel chairs buffed hard and scrupulous.

Don't worry, Greg Hopper said. Caroline and Mike just want a chat. Nothing sinister. OK?

In the foreword of the company prospectus, Caroline's near the back of the staff group shot. The quiet composure of her expression, allied to her faultless posture, articulates her relaxed air of authority. She's a steady hand on the tiller.

Mike, conversely, stands front and centre in the staff group shot, arms folded. The subtle crinkle round his eyes and the playful glint of his smile tells you he's just glad to be part of the team. He's the original Guy Friday.

I'd only been inside the meeting room once before. That was for my interview. My panel that day was Greg Hopper, Mike and Caroline. So this was just like old times.

Walking behind Greg Hopper, I felt a slick wash of dread. All I could think of was William handing me the rubber ball.

You clench it.

The rest I remember like a flicker book.

Mike sat at the far end of the table, Caroline to his left. I sat halfway down the table, on the right as you walk in. Greg Hopper opposite. Mike shared a joke with Greg. Caroline laughed. I laughed. Mike said he was happy I could drop by, and I nodded. Then I smiled.

You clench it to raise the veins.

Mike said he just wanted a chance to discuss my future at The Greatest Gift. He said he was aware there'd been a mix-up with some sushi chefs. A minor snafu, he said. And everyone nodded at once.

He said he'd looked into the situation personally, and that was why he wanted to have this chat with me.

Before we go any further, I said, I take complete responsibility. And I can assure everyone here that nothing like this will happen again.

Greg Hopper nodded. Caroline smiled. Mike laughed, just a little. Caroline said that she and Mike appreciated my candour.

We thank you for that, she said. You've handled a situation in which you were the innocent party with impeccable good grace.

Mike nodded. Greg Hopper coughed.

Obviously, she said, you can't be held responsible for the poor training of your colleagues.

And Greg Hopper notes a tingle square between his shoulder blades.

You've got a cool head under pressure, Mike said. That's a very useful asset.

He feels the tingle turn to metal, a cold burn plunged through skin.

Mike said he'd been hearing good things about me from the team leaders, and the way I thought outside the box could only benefit The Greatest Gift. Caroline said she and Mike believed in rewarding talent, rather than obsessing over hierarchies.

That's why we wanted to have this chat, Mike said.

What Mike's saying, Caroline said, is that maybe the time has come for you to take a step up within the company.

Mike nodded. I nodded.

Specifically, Caroline said, what she and Mike wanted to offer me was a more substantial role. One tailored to my commitment and versatility. She and Mike, she said, would like me to think about becoming the phone crews' senior manager and front desk supervisory co-ordinator, enabling me both to oversee my colleagues' work and build relationships with clients.

Greg Hopper throws his shoulders back, and the entry just goes deeper; wasting flesh, slamming into bone.

We know you haven't been with us long, Mike said. But performances like yours demand recognition. So why don't we see if you're ready?

So, Caroline said, would a role like that be of interest to you?

I smiled, I nodded. I said yes. Yes, Caroline, I said. It would.

Greg Hopper slumps forward, eyes and mouth agape, staring face down on burnished mahogany, a port wine ooze spreading under cream cotton.

Mike said he was glad we could have this chat, and Here's to the future.

Our future, Caroline said.

I nodded, smiled. Thanked them both and prepared to leave.

Greg, Mike said, could you spare us another five?

I'd almost forgotten he was there.

Sure, Mike, he said.

I'm the senior manager now.

When I told the phone room, everyone in Home and Family was great. They shook my hand and slapped my back, said how much I deserved it. Yet for all that, they seemed muted, vexed. Alison took me to one side and explained.

While I was in the meeting room, Naomi had been handed a letter by the temp receptionist. An envelope stamped Private And Confidential. Inside it said that while the company was grateful for her efforts, it believed she would be better served exploring alternative career routes.

They gave her two weeks' pay in lieu of notice, and asked that she vacate her cubicle by the end of the day. When she caught my eye, I couldn't find the words.

She told me it wasn't my fault, that she was really pleased for me and no, moving on's going to be a totally positive thing right now. Then she burst into tears.

Guy and Gal Fridays from every phone crew approached us, attracted by the hubbub, torn between congratulating me and comforting Naomi.

Then Greg Hopper left the meeting room. His every step a muzzle on those around him. All you could hear was breath and the soft glissade of fax machines.

As he walked past my cubicle, he nodded, smiled, but his gaze was three feet beyond me. I was too busy staring to catch Naomi reaching for her bust of Elvis.

She let out a raw, primal yelp, held it high above her head, and flung it at Greg. As he got to the door it struck him across the back of the skull, staggering him til his legs buckled and almost gave way, like a foal chasing its mother. It must have hurt. Even papier mâché must hurt thrown with force from less than ten feet away.

There was a dead thump as it hit the ground, the corner of a quiff sent flying.

He didn't speak. Just straightened up and kept walking. He looked pretty dignified for a man with green shrapnel in his hair. Then Naomi started crying again.

Later that day, Caroline sent a memo round the phone room. *From: Caroline/Re: Personnel*, it said. Then, underneath:

Effective immediately, Matthew Viss has been appointed Phone Crew Senior Manager/Front Desk Supervisory Co-ordinator. I'm sure everyone would like to join Mike and I in wishing him good luck in his new position.

(Greg Hopper will continue as Account Development Liaison Executive.)

In the weeks to come, as I grew more involved with every aspect of the company, even that proved a paper title. Finally he disappeared, excused on indefinite sick leave.

The memo didn't mention Naomi.

The next day, while discussing my revamped employee package with Caroline, I asked where Mike bought the cream cotton shirt he wore in the prospectus. After checking with his PA, she gave me the address. That evening, I bought three the same in the largest size available. They were tight around the collar, but otherwise they fitted OK. I wore one of them home. The weather was getting balmy. Summer was here.

And I'm still falling. Still en route. A speck, descending.

Smiling in the face of Now.

Fifteen floors below, Dutch Street shines like a capsized firmament. Jonah Hoffman pours a drink, carries the tumbler across his private office. At his desk, he reaches into his jacket pocket, savours the lining against his knuckles. Picks out his wallet. Feels heavy in his palm. The way a wallet should do. Inside its compartments are memberships, credit cards, cash, receipts. For a moment, he doesn't recognise the business card peeking from the uppermost slot.

The Greatest Gift, VIP Account Holder.

Now he remembers. Withdraws a dozen notes, mint fresh. They leave a butterfly shiver on his fingertips. It is 11.10 p.m. Without further acknowledgement, he holds the money out to the woman. She leans over and takes it from him, folds the bills, zips them in her purse. Thanks, she says.

Her underwear, some of it, lies on his desk. He hands it back to her like he's returning a dirty napkin in a restaurant.

Oh, she says. Thanks.

Jonah, naked from the waist down, feels a chill around his thighs. His suit trousers hang over a chair on the other side of the office. As he steps toward it he and the woman pass each other, shoulders brushing. An old married couple taking turns in the bathroom. He's never met her before and he'll never see her again.

Inevitably, he isn't satisfied. However intense the euphoria, he never is. He pulls his trousers back on, returns to his desk, sits behind it. There's always something wrong with them. Too fat, too thin, too quiet, too loud. Blonde when he craved brunette, a redhead when he wanted blonde.

The woman straightens her skirt, her back to him. There's a mole on her elbow, a birthmark on her calf. It's neither of those. He can't put a name to it. It's still there. The flaw.

Turning away, he sips at his drink. His gingko tree, three feet tall, stands at the corner of his desk. Slowly, he slides it in front of him.

The tree was a present from an associate. Since receiving it last week, Jonah's been reading up on its care and origins. The genus, he has learned, dates back to the dinosaurs. In ancient China, it was known for its medicinal qualities, aiding digestion and cleansing the bladder. He gently strokes the rigid branches, the fannish leaves, the wire and raffia wrapped loose around the bark.

An adult gingko lives a thousand years. At fifty, this one budded when Jonah was in his cot. These plants are immutable. When Little Boy fell on Hiroshima, a gingko stood half a mile from a Shinto temple. Within a month, it was flowering again.

Jonah spins the pot around, examines it from every angle.

OK . . . 'bye.

He looks up, perplexed. The woman is dressed and at the door. 'Bye, she says.

Oh, Jonah says. Yeah. Turns his attention back to the gingko. Hears the door open, then close. It is 11.13 p.m.

He pictures home. Weighs the small pleasures of the night drive back against the trough of arrival. The half-built fence, blank study wall, his wife glacial in her bedroom, son doing Christ knows what in his.

Pulling his trousers off again, placing them over the chair again, he bears down on the couch, drops leaden into the cushions. In seconds, he's asleep.

71

15, 303, Dutch

A small act of kindness, and it comes around. Except, that isn't why I did this.

Any of it.

You know, every twelve minutes another name is added to the organ transplant waiting list. Fourteen people die each day from the lack of available donors. And all anyone outside can see is you. Squinting dimly at your own reflection.

Obviously, my appearance was of greater importance now. What with the switch.

That's how Mike referred to my promotion.

Matthew. Re: the switch, he'd begin peppy memos addressed to me, CC'd to Caroline. Or his extension would flash red on the caller display of my brand new phone – lighter headset, faster speed dial – while I tracked lost brunch reservations for harried directors of corporate operations. And I'd put them on hold, and he'd remind me that Caroline urgently needed last week's time sheets, or ask me esoteric questions about budget codes.

I was his emissary. Lieutenant. And now he talked to me in expert whispers, arm thrown paternally round my shoulder as he told me all that I needed to know. What to pass on, and what to withhold. Welcome to the club.

I had my hair cut at a salon on Stanlake and Creed, where I drank free coffee while having my roots conditioned by a girl who could have been a model.

I was already working out on a daily basis. Now, I stepped up my regime. Seven miles on the treadmill, for which I allowed no more than an hour, followed by weights, then a circuit.

I spent half that month's salary at Alpha Male. The way I saw it, I needed a wardrobe that reflected my position.

Suitable for the frontline of the company's sphere of operations. These, again, were Mike's words.

Alpha Male sold clothes for the larger man. Not fatter. Just larger. It wasn't like I was troubled by my height. Defined by it. I was tall, unarguably, but never too much so. Just enough for people to look twice. Right there on the cusp. All the same, for me the place was a godsend.

I never liked buying clothes. Usually, it was all low-ceilinged changing rooms and fractious looks from slouching assistants as I shrugged apologetically and sent back yet another dress shirt that stopped two inches above my wrist. This time, it felt different. An investment in blue-chip stock.

The manager was older than me, about the same height. The guy working under him younger, and taller. A courtly giant, with pockmarked skin and a name tag that said Peter Moss right above where it then said Alpha Male.

Hello, Alpha Male Peter Moss, I'm Guy Friday Matthew Viss.

The manager tutted as I walked in. Then he summoned the courtly giant to guide me through racks of massive sweaters, rows of monolithic shoes, around which lofty men silently checked washing instructions or held vast knitwear to their chests before gigantic floor-length mirrors.

I left with two identical suits, near-black, wool, double-breasted. Three identical trousers, black. One bow tie, charcoal, silk. One regular tie, burgundy. Two pairs of Rockport brogues, black, leather. Various belts, socks, jockey shorts.

There wasn't time to go home before Naomi's birthday drink.

Her birthday wasn't til the weekend, but we'd never had the chance to give her a real goodbye. Having torn up her letter of dismissal, she cleared out her cubicle, collected the chippings of the lime green Elvis, and left. She never came back. Now over a month had passed. Alison doggedly stayed in touch, cajoling her into letting us provide a decent send-off. Til we each received an invitation requesting our company at her late farewell, very nearly birthday party.

So I sat with the bags stuffed under my chair in a bar on Ferris Street, around the corner from The Greatest Gift, listening to the story of Greg Hopper and the Elvis bust grow more elaborate each time she told it. And I laughed along with everyone else til someone would catch me laughing, and the laughter would trail away, and we'd all stare into our glasses.

Nobody was ever hostile. Conversations didn't stop when I walked into the room. They just turned antiseptic.

I told myself it was because I was spending so much time on the front desk. Hived off from the day to day, wading through my own minutiae.

It wasn't. Around the bar, within the cubicles, people knew it was my ear that Mike would whisper into, using bland terms with dark consequences. Restructure. Re-assign. But I pursued no agenda. Excised no vendettas. I dealt with my crews' misconducts discreetly, without snitching. I just enjoyed having Mike's attention.

It wasn't like I was enjoying much else. Financially, with a hike in my basic salary, full medical coverage and generous stock options, I was in clover. I'd never felt so valued by my employers.

It wasn't enough. The shortfalls of my reality began to irritate. As I told Mike – respectfully but often – I missed being a Guy Friday.

Though in theory still a member of the phone crew, the amount of time I could devote to clients was minimal, headed for non-existent. I tried to get used to the scalding frustration when a client would ask for me by name, and through the constraints of time I'd be forced to apologise, explain my unavailability, and pass the job on to Dylan in Entertainment, Julia in Personal.

Before long, I had to abandon my old clients altogether. Instead, I sat in my cubicle filling out time sheets and collating holiday forms. My only real contact with the world outside was the meetings I'd take with those interested in opening an account.

Whenever a client signed up after meeting me, Mike made sure I was rewarded. And still it wasn't enough. No one said, Thank you, Matthew Viss. No one was breathless with gratitude.

Don't get me wrong. For all the drudgery, I wouldn't have traded the switch. It just wasn't what I had hoped for. The frustration nipped at me even as I sat at Naomi's birthday/farewell drink.

We occupied a corner, the once and former Home and Family, joined by a gaggle of other Guy Fridays. Around us drones like ourselves, the early evening flotsam, quickly sedating. It took a while to lose the feeling of being at a wake. We'd done this, collectively, a dozen times before. Sat in the corner of a bar, frequently this one, picking over our respective days. Now it was just . . . different.

Alison and Robert kept the conversation going til, after a few bad jokes and cosy reminiscences, the atmosphere finally lightened. We split into fluid subsets, lines of chatter blurring. There were constant rounds of drinks, the table full with glasses.

I drank beer, enough to make me giddy. Naomi drank cocktails, enough to dope a horse. In an ebb of interchange, I heard her voice, gently slurred.

See, she said, that's why I threw it at him. Not because I was angry. Because he was a symbol. A symbol of –

She creaked to a halt in mid-sentence, then began a new one. I hope the bastard dies lonely.

You'll probably get lucky, Robert said. Alcoholics tend to. No one spoke.

You did all know that, didn't you?

No one spoke, again.

Oh. Well, you do now.

And he told us Mike had wanted rid of Greg for years. So when Matthew came along, he said, I guess it was only a matter of time.

As the conversations spun off again, I thought of Greg. His sweating. The endless flamenco pop of his fingers. Wondered where he was now. What he did with his life. Empathy consumed me. And then I forgot him.

The mood at the table grew louder, sillier. Naomi got to her feet.

OK, people. Let's go if we're going.

I glanced confused round the table, til Jon noticed my expression. He said they were meeting some friends of Naomi's over at a bar on Cleave Street.

I mean, he said, come along . . . if you want to.

I thought of home, Bethune and Scala, my weights, vitamins, meticulous bookshelves. I'd go for one drink, then head back. In all likelihood, after tonight, I'd never see Naomi again. So I gathered my bags and followed the rest outside, ready for a stifled groan or muttered oath. Nothing came. They just seemed astonished.

Oh my God, Mr Life and Soul. And so on.

Without warning, Naomi threw her arms around me. Then she kissed my cheek.

Thank you, Matthew, she said.

The tactility bothered me, even in my stupor. I patted her on the back.

It's just up here, she said.

We broke the hug and started walking. I looked behind and ahead of us. The rest of our party was atomised, sundered in twos and threes. I had no idea what to talk to her about.

So, I said. What's the plan?

The plan? she said. The plan! The plan!

She was drunker than I'd realised. Then, abruptly, wholly composed:

We're going to another bar.

Right, I said, and we walked some more.

Actually, I meant . . . professionally.

Oh, she said. Professionally, I'm doing massage. I've already started the courses.

And I nodded as I wondered what to say next, and we kept on walking.

So what made you want to do . . . that?

Well, you know . . . I just tried working out what the one thing was that everyone I knew needed. And what I realised was that we're all unravelling. Coming undone at the seams. Back pain, sinus pain, headaches, inflammation, poor alignment, muscle spasms, RSI, grinding teeth, seizing up, freezing over, shutting down. We, as a people, are chronic. I'll show you.

She pulled up, skipped around the back of me. We must have looked ridiculous. Me 6' 5", her 5' 4", if that. Then I felt hands at the base of my neck.

Jesus, Matthew . . . relax your shoulders.

I knew this was supposed to be good for you. I felt as if I was being assaulted. She began kneading my shoulders in slow, deliberate circles.

It's OK, I said. Really. I do a lot of exercise.

You know, Matthew, you have unbelievable tension in your upper back.

Ironic cheers rang out behind us.

Put him down, Gnome.

Alison and Lisa from Entertainment were approaching, bent double with laughter.

Pick on someone your own size.

I'd never heard her called Gnome before. She let go of my shoulders, and we walked again.

Have you got a girlfriend, Matthew?

She said this with a pure, infant's curiosity.

Actually, I said, I'm married.

God. Really? I never knew . . .

It's not . . . we're not together any more.

I'm sorry.

It's OK.

It wasn't, of course. But that was hardly Naomi's fault.

I hadn't told anyone at The Greatest Gift about Eleanor and Alice, our life together, its ruin. Mr Deedelus, Eleanor's photographs, the forgotten birthday. I wore no ring, I saw no reason to raise the subject. I think, but only think, I once told Alison I had a daughter. I didn't expand.

We walked for another two minutes, maybe three, til I saw the group in front of us – Jon, Robert, Joanna from Business – pause by an awning, a doorway beneath. They stopped, then went inside. We followed, up one flight of stairs into a long, chintzy room with banquette seating around the perimeter. Tables through the middle. At one end was a bar, at the other a stage. A grey, waist-high box filled the corner, swathed in disco lights. Although I'd never been to one before, I knew the set-up immediately. This was a karaoke bar.

As soon as we took our seats, a thick-set guy in shirt sleeves, tie askew, clambered on stage. The lights began to pulse and spin, a synthesised backing track booming from a speaker. I had no idea what the song was and my few suppositions were blown apart once he started howling into the microphone.

His volume only stoked that already rising at our table, a raw cacophony that gathered further when Naomi's friends began arriving. They came in droves, young, well-dressed, ferociously alive. There were more drinks, more singers, our party spilling across four tables. The whole scenario was getting messy.

Jon was the first of our number to perform.

I don't know who instigated it. All I know is, it happened. He sang 'Santa Claus Is Coming to Town'. It was the end of June.

His voice was reedy, brittle.

He's making a list
And checking it twice.

When he finished, a raucous cheer went up from our table, to the obvious distaste of the people beside us.

Naomi was next. She smoked a cigar as she took the stage with one of her friends from outside the company, a woman with her hair dyed fire-truck red. They duetted 'I Got You Babe'.

I was at the point of utter inanity. The junction of melancholy and anaesthesia, where each moment exists in perfect

81

isolation, then dilates, liquefied; where you sit, legs splayed, grinning foolishly at strangers. Eventually, my gaze settled on Alison. She smiled indulgently.

Do you hate me now? I said. Be honest. Does everyone hate me now? Because of the switch?

Because of what?

The switch. Because now I'm Greg Hopper.

No, she said. Of course we don't. No one does. I thought it was what you wanted.

I shrugged.

We're happy for you, Matthew. You just can't expect it to be the same way it was.

We sat, watching Naomi, before she turned to face me.

Are you OK?

I was poised to reply, the words just forming, when I heard my name.

Matthew next.

Robert was standing over me. I looked up, baffled.

Come on, Matthew. Our esteemed senior manager.

A crowd of faces surrounded me, looming in, like through a fish-eye.

Ah, no. No no no no no.

A chant of my name went up as Jon and Robert hauled me to my feet. A list of song titles thrust into my hands. Naomi and her friend were almost through.

Panicked and disoriented, I scanned the titles for one I recognised. As Naomi sauntered off stage, I chose. Trudged toward the stage. The mic had Naomi's lipstick smeared over it.

I sang '1999', by Prince. It had been a while since I'd heard it, but I got a grip once the music started. Inert at the mic stand, I opened my mouth.

As the song went on, I found myself taking the microphone and twirling the lead along the stage. There was whooping from our tables, and it encouraged me to dance a little, dipping my shoulders and twisting my hips in rhythm. I've always been a good dancer. People are always surprised.

The instrumental passages had been all but excised. In just under three minutes, the whole thing was over. I replaced the microphone, stepped down to the floor. Back at the table, all was hysteria.

I have to use the bathroom, I said.

Though the bar was hardly exclusive, the bathroom was clean, an attendant posted at the sinks. It wasn't clear if he was there to maintain hygiene or propriety.

He was in his forties, tactfully urbane. When I was done, he handed me a towel, whistling to himself, almost imperceptibly. Drying my hands, I caught his eye.

Good night? I asked him.

Oh . . . You know.

He carried on whistling, and I asked him what the tune was. It's Bach, sir. Brandenburg number three.

I couldn't think of anything to say to that. Instead I fumbled in my pockets for a tip, lurched for the door.

Crossing the room, back over to our tables, I staggered. Took this as my cue to leave. It was late. Far later than I was used to. I turned to Alison, said I'd see her tomorrow.

Not wanting to interrupt her talking with her friends, I hung back before I said goodbye to Naomi. When I did, she threw her arms around me once more.

We made the customary promises. We'll keep in touch. Have lunch one day. Alison's got your number, right?

She reached out and grabbed my shoulders again.

We can carry on where we left off, she said, then winked and burst out laughing. In another context, I might have been fazed. Here, now, I laughed as hard as her.

Then I grabbed my bags and walked down into Cleave Street.

There were taxis skirting the area. It came as a relief. Cleave Street was the heart of what had once been the city's meat district, a nest of butchers and buyers. After a certain hour, it still had a lurid reputation. Now and then, when the wind blew hard, you could taste history in the back of your throat. A hint of gristle, scintilla of fat.

83

I flagged down the first cab I could and, bags strewn across me, took the short ride to Bethune and Scala. Carl was in the lobby when I came through the door.

Hello, Mr Viss. Do you need any help with those?

I'm fine, I said. Thank you.

I stumbled inside the apartment, threw down the bags. Undressed and cleaned my teeth. Occasionally, as now, I still found the sight of one toothbrush resting in the cup on the sink devoid of Eleanor's beside it unsettling, wrong, the same way I noticed the absence of pickles in the fridge or – though I'd scoured local stores in the effort to find them – the same kind of rubbish bag we used back then.

I got into bed, the duvet wider than I remembered it, my sleep, as always, sudden, absolute. The alcohol just sent me deeper. Felt like I would never come to again.

I must have only been under for seconds before I was roused by a steady clattering. Bear-garden cries. Given how I sleep, they must have been deafening. They came from somewhere down the street.

I peered from the window with the light off. A small group of homeless people stood on the corner of Bethune and Sheridan, right beside the toy shop. They weren't doing much, just milling, carousing. One periodically screaming. Exhausted and rheumy, I went back to bed.

After a while, I guess someone must have called the police. I saw blue lights flicker on my bedroom wall and then, in the beat of a hummingbird's wing, everything went quiet.

The brownies, approaching their sell-by date, need marking down. They go stale under this lighting anyway, the eternal halogen glare that bulldozes day and night. Phillip Reilly takes a price gun, adjusts the number dial, crouches beside them. Keeps the till in his peripheries, the way he was trained to.

This shift is his last at the E-Z Buy General Store, open 24 hours. The last time he'll throw on his stiff yellow uniform, walk among snack food, soft drinks, ketchup, processed cheese in unvarying squares, batteries, condoms, sunglasses. The last time he'll punch in, wipe down the surfaces, change the tapes for the closed-circuit monitor. The intimacies of failure.

He arrived, for the last time, at nine in the evening. He'll leave, for the last time, at six this morning. Four hours from now, he'll stroll into the dawn and start again. He pulls the trigger, bullets the tags.

Phillip Reilly is thirty-eight. A qualified personal fitness trainer, laden with diplomas. An expert in body shape, he once boasted a broad, lucrative client base. Gadfly women wanting better definition, wealthy men with hanging guts.

And then, perdition. The business went in a plume of unpaid bills, house the same way. His wife went with the house. He got used to the repo men.

That was sixteen months ago. Here, under the burning lights, is where he's been since. Conducting his penance. Clearing his debts. Now he's on his way back. A guy with a gym – the friend of a guy he knew from the tracks, another face at the meetings – offered him work at his place. Just while he gets on his feet. The next day, he gave his notice to the duty manager. She didn't seem concerned.

Every Monday evening, he goes to Gamblers Anonymous. There's a new member there at least twice a month. A man, sometimes a woman, will sit in the circle, itemise their downfall. The details are interchangeable. Perhaps it was cards, or racing, possibly slots or the lottery. And they'll break down, and everyone will cry, and together they'll stand and recite the mantra.

We admitted we were powerless over gambling, that our lives had become unmanageable.

A cabbie stands at the counter with a pack of gum, eager to pay and go. Reilly puts down the price gun, gets to his feet. This is his last night, and the hope flows through him.

The fifth of my seven alarm clocks has a shrill, ascending wail, rising to a near-biblical crescendo. I keep it by my wardrobe, in the far corner of my bedroom. More than any of the others, it's the one I've come to depend on. Its four precursors, their rings staggered at one-minute intervals, are hardly polite. Sometimes they're still not enough. The two that follow make the fifth sound castrated, more shock paddles than timepieces. I try to be awake before they ring.

The morning after Naomi's drink it was the fifth that broke my slumber. The other four were already ringing in unison.

I got to the fifth, slamming down the buzzer, then dealt with the rest in turn, tracing a path back to my bedside. I remembered the sixth and seventh only after they each went off while I was in the bathroom.

Considering the amount I'd drunk the previous evening, I felt surprisingly nimble. All the same, I took special care with my supplements and vitamins, increasing the doses where necessary. Put the coffee on. Enjoyed the warm, industrial hiss of the espresso machine as I dressed and showered. While my hair dried, I re-read passages from Eric Handler, drank my coffee and came to, incrementally.

Arriving at The Greatest Gift, the phone room was barely half full. No one from last night's party was there yet. I started my computer, heard it rattle into life. There were budget codes to tally, time sheets to collate. Then, Mike.

I heard him speak before I saw him.

Matthew . . . Just wanted a chat. Thought we'd talk in (he checked his watch, bending his elbow, pulling back his cuff) . . . five?

Sure, I said. Of course.

Great. We'll do it in the meeting room.

Over the next five minutes, I ran through every nightmare scenario. This was the first time since the switch I'd been summoned to the meeting room. I thought of the complainant, returning to destroy me, or a random change of heart by Mike. Rued every minor blunder of the last few weeks, each ephemeral misstep or potential *faux pas*. And I counted down the seconds in my head.

One elephant. Two elephant.

Three hundred elephants later, I got up from behind my desk and headed for the meeting room. Mike was already there. I sat across from him, one seat down. My hands were shaking.

So, he said. How's life?

Oh, great. Absolutely.

This, I thought, is it. The end of the honeymoon. Annulment pending.

Good, he said. Well, here's the thing.

I listened for the chamber being loaded, the hammer cocked.

I want you to know we're delighted with the way you've handled the switch. But we also know you're happiest when you're dealing with the clients. In the trenches.

Here it comes. I braced myself.

So what we were wondering, hoping, was this. We'd like you to continue in your present role. But, given you also want more client contact, I thought you might be interested in someone who's just come over to us.

He leaned in, lowered his voice despite us being the only people here.

An escapee from Lukas Concierge. His name's Jonah Hoffman. Runs an investment house over on Gresham and Dutch. I think we may be looking at a topline account here. So naturally we're keen to . . . show him our best side.

I breathed hard. Reprieve.

. . . He doesn't want anything unusual. Just someone he can talk to directly. Who can offer a real one-to-one service. To do that, I need someone I can trust. What I'm saying, Matthew, is this. I want you to be his Guy Friday.

Mike seemed to be working up into an oratorical fervour. And me, I felt like saluting.

I hope you understand, Matthew, offering a client this level of commitment is uncharted territory for us. You can be, to him, the beating heart of the company.

I'm . . . speechless, I said. It's . . . perfect. I mean, yes. Of course.

Mike beamed at me, and I back at him.

Good. The way it moves forward is this. I told him you'd visit his office today.

He handed me Jonah's address, printed on a Greatest Gift VIP Account card.

Just to get to know each other. It's 3.30. He seems pretty big on punctuality, so make sure you're there on time.

I took this as my cue to leave. Infused for the rest of the day with an open, rosy benevolence. As the afternoon went on, I repeatedly checked the crease of my trousers, the lie of my cream cotton shirt. Then I left for Jonah Hoffman's office.

There was no jolting coach ride across a bleak Carpathian moor. Just the fifteenth floor of a squat, generic block on Gresham Street and Dutch.

In the lift, I went over my lines. Still mumbling when I walked into the foyer. A small brass plaque hung beside the door.

J A Hoffman Ventures and Investment.

Inside, an angular secretary looked me up and down.

Hello, I said. My name's Matthew Viss. I'm here from The Greatest Gift. To see Mr Hoffman. I've got an appointment at 3.30.

She glanced at me again, then at her diary. Then she picked up the phone. Receiver to her ear, she spoke.

Mr Fisk is here.

Viss, I whispered.

That's right, she said, ignoring me . . . OK. I will . . . hm-hm . . . OK.

She asked me to take a seat, said Mr Hoffman would be with me shortly. I sank into a leather couch, my weight pulling me into its cushions, the hem of my trousers lifting to reveal my socks. Embarrassed, I hauled myself upright.

Beyond the secretary was a glass partition, so heavily frosted as to be impervious. With my document case beside me, I felt like a hustler, pedlar, slick, single-minded.

I looked over the magazines laid out on the table in front of me. Obscure periodicals for serious money. I picked one up, leafed through its pages. Even the paper felt expensive. There were ads that looked like reports, reports that looked like ads. Hints on tax loopholes, advice on trust funds, fetishistic homages to tailors, jewellers, island retreats, private aircraft. Brand names I'd never heard of and still to this day remain mystified by.

Matthew Viss?

A man in his late forties with platinum grey hair and drawn patrician features was staring down at me. I stood and held out my hand.

Mr Hoffman?

He nodded as we shook.

Jonah's fine. Do you want to come through?

I followed him to the glass partition, before he paused and turned to me.

Coffee?

Coffee would be great. Thank you.

Bonnie, could we organise some coffee?

His secretary said yes, but he was already walking away. I smiled apologetically, followed him past an unlit room set off the hallway.

We'll use my office, he said, signalling another at the far end.

When we got there, the first thing I noticed was less the grandiose scale of the interior than Jonah's absolute, glitchless self-assurance. He motioned for me to sit on another couch, larger still than the one in the foyer, flush against the wall. The rest of the office comprised a mahogany desk with some kind of bonsai on it, an outsize window from which I just knew the view would be breathtaking, a fax, computer, a couple of phones. Jonah grinning in triplicate from the covers of three more finance magazines, each framed and hung above the desk. That was it. The rest was space. Yet Jonah, at less than six feet and trim, seemed to fill it without even moving. And I, for all my stature, was shrinking here, insignificant.

I take it you weren't attacked by bees on your way here?

Ah . . . no, I said, trying to grasp what he could mean, how I might respond.

You can't have seen the paper today. A truck went over on its side this morning. Just outside Demotte. Seven hundred beehives in the back. Mayhem, apparently. I imagine the place is teeming with arthritics. The stings ease their pain. Did you know that, Matthew?

No, I said, like a question itself.

Hm, he said. And his face turned empty, til he pulled up a chair across from me. Slung his right leg over his left knee.

He held himself the way that only the rich can. Despite the lines etched deep into his forehead, Jonah was always unworried, implacable. The world was always at his service. He got everyone's best side.

So, you're the big man at The Greatest Gift.

Thank you, I said, feeling myself blush. That's very flattering. Ah . . . would you like to see this?

I rummaged in my case, produced a copy of the company prospectus.

No, I've seen that. Your boss already gave me a copy.

Oh, I said, sliding it back in the case. OK.

His eyes flickered with the merest splash of impatience. He cracked his knuckles.

Listen, he said, why don't I tell you a little about what I do? Then we'll move on to what I need. I'm an investor. What I do is also known as venture capitalism. It's very simple. I use my money to facilitate ideas for businesses or products. If I'm convinced of its worth, I inject capital into the enterprise. Sometimes that takes the form of a short-term loan. Sometimes the money stays there indefinitely. Sometimes it's a small sum. Sometimes, much of the time, it's the difference between the idea becoming a reality and not.

The secretary entered as he talked, holding a slim metal tray, on which were balanced a cafetière, cups, spoon, jug of cream, and a bowl of brown sugar in coarse geological hunks.

I smiled at her, but she looked through me.

Thanks, Bonnie, Jonah said as she left.

You'll find, he went on, that most investors operate by committee. They set up companies and fill them with clerks and eunuchs who won't say what colour the sky might be without making sure everyone else agrees with them first. Black or white?

Black. Thank you.

He pushed the cup toward me, then poured himself another, adding a slug of cream and two craggy lumps of sugar. Stirred, fast and relentless.

I'm not like that. That isn't me. I've had partners in the past. Doesn't work for either of us. So this (he gestured round the office) is just me. I'm not a bank. I don't have a mission statement. I don't advertise, and I don't invest often. I invest when I choose to. And the fruits of that approach are any number of products you'll see on the shelves, any amount of flourishing businesses, that exist largely because of me. I could give you the names. You might be surprised.

I wasn't sure if he wanted me to ask him, or if he was being rhetorical.

So where do we come in? I said. I mean, me?

Where you come in is the point at which I need someone to look after certain time-consuming areas of my life. Who'll treat me as a priority, and can be relied on. Someone conscientious to execute tasks I don't have the time or, more to the point, the interest to carry out myself.

I kept thinking I should say something, but he wasn't stopping for breath.

My needs are straightforward. I might need you to book a table at a restaurant, and I might need you to recommend that restaurant first. I could ask you to get my car looked over, or find a painting for my study wall. All I expect is that you treat me with the same respect I give you. If you're going to be away, or you're sick, let me know. I'm not an ogre. I just want someone capable.

I am, I said.

He took a sip of his coffee.

So, what's your story?

I'm sorry?

What do you do when you're not indulging people like me?

My mind went blank.

I, ah . . . I'm into health.

He peered at me, amused and quizzical.

I like to keep healthy. I exercise. That kind of . . . thing.

So you're one of these gym people? Spend your nights sweating in public?

No . . . I do it at home. I've got a treadmill and . . . weights.

Where's home?

Bethune Street . . . the corner of Bethune and Scala.

Hm. I hear it's coming up round there.

He drained his cup and replaced it on the tray.

Do you golf, Matthew?

No . . . I don't.

You should. It's very cathartic. I'm sure if we're together long enough you'll get accustomed to my golf habit.

And he laughed. A fleeting heave.

So what else do you do? Besides lifting weights in Bethune Street?

I . . . like to read. Watch movies. TV.

It was only now, presenting my life for Jonah's inspection, that I realised how it must look.

And socially? he said.

I've just moved to the city. But, you know, I get out.

Of course, he said, with a smile I couldn't quite place. A girlfriend?

I'm married.

And that precludes a girlfriend?

I blushed for a second time. His smile became a smirk.

Relax. I'm just fooling with you. Kids?

A daughter. She's six . . . Actually, we're separated. My wife and I . . . My daughter lives with her.

Right. Must be tough. I'm still married to the first one myself. Our son's fifteen. His name's Julian. Again, in time, I'm sure you'll get to know all about that.

As the last words were leaving his mouth, he got to his feet.

It's been good meeting you, Matthew. And I'm happy with this if you are.

He showed me to the door.

I'm the only man for the job, I said.

Good, he said, cracking his knuckles again. Then we'll see each other soon.

I gave him my card. Wrote my home number across the back. He told me I had lovely handwriting, and I thanked him. He in turn thanked me for coming.

I'll call you when I need you, he said.

Outside, among the throng of Dutch Street, what had just passed didn't feel like a business meeting. It felt like an audition.

When I got back to The Greatest Gift, there was already a list of jobs faxed through from Jonah's office, marked for my attention. Just the basics. A card to be sent. A sandwich lunch ordered.

I liked Jonah. I felt good in his company. Enjoyed the knowledge that someone like him found worth in me. And I fell. And I fall. And I keep on falling.

Belinda Griselda dances for the camera. There is no music. She dances anyway. Eleanor watches as Alice and Aimee take turns with the bear, waving its paws, its stout, abbreviated legs. She notices the fur on its belly is thinning.

The days stay light til late this time of year. In the park, the afternoon mug lingers. Eleanor keeps an eye on the girls' cardigans, heaped under a tree. She focuses, gets ready to take the picture. Shooting in black and white. The lens finds Griselda, then Alice, then Aimee, then Alice again, face cheerfully scrunched while she grapples with her teddy.

This is what Tina Karlsson suggested, prescribed in her office at Alice's school. Before next term, she said, I really think you should spend some quality time with her. Bring her out of herself. Make this summer a special one, for both of you. One to keep in your photograph album.

Normally, she bridles when given advice. With Tina Karlsson, she listened. They talked for an hour, til both realised they were late for appointments.

Besides their shared careers, Tina Karlsson is also a single mother. Two in their teens now, the third a year older than Alice. The key, she said, is to make them know they're loved. Never let them think that he left *them*. And make sure they're socially active. Tina Karlsson put a certain emphasis on that final sentence.

Hence the presence of Aimee, her daughter's one friend from class. Hence the park. Hence Eleanor tirelessly planning outings, trips, excursions, sun-kissed holidays abroad where her child can swim and pick fruit, pal around with the local kids, affable urchins with sweet-natured spirits of adventure. The problem, of course, is the money. So the park it is, for now. At least she got to take the camera out. Hasn't used it in – God. How long *has* it been?

She focuses once more. Belinda Griselda spinning into a dervish whirl. Her lens wanders past, across the park. A group of both sexes play frisbee, a fat guy lounges, shop workers stroll home in shirt sleeves and short skirts, the ice-cream van packs up and drives away. Dogs let off the leash.

Alice still mentions her father. Where he might be. When he'll be back. But less, now, than before. Without the anguish of the first weeks.

Eleanor could use a cigarette. Without a breeze, this heat's right on the point of oppressive. Finally, she releases the shutter and, as she does, she feels herself changing. Becoming other. Like an ice floe breaking.

A Small Act of Kindness

Falling now enough to tell.

Enough to know my body's moving.

To feel my weight as power in the air, compelling me to ground.

A blunt acceleration.

And in my heart, it all seems theoretical.

But I'm falling.

There's no mistaking that.

Not plummeting.

Not yet.

Just

Gathering speed.

Cascading toward the inevitable.

Right now, I'm passing the seventh-floor apartment.

Although it's directly upstairs from my own, I've barely met the guy who lives there. He moved in a month ago.

I hear his music now and then. Only seen him twice. Once when he was moving in. Once a week later. He was outside, crossing Scala Street, being screamed at by a man in a full-face balaclava. Not much of what was said was audible. What I made out was obscene.

That's all I can remember. The guy from upstairs, whose name I don't even know, cowed and raw, humiliated, and when I looked at his companion I only saw the eyes and mouth.

After that, I never saw him again. Who knows what the story is?

In the front room of the seventh-floor apartment, Adam Marcus shuts off his stereo, makes ready to leave. Get the keys, cut the lights. Remember the balaclava.

Khaki, fetid, it lies on the arm of the couch. Elias left it yester-day. Adam shudders at the sight of it.

Elias Toomey is an actor, male lead, ascendant. Adam is his assistant. It started as a joke, back when they were room-mates, and Adam still acted himself. He'd give it up and manage Elias. Then, when the jobs started coming, he did. And, as the money rolled, so his status disappeared. From manager to gopher. He's about to drive him to an interview. Should the location be known, frenzied women will break down the door. That's what Elias thinks. That's why he wears the balaclava.

It started as his TV show began its second run. He'd just appeared on a magazine cover. He arrived at Adam's wearing it. It's military surplus, he said. Now I won't attract attention. Get hassled in the supermarket.

He doesn't even go to the supermarket. But Adam knows better than to say that. Last time he broached the subject, Elias turned nasty in public. And the more money Elias makes, the more money Adam makes, and the worse it gets. He pockets his keys.

And I can't help but wonder if he's watching me now. Gazing from his fume-stained window, observing my fall. And I wonder what I look like from below.

Anyway.

The strange thing about last summer was – in the face of the switch and all that went with it, despite Jonah Hoffman and the summons to Dutch Street – my thoughts kept turning to giving blood. Mortimer and Upas, with an IV hanging from my arm.

I didn't understand it then. I'm not sure I do now. I just longed for the sensation. I kept watching TV, hoping to catch the donor ad, scanning the papers for large-scale emergencies. Ways I could have made a difference.

After my first donation, I'd taken my diary and circled in red the date my rest period ended. Now, I was counting the days.

On the morning my twelve weeks were up, I woke at the

first alarm. Flew through my routine, left with my hair still damp. On my way out, I passed Carl.

Hello, Mr Viss, he said.

Hello, Carl, I replied.

Then walked with vim and purpose, out of my building, left beyond the toy shop. There were more homeless there every time I looked. The city's most successful franchise. I could only imagine where they were coming from.

That morning, I'd read a story in the paper concerning the area's regeneration. Another fragment in the ticker-tape sequence of portents and omens. Now I saw a row of sickly faces ranged against the wall. Plastic ducks at a shooting gallery. Half a dozen, maybe more, standing on the actual corner.

When you first see them, of course, their soiled blankets and need, you recoil. The same way you do at a horror movie. Refuse to accept this as part of your and your children's world. Then you look back.

I recognised one. A sallow guy in mangy sportswear. Young enough for acne, with a brutal scar across his neck. A week ago, he'd asked me for change when I'd had the exact money for coffee. I'd said I had nothing. He thanked me anyway.

Now he approached me again. He didn't look hostile. Just beaten. Defeated. Most of them looked that way. There were the drunks, of course, the angry and abusive. But mostly, irrelative of age or ethnicity, they just looked wounded, bewildered.

He knew that I'd seen him, and I groped for my wallet. Gave him the first note that came to hand. Felt my face redden as I walked away. Whether I was more anxious to get out of there or on to Mortimer and Upas I really don't know. Either way, by the time I arrived, a sweat had broken, my shirt stuck limply to my back. A heatwave was rising.

Swish. Swish. And it all seemed so familiar. The scuffed plastic chairs, the MDF table, Carmen.

I'm sorry, she said, but we've only just opened.

She didn't say it unkindly. Just factually. I shrugged and gazed around, as if returning home from years at sea.

That's OK. I'll wait.

Have you given before? she asked me, reaching for a pale green form.

Yes, I said. I have.

Her hand stopped short.

And you've had breakfast?

I have.

Great.

She stared at her computer.

Sorry . . . It must be tired today.

And we laughed, how you do, til finally she sat back, content with whatever was on her screen. She asked for a name, and I gave it to her.

Great! she said, typing fast, recalling my details. Well, aren't you the eager beaver? Here five minutes after we open, the first day you can give again.

Really? I said. I didn't know.

Twisting in her seat, she printed out a consent form. It verified my willingness to give, confirmed there'd been no significant changes in my health or circumstances over the last twelve weeks. There was actually a dotted line, on which I signed. Ever since Jonah had mentioned it, I savoured the chance to use my handwriting.

She asked me to wait til the nurses were ready. I sat for a minute. The air conditioning, slovenly. An occasional waft, the odd lethargic draught. My cream cotton shirt still clung to my back. I tried to catch Carmen's eye.

Sorry . . . could I get a glass of water?

Oh . . . sure. Just ask the girl in the donors' lounge.

Beyond Carmen's desk, I recognised the semi-circle of chairs immediately. The brunette woman at the counter. The lopsided fold in her cheek when she smiled.

Hi, she said.

Hello . . . ah . . . could I get some water?

Of course, she said, reaching under the counter. Looks like another hot one, huh?

I nodded enthusiastically.

Sheeiiuuwww

was what I said. Like the world's smallest aircraft taking off. Then:

Certainly is. I mean . . . will be.

She handed me the water, cold, in a plastic cup. I drank it in one gulp.

Would you like another?

Oh, no. Thank you.

She stepped out from the counter with the basket uncertainly balanced in her arms.

Here, I said. Let me. And I took it from her, set it on the table.

When I looked up, William was beside me. He held a copy of my pale green form, my declaration of consent paperclipped to the front. His lank blond hair was longer now, over his ears, past his shoulders.

I exchanged half-smiles with the woman as he beckoned, and I followed.

The fruit cake comes in thick, bomb-proof slices, cemented with raisin and cherry. A lot of raisin. Not much cherry. The supplier deals in budget confectionery. Occasionally, someone produces a home-made version, baked that day, plump with morellos. Sometimes it's a random well-wisher. Sometimes Grace Walker herself.

Behind the counter of the refreshment lounge, Grace darts into the stock room. Watches the lanky man she just served marching after William.

It's a cupboard, really. The stock room. On one side are clipboards, pens, diskettes. The other, her stores. She fills the basket. They're out of shortbread. Must have happened yesterday. She didn't even notice. The donors crave it, like pigs for truffles. Once, baffled, she checked the ingredients. Just flour, butter, sugar, preservatives.

Just one of those things she's learned.

Grace Walker has volunteered here for the last eleven months, since the death of her maternal grandfather. The will reflected her status as the family's only viable member. While the old man was never wealthy, his ceaseless austerity left Grace enough to live as she'd like, for a time.

Today, she was the first person to arrive. Within ten minutes an orderly and two of the nurses were drinking store-bought coffee at the kitchen doorway, acclimatising. Carmen the receptionist bustled in afterward, lambasting her journey. I left the house two hours ago, she said. Then they opened the doors.

The shortbread will have to be reordered. It involves elaborate forms, multiple signatories. She counts the cash she has on her. Maybe she'll pick it up herself.

The important thing is to smile. This was the nurses' advice when she started. Don't devalue what you're doing, they said. You're the one who looks after them. Sends them back out there knowing they've done something special.

So she grins when they ask for a Coke or a juice, pallidly clutching their arms. Meets their eyes when every rooted impulse is calling her gaze to the floor.

Slowly, her shyness is abating. With each new face she talks about the weather to, she can feel it lift. It's a reason to be here.

Soon, she'll be able to stop taping conversations. Her own and those around her. She keeps a slim cassette recorder under the counter, in her bag. Practises with the tapes she makes at home. Going over her dialogue, listening to the donors, scripting, interjecting. Making herself a participant. She knows it's working.

She doesn't lie when people ask her why she comes. Just tells them she's got the means to help. That she's glad to support a good cause. Which is true.

When she started, this could have been anything. Any noble design from millions. Mistreated animals or victims of Tourette's, land mines or the rainforest. Now she feels different. She's heard the nurses, with their tragedies escaped or played out in overburdened city hospitals. She believes in what she does. So she fills up the basket, and smiles at the donors.

The last two nurses on the morning shift arrive in summer outfits. Another hot one, says the first. Girl, the second says, I love your hair today.

Grace is wearing it in bunches. She slips the tape recorder under the counter, begins to make the coffee. When it's done, she'll put the basket out.

I took the same bed as last time. Aside from me and William and a pair of female nurses, the place was empty. I lay back as he studied my consent form.

So, he said, you're still at the same address?

Hm-hm.

And there's been no change in your health over the last twelve weeks?

None I can think of.

His eyes stayed on the form.

No steroid use?

I coughed, shifted my position.

No.

Without further inducement, I rolled up my shirt sleeve. As William tied the cuff around my bicep, his grasshopper chorus seemed louder than I remembered. I turned my head toward him.

Hot back here, isn't it?

Hm-hm. The AC's gone.

He carried on prepping me.

How's that cuff feel?

Fine, I said.

Then the ball. As William passed it to me, I wondered how many they had on the premises, where they stored them. Thought of all the hands that had clenched it, the veins raised by its presence.

The rest was as before. The transparent baggie attached to an IV, then to a drip stand behind my head. The fleeting nick, the IV fed into me, this is going to sting, says William, the unsprung pressure as the blood left my body, then William, back, removing the cord, attending to me with a Band-Aid, collecting the baggie.

I sat up, exhaling.

. . . Shall I go and get a juice or something?

Sure. Do that. And remember not to drink any alcohol tonight, or smoke for the next two hours.

Or take any steroids, I said.

He didn't reply. Maybe he didn't hear me. I got down from the bed and returned to the lounge, where the woman smiled as I mooched up to the counter, holding my elbow across me.

She said hello again, and I asked for coffee and juice. The same unearthly yellow as last time. Taking a cup in each hand, I sat at the table opposite the counter, the basket in front of me. Surveyed the cake and chocolate bars. Felt an urge that I couldn't explain.

Excuse me, miss? Do you have any shortbread?

Her features ricked in apology.

There's fruit cake.

The steadfast cheer in her voice made me feel bad. The thought of the fruit cake made me feel worse.

OK . . . Thanks.

She stepped from behind the counter.

Don't go anywhere, she said. Then she walked out of the building.

I picked out a chocolate bar, tore off the wrapping and took a bite. Washed it down with coffee and juice. By the time she got back, I was almost done.

Here, she said. As you're the first of the day.

And she dropped a small tartan packet of shortbread into my lap.

God . . . thank you. There was no . . . I didn't mean . . .

It's fine. I had to get some anyway.

Only then did I see she was holding a plastic bag full of the stuff. In truth, I wasn't hungry now. Obviously, I ate it, murmuring appreciatively. She stood beside me, slotting the packets into the basket. I felt obliged to talk to her. More than that. I wanted to.

So, I said, eventually, do you give yourself?

And she told me that she did. That she had done for years. Every twelve weeks, like clockwork. She glanced over to the counter.

Do you need anything else?

I told her I was fine, and she stayed where she was. One elephant. Two elephant.

Do you . . . ever think about the recipients? The donees?

It was all I could think of to say.

Sure, she said. Every time. You?

And she caught my gaze and held it.

Oh yeah, I said. Sometimes, when I'm on a bus or I'm in a lift or just sitting there at work, I'll look around at the people I'm with and all I can think of is which one's destined for some horrible misfortune. Some random senseless calamity. And if I could help when it happens.

The words were pouring out of me. I dreaded how they sounded. She just kept staring til, as she spoke, she leant in closer.

Me too, she said. You know what? Me too.

She smelled of palm milk hand cream and coffee grounds. Her lipstick a deep burgundy. Eyes cat green. I realised then I liked to look at her.

So, she said, you on your way to work now?

Yeah, I said. I'm over on Pearl Street.

Sure. I know it.

Right.

And she stood, and I sat.

The shortbread's great, I said.

Then I drained my coffee. Told her I should go.

Well, you have a great day.

And you.

By the way . . . I'm Matthew.

Grace.

Nice to meet you, we said together, then burst out laughing. How you do. She said she guessed she'd see me in twelve weeks, and I told her she definitely would.

Heading for Pearl Street, there was the same wooze to my gait, throb in my arm. The same little brilliance. Only this time, it felt even better. Like I was tuned to the city's every psychic wavelength. A lucid, martial drumbeat.

You know, routine heart surgery takes six units of donated blood. Bone marrow transplants twenty. Organ transplant forty, with a further twenty-five of plasma.

By the time I got to work, my head was full of car wrecks and miscarriages, haemophiliacs and burns victims. And I'd never felt more alive.

The day passed in sweltering rapture. The AC collapsed round lunchtime. Through the gripes and decrial of my colleagues, I remained elated. In thrall to something subcutaneous.

It was after six when Jonah called.

Mike had granted me no little autonomy in dealing with the account. I continued to supervise the phone crews, but most of the admin was delegated elsewhere, allowing me to focus on the job at hand. Another concierge service – Definitive VIP – had recently opened up and was advertising throughout the city. I guess he was just eager to maintain our profile. Jonah, as he knew, was not a man without influence.

I had him on speed dial, a line reserved. Looked forward to its red light bidding. Jonah seemed so unimpressed by so much, I couldn't help but savour his endorsement of me.

This time, when my red light flashed, I was getting ready to go home. Obviously, I didn't say that. He'd rung me five times that day already. He'd needed a dental appointment. The golf course at the Avelden Country Club booked. His car waxed. To confirm delivery of the painting.

Of all the jobs I ever did for Jonah, finding the painting for his study wall was easily the most intimidating. The vagueness of the brief – together with my ignorance of art past high-school doodles – left me floundering. Having scoured catalogues and talked with grasping dealers, I inveigled Alison into helping out. She seemed flattered. Together, we visited a gallery managed by a friend of hers. Chose an abstract by a woman from the neighbourhood, who Alison swore to me was highly regarded. A vast colourfield, with random zips of monochrome. It was being delivered to Jonah's house that afternoon.

Fine, he said, when I told him. Christina'll be there. Or Alda.

Christina was Jonah's wife, Alda their maid. I hadn't met or spoken to either, but Jonah already used their names as if we were acquainted.

Actually, he said, could you call and check someone *is* going to be there?

A woman answered when I rang.

Good afternoon, I said, may I speak to Mrs Hoffman?

You are.

The voice was well-bred, snappish. I introduced myself, explained where I was calling from.

Yes, she said. I know who you are.

Her manner made me nervous.

I . . . ah . . . was just calling to see if you or Alda were going to be at home today.

The line crackled, otherwise silent.

There's a painting . . . being delivered . . .

Nothing. Briefly, I thought I'd been cut off.

Hello?

Yes, she said. Then a sigh. An abundance unspoken . . . I'll be here til seven-thirty. Alda's here all day.

Another lonely rustle.

OK?

Ah . . . yes. That was all I –

And the line went dead.

So when Jonah called me at almost seven, I expected it to concern the painting. Instead, he told me he needed a table at Marlowe's. For two, he said, at ten. In the alcove. If the greeter stonewalls you, mention my name.

I'd never been to Marlowe's. Its reputation was one of deals struck and tradition maintained for an aggressively upscale clientele. Old leather, real fire, dark wood, huge steaks, served rare.

Oh, he said, and could you explain to my wife that I'm meeting an associate. I'll be back . . . well, I suspect it'll be late. Flowers might be good.

For your wife?

That's right.

Any preference in bouquet?

No, you decide. Oh . . . and could you call by my office after you're done? There's something to be collected.

It would take me twenty minutes to get to Dutch Street. Thirty more to home. I wouldn't get back til almost eight, and I needed to make the health-food store. I was out of papaya enzyme. It closed in half an hour. Obviously, I didn't say that.

Sure, I said.

Good, he said. I'll let security know you're coming.

When I called the florist I asked for laelias, which only fuelled his peevishness at the late hour of my order. I specified the card should read:

Til tomorrow – thinking of you.

Then I called Christina.

As I told you earlier, she said, I'm about to leave myself. So my husband's whereabouts are really not an issue.

Then I called Marlowe's. With bland disdain, the greeter told me he naturally had nothing available. I mentioned Jonah.

I'm sorry, sir, he said. Would an alcove table be acceptable?

I packed my briefcase, shut down my computer, called the florist to check the laelias were sent. Took a cab to Dutch Street.

The doors were locked. The security guard sat out front, fixed on a small TV. I gesticulated from the street til I got his attention. Scowling, he emerged from his cloisters. There was food on his chin.

Through the glass, I told him I was collecting something for Mr Hoffman. Making no attempt to veil his suspicion, he let me inside. There were exchanges with Jonah's secretary, mumbled clarifications, ID checks and visitors' logs.

The elevator descended from unstaffed floors. Inside, the temptation to goof off was almost irresistible, til I noticed the camera mounted by the ceiling.

Jonah's secretary was pacing when I reached the fifteenth floor. She looked furious, beyond the trite asperity of cities in hot weather.

So you're here, she said.

Ah . . . Jonah told me –

Yes. I know.

Spinning on her heel, she led me into Jonah's office. In the centre of the room, as if on exhibit, stood a gleaming rack of weights. A black steel pyramid, the saddles of which held a full set of dumb-bells. Solid chrome, with contoured handles to aid the grip. On top lay a pair of leather weights gloves and a blank card. Inside, it read:

With thanks for all manner of jobs well done – J.

A gift. A prize. I found myself welling up. I truly hadn't expected this, or anything like it. Now it was here, sublime.

The only problem would be moving it. I glanced over at the secretary, leant up against the doorframe.

No, she said. Just . . . no.

I only need to get them to the street, I said.

And we stood there a moment, in stalemate.

Stay here, she said wearily, then left the room.

Crouching, I studied the weights, recognising the brand from when I'd bought my own. Then, they were out of my price range. Now, the more I thought about Jonah's big-heartedness, the more amazed I was.

The secretary returned with the guard in tow. There was still food on his chin.

God, Bonnie.

I know, Jerrell. But you'll really be doing me a favour. I've got to be somewhere.

Sorry, I said, to her, to both of them.

And he sighed OK.

But you owe me, Bonnie.

You're an angel, Jerrell, she said.

Without acknowledging each other, the guard and I took the weights from the rack. Then, starting with the heaviest, we ferried the dumb-bells out of the office, one in each hand. The empty rack came last.

When we were done, the weights sat in pairs beside the elevator, rack adjacent. Jonah's secretary switched off the lights, and locked the door.

Thanks again, Jerrell. I could kiss you.

Bonnie, you'll get me in trouble.

She threw her bag over her shoulder and took the stairs. The guard and I, we took the lift. Down, then out to the street. Before I could thank him again myself, he grunted and shuffled back inside, locking the door behind him.

I stared down the street, deserted apart from the wrapper of a chocolate bar floating across the road. A garish tumbleweed. There were, of course, no cabs. Why should there be?

I kept looking. Eventually, I counted the seconds. By then, I must have already been waiting ten minutes. Another five and a taxi appeared in the distance. I flagged it down, then watched impotent as it sailed by me.

Seven minutes later, the same thing happened again. This had never happened to me before. With an unfamiliar bulk beside me, I'd slipped down the caste system employed by taxis throughout the city. Nine minutes elapsed before another cab. This time, I took no chances.

Striding into the road, I flailed my arms til the driver braked. He looked at me impassively through the windscreen.

I'll give you twenty to get me to Bethune Street, I said.

He shrugged.

Not with those. They'll kill my suspension.

Ah, come on. It'll just be like . . . having two fat guys in the back.

He just sat there, tapping the wheel, with my hands pressed against his windscreen.

Come on, I said. Come on.

And so it went til, grudgingly, he agreed.

Half expecting him to leave with screaming tyres the moment I stepped from his view, I disassembled the rack, loaded what I could onto the back seat. Asked him to open the trunk and he struggled out, cursing. Flipped it open. I stowed the rack, got in behind him.

No, he said.

What do you mean, no?

I mean no. You're gonna kill the suspension.

Look, I'll give you (I counted what cash I had on me) . . . thirty-nine . . . seventy.

He shook his head.

Well, that's all I've got, I said. And we sat, a symphony of mute belligerence.

OK, he said, a full minute later. Let's just go.

With the weights taking up most of the space, the back seat was hell. Every time we took a corner, the suspension groaned, and I'd see the driver glare at me in the rear-view mirror.

He drove slow. It was forty minutes at least before Bethune Street. Approaching the toy store, the lights turned red. One block down, I saw a police van on the kerb. Half a dozen cops assailed the same number of homeless. It looked like they were moving them on. Like they weren't being gentle about it. When the lights changed and we cruised past, I thought I caught the eye of the scar guy from that morning. An officer's hand at his throat.

We drove on. Pulled up outside my building. I didn't ask the cabbie to help me unload. As soon as I stripped out my wallet, he was gone. With the weights and rack lying on the street, I ran into the lobby to find Carl. He was nowhere in sight.

I brought the weights in alone. Once the last dumb-bells were inside the apartment, I closed the door and checked my watch. It was almost ten. I'd left Pearl Street, give or take, three hours ago. My arms stung from the clinic and the weights. My shirt was drenched. I opened every window. Made coffee, ran a bath. Minutes later, maybe less, I jolted upright. Realised I'd fallen asleep.

Lurching to the bathroom, I caught the water at overflow. By now, my arm was seizing up completely. I stripped and climbed in. When my eyes next opened, I was still there, face half submerged in the water.

It was two-fifteen on Friday morning. The coffee was still hot.

The gravel sprays in tiny arcs as the wheels come to rest. Jonah puts the car in neutral, parks outside the house.

It is 2.16 a.m. A rocket of discomfort jolts through his belly. He thinks back to Marlowe's. Meat, bloody on his plate. Reaches into the dash for indigestion tablets.

One light in the house is on, a single beam from the attic. His wife's bedroom is darkened, curtains firmly drawn.

Jonah steps from the driver's seat, remote locks the doors, takes the short walk back to the fence on the rim of his property. It is, they tell him, complete. A criss-cross of wire, fitted with cameras, elaborate pressure pads, triggers for alarms.

The construction looks slapdash, accidental. He kicks at a supporting post. As he expected, it wavers. He remembers the contractor's site manager, his glib protestations that, You know, Mr Hoffman, most of our customers are moving away from excessive displays of deterrence.

You could plough through this with a motorised scooter. He wants his deterrence excessive. Wants fearsome barbs and high-voltage currents. The kind of fence behind which lurks a relentless sic dog, slavering, unfed. He turns, retreats up the driveway, back to the house. Jesus. There is, he feels, a lesson here. Do favours, what happens? He should never have listened to Christina. Let his instincts be tainted by sentiment. Should have simply ignored her glutinous appeals on behalf of the cousin, or the brother, of the maid.

As he passes the car, he glances inside. A hollow in the back-seat leather, the imprint of bodies recently pressing, warm and insistent.

In the house, he slips off his shoes, wanders into the study. His new painting lies in the corner, rectangular, wrapped in brown paper. He'll look at it tomorrow. Right now, he doesn't have the energy. It is 2.21 a.m. It occurs to him he needs a hair-cut. Grabbing the phone, he calls the concierge. Waits for voice-mail as the pain in his stomach moves into his chest.

And the smoke hangs thick in the attic. Julian Hoffman's red-dened eyes darting across the room. All his. All this. The posters, CDs, vinyl, computer, the ashtrays, bottles, his friends. They bawl over the music, at him, at each other. Through years of experience, Julian knows the precise volume his mother will tolerate. He keeps track of the months since she last barged in here, a long stretch, measured with pride. The attic's security the bedrock of its status as his circle's favoured sanctum. His rules of entry zealously enforced. And the music rumbles on.

He gazes round again, the heads of his friends nodding as one. A hand passes him the bong. He takes the vapour down into his lungs, holds it there, blots out the urge to gag. His friends cheer, and Julian falls backward, hears three conversa-tions at once. Focuses on Balthus and Xavier. The latter, the old-est of those assembled, is nearing his seventeenth birthday. In here, this constitutes infirmity.

Gonna hafta can the jailbait, X, Balthus says. No more ickle twelve-year-olds.

One time, man, Xavier says. That was wu-uhn time.

Julian narrows his eyes, imagines his friends as chimps, loutish and gibbering. More than one calls out to him. He can't make out the words. They either want to use the pool, or the pool room. The answer's no for both.

He props himself up on his elbows, studies them. The bass thumps and they act like children. How much longer can they act like children? What will they be like when they're adults? The worst thing is, he knows.

Spinning out, he drags himself onto the bed, stares from the window. A black BMW sits in the driveway. The only way he knows his father's home. He takes another hit, belches out a cloud of smoke. Prepares to evict them.

When you're lifting weights, you're tampering with the body's conversion of oxygen. As you strain and heave, the relevant muscle is starved of energy. Eventually, with sufficient repetition, it becomes exhausted. If you continue beyond this point, keep hauling when the pain seems insufferable and the lactic acid flows through you like engine oil, the muscle will rip, its fibres rending and tearing.

Only then will anything worthwhile have been achieved. Only when the fibres heal will the bonds of tissue strengthen. And the muscle, the single tortured object of the whole racking enterprise, will be larger, tauter, more powerful.

I thought of this as I stood before the mirror, working my triceps. Threw my elbow up, raised my arm clear above my head. A set of twenty reps, then another. I dropped my hands to my hips, began my upright rows.

Jonah's gloves and weights made all the difference. Previously, my grip would give in the middle of lifts. Now, it was impregnable.

With every elevation, I watched my shoulders ripple. My face, still as tundra while the muscle tore.

As it was a Saturday, I'd allowed myself a lie-in. I hadn't meant to sleep til twelve. Fourteen hours since I closed my eyes on Friday night. Opening them again in the haze of noon, my alarms had run down, and it felt like being hoisted from the sea bed, confined inside a diving bell. I sat for an hour, just drinking coffee, chewing nicotine gum. Already, I was willing the next twelve weeks to pass. I could feel

William feeding the IV into me, taste the juice in the donors' lounge. Except it was dwindling. And the more it did, the harder I pined.

In my vest and shorts, I sauntered down for my mail. Carl was in the lobby.

I grabbed the bundle from my pigeonhole, headed back to the apartment. Inside, I set a water bottle beside the treadmill, stepped onto the belt. Started with a barely-there acceleration, a country-lane stroll to warm the muscles.

The motor whirred as I upped the speed, still genteel enough to let me open my post. A credit-card circular, utilities bill, some form of hustle in a brightly coloured envelope, its plastic window cracked and crumpled, heavily asterisked dispatch informing me I'd already won a substantial cash dividend. A letter from the bank.

As soon as I saw the Two Cities logo, a sliver of unease jinked through me. To me, a letter from the bank meant one of two things: a crude inducement or snarled remonstration. Yet this seemed to be neither.

Glancing down the page, random adjectives detailed the Exciting, Dynamic and Personally Tailored virtues of something called the Gold Ring Trust. It was signed by a woman with a nebulous title. The tone was helium perky.

Near the end, bullet points summarised the Gold Ring Trust's most Innovative and Unrivalled aspects. I had to re-read the entire thing to see exactly what the idea was. Then I realised. It was one of those deals where you surrender instant access to your money in exchange for higher interest payments. And what they – they as embodied by this notional woman – wanted was for me to take the money in my savings account and transfer it into the Market Leading Gold Ring Trust.

That account. Untouched for years. That money, inviolate. The money from my parents.

I felt a long-forgotten swell. History, anger, identity, regret. And Alice. From out of somewhere else entirely. Her ankles, lashes, the peach fuzz on her earlobes. The curve of her nostrils and minute perfection of her fingertips.

Reeling, enraged, I threw the letter to the floor, increased the treadmill's speed.

Faster. Faster. Fastest.

I found my rhythm, lengthened my stride. Tried to banish Alice from my thoughts like I was sending her to bed after supper. This happened more and more.

Work was going great. The previous day, Friday morning, there'd been two messages waiting by the time I reached my desk. Both from Jonah. He needed a haircut and the Avelden booked. I called his office immediately. Thanked him, profusely, for the weight rack. Waited for a reaction to the painting. When none was forthcoming, I raised the subject myself.

It's great Matthew, he said. Exactly what I've been looking for.

We spoke twice more during the day. He needed an obscure nutrient for what I now knew was the gingko tree in his office, a crêpe pan bought for and couriered to an associate on Rush Street. I signed the card on his behalf. And I relished it all. Executing Jonah's wishes, one meagre corner of my life made sense.

It was out of hours the problems started. I'd think of the clinic, the IV cord, the car wrecks and the miscarriages. Then push it all aside, block it out, bury it. Only for Alice to loom in my head.

I won the toy. When we were at the theme park. An overstuffed bunny. I threw my last hoop at the hula stall, saw it waver over the skittle before I looked down and realised I was alone. I don't know if she'd have liked it. I never got to find out. Now she appeared at the edge of each moment. And I was thinking stuff I'd never thought before.

On Friday, having struggled home past nine and slipped into my robe, I'd lain on the couch, picking at the fraying M, staring at the television. I settled on a trashy documentary, part of a series called *Mystic Mysteries* for which I'd developed a minor enthusiasm. I was just getting involved in the secrets of the Bermuda Triangle when it dawned on me the show was ending.

The ads that followed were gaudy hard sells. Frantic demos of strange household gadgetry, missives from plump astrologers, endless spots for telephone chat lines where assured young men and full-lipped young women laughed into receivers, faces shining with erotic promise.

And in their smiles I saw the horrors of the world. An African child, pot-bellied from malnutrition, head shrouded by flies. An army of homeless, massed outside the toy shop, feral, disenfranchised. Day-old crack babies screaming from withdrawal. The wrongfully imprisoned. The terminal, the bereaved, the lonely.

I had no idea where all this was coming from. But when it came it grabbed at my soul, pulling me helpless into its maw.

And I wept. I wept til I shook. A violent, mucusy jag that deepened as their misery took shape in my mind, like black pearls or coal. I sat in my robe and I yearned to hug cripples, unlock the doors of every third-world sweatshop, take the checkout lady from the supermarket on Bethune Street, the one with the gimp and the milky eye, tell her she was beautiful, make her feel loved and look after her. Make everything better. And then I wept some more.

So now, I thought about nothing, intently. Cut the treadmill, legs winding down. Moved on to star jumps. Arms out, legs spread, I flung myself into the air.

Sometimes I thought about joining a gym. Only I didn't like gyms. Didn't like exercising round other people. The money, I felt, would be better used on a proper home multistation.

There was one particular model I'd admired at length when buying my weights, the old weights now abandoned in my bedroom. It was called the Maximal IX 450. A machine to meet my every need. The price equated to three months' salary.

I dropped to my haunches, began my squats.

Six inches taller than me, half the breadth of the room. A hulking mass of steel and leather, cables, brackets, pads and hinges.

I wondered how tall Alice was now. If she'd put on weight, or needed braces.

When it came, it came from nowhere. My daughter, my psychic jack-in-the-box. The dripping tap you go days without noticing, til you hear it in the middle of the night, and then it's got you. Claiming and transfixing you, immune to all remedy.

In the midst of my work-out, I stood, walked to my bedroom. Opened my drawer and pulled out the one photograph I had of her.

It dated from her fifth birthday. Eleanor had taken it as Alice was opening her presents. She was smiling at the camera, surrounded by wrapping paper. In the corner of the frame, you could make out one of my gifts. A wooden box filled with cut-out teddy bears, which could then be dressed in paper costumes. A toy soldier, fairy princess. I remembered I'd been delighted with it.

I looked at the picture, at her, just standing there staring, til I felt my muscles getting cold. I wondered how long her hair had grown. Whether the sun had brought out her freckles, as it had mine. I wanted to call, hear breathless tales of summer adventures. I couldn't. Not yet.

I knew I could only make contact – let alone return – when certain beyond all doubt that I would never again see the blighted look she wore on her birthday, the drained chagrin of her mother. When I'd redeemed myself.

I walked stiffly into the bathroom. After washing, I dressed. Being the weekend, I dug out my weekend outfit. A short-sleeved shirt and jeans. They made me uncomfortable, but I thought I should make the effort. Checking myself in the mirror, I had the same poky expression you see on people in the bad suits they only wear for funerals and job interviews.

Taking the letter from Two Cities, balling it up and trashing it, I resolved to organise a standing order to Mortimer and Upas first thing Monday. If I couldn't give, I could still give. Then I tidied. Dusted. Took my clothes from the wardrobe, refolded and rehung them. I hated Saturday nights.

I sat in my apartment, restless in my jeans. After Friday, I didn't much feel like watching TV, so I took the short walk over to the video store. Joined using my donor and cash cards as proofs of ID.

Scanning the shelves, there was nothing I wanted to see. The only other lone men were scattered round the Adult section, looking up embarrassed as children giggled.

I left without making a rental, picked up some provisions at the supermarket – avoiding the woman with the milky eye – and trooped back to Bethune and Scala.

At home, I cooked myself spinach and eggs.

I shallow-fried the eggs in olive oil. I hadn't eaten fat in the last two days, so I figured I needed it. As I cooked, I gazed again at Alice's picture, propped up on the work surface. When the eggs began spitting, I turned down the heat under the pan.

A gob of fat had landed on the photograph.

Panicking, I turned the heat off completely, ran the tap. Tried desperately to wipe away the grease. Dabbed at the picture with a cloth soaked in washing-up liquid. A half-congealed streak ran down the print. Alice's face, I realised, was starting to dissolve. Fading and distorting the harder I rubbed. Disappearing away from me.

I'd never felt as sick with myself. Maybe Eleanor was right. I couldn't even be trusted with a photograph.

I let the picture dry out. Paced the kitchen as I waited. When it was done, a brownish smear had settled beneath her eye. I threw the eggs and spinach in the trash, opened a can of soup. Sat and ate it, stared at the walls, then peeled off my shirt and stood in front of the mirror.

In bed by 9.30, I returned, as I had so often, to Eric Handler's 15 *Wisdoms*. And finally I lay my head on the pillow, knowing that I would wake tomorrow and by then tomorrow would be Monday, and on Monday I would wear my cream cotton shirt and Rockport brogues, and when I arrived at The Greatest Gift there would be messages from Jonah waiting.

The Romane Valley health resort has a man-made waterfall set in the middle of the gym. It tinkles soothingly amid the grunts.

Phillip Reilly looks down, tells the wheezing figure at his feet, Ten more. Watching him struggle, he coaxes and cajoles.

Nine, *come on*, niiiine, that's it . . . eight, come on, eight, *good* . . . seven –

This is the scene of his comeback. Now and again, the friend of a friend who owns the place stops by. His name is Fergus. Once, Reilly might have found him patronising. Now, he accepts the state of things. That he is, for now, a charity case.

The client stalls at five. If you do this job long enough, you get a sense for when they've reached their limit. In places like these, you don't even come close. You tell them to stop as soon as they're hurting. Learn their goal is not to get fit, just to attain the illusion.

The guy at his feet is flabby in red lycra. Reilly helps him up, tells him to stretch off. It's nice, this place, he thinks. Each step machine lustrous, cycle immaculate. He sizes up the clientele, sees profit oozing out of them. Cash cows, Fergus calls them. He started out as a trainer too. Then he opened his first gym. The beginning of the sure ascent that led to here. The secret, he said, is to aim upmarket. Go solely where the money is.

Fergus has been fantastic. A mensch. He knows Reilly's not planning on sticking around. Even said he'd vouch for him if he wanted to rent out a studio. Even gave him the details of the guy who backed him, right in the very beginning. Reilly pats the number in his tracksuit pocket.

After this, he'll head to his twice-weekly meeting. Sometimes, it seems like a chore. Right now, it feels imperative. He's had a bad morning. An old desire, voracity. So tonight he will stand and declare with particular gusto:

We admitted we were powerless over gambling.

Over horses and roulette wheels, card games and prize fights, over lotteries, dice and the elemental itch that strips you bare and leaves you prostrate on the kitchen floor, unshaven and stinking as your wife walks out for good and the repo van arrives to take your furniture.

He'd like a place like this, he thinks. To be his own boss again.

OK, he tells the guy, let's go for five. Five more, then you're done.

Eleanor Carlin does as she's asked by the automated voice at Two Cities Telephone Banking. Presses the star key now. Waits, and listens. A burst of muzak, a robot oration. Then, her balance.

With a new school year ahead – uniforms, books, assorted kit – the numbers involved are sobering. She could always, she supposes, find another job. Some leafy cloister with richer parents, higher salaries. If only it were that simple. She thinks, instinctively, of Alice. There's been enough rupture already, surely.

She could call Matthew. Ask for help. Assuming he's at the same place. She stares at his note, sent in the mail five months ago. Hasn't heard from him since. A telephone number on a sheet of lined paper, attached to a cheque. No further message or intimation.

The sum involved was startling. Must have all but cleaned him out. She doesn't know how he's living now, or when there might be more. Debates the urge to call him. Just keep it civil, to the point. Neither instigate nor get drawn into contention, recrimination. This is, after all, nothing new. He never did grasp the force of money. Hers, or his, theirs, his parents'.

Alice bounds into her mother's room, Belinda Griselda under her arm. Aimee lurks behind. She says they have to go. Tugs at Eleanor's sleeve. Eleanor pleads til her daughter retreats. Two minutes, she promises.

How, exactly, did this happen? At which specific point did every shard of her identity fall away, til the moment she became, finally and exclusively, her own mother? Sturdy and dependable. What if she doesn't want to be dependable?

It's not that she feels anything for Alice other than she should. Just never expected this to be so unanswerable. The step from what she thought she was, to what everyone else always took her for.

She traces the chronology. It was there at school, she knows, and college too. She would, uncannily, be in and at hand when her room-mate collapsed through the door after her latest tearful break-up. Attend every lecture and gladly pass her notes to those who didn't. Talk in slow, pacific tones to the girls down her corridor freaking out from LSD, feeding them slices of orange as the best parties of her youth raged on without her. As if, unknown to her but obvious to the world, God had appointed her designated driver. And now she sees all she wants to be and do as stripped, boiled down, remaindered.

She has to find her shoes. Spent so long getting Alice and Aimee ready, she hasn't had the time to find her shoes. Then she'll make sure the girls have everything they need (or will need), shepherd them into the car, get to Tina Karlsson's by two, whereupon she will collect Tina Karlsson, Tina Karlsson's daughter Chloe, and Chloe Karlsson's best friend Leah. And the six of them will squeeze into Eleanor's car and drive, slowly, noisily, to the Children's Onestop Playshop.

This was Tina's idea. She called last week, to see how Alice was doing. Mentioned she was taking Chloe out on Monday, and maybe Alice would like to come too?

The Children's Onestop Playshop is organised for kids and untethering parents nearing the end of expansive summer breaks. In the main hall of the college on Cale Street, there will be magic shows and puppetry, clay sculpture, origami, something called a Percussion Explosion, sundry other games and diversions. And so the six of them – seven, including Belinda – will be there.

Eleanor gets down on all fours, sees her shoes lodged under the bed. Drags them out and pulls them on.

It was the same with her family, she thinks. The eldest of six, three brothers, two sisters. Born practical, her father would say, the way you would with a boy, at the same time her mother was enlisting her in the kitchen.

She babysat. Of course she did. At home, she liked the noise that filled the house, aware even then she would miss it when it ended. But even more, she felt the keening for something that belonged to her. Not shared among the rest of them, pawed over and appropriated. Just hers, alone.

With Matthew, she got it. For good and for bad. She hesitates. Recalls what drew her to him. The way, out of the murk of his timidity, he'd be funny, guardless, oddly charming. It was, she told her friends, like having her own ET. Curious and uncorrupted. His proposal came in the form of a note, a gold band taped to the back. It said: Can we be for ever?

He excelled at the romantic. Hotel suites filled with roses, cruises on the river. Her birthdays – at least til Alice – marked by a gift for every year. Sweet, considerate Matthew. Always one for the gestures. And if it was never quite fairytale, she could live with that. By then she knew better. With him, whatever else, she would never become one of those women she saw at her parents' dinner parties, drunk, hollow, deformed by menopause and bitterness.

Because she could have.

His name was Vale Stoningham. He was older than her. Enough for her to play the ingenue, not so much to vex her parents. Sway them from believing he was all a girl could hope for. She was, in truth, convinced of that herself. Successful, worldly, ever confident, fluent in countless languages, at home in any social context. Profoundly good-looking. She found the envy of her peers seductive.

They got engaged twelve weeks after meeting. The ring, fourteen carat.

She was with her family when the phone rang. A month before the wedding. His father told her to sit down. Vale's clothes had been found by a dam. Police divers were at the scene. No one was optimistic. She heard his mother wailing in the background.

And somehow Eleanor knew. She knew at the funeral, mourning an empty coffin, the graveside packed with old girlfriends. At the morgues she was summoned to whenever a white male was pulled from the river, bloated, unidentified. She knew it was a lie.

Months later, his father called again. Told her Vale had been found alive; found alive then arrested for fraud. He'd been in the Caribbean, a pregnant local woman by his side. Eleanor skipped the trial.

She never told Matthew the whole truth. A bad break-up, she said. Anything more would have wrecked it. And he brought her everything she needed now. When they were out, she felt no call to swoon or dazzle, the way she always had with Vale. He'd listen to her talk, rather than just letting her. And when she did, his eyes would fix, not glaze or wander. He only wanted her. So she read his proposal and thought she was safe. That he would never leave her.

She folds the number back inside her diary. Selfish, careless Matthew. Matthew, and his money. The money from his parents, that planted the seed that choked their marriage, instructed every fight. Who knows what latent traumas they dealt Alice? And then to leave and not come back. Abandon her in this minefield, each scold or praise so freighted with consequence. She'll take her daughter's hand and say, Angel, none of this is your fault. And Alice will nod, and Eleanor knows that the thought may never have entered her head had her mother not just put it there.

Clumsy Eleanor, selfish Matthew.

Once, he was all she thought she wanted. She delighted in him. Spent film after film mapping their bond. Matthew and her camera. They were going to be her life. And if his side of their future was less precise, there was no cause for alarm. He just needed time.

Except, instead, year on year, every trait that had drawn her to him began to pall. What charmed in youth turned ugly adult. His patient wait for vocation became a gruelling flit through situations vacant. His willingness to pledge himself, her entry to an airless breeding programme. The constant fucking sleeping.

His bashfulness would prove itself a curse. At the rare social functions she convinced him to attend, he wouldn't leave her side. If she needed the bathroom, she'd return to find him where she left him, still alone. Had anyone approached, she would see him blushing, panicked. And as they walked away he'd clutch her hand, and say they'd asked what he did for a living, or questioned him about his family.

His reasoning – his alibi – was that he missed the basics growing up. The only child of distant parents, moved around like so much furniture. For him, he said, this was all an education. And he'd say how much he wanted people to like him. Just didn't know how it was done.

Maybe, in part, it was her fault. Her refusal to admit that the problem wasn't shyness. It was that he wasn't interested. In strangers or acquaintances. At heart, in either her or Alice. Didn't want to know how their days had been, what they might want to do at the weekend. Just needed the measure of their adoration.

Alice is at the door again. Belinda Griselda, she says, is very cross, and she wants to go this instant.

In less than two weeks, they will all return to school. Alice, Eleanor, Tina Karlsson. Summer's almost over. She gets to her feet, takes Alice by the hand.

The next time I saw Grace, I was in the toy shop on Bethune and Sheridan. It was early, and I was carrying a teepee.

Having gazed in the window who knows how often, this was my first venture inside. I was looking for gifts for Alice. I wanted her to know that I hadn't forgotten her. That I was still here for her, even in my absence. Especially in my absence.

The teepee came in a long, rectangular box, the size of a deckchair or a coffee table. Erect, it would stand over seven feet tall, a soft canvas veil supported by hardwood. I figured she could use it outdoors til the weather turned hostile, then bring it in through winter. We had a spacious basement, albeit full of tools and paint cans.

I was at the counter when I heard her voice. A hesitant tap on my shoulder.

Hello.

I turned, and I knew her. I just couldn't place her.

Planning a camping trip?

Then it clicked. Mortimer and Upas. Grace, the donors' lounge. She smelt of palm milk hand cream again. Today, her lipstick was plum. I realised seconds had passed.

Hi. Ah, yeah. I mean, no . . . it's for my daughter.

I stepped up to the counter, where the sales assistant – with whom I had already exchanged introductions, and whose name I had learned was Scott – grappled the teepee from me.

So, I said, how are you?

Oh, good, she said.

She held up a crocodile glove puppet.

Nephew's birthday.

Is that everything? Scott asked me. I told him it was, and he reached into the basket that I'd left behind the counter. Ran each item through the bar-code reader.

First came the Jam Board, a wipe-clean easel that doubled as a keyboard. The pressure of the pen created an electronic melody. You could, if you wished, sketch to a backing track. Next, the Felt-Play space station, a basic fuzzy board on which were mounted a pair of astronauts and several aliens – green, cyclopic – an alien spacecraft and rocketship. Miracle Johnson's Bead Shop was a vast selection of coloured beads, ice blue, peridot, copper, lilac, to be placed in a battery-driven vortex that threw them into motion in the manner of popping corn, before mechanically threading them onto a necklace. Mister Pig was the one soft toy. He/it had a plaintive expression and an oversize dickie bow tied around his/its neck. Watching Scott load him/it into my bag, I was suddenly conscious of the strip of charcoal silk furled inside my pocket. Plus, of course, there was the teepee.

When he was through, Grace turned and asked me if all of these were for my daughter. I said they were.

Well, she said, she's certainly a lucky girl.

While I paid, we talked. As I handed over my credit card, she told me she'd been looking at an apartment on Foley Street. Been trying to find a new place for months.

I said that I lived over on Bethune, and she told me she'd heard this whole area was really coming up.

As I signed my credit card slip, she said she wasn't going to take it. The apartment on Foley. Too cramped, she said. Too expensive. Handing back the slip, I said I thought I'd landed on my feet, because my place had been the first one I looked at.

As Scott gave me my receipt and my copy of the credit card slip, she asked me what I did for a living. If I didn't mind her asking.

I'm a concierge, I said. I do everything. For anyone.

And she laughed, although I wasn't joking.

Scott hauled my bags over the counter. I was going to need to make two trips. I told him I'd leave the teepee here, and pick it up in a few minutes. As he ran Grace's puppet through the till, he said that was fine. She paid in cash, then yawned. Covered her mouth in embarrassment.

Sorry, she said. I'm just exhausted.

Me too. It'll take another three coffees before I wake up.

She laughed, again. This time I was at least trying to be funny (notwithstanding the fact it was true). Struggling just slightly with my bags, I held the door open for her.

Outside, we stood facing.

Well, she said.

Well, I said. I guess I'll see you at the clinic.

I guess you will, Matthew. And I'll make sure there's short-bread.

I was halfway back to the apartment before it struck me as noteworthy she'd remembered – and used – my name. Laden down, I went carefully, my pace slow, each step considered.

There was no great urgency to get to work. Last night had been my finest hour. My *tour de force*.

The spark was Clarissa from Personal going sick. She'd been battling with flu all day. I sent her home. She'd just taken a client call, and I took the job. Jonah was at the Avelden all day, his evening already booked up, so I – for once – was free.

Clarissa's job was for a Mrs Blum, a Senior VP of Corporate Acquisitions. She needed something special for her anniversary. Silver. That evening. Her plans, she said, had fallen through. She sounded distraught.

After running through the options, we settled on a musical. She and her husband, she said, had heard wonderful things about *Different Drummers*.

Different Drummers, I said, and heard the phone crew's whistles.

We were always being asked for tickets to *Different Drummers*. Having opened in the spring with a pair of movie actors in the lead, it soon became the talk of the city. Every night sold out; queues around the block for single returns with restricted views. A pair of tickets on the night itself were as close to the impossible as we ever had to deal with.

I told her I'd see what I could do, and I did what I always did. The very best job I could. Til finally I ran out of numbers.

I left the office and headed downtown.

There are places you can go to in this kind of situation. Addresses you visit when you're desperate, that you learn about from other concierges, who give you the details in stealthy tones. I'm sure there's other things you can find at these places, like I'm sure there's other names they use for what they do. But part of what they do, the part I was concerned with, is scalping tickets.

There'll be a dowdy shopfront, with a bare interior. A guy will stand behind a counter. You'll tell him what you need, and he'll shrug. Then perhaps he'll make some calls. There's no standard pricing. Just whatever they can get.

I went to such a place, and talked to the guy behind the counter. There were coughs, mumbles, the trappings of subterfuge. He told me to wait while he called some people. He was gone half an hour.

And then, with Mrs Blum paging me at literally five-minute intervals, he returned with two tickets. They were at the back of the stalls, admittedly. Two tickets, all the same.

The price was grotesque. Completely out of her budget. I bit my lip. The way I saw it, I didn't have a choice. I made the difference up myself. Out of my own pocket. Half resolved to claim it as expenses, but now I think of it I never did.

It didn't matter. I had them now.

I called Mrs Blum, who sounded fit to cry. Said she'd ring her husband then and there. He'd be overjoyed, she said. I told her the pair of them would be collected from her office, in a white stretch limo with chauffeur. She was definitely crying now. She called me a darling. Said this was the sweetest thing anyone had ever done for her.

I booked a restaurant for after the show, flowers to be waiting at the table. Then Mrs Blum called back. Her husband, she said, was stuck at the office. Wouldn't get out til past ten.

So I offered to take her instead. It seemed like the right thing to do.

I can't say I enjoyed the show, but Mrs Blum was rapt. At the end, she grabbed my arm and made me stand for an ovation that went on til I thought I'd faint. As I took her back to the limo, she kissed my cheek and told me – again – I was a darling.

Anyway, such was the hour that I finally got home, I thought this one time I could be late into the office.

Now, breathing hard, I reached the apartment. Made a coffee and unpacked the toys. Found myself staring at the fuzzy felt space scene, unable to look away.

The spacemen had blandly smiling faces, half obscured by the visors of their helmets. Their suits looked flexible, legs bent at the knee. Given that their lower torsos would be sheathed in thick layers of urethane-coated nylon, I thought this less than realistic. Plus their backpacks were far too small in proportion to their bodies to maintain any decent supply of oxygen.

I know about this stuff. My father was an astronaut.

And I know how that sounds. Exactly how it sounds. As soon as I was old enough to keep a lie afloat, I'd say he was a dentist, plumber, truck driver. Anything but the truth. For me, it was about the judgement of my peers. I felt unlike enough already. My father did the same himself. He just never wanted to engage, explain.

All the same, that's what he was.

At home, he never talked about it. No one talked about much in my house, bar functional requests to pass the salt or switch off the TV. We avoided needless conversation with the zest of Trappist monks. If I raised the subject of his career – which I rarely did – he'd say:

It was only a job, Matthew. Someone's got to do it.

My mother showed me the pictures. My father, training in zero gravity, laughing as he hung in the air. She kept them stashed, out of his sight.

They had a wedding portrait framed in the living room. Him in his pomp, her the eggshell beauty. They looked almost magically happy. Their features were much the same, tighter jawlines maybe, smoother brows. The fleeting perks of youth. Still, I hardly recognised them.

I was three when he went into space. He was there to help fix an orbital workshop that had gone up six months previously. Two of its solar panels had come loose. Along the way, there were studies in solar astronomy, a legion of medical tests. He was gone for sixty days.

My mother told me these things in the years that followed. I couldn't remember him going and, like I say, he rarely discussed it. There were no glorious discoveries or cinematic near-disasters. He went up, he came down, and in between he gazed at Earth through skies of cold indifference. Saw the infinite, himself within it.

Seven years later, they diagnosed him as depressive. He

got a medical discharge, the regulation plaudits, a generous pension. We moved to the other end of the country to start again. And as time went on, his retreat intensified.

Mostly, he kept to his watches. Late at night, he'd lay them out, mechanisms in disrepair. Tinkering, scrutinising. Sometimes I'd see him sitting in the back room of the house in his underwear, poring over a damaged mainspring or troublesome escapement, and sometimes he'd see me, and he'd look up and say:

You know what this is, Matthew? This is a postscript. An epilogue. A scrawled afterthought no one's going to read. This is dead air after the programme's finished. This is the waiting.

I never knew what he meant. It was years before I realised. They were, aside from cursory potted reports on my day at school, the only times we talked.

He gave the occasional lecture to Women's Institutes and physics students. Such was the gloomy ennui with which he delivered them they soon stopped asking him. After that he left the house less and less. Inside, he had his watches. My mother said his downfall was self-indulgence. The irony, as she spruced the house for a social circle long since disintegrated, didn't escape me even as a kid.

The last time I saw her, she was talking about Jesus, as she often did by then. They were the only times I saw them argue, after she got God.

One afternoon, I came home from school, and I could hear the yelling from outside. My mother hectoring, quoting scripture, manic, frightening. As I walked into the living room, my father spat on her Bible.

Both my parents are dead. They died in a fire at the two-storey house on the edge of the city that we'd moved into five years before. I was nineteen when it happened. My father was forty-six. My mother a year older. I remember them now and they're just one more detail.

For a long time, I couldn't bear to recall them. More than the crack babies, more than giving blood, more than Alice or

131

Eleanor or the life I had before, I devoted so much energy to not thinking about my parents. I never shook them off. I was riddled with them. All the clichés are fact.

I put the space station with the rest of the toys in a pile over by the wardrobe. Then I finished my coffee and left. Locked the door of my apartment, started back to the toy shop in order to pick up the teepee.

Approaching the corner of Sheridan, the first of the homeless were assembling. The guy with the scar was among them. A wicked bruise above his eye to accessorise his neck. I looked down and hurried inside the store.

Leaving a few seconds later with the teepee, I glanced around the block. Accidentally caught his eye.

Is that for me? he asked.

I was at a loss.

It's for my daughter, I said.

Oh, OK . . . I thought it was for me.

I still didn't know how to respond.

It's OK, man. I could always just come and sleep on your floor.

I laughed – kind of – propped the box against the wall. Reaching for my wallet, I handed him a note.

Thanks, man. Thank you.

Ah . . . what happened to your face?

I couldn't help but ask. He began a long and complex story that I think involved the origin of his scar.

No, I said, I meant . . . the bruise.

Oh, that, he said.

And he told me the police were there night after night now. Moving everyone on to hostels across town, where your stuff got stolen and the mattresses stank. They arrested anyone that wouldn't go. From what he was saying, I figured he got the bruise the night I got the weights from Jonah.

He said it had started, so he'd heard, with complaints from local businesses and residents. Suspecting he knew I was a resident myself, I tried to sound outraged. It only made me sound guiltier. I was thinking I should really get the teepee home, then make my way to work.

Another man approached, calling out to the scar guy. His right arm was missing. Sleeve hanging empty. I reached into my wallet again.

Oh, the scar guy said, surprised. Thanks.

Sorry. It's just I've got to –

I gathered up the teepee and stepped away.

Thanks, man. Have fun in your wigwam.

An hour later, when I got to The Greatest Gift, there was an atmosphere I couldn't read. Walking in, everyone was looking at me. Then Mike and Caroline bustled out of the New Client Liaison Room. They were both clapping. Caroline gestured for the phone crews to join in.

After a while, Mike waved for hush. Then he gave a short speech. He explained that an hour ago he'd taken a call from a client named Mrs Blum. That call, he said, had only confirmed what everyone here knew already.

That Matthew Viss is an inspiration. A role model to us all.

Then Caroline had everyone clap some more. I scanned the faces of my colleagues, and it made me feel fainter than I had at the theatre.

Inside my cubicle, my voicemail was flashing. I noticed Mike beside me.

Matthew, he said, I just wanted to thank you. You've made us very proud.

And all the thoughts I wished I didn't have careened straight through me.

The next day, I had Alice's presents couriered to the house.

And so proceeds the waiting.

City Air

The sixth-floor apartment is my own. My fall now gathered to a swoop. Still subject to a brisk acceleration. As if the ground below were only there for me.

Right now, I'm thinking of the newspaper. If – how – they'll report this. My name, age, a brief description of the manner of my death. Perfunctory speculation concerning my motives. A nonplussed quote from a neighbour or a colleague. He leaves a wife and daughter, from who he was estranged.

And so my window flashes past. On the kitchen table, there's a copy of The Greatest Gift prospectus. Beyond that my possessions. Memory prompts and ligatures to everything I am. The money spent. The money earned. Each prize I've won and book I've read and every film I ever saw. The card tricks witnessed, conversations overheard. Each haircut, blister. Every time I've eaten squid, or seen a corpse, or swum, or flown. Lost a button off a shirt. Felt snow against my skin. Played the piano. Fallen from a bicycle. Been stuck inside an elevator. Rolled in grass downhill. Had a full shopping bag split on me in public. Convinced myself I was suffering from something incurable. Smelt petrol, menthol, wet paint, dough-nuts. Laughed in genuine surprise. Run through a thunder-storm. Talked to a salesman with no intention of buying anything. Lent back in my chair til I almost tipped over.

And then I'm gone. Beyond it all.

By the end of summer, I was knee-deep in jobs for Jonah. Every morning, something else. Another batch of messages. More instructive dialogues.

Call his wife, maybe flowers. Find his son a birthday pre-sent, then sign the card. Run over to his office and tend to his gingko, or pick up his new socks and underwear. (He bought a fresh supply each month.) Find two steel meat cleavers for the address on Rush Street.

And each time I'd get a box of gym chalk, or an adjustable leather weights bench.

Til I crossed the line. Not that I realised it. The nature of these things is you don't notice yourself in the act. The cracks always open with your gaze somewhere else.

There was a document Jonah wanted me to look at. Just cast my eye over it and give him my thoughts.

You'll see what I mean when you get it, he said. It's more your area of expertise than mine. No urgency. Just take a look and get back to me.

Within an hour, a courier arrived with a brown A4 envelope. Inside was a business proposal in a green plastic folder. It outlined plans for an executive health retreat. There were sketches, cost assessments, forecasts of growth displayed in graph form. A CV from the guy behind it, a man called Phillip Reilly, a personal trainer of wide and illustrious experience.

Although the package as a whole looked impressive, you could tell it had been assembled at a copy shop. On the uppermost right-hand corner, increasing in size page by page, a sooty grey smear of cartridge ink next to the edge of the paper.

Within seconds of opening the envelope, my phone flashed red. It was Jonah. Checking I had it. I told him I did.

OK. Good. Just give me your thoughts. Take as much time as you need.

I wanted to ask him how the painting was working out. He hung up before I could. He hadn't mentioned it since the day after delivery. I couldn't help but worry.

I wanted to discuss it with Alison, but her role in the original purchase made the issue sensitive. I'd be lying if I said it wasn't subtly affecting our relationship.

Normally, she was the one person at The Greatest Gift with whom I had a rapport. We'd seek each other out in the mornings, just to say hello, make chit-chat over coffee. There was no sexual attraction. We just got along. She even sounded interested when I talked to her about Eric Handler. At Pearl Street – and elsewhere – that was unusual.

Now, fretting over the painting, I felt totally alone. I couldn't bear the thought that my work was shoddy in his eyes. I liked Jonah. I liked him more and more. His generosity, both to me and his associates. The way he'd ask how my training was going, if I was enjoying the weights he'd given me, or offer up some curious, tangential nugget on any one of the range of subjects with which he was familiar. Just drop it into the conversation, whatever had struck him or caught his attention.

You know what I was reading this morning, he'd say, or, Do you realise what today is, or, You know what it makes me think of, Matthew? And then he'd tell me – just for instance – that Harry Truman's grandmother had been scalped by Native Americans, and that as a mark of respect he kept the woollen cap she wore til her death on display in his Kansas menswear store and later in the White House.

Much of what he talked of was inclined toward the morbid, or strangely concerned with physical quirks – noting the guy he'd just met for lunch had a criminal ear, obsessing over vestigial tails – but then he'd segue into politics, history, the arts, sociology, the healing properties of golf. And he'd talk and I'd listen, til he'd say:

Did you know that, Matthew? Did you *realise* that?

As if he was truly interested in me. Wanting to share, connect.

In sombre moods, I brooded over the thought he would become unhappy with my work and request another Guy Friday. I'd look around the phone room and identify potential replacements. It only made me more grateful for the freedom he allowed me in escaping Pearl Street.

The atmosphere was close there, staticky. I didn't want to be around it. I still relished being a Guy Friday. I just didn't want to be in the office.

I put it down to Greg Hopper. He was back now. Had been for a week or so. I hadn't spoken to him. Wasn't even sure what he was doing. He sat in a lone cubicle off to the side of

Entertainment. He'd take his seat and his eyes wouldn't leave his screen all day. There was no snapping of the fingers, managerial strut. All the same, his being there made me uneasy.

Mid-afternoon, I picked up Jonah's dress shirts from his tailor and collected a set of caviar spoons for Rush Street. I'd have them delivered the following morning. Then, rather than go back to my cubicle, I went straight home. Which wasn't like me at all.

I figured Jonah and Mike both had my pager in case of emergency. I'd read through the proposal later. I'd been tired all day. Sapped. My limbs were heavy, eyesight blurred. I could have slept at any juncture.

The empathy was only getting worse. Each time I looked out of my window, the city seemed convulsed, and I felt each tragedy as if it was my own. Retched with every overdose, bore the sorrow of mass redundancies, wept at schoolgirl abortions.

We give these things names in the hope we might shackle them.

Inside my apartment, I slumped on the floor. I could have looked in my diary and confirmed how long it would be til I could next give blood, but I knew the date by heart. I could have called Alice, asked if she liked her presents, but I didn't.

Changing from my cream cotton shirt and single-pleated trousers into my vest and shorts, I set about my weights. Took the 7s off the rack, wrapped my fingers round them, leaned forward on the bench and began my preacher curls.

My arms were rubber after less than ten. I was breathless and queasy. There was simply nothing there. And everything that followed seemed, at the time, perfectly logical.

Replacing the bells in the rack, I rummaged in my kitchen drawer and found the miniature sewing kit I'd had for years and never used. Pulled a needle from the packet. Walked into the bathroom. Sat on the rim of the tub. Took a bottle of anti-septic and a cotton-wool pad down from the cabinet. Wiped in a circle just above my elbow, tied off my arm with the belt of my robe. Listened to my breath over the extractor fan.

Then I rolled the needle between my fingers, pressed it to my arm. Closed my eyes, took a breath and pushed harder, feeling the point of the needle sink into me. Held it there. Let the blood drip to the bathroom floor. Placed the needle on the sink. Swabbed myself down with the cotton wool and antiseptic, applied a Band-Aid to the puncture. Turned off the light, and sat again.

I didn't even think about what had just happened. It had just happened. An instinct, a reflex. And it worked. Exactly like I hoped it would.

Of course, it wasn't the same as if William had been there. The IV cord, the baggie. It could only ever be approximate. But in the darkness, I felt a spotlight trained on me. Picking me out, washing over me. Restorative. A little brilliance, regained.

I wanted to see Grace.

I hadn't thought of her since the toy shop. Now I couldn't get her out of my head. Palm milk and burgundy lipstick.

I turned on the light, and checked my watch. They'd still be open. So I headed into the bedroom, changed and left the apartment. Then out, around the block, walking fast. It was only when I got to Mortimer and Upas that I paused. I honestly couldn't tell if my mind was coming into focus, or misting over. I went inside anyway.

Swish. Swish.

I told Carmen I was here to see Grace. I'm not sure she recognised me. I strode through to the donors' lounge anyway, stood in front of the counter.

Oh, she said, reaching underneath her. Hello. How are you?

Good, I said. I'm good. Listen . . . I want you to know I don't do this . . . I mean, I know I'm doing it now, but it's not something . . . that I do. Typically.

She made then held eye contact.

OK, she said. Did your daughter like her presents?

Ah . . . I guess . . .

Still the eyes.

I don't live with her mother any more. We're separated. So I had them couriered.

She nodded, said she understood. And I opened my throat. Let the words come.

Would you maybe like to have a drink or a coffee some time?

The question hung there, radiating. Her eyes dropped to the counter, then flashed back up at me.

Yes, she said. I'd like that.

I didn't know what to do next. Shaking hands seemed inappropriate. We stood, facing, til I asked for her number. She gave it to me, said I should call her. And that was that. The whole exchange.

I told her I had to be somewhere, which wasn't true but got us both out of what was fast becoming an awkward exit. I said I'd call her tomorrow, and she said she looked forward to it.

Walking home, I wasn't even sure why I'd gone there. I didn't even know if she was single. I'd just felt a compulsion and followed it.

My senses were so acute now; antennae fixed to a shell.

Before I even turned into Bethune Street, I could hear the commotion. A crowd had gathered outside the toy shop. There were placards, chants.

Maybe fifty people stood on the corner. Half were obviously homeless. The rest, earnest in clean clothes, gave out leaflets to passers-by. I saw the scar guy, wearing one shoe and holding up the other. Peering at a limply disattaching sole.

Then the priest. Fifties, stocky, bald. He handed me a leaflet. Stop Corporate Greed Wrecking People's Lives! it said, beside a cartoon of a wrecking ball slamming through a brick wall. People Are Not Commodities!

My name's Vincent Cole, he said. I don't know if you're aware what's been going on here lately, but –

Yeah, I said. I live just up on Scala Street.

Oh. Then you know.

Kind of. The broad strokes. I've seen the police. And the guy over there with the . . . neck . . . he mentioned something.

Right, he said. And then told me that the homeless community throughout this part of town were being hounded on behalf of neighbourhood landlords and businesses who were, he said, eager to improve the area's image and thus drive up rents and prices. The police, he said, were simply being used as removal men for local government and corporate interests. And all this, he said, was being carried out without even lip service to the need for adequate shelter.

He said his church ran a soup kitchen every Tuesday and Friday, but there was only so much one could do faced with the indifference and outright hostility of the authorities. I made disapproving noises.

People don't want to sleep out here, he said. Who would? But this is what happens when hope is stripped away.

Right, I said. Exactly.

I signed a petition. Gave some money.

You know, he said, we can always use volunteers down at the kitchen –

Oh, I don't know . . . I have work and . . . you know –

Listen, he said, I'll give you the details (he took another leaflet and wrote the address of a church on the back) . . . and if you do have an hour or so free one evening, then –

Sure, I said.

It's up to you. Tuesdays and Fridays, six til ten. Just ask for Father Vincent.

And the scar guy pulled the sole away completely.

They stand inside the gallery, the two of them. Staring, centred. Around the room, under the high ceiling, in front of each white wall, two dozen more do likewise. A further throng outside, waiting for admittance.

Alison bends at the waist, leans in to read the card beside the frame. Glancing left, she senses Naomi getting bored. Sees the earnest tilt of the head betrayed by the childlike shuffle, a furtive puffing of the cheeks. Everywhere are sculptures, films and installations. A lifetime's canon by the Japanese artist to whom the Hanway Museum of Modern Art has devoted this single massive room. Four glass keys set inside a glass frame, an all-white chess set.

This is Alison's day off from Home and Family. The one day a week she doesn't answer to Gal Friday. She peers ahead, intent and awestruck.

It's really . . . powerful, Naomi says. Alison can tell she's worked on her response. Sweet of her. This isn't her thing.

In three weeks' time, Naomi will take her exams in therapeutic massage. Already equipped with her own cushioned table, burgeoning knowledge of physiology. Never paid such attention to the thickness of towels. In addition to her classes, she's been practising at home, treating an array of friends. Alison stops by twice a week. Insists on leaving money in spite of Naomi's protests.

The exams should be a formality. Her teacher calls her a natural. She leans forward, the way she sees Alison do.

Do you want a coffee, Gnome? Alison says, and she almost screams with relief.

Although it's been months since she left The Greatest Gift, she and Alison are closer now than ever. Aside from the massages, they'll talk on the phone every other day, have lengthy, free-ranging dialogues in which Alison tells Naomi how much she admires her. Respects her for making the break. Starting over. Now they walk from the room, to the stairs that lead to the cafe in the basement.

Alison wishes she could follow her friend's example. Give it up, cut herself loose. Maybe even paint again. Just picking up the brush would be a start. The confidence eludes her, sand through her fingers.

The cafe heaves with occupation. Naomi slides a tray along the counter rail. I'll get them, she says. You find a seat.

Over by the window, a middle-aged man in shirt sleeves rises to his feet. Alison hovers til he's done wiping his mouth, then takes the chair opposite and thanks him. He makes no acknowledgement.

144

Settling at the table, she notices he's left his paper. She thinks of calling after him, but his pace is such it would simply be futile. Instead, she starts to read.

It is 11.15 a.m. Jonah Hoffman pulls on his jacket and takes the stairs from the cafe of the Hanway Museum toward the exit. An hour wasted. He half turns back, contemptuous. He came here for inspiration. What did he find? Rubbish.

Jonah sat alone in his study last night, scrutinising the painting from the concierge. Still unsure of his reaction. He has a hunch he doesn't like it. If he liked it, why would he have come here? Why would he be looking at alternatives?

Outside the museum, approaching his car, he calls the office.

Bonnie, he says, it's me. Hm-hm . . . right . . . Well, in that case I'll be at the Avelden. Back around five . . . No, I'll eat there.

Next he calls the concierge. Gets his voicemail. Runs through tomorrow's jobs. The moment he ends the call, his phone rings. The trumped-up site manager from the security firm. Earlier this morning, Jonah called him about the fence. Left a message. Now he repeats its contents, listens to the answer.

Hm, he says. Well, to be candid with you, I actually don't care. Your company's work is unsatisfactory, and I'm asking you that it be carried out again at no further cost. I was promised a certain level of performance. That level has not been reached.

He unlocks the car door, listens, climbs in.

I would remind you that my name carries a certain weight within the financial community . . . Well yes, that's the least I'd expect.

It is 11.21 a.m. He settles into the driver's seat, shuts off the phone. Pulls the safety belt across himself and fires the ignition.

It is, of course, if you think about it rationally, absurd. The notion that this strip of cloth could be so entwined with destiny. Could be anything but fabric. But Phillip Reilly believes it. Invests his faith within it. So his lucky tie hangs around his neck, a blue and salmon talisman, cherished and relied on.

Reilly breathes deep outside Romane Valley, holding his phone, his free hand clutching the plastic folder. The collaboration it contains. It's amazing the people you meet at GA. The accountant who did the numbers for a beer. The architect, sketching for the same. Fergus at Romane Valley, who gave him time off and a raft of advice. All donated what they could, and gladly. Would take nothing for their efforts. Refused point blank.

And Reilly adjusts his lucky tie, and dedicates this one to each of them. Dials. No signal. So he finds a call box. Feeds the slot. Dials again, tapping out the number for Fergus's guy. The investor. The guy he mailed the proposal to last week.

Hello? Is Mr Hoffman there? . . . He is? . . . Ah, this is Phillip Reilly . . . that's right . . . Ah, could you maybe have him call me when he's back in the office? . . . OK. Thank you.

And he hangs up the phone. Still wearing his lucky tie.

Grace and I met in a franchised coffee bar on Mulberry Street. We figured it was equidistant between her workplace and mine.

She took hers black, as did I.

Ringing her proved easier than expected. I set a random time at which to call. My nerves buzzed and sparked as it approached. With half an hour remaining, I was troubling the nail on my left-hand index finger like a dog after a ham. Soon, it was down to the quick. I nibbled round the skin, pushed the cuticle back with my teeth.

You know, the fingernail is largely made up of the protein keratin. It acts, along with the tongue, as a guide to the body's general health. Ridges in the nail, for instance, denote insufficient stores of vitamin B. Ragged cuticles are symptoms of calcium deficiency. I always keep a close eye on my nails.

Then, seconds before the deadline, my head cleared. I dialled, she answered, and I said hello. She said she couldn't talk for long, and I told her me neither. She had an hour free after work. Could leave at six, and how was that for me? I told her I'd check my diary and call her right back.

I called Jonah. That morning, I'd already had three of his suits dry-cleaned and rung Christina to say he'd be away for two nights during the week of the 20th. For the first time since meeting him, I felt relieved when he proved uncontactable.

So I called Grace back. Told her six was fine. I'd been at Pearl Street since seven that morning. Mike had asked me to come in early every day that week.

OK, Matthew, he'd said. We're looking at a code red. Use the meeting room as base camp.

Mike always dealt in hyperbole, usually laced with military imagery. Without it, I sensed, his days would lack impetus. The gist of it was there was a bug going round. The traditional omen of seasonal change, tearing through sick buildings across the city. I'd been drinking echinacea like chocolate milk.

When Grace arrived at the coffee bar, she was holding back a sneeze. Halfway to the counter it exploded. I discreetly kept a hand over my mouth as she walked toward me.

In my defence, I was feeling especially vulnerable to germs. I was tired, stressed. Wiped, but twitchy with it. Half the phone crew were off sick. It seemed like I was covering them all. The only reason I left Pearl Street when I did was my prior insistence with Mike. I so rarely – in fact, never – demanded to leave on time, I guess he could tell I was serious.

I had somewhere to be, even before the call to Grace. I told everyone relevant what I was doing. Just in case they thought I was being indolent. Had my sports bag with me as proof. Alison said it was the sweetest thing she'd heard all day.

The last two hours of the day were spent organising a corporate getaway. A weekend at the end of the month for a group of junior Vice-Presidents. The PA I was dealing with was curt, aggressive in the implication she had many better things to do. And the whole time, I could see Greg Hopper slumping at his cubicle. And I realised how much I missed the old Greg. The Greg who had become what I always hoped he would. A half-forgotten memory.

Within days of his return, Robert had given me the story behind Greg's absence. How he knew so many of the details remained a mystery. Still, he seemed sure of them. On the day of the switch, Greg, he said, had left Pearl Street and retreated to a nearby bar, traces of Elvis stippled down his back. There he negated two years of abstinence by drinking himself into a stupor. That night, furious at what he saw as his mistreatment, he returned to take physical issue with Mike. Somewhere between the ground floor and The Greatest Gift, he passed out in the elevator.

One of the cleaners discovered him. Apparently, they thought he was dead. Mike would have gone home hours before, but I suppose Greg wasn't thinking things through. For the rest of the summer, he was given leave to consider his future. He tried to find ins at Lukas Concierge and Definitive VIP, but they weren't hiring. They weren't hiring Greg, anyway. So he came back. He was still drinking, Robert said. You could smell it on him. Me, I hadn't been close enough to tell. When we passed each other, he just stared through me, ashen and dishevelled.

Anyway, eventually, I finished booking the corporate getaway. Filled my last white box of the day. By the time I got to the coffee bar, I was becoming aware of a prickle in my throat.

I ordered coffee. Took my seat as Grace arrived. She was wearing the burgundy lipstick. Then, the sneeze.

Bless you, I said, watching her slide into her chair.

In the hour that followed, we didn't talk about anything momentous. We just talked. The prevalence of the bug and the changeable weather that nurtured it. How our respective days had been. The recently released movie everyone was talking about, which it turned out neither of us had seen yet, and how that was happening more and more. The progress of her search for an apartment, or the lack of it.

It wasn't like a date. It was just two people meeting for coffee. And I felt comfortable here, with her. Able to talk freely, without vetting or self-reproach. She'd listen, then respond. It seemed we got along.

Ten minutes in, she wiped her mouth with a napkin made from recycled paper. Her lipstick didn't smudge at all. Twenty, and she sneezed again. Twenty-five, and our feet touched under the table. Neither of us acknowledged it except to recross our legs. Thirty and she asked what I had in the bag. I told her, and I told her why.

Oh wow, she said. That's . . . fantastic.

Forty-five minutes in, I saw that the nail on the index finger of her left hand was bitten back in the exact same place as mine.

By seven we were outside, facing. Agreeing we were both worn out and had a whole stack of things to do at home, but also that it had been a lot of fun and that we should definitely – without question – see each other soon.

She was single. I knew that now. She was single, and I was separated.

OK, I said.

Well, she replied.

I found myself speaking without thinking.

Can I take you to dinner?

Yes, she said. I think you can.

Great. So I'll call you.

You do that.

We nodded at each other, emphatic, and I found her a cab.

The next taxi that came, I took myself. I needed to get back. Get washed and changed before heading out again for my prior engagement.

After a while in the city, you learn to appreciate a good cab driver. The one that answers when you ask them a question but otherwise keeps to themself. Who drives fast but safe, doesn't sling you round the back seat like a sack of flour. The driver I had was good. We swept elegantly through the dulcet calm that follows rush hour, past street signs and shopfronts and speed-walking pedestrians. Cocooned in transit. Nowhere for long.

At the lights approaching Sheridan Street, I looked out at the toy-store window, its metal grill half down. Leant forward and spoke to the driver.

Make a U, I said. Head north. Head north and keep driving. He spun us around and accelerated.

This part of the journey wasn't the plan. Just something I realised I needed to do. We drove back the way we came, til we reached the junction that sends you north. The city receded, bars and office blocks giving way to warehouses and business parks, til they in turn began ebbing into the suburbs. Midway into the journey, he flipped on the radio. I heard a snatch of news as he tinkered with the dial. Settled on a music station. Didn't ask if I minded, but that was OK.

It was loud enough to have listened to if I'd wanted, sufficiently quiet to blot out otherwise. As it was, I let it filter in and out, a muted accent to the tick of the meter, the occasional sputter of early evening rain.

The journey seemed to take for ever, and it seemed to be done in a flash. In fact, it took just under an hour til we reached the house. The street I used to live on.

It looked the way it always had. Two identical rows of houses, three bedrooms each, lawns out front, beech trees lining the kerb. Eleanor's car was outside ours. Our car, outside our house. In which was our child.

The cab driver switched off the ignition, turned and asked me, not ungently, if this was where I needed.

I just want to sit for a while, I said. Is that OK?

Your money, he said.

All through coffee with Grace, I had this house at the back of my mind. Reruns of my life here. Now, the first time I'd returned since leaving, they played again.

Moving in, Eleanor pregnant and showing. Eating take-out off packing cases. Painting the living room, buying furniture, a sofa, a cot.

Leaving here, sneaking out, ashamed. The weeks beforehand. The silence only broken by fighting. Screams inside a vacuum. Eleanor berating me about the money. She was the only person I ever told, and she threw that back in my face.

We have a child now, she'd say, like this was unknown to me. There are things we need. That she needs. Our life has changed. Our needs have changed. And that money does nothing, she'd bawl, when it could meet those needs. A car that worked. That'd be a start. A car that worked, like normal people's do. What good are presents, Matthew, when we can't even drive her to school?

And then she'd cry. The way she did. An indictment.

It was a long time coming. My going. I was a cross to them both. And knowing that only made it worse. Drove me further into withdrawal.

Never was good enough. And til I could change that, they were better off without me. I couldn't even remember my own daughter's birthday. So I bound us in this act. Like any vital surgery, it hurt. But she'll see what kind of man her father is, or could be. Soon.

I looked up at her window. Saw her light was on.

None of it had worked out like I hoped. In the days after she was born, I waited. Stared at this pudgy assembly of mouth and eyes, and waited. Waited as she took her first steps, lost her first tooth, spoke her first word. (Moon, incidentally, or something like it. I didn't hear it myself. Eleanor told me later.)

And still it never came. The point at which everything fell into place. When her presence gave me meaning, shape. The way it was supposed to. I just felt the same way I always had, for as long as I could remember.

Eleanor taught to make sure the bills got paid, and I carried on searching for my calling. We met when I was training as a prison officer. She was taking pictures there. It was my fifth career change in the two years since finishing my studies. By the time I asked her out, I'd already decided to hand in my notice.

This was before I got into retail. You name it, and I promise you I've sold it.

Eleanor described it as negative momentum. I guess she

was right. Us coming here, me leaving here, me coming back to think of me leaving here.

I saw the light go off in Alice's room. Leant forward again, asked the driver to take me back to the city.

Then noise, all around me. Bludgeoning, cacophonous. I cried out, terrified.

The radio was on, full volume. I realised I'd fallen asleep. Now I was waking. The driver swivelled in his seat and stared at me. We were at a set of traffic lights, in a generic outskirt. I couldn't tell which one. He lowered the volume, turned back.

I didn't know what else to do, he said. You've been out cold.

Right, I said. I'm . . . a . . . heavy sleeper.

He asked me where I wanted to go, and I told him I didn't know where we were. Demotte, he said. I told him where I needed to be, and when the light turned green he pulled away.

I had no idea what time it was. Checking my watch, I exhaled. It was fine. My destination would still be open.

Back in town, I had to stop at a cash machine to make the fare. Then we arrived. The church of St Jude Thaddeus, on the furthest tip of Bethune Street.

I paid the driver, made sure to remember my sports bag. Stepped out of the cab, looked up at the wood and stone, walked in. Stood beside the candles, absorbing what lay before me. A long table had been set up in front of the altar. Scattered round the pews were maybe forty homeless. Most I thought I recognised from the corner by the toy shop. The others were volunteers. Some I'd seen at the demonstration. Fresh-faced, enthused, undisappointed.

The homeless, by contrast, were doleful and glassy, slumped between pulpit and exit. I stood in the nave. No one appeared to notice. Eventually, I walked up to a volunteer.

Excuse me, I said. Is Vincent Cole here?

And I felt a nudge in my back as someone brushed past, heading for the table. The volunteer turned to his left.

Someone to see you, Father.

Following his line of sight, I saw the priest in the row adjacent. He was down on his haunches, talking with a ramshackle woman. The lights above gave his head a vibrant sheen. He looked back at the volunteer, then up at me. Whispered something in the woman's ear, clasped his hand over hers, then stood and came over. Offered his hand, grinning broadly.

Hi. You made it. Welcome.

We shook, his grip the kind you check your hand for fractures after. His dog collar worn under a chunky knit sweater.

I was . . . passing, I said.

That's great, he said. *Great*. You know, we're trying so damn hard to do something worthwhile here. It's so good to see members of the community getting themselves involved. Anyway, let me introduce you to some friends.

And he put his hand on my shoulder.

You must forgive me. I can't remember your name.

Matthew, I said.

Matthew, he said, directing me to one end of the table, which I now saw was four smaller tables pushed together and covered by a linen spread.

Hayden, Zoe, he said, and two cheery faces jerked up at me. This is Matthew. He's with us for the first time.

Hello, Matthew, they said, as one.

I'm Hayden.

I'm Zoe.

Do you want to come around?

I shuffled behind the table. Vincent Cole patted my arm and wished me good luck.

In front of me were several plastic flasks, ceramic bowls of rice and peas, soup, pasta, squishy white bread. A tower of paper plates. Hayden and Zoe stood on either side. I looked to my left, and Hayden smiled. I looked to my right, and Zoe did the same. I smiled at them both, then looked down the nave at the steady influx heading our way, a grisly nocturne of missing teeth, DTs and psychoses, clothes fouled or simply disintegrating. Late-stage addicts, waiting for the inevitable.

The worst was the eyes. Their cruel biographies.

The scar guy was in the fifth pew back. I don't think he'd seen me.

It's like a bar, I said. Gets busy right before it closes.

Uh . . . yeah, Zoe said. I guess.

A kid no older than seventeen approached my end of the table. I looked at him, his matted hair, his limp, til I realised Hayden and Zoe were staring at me, expectant.

Ah . . . I said. Hello. What can I get you?

Rice, he said, so quiet I could barely hear him. I asked him to repeat himself.

Rice. And can I please have some tea with that?

I doled out the rice onto a paper plate, then poured the tea into a styrofoam cup. Passed him both and he thanked me, twice, before sitting in the pew in front of us.

The despised, Hayden said. The unclean. That's all these people mean to the world outside.

It makes me so angry, Zoe said.

The next guy to approach began hawking a few steps from the table. When he asked me for soup, an oyster of phlegm was rolling in his mouth. And Hayden smiled, and Zoe too. As he grabbed the bowl, his hand touched mine and I couldn't help but shudder. His arms a flower garden of scabs and lesions.

In the next twenty minutes, I served maybe thirty people. Every one made me feel worse. I was starting to dread the weary procession of hungry mouths. Hayden and Zoe, conversely, seemed to grow a little taller with every one.

By now I was constantly rubbing my eyes. My shoulders hunched. I drank some of the coffee, which I could tell Hayden and Zoe disapproved of.

Sorry, I said. It's been a long day.

Smiling unconvincingly, they asked me what I did. I told them I worked at The Greatest Gift. Noting their lack of response, I described the nature of the company, my position within it.

Oh, they said. Right.

And silence. Another hapless body, another plate of stodge.

Personally, Hayden said, I couldn't commit to a full-time job. Not when there's so much *real* work to be done.

Exactly, Zoe said. What boss would let me spend six months of the year in India?

I caught her eye, curious despite myself.

Oh, she said, I've been working on sanitation in Delhi. Got back last week.

I've been in Uganda, Hayden said. Distributing healthcare information to end the spread of HIV.

I'd *love* to do that, Zoe said.

I tried to explain I had rent to pay. A child to support. Silence, again.

I've always thought, Hayden said (as if to no one in particular), it beggars belief that someone could bring a child into this world when we in the West still rely on the suffering of others for the maintenance of our lifestyles.

Zoe peered at me over the ceramic bowls.

How did you say you knew Father Cole?

I glanced round the other volunteers. Not one, Hayden and Zoe included, was beyond their early twenties. I turned back to Zoe and told her I lived near the corner of Bethune and Sheridan.

Oh, she said, suddenly chipper, you were at the protest? I so wanted to go, but my parents had this ski trip organised and –

No, I said. I was just passing . . . I live round there.

Oh . . . Right.

Father Cole is a great man, Hayden said. His energy astounds me.

Hayden's right, Zoe said. He's helped me with a lot of painful issues in my life.

I was strangely grateful for the next arrival at the table. A girl about Hayden and Zoe's age, sleeping bag draped over her shoulder. I ladled out the rice. She thanked me, then looked over the ceramic bowls.

Um . . . is there anything with meat?

Meat? Hayden said. No. There isn't any meat here.

As I passed her the plate, Vincent Cole appeared beside us.

Zoe, he said, can you help me close up? See that everyone has somewhere to go?

Of course, she said, stepping out from behind the table.

I'm sure I saw Hayden glower at her. I turned to face him.

Ah, listen. I have to go.

You're not staying for evening prayers?

No, I really should get –

I eased myself round to the front of the table, sports bag in my hand. Gave the priest a healthy berth, made for the scar guy. He was still in the fifth pew, showing a companion his worn-out shoe.

Hi, I said.

Wigwam man! I thought that was you.

Yeah. Listen . . . ah . . . I hope you're OK with this . . . but the other day, I couldn't help noticing . . . your shoe. So I brought these.

I lay the bag on the floor, squatted and unzipped it. Removed the contents. My Hush Puppies. The ones I spent my first weeks in the city wearing, til I overhauled my wardrobe. A few scuffs aside, they were in prime condition.

You brought these here for me?

They're old, I know. But I thought you could use them.

Christ. Thanks, man . . . That's . . . incredible.

I thought they might be good for the winter.

Ah, man. That's just . . . amazing. Thank you.

He took off his shoes, feet raw and blistered, and I handed them to him. As he pulled on the left, sniggers broke out around us. With the right, they got louder. Spreading down the pew and into the next row. I stared down at the shoes.

They were, conservatively, three sizes too big.

They're great, he said, the laughter now a gale. I'll just have to wear thick socks.

I couldn't take my eyes off them.

Listen, man, he said, I'm really grateful. It's just –

My eyes, I realised, were welling up.

– you're big. A big man. You know?

And I fled. I turned and ran. I ran from the church with my lungs on fire and tears streaming down my face. And I didn't stop running til I reached my apartment.

The door ajar, Eleanor slips into her daughter's bedroom. A practised tiptoe. She always checks her around this time. Makes sure she's sleeping. Not beset by panics.

Her head lies on the pillow. Face angelic beneath the Glo-Star constellation of the ceiling. A hundred tiny points of bright fluorescence, glinting in the darkness. Still rare for her to sleep without the nightlight.

The time invested over the summer looks to have paid off. A month into term, her conversation is of new classmates, teatime invitations. She mentions her father only sporadically. Her relationship with Belinda Griselda, once monopolistic, now stands open to select third parties. The last time Eleanor spoke with Tina Karlsson, on the weekend just passed, she said she'd never seen Alice so happy.

Satisfied, she retreats. Returns downstairs. On the living-room table, an envelope. Inside, a cheque from Matthew. Arrived that morning. Again, no message. Looking at his signature, she realises some part of her is glad he's OK.

She opens a window. Reaches inside her bag. Takes out a cigarette, lights it, inhales, waves the smoke from the room.

If only the breach had been contained between them. But it wasn't. Alice was touched by it too. Like always with Matthew, the theory adored, rejected as reality.

While she was pregnant, he'd pat her bump to the point of irritation, singing, burbling, cooing possible names. After the birth, he wouldn't hold the baby til past six months.

Stretching across the room, cigarette by the open window, she gropes for the remote control. Switches on the television.

Birthdays and Christmases were different, naturally. The card always specified which gifts were from him. Eleanor's would have to wait. Matthew's first, gleeful, ceremonious. Alice tearing at the wrapping, face alight. His even more so. Ready for her joy. His validation.

She leans out of the window, stubs her cigarette on the exterior brickwork, pulls back inside and folds the butt in tissue paper. Casts it into the garbage. Closes the window, moves to the couch, gazes at the television. A movie is playing. She finds herself watching.

On a sunny Technicolor morning, a redhead pulls up on a smalltown street in a powder blue car. She approaches a second woman, relaxing in her garden. As usual, Carrie, she says, you're way ahead of me. I haven't even had time to think of my trees, much less get them pruned.

Presents from Matthew to Alice are scattered in one corner of the room. The last batch received. The usual excess.

Earlier, over supper, she looked into her daughter's eyes and asked – the asked, she feels, is important – if some could be given away. Explained to her there were children who didn't have toys, and it might be a nice thing if they could share hers. And she nodded. An understanding denied to her father.

Eleanor tried persuading him to see someone. A shrink, specifically. It just fed the silences between them. There were no real friends of either sex. Between his lurch from job to job, there was just no chance to make them. He'd say, as he always did, that all he wanted was something he was good at. Something to take pride in.

Before Alice, that was fine. Truly, she admired him for it, even as she packed away her cameras. Five years and Alice later, she felt no admiration. She'd sit here in the evening with her marking, wait for him to come home. Blithely announce that he'd quit again. He was never out of work for long. Always had something lined up. That, as she told him, wasn't the point. And meanwhile a sum larger than either of them would earn in a decade sat idle in a bank, in Matthew's name. It was Alice's, he'd say. For when she's older. And Eleanor would try and raise the issue of its use, and Matthew with his Fort Knox will would walk away, fall silent.

What was the low, she wonders? So many times she thought this must be it. Alice's fifth birthday? A week til their first holiday since before their daughter came. Matthew watching spellbound as Alice tore open the paper, first from the usual regiment of toys, then a hand-stitched leather diary and a solid silver chain. And the fight they had that evening – Matthew, she is five years old! – him mystified, explaining she would value them in the future, and by the way, the latest job wasn't working out for him, so the holiday might have to wait. She knew better than to mention the other account.

And then, of course, her sixth. Meant to be the new beginning. A line marked under the last months' trials. The breach at their centre, his later unravelling.

Naturally, she tried to rouse him in the morning. Dutifully nudged him the moment she heard Alice stir, a nudge that became a shake, knowing he'd want to greet their daughter. Didn't hear him come in the previous night. Must have been late not to even hear him. Now, he lay there at his most unwakeable.

Til Alice skipped into the room, and Eleanor sang 'Happy Birthday' and threw on a robe and ushered her downstairs. Made pancakes for them both, watched TV, took photographs. Waited for Matthew, for the usual ceremony. Waited all morning. Left Alice with the TV as she trooped back up, saw him still unconscious beneath the covers. Shook him again without success. Finally lost patience. Gave Alice the presents she'd bought alone. Nothing like what he must have massed and hidden, just a small collection of simple toys. And as she watched their daughter open them, she thought he must know they were leaving for the cinema at noon. She'd told him more than once. The first time Alice would enter such darkness since the week before the theme park. And all that represented.

It was almost twelve by the time he came down, stumbling, unshaven. And she knew he had no idea what day this was. That somehow, amid his disorder, the birthday and the cinema had each been forgotten.

And she saw Alice look over at him, not with pique but blank confusion at his rumpled appearance and lateness, and in that moment she didn't want excuses, just to take her daughter out as she'd promised her. And when they came back he would have bought gifts and the cake would still be in the fridge and the rest of the day could go on as planned.

She found his note on her bedside drawer.

The woman in the movie stands on her doorstep with a man, older, avuncular. I'm sure you feel like I do, he says. That companionship and affection are often the important things. And Eleanor keeps watching, begins to drowse, and wonders if that's true.

The sun wavers uncertainly, as if it's surprised to be here this early. On the first hole at the Avelden, Jonah Hoffman takes a breath. The mist still hangs in the trees. It is 6.16 a.m. Adjusting his posture, he asks the caddy for a driver. Accepts it, turns it over in his hands. Listens to the absence. The reason he came here at this time of day, just five hours after falling into bed.

He hasn't slept well. The five hours spent beside Christina have not refreshed him. In wisps, fragments, he remembers his dream.

He was in his office. Calling through to Bonnie. All he could hear was dead hum. So he called the concierge instead. The exact same happened again.

In his dream, this failed to perturb him. Poised, almost brash, he walked to his window. Surveyed the city below. Heard a rush of something in the distance, coming fast, getting louder.

A sheer wall of water, a hundred feet high. A tidal wave, advancing over the city, burying the tops of skyscrapers. And he stood and he watched as it tore toward him. And all he could think was how far he was from the ocean.

It is 6.17 a.m. He takes his shot.

The Stretcher Case

The first kick lands an inch below the ribs. Where you get a stitch. The soft place there. The second goes higher, to the ribcage itself.

The school grounds are deserted. Early classes started now. Julian Hoffman lies prostrate, on the fields his parents pay for. Instinctively, he curls into a ball.

The third kick is heavier. Delivered to his kidneys. Then his ribs again. Then his back again. Then both at once, repeatedly. His hands are raised to shield his head. It just provokes a battery.

Soon, his knuckles bleed and blacken. He thinks his fingers could be broken. Feels the air escape his mouth. A flurry of precision now. Tempo and brutality. His face, his gut, between his legs. And on, and on.

Above him, finally, they tire. Huffing and panting. He sees a teacher at a window. His notice this will soon be done with. The last kick connects with the side of his head. That's all he remembers.

I never went back to St Jude Thaddeus. Every time I thought of it – my shoes, the scar guy, Hayden and Zoe – I flinched. Physically flinched.

I felt no brilliance. No inner glow. Just impotence and humiliation.

Grace had left a message by the time I got home. She was, she said, really looking forward to dinner. Call me, she said.

By the time I woke the next morning, Jonah had left one too. He was phoning from the car. He needed me to book him a table at Marlowe's. Call Christina and tell her his trip of the 20th was now extended through the 23rd. Collect a golfing lithograph he had on order from a dealer. Bonnie had the details.

Oh, he said, and if I could get your thoughts on the health retreat thing . . . that would be great.

Going by his tone, as much time as I needed was up.

An hour later, in my cubicle, I called Bonnie. Asked her for the details of the lithograph. She said she'd fax me something over. Then I spread the proposal across my desk. Peered at it, scrutinised. Looked at it front to back, then back to front. I had no idea about pool tiling or locker-room furniture.

I popped a gum and headed to the kitchen. There was coffee in the pot already. Alison was in there. I guess she must have made it.

We said hello, enquired after each other's health. Remarked that, given the crowd in the phone room, the worst of the bug must be over.

Yes! she said, while I poured. That's what I meant to tell you!

She ran from the kitchen. I figured I should wait to see if she came back. When she did, she was holding the paper, leafing frantically. I sipped at my coffee.

There! she said, standing beside me, the paper open.

She was pointing at a column that ran half the width and the whole length of a right-hand page. At the top was a small white box that said:

Your Good Samaritan.

Directly beneath was the name of a supermarket chain. Sponsored By, it said.

The column itself concerned a teenage boy from a housing project who'd built his own organic garden on a plot of waste ground near his home. He distributed the produce to local hospitals and homes for the elderly. There was a photograph of him in his garden, surrounded by his vegetables.

And that's why Josephus is Your Good Samaritan, it said at the end.

I still didn't understand why she was showing it to me.

They have this once a week, she said. I'm going to nominate you.

My right hand began shaking, a drop of coffee spilling. I felt like I was going to combust in a shower of unchecked emotion.

You'd do that for me?

164

Yeah, she said, like it was no big thing. I thought of you immediately. You know, with paying the mark-up on Mrs Blum's tickets and taking her yourself, and you giving blood . . . and the soup kitchen.

Ah, I said. Right.

The mechanics seemed simple enough. Readers wrote in to nominate those who'd performed or were performing a notable act of humanity. Every week the paper announced a winner. I just had to let her give them my number.

There was a cash prize, to be given to a charity of the winner's choice. I thought of Eleanor showing Alice my picture. Reading her the tribute.

I'm just so touched you would do that for me, I said.

Well, you know . . . Don't shield your eyes from the light around you.

I recognised the line immediately.

You've been reading Eric Handler, I said, and wowed and hummed as she told me she'd just started *Reinventing the Soul*, intrigued by my ceaseless promotion.

I told her I was in awe of the imagery he used throughout. Chapters three and four especially. She said she knew what I meant, and we each sipped at our coffees.

Well, I said, I think you're going to find it incredibly powerful. He's just . . . the master of his form.

In contrast, I said, I'd recently been reading Suzanne A. Lee's much-hyped *The Me Within*, but having spent the last week ploughing through it I –

Alison hopes he's right about the book. God knows, she needs something. Something to curb the racking self-effacement. To stall the modesty before it turns to diffidence and then to self-denial. The unseen hand that drags her from the easel, corrodes her future, keeps her penned and docile.

All she wanted was to paint. But she can't. Physically. Can't bring herself to hold a brush. She doesn't know how it started. Can't pin it on a single moment. Only knows that somewhere she became convinced, deeply and unshakeably, that she doesn't quite deserve it. Doesn't have the talent. Was never going to make it anyway. And she'd sketch instead with charcoals, til even that made her cringe and go rigid.

Her friends, of course – even those she suspects think she's dipping for praise – tell her not to be so stupid. Garland her in flattery, affection. You were always so good, they say. Just bite it and start over. And she hears them. She does. But then again, she doesn't.

really felt it lacked a certain clarity.

Really? she said.

Oh yeah.

We smiled at one another, then down at the paper.

Maybe you should write a book, she said. Matthew Viss's tips for personal growth. *Secrets of the Happy Concierge*.

I knew she was being flippant. But it didn't sound so ridiculous. Of the myriad books that lined my shelves, there were many by professors and clinicians, admirable minds boasting graceful prose styles and profuse certification. More, however, came from ordinary men and women just like me, simply granted an intrinsic horse sense and a willingness to share it. Eric Handler sold freezers before 15 *Simple Wisdoms* was published.

It could even be For Alice.

Owen from Personal walked in with the fax from Bonnie.

For you, he said.

I should get back, Alison said. I've got a banquet to organise.

And she held up the paper.

Fingers crossed!

Sometimes your luck can change before you. A swerve in the road that you never saw coming. Of course, I wasn't seeking kudos. But the thought of it felt good.

I tackled Phillip Reilly's proposal with a new sense of vigour. The more I read, the better it sounded. I honestly didn't see how it could fail.

I went out for lunch just after one, was back within fifteen minutes. Ate at my desk. The next time I looked at the clock, it was almost four and I'd filled six pages with my thoughts on the health retreat.

I recommended Jonah give it serious consideration. Said it appeared a fantastic opportunity, and couriered the report over to Dutch Street.

Only now did I realise how badly I'd been needing some words of kindness.

When I got home, there was a box in the lobby. A present from Jonah. An abs crunch bench, for honing my obliques and abdominals. That night, I wrote for hours, in longhand, in a legal pad. Just put it all down, untrammelled. I wasn't thinking in terms of a readership. That said, it didn't look too shabby.

I walked to the all-night copy shop on Barton Street, used a computer there to type it up. Printed out two copies. One for me, the other attached to a covering note and mailed to Eric Handler, c/o his publishers. I didn't know who else to send it to.

The empathy remained, persistent, invasive. I sighed for the melancholy girl behind the copy-shop counter, dreaming of escape from whatever stifling circumstance compelled her to be here, changing toners in the dead of night. Offered a silent commiseration to the plump young man in the back room, guillotining leaflets and casting lovelorn glances at the girl (oblivious).

Hello, Carl, I said, returning home.

Hello, Mr Viss, he said.

I was, I realised, whistling.

I spent twenty minutes on my new abs bench, then moved over to the treadmill. Ran nine miles as I watched TV.

A lot of times I find when I'm running that I need something to focus on outside the burn in my thighs and the heaving clench of my chest. Music videos can be useful. Sports are also good. I wound up with a news show. I hadn't seen the news in days. This was the localised segment. All the world in a fifty-mile radius.

We began with a stock suburban house, then cut to the interior. A couple about my age were sitting at either end of a floral-print couch, holding hands in the middle. The woman was obviously distressed. Occasionally, her husband would lean across and put his arm around her.

They were talking about their daughter. I didn't catch her name. She was critically ill. A rare disorder of the lung. We saw her playing in her bedroom. The voice-over explained that her parents couldn't afford the treatment she needed.

Her face was a lead-poisoned white, thick lines of purple ringing her eyes. An IV tube hung from her nose. She needed a transplant as a matter of urgency. That was only the beginning. The operation itself could kill her. At best, there would be arduous years of convalescence.

Then we cut back to her parents. We just want our baby to get better, the woman said, breaking down. And her husband put his arm round her once more.

Afterward, the anchorman said a fund had been set up to handle donations to the family's medical bills. Cutting off the treadmill, I scrabbled for a pen. Wrote the details on the back of the legal pad. Started warming down.

I found my chequebook, settled on a figure to give to the appeal.

The phone rang, and it was Grace.

When I took her to dinner, we had Chinese food. We met in a bar next door to the coffee shop from last time. There we chose a restaurant.

I had considered Marlowe's. Jonah always told me that if I needed a reservation myself, I should feel free to drop his name. Eventually, I decided against it. I thought it might seem ostentatious. Also, I was certain that she'd mentioned being vegetarian. Or only eating fish. Either way, Chinese food it was.

There was a place five minutes from her house, she said. If that didn't sound too selfish. I told her no. That sounded great.

I've always liked Chinese food. My taste buds have been so degraded by coffee and nicotine gum, it's one of the few meals I actually enjoy. That's how I can maintain the kind of healthy diet most people think of as boring. To me, it's all the same.

She was wearing a pale grey rollneck, lipstick a shade darker than usual. We sat at a corner table, like the others covered in a rouched pink tablecloth. Smiled and said how good it all looked while studying the menu. Made chit-chat over starters. I noticed, and remarked on, her dexterity with chopsticks.

The rapport we'd established in the coffee shop returned almost immediately. That was the thing with Grace. It always felt like you were carrying on a conversation. Not like those people where no matter what's gone before, it's always the first time you've met them.

We mulled over our days at work, the fact we still hadn't seen the movie that everyone was talking about, her continued search for an apartment. She had this tic of rooting through her bag, but that faded as the meal progressed.

Over the main course, we talked mostly about the food itself. As she finished her noodles, I told her about my hypersomnia. I was just so at ease with her by then, I could have told her anything. She didn't seem fazed. Just curious.

The fuller memoirs came between the removal of our bowls and the arrival of coffee. (Neither of us had dessert. We shared, we learned, an aversion to lychees.) She discussed her education, fears, ambitions. Told me she loved working at Mortimer and Upas. I told her about the soup kitchen and the Good Samaritan award. Like we had something in common now.

She said if there was one good thing to come out of her grandfather's death, it was the chance to work as a volunteer. There'd been a small inheritance, she said.

Right, I said. And left it there.

In time we got round to our parents. I hedged for a while, then came out with it.

. . . My father was an astronaut.

169

She didn't laugh or plainly disbelieve me. She even asked what missions he'd been on. Pondered zero gravity, dehydrated food.

So, she said – and by now I didn't mind that she was grinning as she spoke – did he ever see anything . . . unidentified?

No . . . I mean, he didn't like discussing it. Any of it. But I asked him about that. And he told me there was nothing. There was nothing out there. Just cold and dust and silence.

I must have had something at the corner of my mouth. She made a gesture too subtle for me to understand, then leant over and brushed whatever it was away with her napkin.

But, she said, you didn't want to go into that . . . field . . . yourself?

Oh, no. I don't think I've got what it takes.

Our backgrounds, we discovered, were really not dissimilar. She was an army brat. Both our families had pursued a drab itinerancy, then settled in the suburbs that girded the city, mine to the north-west, hers to the south. That, she said, was where her shyness started. A shyness I hadn't even noticed, that she talked of as an affliction, to be overcome, rid of.

You really don't seem that way, I said. You seem very . . . assured.

Thank you. That means a lot to me. I still have to work at it.

I know exactly what you mean.

She had two brothers, but they were older, already mired in adolescence as she was starting school. I told her I was an only child. Neither of us close with parents who had their own lives to deal with.

So here we are, I said. Born to silent houses.

Well, she said, we're doing OK now.

I guess we were.

After the discussion of my father's job, I spun the conversation away. I don't see them any more, I said, with enough emphasis to close the subject. When she asked about Alice and Eleanor, I tried to be as honest as I could.

She made it clear she had no interest in getting involved

with a married man, and I told her I believed my marriage was over. My daughter, however, was my world. And as she talked, I thought about what I was here for, and I didn't have the answer.

– and then I knew I had to start over, she said.

She'd been married before as well. Divorced now. His name was Jerry. She met him young. Too young. It ended badly.

When the coffee came, we took the bill at the same time. There was a friendly squabble over its payment. Though Grace insisted we split it, I was adamant on the issue, placing my hand over hers as she reached for her bag.

No, please, I said. These things are important.

The same way it was important that I helped her on with her coat, held the door open for her, then swept in front so I was standing on the kerbside.

Afterward, I saw her home. She slipped her arm through mine as we walked. My back straightened at the urge of some primal directive.

Her area was a medley of boarded-up shops and waste ground. I could see why she might want to leave. As we turned into a side street that she told me led to hers, a terrier bolted from a house, low and hurtling. By the time I'd absorbed the size of it, I'd already flung myself backward.

I thought of how we must look. A man of my height and frame, cowering as Grace stood in front of me, the dog – its stomach barely off the ground – yapping at us both.

I felt I owed her an explanation. As soon as I righted myself and sidestepped the terrier, I told her about Leon.

Leon came into my life just after my twelfth birthday. He wasn't a present. Wasn't even mine. He belonged to the family. A German shepherd, eight weeks old, overbred and nervy. Beautiful.

Back then, as children do, I believed that animals could see what lies inside you. Mute but uncanny character witnesses. The first night my father brought him home, he seemed to take a liking to me. We spent an hour tussling on the floor before I was sent to bed. He was locked in the kitchen overnight, whining and scrabbling.

Around twelve, when my parents had gone to bed, I snuck downstairs. Crept into the kitchen. Saw him doleful in the corner, got down on my knees and patted the floor. Whispered quieting noises.

He stared at me a second. Then he went for me. I blinked, and he was at my throat. All I could see was his teeth.

Realistically, it must have been over in a second. He was still just a puppy, and I was big even then. I grabbed a handful of fur and threw him across the room, yelping. I was fine. He seemed the more shaken of us. All the same, I thought I should tell my parents.

At their bedroom door, I coughed, then knocked. Then knocked again. My father was the first to wake.

Matthew? he said. What is it?

Before I could answer the light was on, and I heard my mother screaming.

I spent three nights in hospital. Leon had drawn blood in several places, but the serious damage was done to my scalp, where a marshmallow clump of skin and tissue had been torn away from my skull.

Slowing, I pulled my hair away, showed Grace the alabaster scar.

There, I said. Can you see it?

I can, she said.

So that's why I'm bad around dogs.

She tightened her arm inside mine, asked me what happened to Leon. I asked her what she meant.

Well . . . it was put down, right?

No, I said, aghast at the suggestion. My dad was already really fond of him. Besides, he was so placid with everybody else, I think they assumed I'd provoked him. He was usually very even-tempered. Apart from that one time.

By the time I'd finished telling Grace about Leon, we were at her building.

This is where I live, she said.

A beaten-up mansion block, rubbish on the bottom step. Outside, we stood facing.

I felt no little relief when she spoke. Even more when she told me it had been a lovely evening, but she had an early start, and –

Sure, I said. Me too.

OK. Well . . .

And we each stepped forward. An inch from her face, I still wasn't sure if this was a kiss on the mouth or the cheek. I don't think she was either. In the end, our lips half mashed against each other, til both of us withdrew. At the top of the stairs that ran up to her building, she turned.

Call me, she said.

I said I would, and then I started home.

First, she sits on the edge of the bed, pulls off her shoes. In the bathroom, removes her make-up. Wipes away, cleanses, rinses.

Back inside her living room, Grace Walker reaches for her bag. Combs through the interior, the diary, address book, tissues, lipstick. In the open pocket with the zip is what she needs. She removes the cassette recorder, releases the tape. Walks over to her stereo, slips it inside. Rewinds one side. Watches as the spools turn back til the tape jars silently against the rollers. Play.

A skirl of hiss, then voices. Hers and Matthew's. She listens to their meeting in the bar. Mouths along to her lines.

The taxi ride, as she expected, is buried under background noise. The radio, the engine. Forward to the restaurant. Her shoulders tense and rise. The tape, as expected, cuts out. When she glanced into her bag, there was no light to signify recording. She remembers trying to sound casual as she frantically attempted to disengage the pause. Terrified he might lean over, see, and learn.

Finally, she traced the button, saw the light reappear. She hears herself exhale. Settles back. Reviews the main course and the conversation afterward. It pleases her, her performance. Fluid but demure. No stammerings, *non sequiturs*. Even the stuff about his father she dealt with comfortably. For the most part.

But you didn't want to go into that . . . field . . . yourself?

She winces at her gaucheness, the dopey catch in her voice. Plays on.

. . . There was nothing out there. Just cold and dust and silence.

And she presses pause. Revises the exchange. Chews the inside of her cheek in concentration.

That must have been . . . disturbing, she says now, alone in her apartment. Frowns and sighs in irritation. Why would she say that? Why would anyone say that?

Releases pause, rewinds again. Waits.

. . . nothing out there. Just cold and dust and silence.

She falters, stutters, unproductive. Rewinds again.

. . . cold and dust and silence.

I guess, she says, that kind of thing must change someone.

Relief consumes her. Not great, but it'll do. And the tape plays on. Born to silent houses, he says. A gentleness to him. His manner – she noticed then, and now again – sweet beyond just etiquette. Made her feel secure as he gangled beside her. Alive. Visible. Like she always thought she would with a man's arm slipped through hers, but never did.

Now, she hears herself peeling open. Talking of Jerry, their marriage. Not the whole debacle, of course. Only the gist.

And then I knew I had to start over.

She closes her eyes, just listens.

No, please. These things are important.

She wants to give this one a chance. It's taken her too long already. To recover from Jerry, the years being hawked round like a pack of gum.

Jerry was a cuckold. That was the name for it. There was a whole scene, a foul culture, a world she discovered in the first few months of her marriage and was duly claimed by. Bulls, cuckolds, and the wives they shared. Jerry, she found, could only be satisfied watching her with other men. He advertised in magazines. And she would go along, be pliant, scream in ersatz frenzy through her tears, believing that if this was what she had to do for him, then she would do it.

Til the point at which she couldn't. Til it made her sick to see herself in the mirror. The memory hasn't faded, even without a recording.

There. Can you see it?

She listens to her own voice, bright now, unafraid.

Call me.

And she turns off the machine.

Jonah Hoffman sets his left foot on the ground, leg bent. His weight placed there and only there, he throws his right foot up til it's flat against the fence. Lunging, he reaches toward it with his right hand, clawing his fingers through the tight wire links. Secures enough grip to let him roll back on the ball of his supporting foot while his left hand follows. Hauling now with his fingers alone, the demands on his left leg abruptly subside, leaving it to join his right. The iron of the fence beginning to strain, he holds perfectly still, waits for the frame to adjust. Fingertips white and agonised, feet splayed, halfway up this supposedly invulnerable structure.

It is 11.42 p.m. The rebuilding of the fence was completed today. The site manager called, brimming with assurances about his men in overalls and the quality of their work. The cousin or the brother of the maid included.

Now Jonah clings to the wire in his hand-tailored suit, attempting to break into his own property. His posture classically simian. This, he feels, the only reliable test.

With what leverage he can muster, he throws his weight back, allowing his right hand to grab at the wire that runs along the fence's summit. His left leg follows, til he hooks his foot around the top, carrying his left arm up beside. Then, nudging forward without – he hopes – inducing a headfirst sprawl, his right leg joins the rest of him before, in one motion, he relinquishes his balance and drops to the grass. Lands torpid on his side.

His hands are cut. Palms skinned, fingers shredded. The trousers of his suit are snagged. Standing, he feels a dizziness. Looks up, inside his grounds, to the electronic box mounted on the supporting post. No flash of recognition. A moment later, still nothing.

And now, only now, he sees the white light that represents a distress signal sent to the police. Were he a genuine criminal, precious seconds would already be his.

Jesus. It is 11.44 p.m. Limping slightly, heading toward the house, he calls the police station. Tells them the signal was just a false alarm.

His mind is made up. Tomorrow morning, before he leaves, when the maid has performed her duties at breakfast, he will ask if she could come to the study. Invite her to take a seat beside the fire, under the painting he has now concluded he really doesn't like. And when she has, he will say to her in reasoned, non-aggressive tones that there are two courses of action available to her.

With the first, she can agree that the work carried out by the security company recommended by her, via his wife, under the auspices of her cousin or brother's employment, has been disgraceful and he is therefore entitled both ethically and legally to call the company, complain in the strongest terms and – given the basis on which the contract was awarded – demand that her brother or cousin be dismissed.

Or she can leave her job here. The decision will be hers.

Inside the house, he calls the concierge. Waits for his voicemail. Leaves a message requesting that, at the earliest opportunity, he find and hire the best home-security firm he can.

The walk home took longer than I'd thought it would. I was vague on where I was for much of the journey. I kept to the main drags, avoided cut-throughs. Couldn't help wondering if this was the end of me and Eleanor.

Only now did it cross my mind that she might have found someone else. Maybe that she hadn't yet but hoped to.

I walked, kept walking, past the disuse and abandonment, back to what I knew. I was fifteen minutes from Bethune Street when I passed the hospital. The busiest in the city, seven storeys of decline, diagnosis, finality.

A siren whooped. An ambulance swung into the parkway. Two paramedics jumped from the front seats as an orderly scurried to help. There were shouted injunctions, the back doors pulled open. Amid some jargon that I didn't know the meaning of, I heard one say:

It's a bleeder.

The three of them hauled out a stretcher. A body, prone beneath a lime green blanket, soaked black in patches. I stood and watched. Then followed them. They, of course, were at full pelt. I lost them before I made it to the entrance.

Past the din of the admissions desk, I saw them ahead, spinning the stretcher on its wheels like an expert grandmother in a crowded supermarket. And I followed them again. I don't know what I'd have said had anyone queried me. As it was, I caught up with them just as the doors were closing on a lift.

You can't use that one, sir.

A small, birdlike porter was standing behind me with a trolley full of laundry.

That lift is for emergencies only. The regular elevator's back the way you came.

He pointed back past the admissions desk, polite but stoic.

Oh, I said. Right. Thank you. And the stairs are –

The stairs are right over there, sir.

I had no idea which floor the stretcher case might be on. I had no choice but to check them all. From the vulcanised staircase that spined the building, I strolled into each, affecting to gape in confusion til an orderly or duty nurse would see me and sternly explain that visiting hours were over til tomorrow.

The hallways looked identical, all tan plastic and thick, cushioned flooring. The theatres were on the fifth.

A wide corridor – wider than the rest – I think possibly soundproofed. To my right, down the beige expanse, a middle-aged man walked out through a set of double doors. He wore a surgical gown, the same green as the stretcher blanket, his mask around his neck. As he entered the room adjacent, a nurse appeared from the one opposite, carrying a pair of blood bags. They were just like the ones at Mortimer and Upas. She took them straight into the theatre.

I stood there, rooted. Wondered how many bags they might

use. Where, exactly, they came from. Small acts of kindness, sealed and frozen.

There were maybe twenty seconds before the guy in the gown re-emerged. I thought for an instant he saw me. Dove back into the stairwell.

For the next thirty minutes I observed the to and fro, til an orderly carrying a box of surgical equipment dawdled round the corner.

Heymanwhatchoudoingthere? he said.

He looked ready for any eventuality.

Youainsposedtobeonthisfloor.

Sorry, I said, and made for the stairs.

Nobodysposedtobeonthifloorceptfudocorsnnurses.

I returned to the ground-floor waiting area. Took a seat on one of the plastic chairs bolted to the floor, set in a block of twelve by fourteen.

I guess half of the people there were waiting on friends or relatives, the rest seeking treatment themselves. A bearded guy with a tattoo across his neck had his right foot bare and propped on the seat in front, a fresh gouge at the ankle.

I rose again, walked over to the coffee machine. Found enough coins in my wallet for a single tepid cup.

I hate machine coffee. I hate hospitals. Sterile yet somehow always dirty.

After Leon attacked me, I was dispatched to the nearest paediatric ward. It was the only time in my life I couldn't sleep. That alone was enough to unsettle me. I'd get up in the middle of the night, kept awake by the noises from the other beds, and wander through the corridors, looking at the other patients where I could. My parents came once daily at six. Thirty minutes before dinner.

The first day, I was staring at the wall when I heard my father's voice. I sat up in bed, a turban of bandages around my head. He was at the far end of the ward, arguing with an orderly. Leon at his feet.

The orderly was telling him to get that thing out of here.

My father just brushed him off. Strode down the ward with my mother on his left side and Leon on his right. I discreetly gripped the sides of the mattress in fear.

Maybe ten steps later, a bevy of orderlies surrounded him. He was big like me but he knew when he was outnumbered.

My mother sat with me as my father chained Leon up outside. When he came back, I could tell he was preoccupied. He could sit for no longer than a minute at a time before peering from my bedside window, down to the railings below. My mother just smiled. Occasionally, she'd pat my arm. Then they left.

Yet now, in spite of it all, something had drawn me here.

I sipped at my coffee. Swallowed fast. Went back to my seat. There were now two men with bare feet. A teenage girl to my left being helped off with her jacket by – I assume – her boyfriend. Her arm looked broken. The atmosphere was one of bad diets and complex social-security claims, a kindling resentment choking the air. I guess people with money go elsewhere. Maybe the poor are just clumsy.

Now and then, someone would berate an orderly over the waiting time, to be told with varying degrees of sympathy they would be seen just as soon as was possible. Less frequently, a nurse would call out a name, and a sorry figure would be led away from the graveyard of plastic chairs.

I could feel myself beginning to drift. It wasn't like anyone was paying me much attention. I didn't look wounded or dangerous. My eyes were drawing to.

A second later, my head jerked vertical. With drool running from the corner of my mouth, I checked the time. I'd been at the hospital for over an hour and I didn't even know why. I guess if you asked me now I'd say I was curious about the bleeder. Maybe admit that I felt some involvement. Possessiveness, even.

I stood, considered another sally to the operating theatre. I could have tried the admissions desk, but I didn't feel coherent enough to pass myself off as a relative. It was time for me to go.

As the automatic doors slid open, a paramedic stepped

through, wheeling in another stretcher. A child was lying on it, rigged to a mass of breathing apparatus. A pair of adults run-walked beside, faces drawn.

It clicked then. I knew them. From the television. The local girl with the lung disorder.

I tried to catch the mother's eye, but she looked straight through me. I could understand that. And in her blank dejection, I knew why I'd come. So I could see this for myself. Not through a screen, but here.

I watched them troop toward the emergency lift. Then walked the fifteen minutes back to Scala Street.

The next morning, I overslept. I hadn't overslept since I came here. My clocks had worked fine. They just hadn't woken me. Only the fifth and seventh still rung out, an enervated death rattle.

It was after nine. I should have already been at Pearl Street. I called the office, told Caroline there'd been a gas leak. Collected my mail as I sprinted downstairs, read it sitting tense in the back of a cab. The usual bills and pitches. An A4 envelope from the bank, inside which lay yet another letter pleading with me to transfer the money from my savings account. This time, there was a glossy brochure enclosed, printed on sensually textured paper, featuring a riot of associated imagery: sportsmen, cellists, orchards, nurses. At the traffic lights on Creed Street, I rolled down the window and threw it all in a waste basket.

Six days later, having sent another donation to the girl with the lung disorder's appeal fund, I returned to Mortimer and Upas. For the last two weeks, I'd drawn blood from my arms at least once every night. It kept me ticking over.

Now, I was here to meet Grace. I'd called her, then she called me, then I called her again and so on, til we arranged to have dinner for a second time.

While she was getting ready, I waited at reception. Carmen kept staring at me from across her desk. I'd catch her eye and she'd smile.

So, she said, after minutes of this, you're Grace's new man.

I tried not to wince at her phrasing.

I guess so.

She smiled again, and I drummed my fingers on the MDF coffee table. Stood and moved over to her desk.

Hi, I said. It's Carmen, isn't it?

She looked up, beaming.

It is.

Ah, the thing is . . . I'm actually a donor here . . . and I was wondering when I could give again? When my rest period was up?

I knew when it was, to the day. I was just looking for an opening.

Right, she said. I thought I recognised you.

I'm Matthew Viss, I said.

OK! Let's take a look! V-I-

Double S.

She tapped at her keyboard, rested her head in her hands.

Eight days. You've got another eight days.

Ah, I said. I may be away then.

I brought my voice down to a murmur.

There's no way I could give now, is there? You know . . . as I'm here?

Whatever she thought of the question she kept it to herself.

We're pretty strict about that kind of thing she said. It's important your body has a chance to recover after each donation.

Of course, I said. I mean, that's what I thought.

If your plans fall through, she said, we'll still be here.

Grace and I ate Vietnamese two blocks up from the clinic. I felt distracted throughout. Couldn't keep my mind on the food, or her. It wasn't til the main course that I noticed her lipstick was a shade lighter than usual.

Outside, she asked me what I wanted to do now. I said I was exhausted, but I'd call her tomorrow. And we kissed, the same way we had before. Then I found her a cab.

The next I took myself.

*

And right now, I'm still falling.

Somewhere else entirely.

Closer to the end than the beginning.

Limbs fanned out, unbounded.

Pledged to Newton's tyranny.

And so the fifth floor passes.

The couple who live there are somewhere in their forties.
With them living directly underneath me, I often find myself
running into them.

I've never seen them separately.

A lot of times they'll wear what look like matching outfits.
You just know they call themselves a team.

*Does every shoe have to be stuffed? Reuben Toller stands over
their largest case, oatmeal canvas with chocolate leather trim.
Addresses his wife in taps and gestures. Fluent bursts of sign
language. A mass of tissue paper sits before him on the bed.
Surely you don't stuff running shoes?*

*But you do, Kaye Toller says, palms and fingers jiving in
reply. They'll get crushed otherwise. Be flattened when you
want to wear them.*

*In twenty minutes, a taxi will arrive at their building and take
them from the city for a national three-day shooting competition.
One of six they enter each year at ranges across the country.
Barring loss of form or act of God, Kaye will win her class. She's
always been the marksman of the two. People used to pull
Reuben to one side, ask if she was OK to do this. And Reuben
would watch her decimate another target and tell them – as Kaye
would do herself – that yes, she's fine. It isn't like she's blind.*

*At the end of the bed, a toiletries bag lies next to the guns. Kaye
looks over the equipment, the twin Berettas, vest, the goggles,
cotton buds. They're going to be late if they're not packed soon.*

Are you sure? Reuben says, the tissue still unused.

*Reuben, she says, impatience rising, will you please just stuff
the shoe?*

*

At work, there were still more jobs for Jonah. Always the messages, orders. Collect a prescription for the eczema that, he said, routinely flared up at this time of year. Get his suit trousers to his tailor for repair. Secure estimates and hire a security firm for work to be done at his home.

One time, having booked Marlowe's and reserved the hotel suite, he asked me to call Christina and say he was driving overnight to meet a potential investment.

You don't need to lie for him, she said. I know what goes on.

And every time, there's a present. Til I found myself creeping round metal when I needed the bathroom, tripping over dumb-bells coming home from work.

Even as I grew more fastidious, my space kept dwindling. I tried moving things around, then on top of each other. It did no good. I needed to clear, not putter.

Downstairs, Carl was fixed on the middle distance. I took up position beside his desk.

Hello, Mr Viss. How are you?

I'm good, Carl.

Good.

And you?

Me too.

I blew out my cheeks.

Is there something I can do for you, Mr Viss?

I explained the situation in my apartment. Gently broached the subject of the loft. Wondered if there was any way I might be able to store some boxes there.

He shook his head. Sucked his teeth. Said the loft was still being renovated. That the building managers had expressly told him it wasn't to be used for storage.

I knew what he was getting at. Chris and Helena kept all kinds of stuff there, and I was sure they weren't alone. I reached for my wallet, produced a note.

Carl Haczek considers the issue. The loft is where he practises his reading. For almost three months, he has studied literacy at

Cale Street Community College. Every week on his one free evening he attends a class and leaves with homework. He began on the suggestion of Ruby, his wife. It's called the Basic Literacy Certificate, she'd say with hopeful animation. Only takes a year. And he'd grimace and find excuses til, finally, he gave in.

At the first class, he found himself the oldest there, the rest late teenage drop-outs. Yeah, he said, when they had to introduce themselves, I'm one of those defectives you hear about. And the teacher, half his age herself, said:

Carl, you're not a defective. No one here is.

They tried to read words aloud and write them into notebooks. At first, it made him think of school, want to break the pen, smash his skull against the desk. Then, almost without noticing, he grew absorbed. Came home ebullient. Told Ruby everything with childish glee.

And, as the college workload surged, he started to use the loft to read. To study, unriddle. The others, they don't bother him up there. This one, he suspects, will be in and out constantly. But then, there are the books to pay for. He stares at the note, considers the issue some more.

OK, Mr Viss, he said. Here's what we'll do.

He told me I could sub-let a portion of the loft on the condition that, should the building management actually begin their renovations, the arrangement would be cancelled and all property removed immediately.

He took the note as down payment. Said he'd get me a key cut. The next day, I gathered up my boxes and took them to the loft.

The next day, Jonah called me in the morning.

You know what I've just been reading? he said. Scientists are implanting electrodes in the brains of rats. They intend to remote control them. Have them turn this way, that way, navigate rocks, climb trees. They want to fit them with video cameras and have them search for earthquake survivors. Rats. With cameras. Saving men. Did you know that, Matthew?

I told him maybe, but I –

Anyway, he said. And he told me he'd finished my report on the health retreat. Said it made for interesting reading. He'd had Bonnie contact the guy to make a lunch date immediately. He would have had me do it, he said, but she'd expressed some disquiet about the volume of work I'd already taken over from her.

I said I understood. That I was just pleased he found my input useful.

The only problem, he said, was his trip of the 20th. With that impending, he had so much to get through he didn't think he had the time. And he thought – as I had such an obvious understanding of what he should be doing in this area – that maybe I could represent him.

Flattered as I was, I wasn't sure this was appropriate.

Jonah told me to relax. All I had to do, he said, was talk through the plans and establish what kind of guy this was.

Character, he said, is really all that matters in my business. In any business.

And then I crossed the line again. Agreed to meet the guy. And still it seems like nothing's changed. Technically, there was no way my job spec covered this kind of engagement. But then, by now, I was working to a higher ethos.

I consulted my diary, asked when the lunch had been scheduled.

It's the one you booked for today, he said. Did I not mention that?

I must have forgotten, I said.

He hadn't mentioned it. I wrapped up the call. To get where I needed to be on time, I was going to have to leave now.

Rising from my desk, I glanced around the phone room. Greg Hopper was at his cubicle, talking with a client. He'd only recently been allowed back on the phones. His voice was high, flecked with antagonism. Then he started the profanities.

The phone room stalled dead til Caroline ran from her office, snatched the receiver and took over the call. In the furore, Greg fell from his swivel chair. Crashed head first to the floor. I walked away, took a cab to the restaurant.

I arrived five minutes late. The reservation was still in Jonah's name. Originally, it had been for Marlowe's. Then he'd asked me to make it here instead. It was the same basic idea, sirloins and power. Just slightly less expensive.

There was a moment of confusion with the maître d' over whether Mr Hoffman would be joining us. Finally, wearily, he showed me to the table. The health retreat guy was already there. Shorter than me, but broader, more expansive. Late thirties, mixed race, in a starched white shirt with a blue and salmon necktie.

He stood as I approached. I assumed he thought I was Jonah.

Mr Viss? Phillip Reilly. It's great to meet you.

He thrust his hand across the table.

Hi, I said. Ah . . . I take it Mr Hoffman told you –

Bonnie called. She said he'd been held up and you were coming instead.

He used Bonnie's name like they went back years.

Right, I said. I hope that's OK.

Of course, he said. It's a pleasure.

I don't know whether he was aggrieved at Jonah's non-appearance. If so, he hid it well. The manic tapping of his feet I took to be nerves.

When we talked through his proposal, he spoke with a heady conviction. A zealous faith in his destiny. Emphasised the need to attract a certain stratum of client. For the retreat to be the kind of place his wife would be happy to visit. He asked, if it wasn't too presumptuous a question, how close was I to Mr Hoffman? How much . . . weight I carried with him?

I told him it was my report that had led to this meeting. That Jonah and I enjoyed an uncommonly strong working relationship. That he'd asked me to get involved because of my expertise in this area.

I knew it, he said. I knew you were a gym rat.

Oh, no . . . I mean, I work out at home. I lift a little.

With those delts? Come on, champ. I think you lift more than a little.

For the rest of the meal, we talked gym gear. The top-of-the-line equipment the retreat would be stocked with, the quality of the seam stitch on the Cobra flat bench. Til we finished eating. Sat back, digesting.

So, he said. Ever taken 'roids?

I looked up from my plate, saw the trace of a grin.

No . . . I haven't.

He nodded, shrugged.

Me neither. I used to know a lot of guys on Stanozol. That gets pretty ugly. You heard of Stanozol?

And I told him that I had.

Stanozol is an anabolic steroid, chemically related to testosterone. At one point it was a bodybuilding staple. Now it's best known for getting Ben Johnson busted after winning gold at the Seoul Olympics. The world's fastest man, turned overnight into an abhorrence, eyes the same colour as his own filthy urine sample.

There was a moment of silence. We each took it upon ourselves to move the conversation on. Compared training regimes, swapped notes on technique. He offered me pointers, minor but enlightening refinements. Told me he'd give me

the deluxe programme, gratis

should the deal come off.

As I took care of the bill, I said I'd let him know how things panned out. He seemed eager to pin me down on when.

I'll speak to Mr Hoffman this afternoon, I said.

Outside, he thanked me for my time.

It means a lot to me, he said, that someone of your calibre would look on me as a serious proposition.

In the cab back to Pearl Street, I further assessed his character. Wholeheartedly decided I liked him. I was sold on his plans but, more than that, I admired his drive. His dynamic strength of purpose. He knew where he was going. I could see that. I thought about how long it had been since I'd had a friend. A real one. Had I ever?

Back in my cubicle, I called Jonah. Told him the lunch had been highly productive, and he should at least meet Reilly in person. He said it all sounded very exciting, and he'd think it over while he was away.

Talking of which, he said. Then he gave me my jobs for the duration.

I was to book a limo to the airport for the morning. Marlowe's for the night of his return. Send a pâté mould to the address on Rush Street. Order various items of furniture for a pastoral cottage he'd just bought in Marvendean. Provide a selection of domestic assistants to be interviewed by Christina on Monday afternoon. And then he paused.

Jonah never paused. I'd heard him have three conversations at once while grinding through rush-hour traffic and not stop for breath.

Is there anything else you're going to need? I said.

Yes, he said. I think there is.

The facts as he presented them were these. There had been a fight at his son's school. Fight didn't really cover it. His son had been severely beaten. He'd spent a night in hospital. Christina was beside herself. Jonah believed this kind of thing was inevitable with boys, but he'd promised her he would deal with it. I could sense what he was going to say next.

Do you sail, Matthew? was what he actually said next.

The gist was the same. He'd told Christina he'd take the boy sailing to recuperate. He had a boat, off Halo Point marina. Before he went on, I did make it clear that I'd never sailed in my life. He said that wasn't important. Julian could sail. I told him I had no feasible way of getting to Halo Point.

You can drive, can't you? he said. So hire a car on my account. You know the details. Get something nice. I just need someone to talk to him. Find out what went on. He won't talk to his mother or the school. I realise it's an imposition, but I'd really be very grateful.

I guess, for Jonah, once you crossed the line, you were over it for ever. I guess the same was true for me. The trust – or what felt like it – was intoxicating.

All the same, for the only time in our entire professional relationship, I asked him if I could think about it.

Of course, he said, that was fine. He understood completely. I should just call Christina when I'd made up my mind.

I told her I was going to ask you, he said. So she'll be expecting your call.

Then he thanked me. Said we'd speak on the 28th.

That night, when I got back to my building, there was a box the size of a dining chair waiting for me in the lobby. A rowing machine, built by hand from natural ash. The wood construction cut down on vibration, but the most striking feature was the water tank, a five gallon drum through which the oars connected.

I'd read about them in a magazine. They cost, to me, almost a month's salary. I'd mentioned them to Jonah once, at least three weeks beforehand. He'd remembered. There was a card. Inside it read:

For Matthew, with boundless appreciation – J.

Are you taking this to the loft, Mr Viss? Carl said.

No. Can we just take it up to the apartment?

Inside, I unpacked it. Set it up in the living room. I didn't use it that night. Just looked at it, and Jonah's card. I ran ten miles on the Pro-Form, wrote another cheque to the sick little girl's appeal fund. Then fell into another long night of dreams that I would never remember.

The first time Grace and I slept together was the night we saw the movie that everyone was talking about. Of course, by then, everyone had stopped. The cinema was pretty much empty. We'd sat in the dark, in a fust of stale mustard and popcorn shavings, holding hands like kids. Afterward, we lay facing. Her bed was the kind you sink into. Everything feathered.

I watched her features moving. Her eyes would meet mine, then drop away, absorbed in the internal. I guess that's how women get. Eleanor always did.

Her hand moved across me, stroked my face. Pulled my head toward her, then parted my hair. She put her lips to the white glaze of my scar, and kissed it.

Three years, a month and fifteen days. The exact time passed since Grace last did this. Lay in bed with another body next to her. Longer since she wanted to. Since she could stand to. Much longer. Through the iron conviction she would never be able to do so again, when the mere idea made her weep and fit.

Is he good, this man beside her? Does she trust him? She thinks that she does, and that thought makes her glad. She's watched him for the scuttle of the eyes that Jerry had, the squalid desolation she was then too green and in need to recognise. He doesn't have it.

She could tell this person all the things that she's never told anyone. That Jerry was never interested in. That no one was ever interested in. The girl at the back of the class who never spoke, who the teacher left alone, forgot was there at all. That she forgot was there at all. But this is different. Will be.

Her machine lies in her bag, in the corner of her room. She will, she's decided, no longer use it. Has made her last recording. Preserved and recycled her final conversation.

It just feels right. Necessary, even. An emergency measure no longer required. The belated removal of an outgrown safety harness. Just comes a point when rehearsal must give way. To create a life undefined by others.

She was fine before. Getting by. Used to the solitude, here with her tapes, so long in preparation. And now he's come, she's set off-kilter, scared, bewildered. But glad. To overflowing.

We could have been in a bubble, or the cage of a hot-air balloon. Til, clearing her throat, she got out of bed. Started rifling through her handbag.

It was still odd being naked in front of each other.

She searched her bag and I stared up at the ceiling. Half dozing, I thought of Eleanor. What she might be doing as I lay here in another woman's sheets. A chill rushed through me.

Needing a distraction, I spoke. Watching Grace rummage, I mentioned Jonah. The quandary with his son, the sailing trip. Said I was uncertain whether I should go.

She answered from the corner of the bedroom, talking low with her back to me so I couldn't be certain exactly what she said. But what I heard was:

Yes, Matthew, it sounds like that boy really needs a positive influence.

Right, I said. That's what I thought. Have you lost something?

No, she said. It's here. Sorry.

She stood now, and I could see she'd been retrieving a hairband. Scraped back her fringe and returned to bed.

We lay there a while longer, then threw off the covers and dressed. She made me a coffee. Had tea herself. I explained I couldn't stay. I didn't have my clocks. Couldn't risk sleeping in again. She said she understood.

Now, it was settled.

The next day I called Christina. Hired a car on Jonah's account, cleared a date in my diary. And, on a gusty midweek afternoon, I drove for ninety minutes in a jade green automatic to Halo Point marina. Stood clueless on the promenade.

I was to meet Jonah's son on the third jetty down. That's where the boat would be. The *Sven Foyn*.

As I peered at the names of yachts and sloops, I attracted stares from the people around me. Sinewy owners of tackle and bait shops, retired couples in fishermen's smocks. I was wearing a windbreaker, fat-soled deck shoes, knee-length shorts in tan. I'd bought them especially. I guess they could tell I was a lubber.

I found the third jetty, then the boat. Sleek but doughty. I paused beside it. Waited for proof of occupation. Gingerly, I climbed aboard. A boy in his middle teens was lying on a couch inside the cabin, headphones over his ears.

He was the spit of his father. The wear of age aside, the only real difference was the rotten fruit contusion down one side of his face. His right eye was almost closed, a bloodshot slit in swollen flesh.

I knocked on the porthole glass. He rose, and the door opened.

So, he said, you're the concierge. I'm Julian. Shall we go?

I held out my hand, but he bowled straight past me. Began preparing the sail. There was hoisting, the tying of knots. Probably some splicing. The sea looked murky, choleric. He threw me a lifejacket.

Make sure it's tied at the back, he said.

Jumping from the ledge, he undid the mooring. Got back on-board, dragged the rope after him. More than once, he asked me with threadbare courtesy to move out of his way. Til we eased out between the other boats.

He sat at the back, hand on the tiller. Occasionally a wash would hit us, coating the deck with spume. I'd look over and he'd stare past me. I didn't know if he was affecting a sea dog languor, or if this was just how he was.

Ten minutes in, we hadn't spoken. The wind was picking up now. The sail billowed irascibly. We were losing sight of the marina. Finally, I'd had enough.

Everything OK?

Everything's fine. Why don't you just go into the cabin and relax?

I asked if he could see OK.

Is that why he sent you here? To see if my eye was OK? Seriously, man. I'm interested. What kind of thing does he have you do?

I turned back. Told him the basics of The Greatest Gift. That, dealing with his father, my duties could include any-thing from taking care of his gingko to liaising over his schedule. Currently, I said, I was working closely with him on a possible investment that we were both very excited about.

Well, he said, aren't you the golden boy?

Then he told me he hadn't set eyes on his father since August. I said I found that hard to believe, and he asked me why he'd lie. Made an adjustment to the tiller.

Can you get me a Coke?

Sure, I said.

I needed a coffee anyway. I'd exhausted my thermos driving out.

The cabin was about the size of my living room. Beyond were bunk beds and another room. I made coffee and filled my thermos. Returning outside, a breaker spat against us. I handed him the Coke. Watched the gulls cruise overhead.

So, he said, why's Alda been fired?

The maid?

Right.

I said I had no idea. Jonah hadn't mentioned that.

The minutes passed. I asked him how often he sailed. Not as much as he liked, he said. Though sometimes he had parties on the boat.

Tell my father that, he said, and I'll kill you. Seriously.

As the wind blew directly into my face, I shivered. He started laughing, a scratchy cackle, and I asked him why.

Those shorts, man. They're ridiculous. Do you not realise it's almost winter?

I looked down at my calves, raw, exposed. It was true. I did look absurd. I still thought he was being offensive. And I said so.

Oh, I get it, he said. So now I say sorry by telling you what happened?

That wasn't what I'd meant. But if it was how I could justify the faith his father had placed in me, I'd go with it.

So what do you want to know? I got my head kicked in. It happens.

Why'd it happen to you? I said.

193

Because I'm clever. Because I'm stupid. My father's too rich. Or he's not rich enough. There's always a reason, isn't there?

Then he told me he was being bullied. That it had been going on some time. That most days at school he spent in fear. He wouldn't tell me who was responsible, because then I would tell his mother and she would tell the school, and then it would only get worse. I knew I had to act.

I put my hand on his shoulder. I never could stand bullying.

It wasn't like I was bullied myself. My father's job could have rendered me a target, but my height granted me immunity. Bullies have a grudging deference for the tall. School, for me, was tolerable. At least I understood how it worked.

All the same, I kept my hand on his shoulder. Grace was right. He did need a positive influence. And Jonah needed another pair of hands.

On the way back, Julian disappeared inside the cabin for over five minutes. The stench of marijuana mingled with the brine.

I disapproved. Particularly here, at sea. This one time I'd let it go. If there were a next, he wouldn't find me so forgiving.

In truth, I liked minding the tiller.

Music like this makes her teeth itch. Ambient, twittering. A pastiche of whale song. But the clients adore it, fall deep into repose as it wafts around them. And so she'll learn to live with it.

Naomi adjusts her posture, moves unhurried round the table. Begins to coax and pummel. Having passed her exams with honours, she now works here, in this small, white room at the Central Clinic of Physical Therapy, Mohren Street. Three days a week devoted to the muscular cricks and spinal curvatures of office workers from across the city. From next month, another will be spent in the Simonsen Hotel, where the tips are as plump as the clients. The fifth, in time, at a hospice for cancer patients. For her, it all just came together. That's the only way, she thinks. Don't chase it. Let it come to you. She stares down at the table.

Are you sure the music's OK? I can change it.

Honestly, Gnome, Alison says. It's fine.

And Naomi keeps working as Alison's face drops through the headrest at one end of the table, tissue paper against her cheeks. Downy towels covering her. Her arms loose by her side. Hands knead, supple, warm, fingers ply between her shoulders. One stroke causes her left arm to convulse, rising like a Sieg Heil.

Alison comes here for a massage once a month, to relieve the strains that leave her hunched and taut. After protests from Naomi that she wouldn't take a penny for her time, she now pays a discount rate for an hour.

This, Naomi says, is the root of the problem. It gathers in the shoulders. The stress.

She lays her hands at the base of Alison's neck, recommences.

So, what's been happening? Painting yet?

Alison's painting – or her failure to pursue it – is a regular feature of their conversation. Despite having only seen Alison's work once, Naomi often voices a stern insistence that she must fulfil her talent.

Not yet. I've been reading these books though . . . Self-help stuff. God, it sounds cheesy. But they're useful. I think. Matthew Viss kept –

Matthew Viss! Oh my God. I haven't thought of that name in so long!

He's pretty much the same as ever.

Does he still never swear?

Not that I've noticed.

Matthew Viss . . . God. So be honest. You and him were pretty close . . .

And Alison says, No, not really, but Naomi says, I think you were. You were the only one of us he ever spoke to. So did you ever think about . . .

What?

You know.

He's just a guy at work, Gnome. He's nice. That's all.

OK. Fine. I just thought you might like that whole gentlemanly thing.

He's really not my type. Really. And that isn't gentlemanly. It's . . . repressed.

If you say so.

And they each collapse into laughter.

OK, Naomi says. Can you try and relax the muscles here for me?

And Alison tries, her eyes closed, thinking solely of her breathing. Her world becoming nothing but the oiled warmth of her body. The music like caramel. And Naomi flattens her palms into Alison's shoulders. Drives out another ball of tension.

The water felt heavy, purposely weighted. My limbs shrieked with fatigue.

I pulled the towel from around my shoulders, stepped from the natural ash rowing machine. It was just as good as I'd hoped it would be. Now I was nearing the perfect range of equipment. There were still omissions. I made a list of what I needed, called the store and placed my order. A cross-trainer, stepmill, Smith machine. They came the following week.

I could feel myself evolving.

I cut Alice's face from the grease-stained photograph and kept it in my wallet. Drove to Eleanor's in the jade green automatic. Sat and watched the house for hours. As I did, I felt charged, ascendant. Like Alice was still with me, but now my arms outstretched, extended, supporting all in need.

I stayed with Grace again the night before my twelve weeks were up. This time I took my clocks. In the morning, we walked to the clinic together.

William's hair was longer now than ever, verging – I thought – on the unsanitary. I lay on the brown leather exam bed, rolled up my sleeve. What with coming here again and Grace seeing me undressed, I'd stopped drawing blood from my arms. I thought it might look suspect. Now I took from my feet instead. Afterward, Grace kissed me goodbye.

Then I left for Pearl Street, the same as usual. Only now the brilliance was dulled. Insipid. Hardly there at all.

I needed more.

Just a Drop, Soaking Through

In every aspect of my life, I was reimagining. Finding new structures. I bought more shirts, cream cotton like always but tighter in the chest and arms. Changed my brand of coffee. Painted over the magnolia of my bedroom walls with pure matt white, having first OK'd it with the building managers. Collated my bank statements and sat down to order my finances.

I've always been frugal. My only real overheads were rent and the cheques I sent for Alice. I looked at the figure in the savings column. Idle, redundant. Waiting.

Then I spent a week of lunch hours arranging standing orders to charities. Used the phone book to find them. Of course, I savoured their reaction when I called them for their banking details. Just the warmth in their voice was a tonic.

Thank you so much, Mr Viss, they'd say. Would you like us to send you an information pack?

No, I'd tell them. That's fine. I'm sure you're doing wonderful things.

I doubled my existing order to Mortimer and Upas. Made another contribution to the little girl with the lung disorder. At the end of the week, I slipped a cheque inside an envelope, and tacked that envelope to the door of St Jude Thaddeus. The next day, I ordered the home gym. The one I'd always hankered after. The Maximal IX 450. I put down a deposit. The balance would be paid in monthly instalments.

There were four workstations beneath a gleaming canopy of bars and wires. Every feature tuned in fine increments. Soft black pads framed with powder-coated steel, its cables the same density as those used on passenger jets. It came in a shade of burgundy the manufacturers called Carnival. Now every inch of my body could be isolated and enhanced.

When it arrived, Carl and I brought it up to the apartment. It barely fit inside the elevator. Both of us were exhausted by the time we were done.

I would have liked to have had it in the living room, but Jonah's gifts and my own recent purchases already blocked out the sunlight. Instead, I took it into the bedroom, where its high beam scraped the ceiling and dusted my shoulders with plaster. I pushed the bed into the corner. Everything superfluous was gone now.

When the hire agreement ran out on the jade green automatic, I renewed it in my name. Took a day and a further three mornings off work (available to Jonah in case of an emergency). The logistics were simple. Anyone could do it. I just had to upgrade my diet and training schedule. Then I could give every month. More, if I was lucky.

I visited the health-food store, bought vitamins, supplements, herbal extracts. Took passport photographs, ran off fake IDs at the copy shop. Found the address of every donor centre within ninety minutes of Bethune and Scala.

Drove there, registered, gave.

At the Weedon Healthcare Clinic, I was Andrew Schofield. At North Duke Blood Centre, Malcom Dunne. An interchangeable procession of doctors and iron tests and pale green forms that were sometimes blue and sometimes orange and all of which asked about pituitary glands and trips to Africa before I was shown to a leather exam bed and later fed chocolate and orange juice. Thanked and shaken hands with.

And every time, my route home took me past Eleanor's house, where I sat watching the lights go on and off. Like I was being shown different reels of a film, trying to remember the chronology.

The same scenes would play, over and again. And just as all my journeys in the hire car led back to this house, so every recap outside it found me walking with Alice's hand in mine through the turnstiles of the theme park.

When Eleanor and I were with the police, we saw their file of missing children. Brown card, filled with photographs. A picture book of seismic loss. And after Alice came back to us, I'd look at her and see that blur of faces.

Now I sat outside the house, reckoning my debt to her. So much of me longed to return. Only I knew that to go back now, ahead of time, would be to admit I should never have left. That I lacked the mettle to see this through. For both of us.

And I'd make it better. Soon.

The memo from Caroline simply announced that:

Greg Hopper is stepping down from his post within the company. His resignation will take effect immediately. Greg was among our first Guy Fridays, and his hard work helped build us into what we are today. We wish him every good fortune.

I looked over to his desk and saw him clearing his stuff. I didn't know what he was planning to do. There was conjecture in the kitchen. Robert made a swigging motion. Over the course of the morning, the occasional Guy or Gal Friday would approach, shake his hand or pat his back. I didn't. I just made my calls, watching as he packed his things into two brown boxes.

The whole exercise took half an hour. When he left, he didn't even look back. Just carried out the boxes, one under each arm. His own pallbearer.

I thought we caught each other's eye as he shouldered open the door. I could have been mistaken. By the time it closed behind him, my phone was flashing red.

I took a moment to answer. There was one particular call that I yearned for it to be and, while I knew in my gut this wouldn't be it, I wanted to prolong the expectancy.

I know you have to be patient. I was still upset I hadn't heard from Eric Handler's publishers. Not even an acknowledgement of receipt. I'd called their head office, where a practised receptionist told me all submissions would be responded to just as soon as was humanly possible.

I tried explaining that I simply wanted mine passed on to Mr Handler, but she just repeated herself and put the phone down.

When I had the time, I worked on it anyway. Amended it, polished. So there would be more at hand when it finally got to the reader it was meant for.

As it says in 15 *Simple Wisdoms*:

To stop the past impeding you, make the present your bridge to the future.

Now, I watched the door close behind Greg Hopper. And I looked down and saw my phone was flashing red.

When I answered, a woman asked me if this was Matthew Viss.

I said it was. She told me she was calling from the paper, and was delighted to tell me I was this week's Good Samaritan.

I said nothing. Confirmed this wasn't some cruel idea of a joke.

No, she said. I am who I say I am.

I may even have sworn in exclamation. I thanked her, more than once.

This really means the world to me, I said.

She told me she loved the story of me and Mrs Blum. Such a wonderful gesture, she said. She didn't mention me giving blood or helping at the soup kitchen.

Ever since my nomination, I'd read the column every week. All the winners seemed far more philanthropic than me. Now I'd be among them. She asked when might be a good time to have my picture taken? I gave the issue some thought. I would need a haircut.

How about three this afternoon? she said. It is for tomorrow's issue.

I swallowed hard. Told her that was fine. Wrapped up the call and ran to Alison. We nearly hugged. Then I called Grace. She said she always knew that I was going to make it, that she'd take me to dinner to celebrate. I called Jonah, only he wasn't available. (Bonnie said she'd tell him just as soon as he was back.) I tried to think who else I should contact. There wasn't anyone.

Mike and Caroline were ecstatic. They suggested I have the picture taken in the new client liaison room. I agreed. As three drew closer, my bones seized, palms sweated, and I took my seat. The second-hand on my watch crawled by.

At a smidgen past 3.20, a gaunt man with a canvas rucksack walked into the room. Mike stood outside, giving me the thumbs up. We shook hands and he told me this would only take a couple of minutes. Frankly, I was hoping it might take longer.

He tinkered with the lights. Drew the blinds then opened them. Moved me from one side of the office to the other. Settled on me sitting at the far end of the table. Staring into the lens, trying not to look the way I always did in photographs – simple or insane – I started to blink uncontrollably. He asked if I was OK.

I'm fine, I said.

He disappeared behind the camera and released the shutter one, two, three, four times. Then he asked me to turn my head just slightly, and he did the same again.

I grew more relaxed. Felt the muscles in my jaw begin to calm. And then he said:

OK . . . that's great. Thank you.

Oh. That's it?

I had thought there might be props. An oversized cardboard cheque, maybe.

We only need a mugshot, he said. Then he packed up his equipment and turned toward the door.

Ah . . . Do I talk to you about the prize?

Nothing to do with me, he said. They'll call you.

I told him I'd decided to give the money to Mortimer and Upas. That although I'd originally thought of dividing it between several different charities, I felt with a relatively small amount like this, a single donation worked best.

Oh, he said. Great.

In the morning, I bought a dozen copies of the paper. Stood in the street and raced through the pages, the rain half pulping those exposed.

I found myself on page seventeen. Your Good Samaritan, it said above the name of the supermarket. Then a photograph of me, smiling in my silk bow tie.

The column quoted chunks of Alison's letter, referring to my voluntary work at St Jude Thaddeus and blood donation, then describing the episode with Mrs Blum.

And that's why Matthew is Your Good Samaritan, it said.

I read it through, and I read it through again. Watched commuters at news-stands to see if they bought the paper, knowing when they did that I'd be there, waiting for them. I took the subway just so I could look at people reading.

At work, at least half the phone room stopped by my cubicle to congratulate me. More, I noticed, than had said goodbye to Greg. Mike sent round another memo, to let people know to buy the paper.

I took the two copies closest to mint, checked for creases and newsprint blemishes, folded them inside an envelope and mailed them to Alice, c/o Eleanor.

The news stayed unread til the evening. On page nine, a headline said:

Please Save Our Angel, Plead City Parents.

Underneath was a photo of the girl with the lung disorder. She was still in hospital. The report had more details on the nature of her condition. A steadfast malevolence engulfing her body, carried in a single gene. Most cases, it said, were fatal. What treatments there were were erratic and primitive. A transplant the only real cure.

It said she was deteriorating. Her doctors losing hope. In the short term, the medical bills were spiralling. Right now, there was only the short-term. Both her parents and the hospital were issuing a call for donors.

This wasn't just a drip and a baggie. Almost half your lung would be cut from you, the tissue spliced with hers. That is, if you got that far. She needed a protein only found in five per cent of the population. A lengthy screening process would have to precede any transplant. At the end, there was another mention of the appeal fund.

I kept her face in mind as I pummelled my body on the Maximal. As I drove to new clinics in the jade green automatic, booked hotel suites for Jonah Hoffman. As I read Eric Handler and filled my own pages in feverish longhand. Applied for and received three credit cards. Lay in bed with Grace, trying not to fall asleep til she was finished talking.

And I see it now, in the beat of a hummingbird's wing.

They sit on hard-backed wooden chairs, expressions ranging from bored to hawkish. Eleanor stands at the front of the class-room, perusing their faces. Eight in total. Pulls her bag onto her desk.

This is Room 26 of Cale Street Community College. These eight are her pupils. Students of Beginners' Photography. The adult education course she will teach one night a week from now til the spring of next year. And this is her first lesson.

She saw the ad in a trade magazine. Realised she needed something else, something of hers besides Alice (tonight she's with the Karlssons). The money barely covers her petrol. The money's not important. She looks across the faces again. Realises how long it's been since she was last in this position. At school, she takes class only in emergencies. She'd forgotten the itch of the skin, the dryness of the palate.

All eyes train on her, waiting for speech. Hers drop to her desk. A grey cyst of gum, stuck to the corner.

She reaches inside her bag, unpacks her camera. The Leica she's used for years, that she bought second-hand when she was a beginner too. The size of a pack of cigarettes and half as much again, small and black and treasured. She wipes a smear from the viewfinder, places it on the desk.

The eight assembled gaze upon it as if it were a strange animal. She looks down, feels herself slip into the stillness of purpose.

Instantly comfortable, inspired. Clears the misgiving from her throat.

Hello, she says. My name is Eleanor Carlin.

Falling now more like a stone.

In the past, there would have been a net here. A baggy hammock, strung into a smile across the face of the building.

There is no net.

And so I pass.

The woman on the fourth floor is called Luders. She must be in her sixties. Older even. I see her in the lobby and she looks at my cream cotton shirt and bow tie with a sadness I can never fathom. I know she's lived here for years. Longer than any of the other tenants. An unfamiliar permanence.

It all seems so long ago. Another life entirely. Ingrid Luders gazes round the articles that fill her apartment, the photographs, mementoes, trinkets, bookshelves whose slats buckle under their contents. Grundrisse, Notes on Dialectics, Their Morals and Ours, Long Live the Victory of People's War. The Manifesto, in three languages.

Many were gifts. Tokens from when this was a place of safety, hot with the noise and belief of those who stayed here. She thinks of her comrades, Gudrun, Andreas, Jan-Carl. Her pretty namesake Schubert, the doctor girl.

How long ago was it? The dream of something better? All lost now, of course. Forgotten. A road closed off and overgrown. Yet still she watches for the signs, the rise of those excluded yet unclaimed by the madness of religion. She looks to them for the spark of resistance. Sits among her keepsakes, defiant, unco-opted. Hopes that it will not end here. The struggle of history reduced to this. A lonely old woman and her books, growing dusty in a portered apartment block.

I was sleeping like ballast again. Too long and too deep. Waking later every day, clocks wailing futile. At first, I put it down to my exercise regime. But that kind of fatigue always passes by morning. Now, swilling with coffee and Provigil, it was taking me til lunchtime to clear the scurf from my eyes.

I thought my tours of the clinics would help. In the back-wash of each donation I felt euphoria. Driving home in the jade green automatic, scouring the radio for something anthemic. I was taking care of my body with a fervent attention to detail. It just wasn't working out the way I thought it would. I was in a rut. Grace; the clinics; Jonah. Forever Jonah.

Given the weather's inclemency, he wasn't at the Avelden so much any more. There was still always plenty to do.

Late in the afternoon, he called me.

Matthew, he said, I've got a problem.

How can I help?

He sighed before he answered.

You know I'm having dinner in Demotte tomorrow night?

You want to change the reservation?

He told me no. Then explained his predicament. He and Christina were booked at a school fundraiser later the same evening. He couldn't be sure he'd make it back in time. Said these things meant a lot to her. That she hated attending them alone. The kind of woman who needs an arm, he said. That's just how she was raised. She's fragile, he said, if I knew what he meant. Asked if I could see his dilemma.

I can, I said.

He said nothing for a moment, and I asked if he'd had a chance to think any more about the Reilly deal. He said not yet, but could he take it we were agreed on the fundraiser? And I said of course.

The evening in question, I had a date with Grace. We'd planned to eat, then take in a movie. She was obviously upset when I called to cancel, but she knew sometimes my work had to come first. She understood that.

When I think of it now, Grace understood pretty much everything I ever told her.

The next evening, a limo picked me up at 6.30. In accordance with Jonah's wishes, I was dressed in a dinner jacket and slacks, each bought that afternoon. The limo wasn't a stretch, just a luxury saloon. I sat in the back toying with the in-car TV, running my fingers along the walnut trim.

We headed north, took the same route out of the city I used to visit Eleanor. After maybe half an hour, we diverged. Swung off at a junction I'd never even noticed.

You don't see the difference for maybe fifteen minutes. Then it hits you. The scale of the houses, the cars outside, ever increasing til they suddenly vanish, the cars spirited into unseen garages, the buildings withdrawn behind high walls and trees.

I guess if you were to draw straight lines between Bethune Street, Eleanor's house and where I was now, you'd have an equilateral triangle.

We pulled up at a house with a quarter mile of nothing on either side, a fence of thin steel further enclosing the land. The driver spoke at the intercom, took us up to the door. The exterior was magnificent, gabled, lavish. I could only imagine what it looked like inside.

Ten minutes later, Christina emerged. Underweight but elegant in a black trouser suit. I held out my hand as she climbed in frowning.

Hello, I said. I'm Matthew from The Greatest Gift.

Yes, she said. You are.

There was the swift reckoning of misconceptions that comes when you meet those you've spoken to but never seen. I tried to sneak a glance where I could, study the hang of her mouth or the rucks beneath her eyes. I guess she was doing the same.

We quilted together a conversation. I asked her a little about the evening ahead, and she told me the idea was that parents and their business contacts paid for an invitation to drinks with the headmaster. Throughout the evening, further collections would be made. The total received was then donated to the school. Its sports facilities, extramural activities, so on. I asked her what I had to do. Nothing, she said.

And we drove on in silence down cloistered roads, til she told me how grateful she and Jonah were that I could spare the time to go sailing with Julian.

I really think you got through to him, she said.

I asked how he was.

Hasn't he called you?

I told her he hadn't, and she tsked.

I asked about the bullying situation, unsure of how much I could say without breaching Julian's confidence.

It's OK, she said. He told us.

She made sure to catch my eye.

Thanks to you.

I thought of showing her the cutting from the paper. Just as I was preparing to retrieve it from my wallet, the car slowed. A single left turn took us from what, despite its affluence, was still recognisably suburban into a dense expanse of woodland. I realised this must be the grounds of the school.

The building itself sat at the end of a sylvan approach road, a weathered red facade inlaid with bay windows. Floodlit and stripped of children.

We pulled up, left the car. I followed her to the main entrance. Inside, portraits of alumni hung beside photographic montages of pupils in spacious classrooms, eternally patient teachers leaning over them.

It's right through here, she said.

The headmaster's study was already full. Choked with couples at various points of middle age whose bearing alluded to holiday homes and rarely dealing with their own laundry. They stood in circles, a phalanx of waiters moving among them with trays of canapés and fine white china. I hoped when I thanked them they would see me as I was – as one of them – but they just gave me the same impassive nod as they gave everyone else.

The whole room seemed to know Christina. As soon as she appeared, they would bring their glasses from their lips and call her name. And every time, afterward, they would turn as one and stare at me. She introduced me as a friend of the family.

When the headmaster came by, we discussed his plans for an expanded language lab, new lawns for the tennis courts. Through hunger and nerves, I kept busy with the canapés. Someone, invariably, would ask after Jonah, and Christina would say he sent his best to all. Every bitter note I heard when I'd call her with his schedule had been quashed and swallowed down.

Occasionally, a man in a dinner jacket or woman in evening dress would take her arm and lead her away. I'd glance around and gravitate toward the corner. Returning, she would nod at me and we'd work the room in tandem.

I know this is awkward, she said. But you're doing brilliantly.

Her breath smelled of olives and alcohol.

Twice while I was on my own, a functionary approached with a plate stacked with bills and cheques. The second time, Christina saw me and burst out laughing.

Matthew, you don't have to do that. Tell my husband what you've given and have him reimburse you.

In truth, I was glad to be here with her. In person, she made me feel healthy, poised. With Grace, I just felt like myself.

It was gone eleven when we left. I could tell she was a little drunk. On the drive back, she said there'd been a time when she hated going out without her husband. Acting as his delegate while he indulged himself. Now, she said, she considered his absences a boon. They'd taught her the value of her own company.

All that worried her was Julian. What he was growing up with. His father's influence, or the lack of it. Whichever was worse.

I didn't reply. I hoped if I didn't reply she might stop abusing Jonah. It didn't work. In the end, I faked a coughing fit to keep her from continuing.

Arriving back at the house, she thanked me again. I watched her sway inside as the driver turned us round.

Julian called late the next day. Said he wanted to thank me for the sailing trip. I guess his mother had put him up to it. I asked how he was and he mumbled at me.

Right, I said. Well, that's good.

Puncturing the void that followed, I asked him if he'd been back out on the boat. Eager now, he told me an involved story about a botched on-board party, which then segued into a long tirade about the failings of his peers, his family, the species. The universal complaints and delusions of his age.

I told him I'd been to his school last night, and he said he knew. I said I'd been very impressed. He said he was sure it looked great when you didn't have to go there.

I couldn't believe my insensitivity. I could have slapped myself.

Has it happened again? I said. The bullying?

He told me no, but he still felt oppressed by the memory. Becoming phobic, brooding. I could have sworn I heard a sob, but he denied it.

I tried to console him without attracting the phone room's attention.

Listen, I said, don't worry. I'm sure it'll . . .

And then I was at a loss.

From where he is, Jonah can see the gingko's leaves are wilting. Yellow and dried out. The body itself seems listless, glum. He just can't understand it. He pays a ridiculous price for the nutrient. Employs only as directed. He feels victimised. Tormented by his ignorance of what he might be doing wrong.

It is 10.54 p.m. His attention wavers, fleetingly. Legs fold around him, breath in his ear. Certain words used in a specific order. He loses himself in the moment. The release. His eyes roll up then close. Like a sneeze, he always thinks.

They lie there on his office floor, til he raises himself on his elbows. Lifts his hips. She levers out from underneath.

His focus returns to the gingko. He wonders what he should do. More nutrient? Less? A change in lighting? Different soil?

Perhaps he'll call someone in. An expert.

The woman dresses now. It is 10.57 p.m. Naked from the waist down, he walks over to his desk. Reaches inside his jacket pocket, removes his wallet, plucks the notes. A minute passes. A dour transparency. He looks from the gingko to his window, down at the teem below.

OK then, she says. And Jonah turns back, his eyes shot, face streaked, and he says to her, Could you love me?

And the woman peers back at him.

I'm sorry?

I said – could you love me? he says, again. Then again, then again, then again, again, each time louder, more hoarse, incantational.

Could . . . you . . . love . . . me?

The faintness had been with me a while. The summary withdrawal of strength, co-ordination. If I stood still too long or got up too fast, I was overcome. My head sang and my legs shook. I was trying to compose myself when my phone flashed red.

Morning, champ, the voice said.

And to you, coach, I replied.

Champ was how Phillip Reilly referred to me. Coach was what I called him.

I had an idea what he wanted. He wanted to see if there'd been any progress with Jonah, or to find out when there might be. He rang me three times a week. In another context, I might have found it irritating. With Reilly, I didn't.

He was just so irrepressible. Doing everything he could to realise his dream. Become all he yearned to be. In truth, I looked forward to him calling.

As we talked, he suggested maybe we should meet up next week. Take a run in the park. I gave it a moment's reflection. Thought it might actually be pleasant. If nothing else, a chance to gauge my fitness with a professional.

OK, I said. Let's do that.

And I assured him, as I always did, that I'd harry for an answer in the meantime. Then I called Jonah's office to see how everything was, ask if he needed anything and enquire, just in passing, if he'd thought any more about the Reilly proposal. This time, Bonnie told me he was out til lunchtime.

I was actually pleased. Though obliged to make the call, I couldn't afford to be delayed. I had to be gone by 10.30.

I told Mike I had my pager with me, and I left on time. Took the jade green automatic and headed north. Did my best to remember the route. Made the appropriate junctions and turnings. Arrived at Julian's school a little after twelve.

The receptionist was a tiny woman in her mid-sixties, with the crabbed air of having been distracted from a truly vital dropped stitch.

I gave her my name. Said I was a friend of the Hoffman family. That I had an urgent message from Julian's father.

Well, she said, then I'll make sure he gets it.

Ah . . . the thing is, I really do need to give it to him personally.

Every withering look I'd ever had in my life was nothing as compared to this.

And you say you're a friend of the Hoffmans?

I told her I was, and perhaps I should run this by the headmaster? Casually related my meeting him at the fundraiser.

A muttered phone call later, he appeared beside her.

Mr . . . Viss? Good to see you again . . . so soon.

I greeted him warmly. Appraised him of the situation.

It's really nothing serious, I said, but as you know, he has been having . . . a difficult time. So I think Mr Hoffman might prefer that I deal with this myself.

Ah, he said. I understand.

He said I should – of course – do as Mr Hoffman asked, although he would rather I didn't disturb a class in progress. They'd be breaking for lunch soon, he said, and would I like a coffee while I waited?

213

I thanked him, but said I should probably just head down to wherever Julian was and then be on my way.

Fine, he said. As you wish.

He asked the receptionist to direct me, and we shook hands before he left.

He's in room twelve, she said, irked I could tell. That's in the Schuster Wing . . . Just follow the signs.

The Schuster Wing seemed designed as some kind of walk-in IQ test, a dingy ravel of hallways conjoined to the main building, panelled with old wood and more fond portraiture. More than once, I thought I was at room twelve only to be confronted with a dead end or stationery cupboard.

Finally, I stumbled onto it. Saw nine pupils and an owlish teacher. It looked from the notes on the board like Physics. Julian was hunched in his chair by the window. A parody of teenage indolence.

So, Mr Steveland says, if we take g as 10N a kilogramme, what might be the loss of gravitational PE in the downward motion?

Julian turns back from the window, the endless grounds outside, stares unfocused at the front of the classroom. The board and teacher. Notes an irritation beneath his right eye. Brings his index finger up to deal with it, the tip barely touching beaten flesh before he jolts back in pain.

Mr Steveland taps his foot, smiles optimistically.

Julian knows the answer. Knows all of this already. Mastered it a year ago, longer, now – like always – waiting on the rest. It just comes too easy for him. Everything. He glances across at his classmates then back to Mr Steveland, as the boy at the desk adjacent flails at the equation. Accidentally meets his teacher's eyes. Observes the usual disillusion.

From eleven til thirteen, Julian was Mr Steveland's favourite. The youngest but most celebrated member of the school's science quiz team (The Mighty Atoms, undefeated champions throughout Julian's tenure). Possessor of an arctic nerve and startling breadth of knowledge. Science wasn't even his strongest *discipline. But science was what he chanced to win trophies at, the source of his father's approval, recognition. Except it wasn't. His father never saw him compete with the team. Didn't once acknowledge two years of unsullied excellence.*

Had nothing from him ever bar all that he could ask for.

So in the summer that followed his second championship, he quit the team – consigned from then to mediocrity – and ever since, when his eyes meet Mr Steveland's, he catches the same baleful expression. He sees it now, and it makes him look away. Turns instead back round his peers. Most, his debtors.

Oliver Pennyman, scrawling in his notebook, lent 100 three weeks ago. First instalment due on Friday. Next to him, even blanker than usual, Mark Boddinger, repaying 400 over a six-month period.

Julian has been moneylending within the school since the middle of last winter. Heard the continual whining of his peers, their aggressive want for those few things not granted by their parents. So he brought himself to market. And now business is flourishing. His original investment multiplied tenfold. Tonight, he has decided, he will tell his father – or more likely ask his mother to tell his father – that he can do without his allowance. Prove he's more than a pampered scion. Worthy of regard.

OK, Mr Steveland says, so that's something to think about, but the bell has already rung, and his pupils are leaving the classroom.

I waited outside til the door squealed open. The teacher kept talking as his charges filed out. I called Julian's name, and he spun, double took. His face remained a mess.

What's going on? he said. Has something happened?

I told him to relax. Said everything was fine. That I'd given this a lot of thought. He had the right to pursue his education without threats and assaults, and I'd do what was needed to safeguard that. Not just because of my relationship with his father. There was, I said, a principle at stake.

Look, he said, I already told you I'm not naming anyone.

I told him he didn't have to. He just had to show me who they were. He asked me why, and I explained. He should trust me, I said, as an adult, when I told him I believed this the only solution. He protested, kept arguing, said it wouldn't help, but I was insistent. Stern in my assertions that I wouldn't leave til this was done. Finally, I wore him down.

We paced back through the maze as classrooms emptied. Three hallways in, he gestured at a boy his own age, alone, pimp-rolling. We followed him down the corridors til he cut into the bathroom. Julian slowed.

You can wait here, I said. He told me no.

Inside, the kid was at a sink, patting down his hair in the mirror. I asked Julian to watch the door. His bully turned, uneasy, squinted.

I took three steps forward, broke into a trot and grabbed him. Felt my thumb and middle finger tighten round his collar. He jittered backward. I knew better than to think of what I was doing.

See? I said. Not funny, is it? Not when it's happening to you.

He attempted to push me away. It was useless. I was nearly a foot taller, half his weight again.

Listen to me. I know what you did to my friend. And I want you to promise me it won't happen again.

All that came was a gargle. If I'd been the sadist he was, I could have dragged this out. But I wasn't. That was the point.

I'm only asking that you show people some respect. Not just Julian. Everyone.

I could feel him nod. I lifted my hand. He gagged with his back to the mirror, struggling for breath. I told him to go about his business, that what had just happened should remain a private matter. He said OK. Then he bolted.

Julian watched him leave, then turned to me.

OK? I said.

He must be insane. It's the only explanation. A lunatic, past skewered with derangement. Yet there's no sign of relish. Nor,

in fact, much vicious competence. Julian backs against the wall.
Sees the concierge exhale.

He tries to recall why he picked the boy he did. Thinks he
might once have looked at him sideways. He could be wrong.
That might be someone else. The two that beat him up, his
quarrel with them is over. A business dispute got out of hand,
now settled, even amicably. (They got the loan he originally
refused; so now, in their way, valued customers.) Only bullying
sounds better than a whipping over money, safer, less incrimi-
nating. And he can't go changing the story now.

He said that he was, which I was glad about. Now I simply
wanted out of there. My right hand trembled. I tried using my
left to steady it, but that just set them both off. I've never been
a violent person. I don't think I've been in a fight in my life.
Now, I was reeling. I gauged the objects around me. The sink
would crack my head. The floor, at worst, break a rib. I was
starting to topple when it passed.

Grateful, I straightened, wolfing for air.

How long have we been here? How long since he left?

It was . . . just now, he said. Are you OK? You look –

I'm fine, I said. I just need some air.

We walked fast, left through a fire exit that led in turn to
the parking bay. He told me I looked pale. At the car, I
checked the wing mirror. Had to agree.

Let's just keep this between us, I said. I don't want your
parents more worried than they are already.

Driving back was hell. I got marooned in traffic, then lost.
Twice I caught myself dozing at the wheel. Seeping from day-
dreams into unconsciousness. The second time, a lorry blast-
ing its horn at me as I wavered on the lane boundary was the
only thing that snapped me to.

I turned the radio as high as it would go, drained my thermos, and drove on. Went straight home rather than return to
work. I meant to call Mike as soon as I got in, but that didn't
happen. This was how life was now. The moment I stopped

moving, I was out. My body had mutinied. In the office, I ran on caffeine, staving off the crash. Evenings and weekends, I barely made it out of bed. Sometimes, the phone would ring and I'd answer, and it would be Jonah, wanting to thank me for that day's jobs, or Grace, calling because I should have been at her place an hour ago. Other times, I'd sleep right through it. Wake to find their messages.

This was one of those. I got home just past three, fired up the espresso machine, sat and popped a gum before preparing to call Mike. Next, all I could see was the sofa cushions my face was pressed down into, the rest of me foetally tucked.

It was after ten. I'd slept for seven hours. A number nine on the answerphone's display, nine calls of five rings each, followed by my voice, then others. None of them able to bring me back.

The first, fifth and sixth were from Mike. Wondering, more fretfully each time, if I was coming back this afternoon and could I call him as soon as I got this. The second and seventh were Jonah. Another slate of errands and commissions.

The third was a woman from the bank whose name I never caught but who weekly left a message here to keep me informed on the latest news about the Gold Ring Trust.

Grace had left the fourth and eighth. Just calling, she said, to see how I was doing, and did I still want to see her Thursday? Call me, she said.

The ninth was from Alison. She'd never rung me at home before, though we had each other's numbers from my time at the hub of Home and Family. She apologised for calling me here, but she just wanted to let me know something that she thought I might be interested in. A friend of hers had seen it advertised. Eric Handler was doing a signing at a bookstore in the city. Let me just check the date, she said.

And, just for an instant, before returning to the black – while I tried to find a pen, Alison and I scrambling together hours apart – I was rested, elevated.

Somewhere else entirely.

Blues for Joselyn Whitehead

Helping Grace move could have been a misjudgement.

I was fine with the smaller items, the books and clothes, the kitchen equipment, cutlery, TV, knick-knacks. It was just the furniture that troubled me. She was leaving the couch. I'd always disliked it. Pleased to discover it wasn't actually hers. Had simply been abandoned by the previous tenant, as Grace herself was now poised to do. There was still the armchair and the kitchen table which – though the chair was light and the table folded – proved fiendishly hard to manoeuvre.

My breathing was short, my head swam. I still felt I had to be there. Otherwise, she was going to have to hire movers, pay hirsute men to come and break her valuables. And what kind of person would that have made me?

She'd rung me, I'd rung back, and when I did she told me she'd found what she called the peachiest one-bedroom. Out in Vimont, a half hour from Bethune Street. She was moving Sunday. Had been so enamoured she put down the deposit right there. Then she came home, hired the van, packed what she could into brown cardboard boxes. The kind you assemble yourself.

I didn't mention it, but I felt a minor pique that I hadn't been further involved. I guess she just got seized by the moment. She asked if I might be able to help out with the bulkier articles. Of course, I said. It wasn't like she had much to take. I guess she'd left a lot behind with her husband. It all went in one trip.

Her new place was a basement, a scrub of garden at the back. Afterward, I suggested we get take-out. I thought we could eat on the packing cases. She told me she wanted to get on with things alone.

I could understand that. I'd felt the same when I moved into my place. Besides, while I tried to keep her from noticing, I was in a pretty bad way by now.

The Friday before I'd given again. The sixth time that month.

I said I should get going. That I was a little tired. Maybe coming down with a cold. She told me she'd thought I'd been looking washed out, and I said I was fine, really, just beat. I'd see her tomorrow. Pick her up at seven.

I didn't tell her I was planning something special. A celebration of the move that, as she'd reminded me on the fluttering drive to Vimont, had been kind of what brought us together.

Remember? she said. The apartment by the toy shop?

So, something demonstrative. Sweet. A meal, then the opera. I always recommended that to male clients. Maybe a walk by the river to end.

I'd iron out the details next day at work. I had nothing too pressing to deal with. In the morning, I even took a handful of calls from regular clients. That afternoon, my only real commitment was the horticulturist. Jonah had asked me to screen potential saviours for his gingko. He was plagued with anxiety about it. I put together a shortlist. One I was seeing today. The rest tomorrow.

My only other job was the purchase of a gift for Christina. Jonah said she could use a pick-me-up. That things had been rough lately, what with him away so much and the whole Julian scenario.

I asked him how Julian was now.

Oh, he's fine.

Enquired what he had in mind for Christina.

I'd hoped, he said, you might be able to answer that.

Just after twelve, I left for my prior engagement. My lunchtime run with Reilly. I slipped into the men's bathroom and changed, re-emerged in sportswear and training shoes.

It was drizzling as I reached the park. He stood by the gates in a sheeny red tracksuit that he wore as if born in.

Afternoon, champ.

And to you, coach.

We talked about the weather as we limbered up. Began a gentle canter round the tarmac path, skirting rubbish bins and grey wooden benches. In seconds we hit our stride, falling into rhythm, silent, metronomic.

So, he said after maybe ten minutes, any word from the top man yet?

I'm on the case.

I know you are. I'm just so psyched. You should see the pec decks I'm getting hold of. Smooth like you wouldn't believe.

I'll do everything I can to make it happen. Trust me.

I do, he said. OK. Let's see what you've got.

Without further notice he broke into a sprint, knees high, driving. I did the same, catching him, speeding beside, til a hundred yards on he pulled away. Initially, I thought it might be arrogance, his ego getting the better of us both. Then I realised quite how slowly I was moving, heart thumping despite my languor.

He eased up and waited at the ornamental garden. That was good, he said when I finally got there, though I knew it wasn't.

Once I'd stopped running I felt fine. Just puzzled and abashed as Reilly soothed me the same way I assumed he did with the dabblers at his gym.

And so we started to jog again, grinding up inclines, loping down them. He asked what I'd been up to, and I told him about the Maximal – a quality machine, he said – and my having been invested as Good Samaritan, though as I did I remembered I'd left the cutting back at the office, in my wallet. He cooed as I explained the nature of the award, then told me a lengthy anecdote about a date he'd once had with his future wife, a farcical episode in which he'd tried impressing her by helping a blind man catch a bus. In his phone calls, Reilly often spoke of his wife. They had no children, but I could tell from his tone that he wanted them. In the spirit of

223

mutual disclosure, I'd told him a little about Alice, the gist of my separation from Eleanor, that I was now seeing another woman. We were, I realised, bonding.

I enjoyed Reilly's stories, despite a weakness for repetition that meant even at this early stage of our friendship, I'd heard the same ones – this included – a couple of times already. And it was fine while he was talking, because then I could listen, and not worry about the next time he was going to up the pace.

Of course, it couldn't last. OK, he said at the perimeter wall of the zoo, and took off at full pelt again.

Twenty yards in, we were almost level. Twenty more and I was on the ground, breathless and heaving. He looked over, saw me. Ran back.

Everything all right? You going to be sick?

No, I said, like the idea was ridiculous, and not just what I was wondering myself. I saw stars as I brought myself upright. Couldn't suppress a groan.

Maybe you need a booster, he said. Something to keep the energy flowing.

He asked if I wanted to carry on, but I guess my expression gave him the answer. We walked back to the park gates as the drizzle thickened.

I'll let you know as soon as I hear from Jonah, I said.

Thanks, champ, he said. And you take care in the meantime.

When I got back to Pearl Street, I showered in the bathroom there. Ate a sandwich lunch in my cubicle, prepared for the afternoon.

Leery of taking the car after the drive home from Julian's school, I grabbed a cab to the nursery. The horticulturist, a donnish woman in mittens, had matter-of-factly well-informed answers for each of the questions Jonah had primed me with.

On the way back, I had the taxi drop me in Windmill Street, in the centre of the jewellery quarter. The deals you got in these squat ground floors of old tenements had the beating on anything you'd find in department stores.

I thought a pendant might be apt. At the third shop I visited, I found one I thought Christina would like. Fine silver with a heart in pale rose quartz. Gazing through the reinforced glass of the display case, I asked to see it.

And I felt myself getting short of air. The pound behind my eyes. I breathed, breathed again, kept breathing. My upper body lurched forward just as my legs began to give. A hand at my elbow. The jeweller.

Are you OK, sir?

I wanted to speak, except I couldn't. One instant everything was black, the next a glut of colours in grim lysergic trailbacks. Then a blitzkrieg strobing of the two. I tried looking for something to hold on to. It was too late.

I just remember the display case. All those rocks and metal, so intricate, so beautiful, the light dancing as I swept toward them. And

then

And then the coming to. The groggy panorama of faces looming over you. How the world must look to babies. You hear them speak, their voices one.

Are you OK? Is he breathing? Can you hear us?

There were three of them. The jeweller, his assistant, the only other customer. One of them had their hands on my shoulders.

More than anything, I was embarrassed. Lying here on the balding carpet of a Windmill Street jewellers. My head smarted from where I must have struck the case. I lifted my hand to my scalp, but they pulled it away.

Am I bleeding? I said.

No, the jeweller said. Gave yourself a bump though.

How long was I out?

A second, the customer said. That's all.

I raised my head experimentally.

He should lie still, the assistant said.

Then she turned to me.

You should lie still. Don't worry. We've called an ambulance.

I didn't want that. The rigmarole, the explanations. I told them, but they wouldn't listen. As I tried to hoist myself upright, one of them even pushed me back down.

I shrugged off their insistences, rose to my feet. Thanked them but said I was fine. Saw the jeweller had the pendant on the counter. I lay some notes adjacent, put it in my bag and left.

By the time I hopped in a cab back to Pearl Street, I was feeling spry. I skipped the elevator, took the stairs. Marched back into the office, head high, chest out.

I made it as far as the front desk. Then the same stifling of breath, loss of authority over my body. The same obstinate momentum and the same rush of colour.

And

then

again.

And then, again, the faces above me. This time, of course, I knew them. Robert, Alison, Noel from Business, Isabel the receptionist, Caroline and Mike. All wearing the same look of deep concern and naked curiosity.

It's OK, I said. I'm fine. No one's called an ambulance, have they?

There was a flashpoint of debate over whether they should have, or if they should do now. I told them there was no need. Got up and sat in the new client liaison room. After maybe five minutes, Mike knocked on the glass. Came in, pulled up a seat. Asked how I was feeling.

Oh, fine, I said.

He asked what had happened and I told him I got dizzy. He sucked his bottom lip.

When was the last time you took a holiday, Matthew?

I gave it some thought. Told him I didn't remember.

I'll tell you, he said.

And then he said that in the seven months I'd been with the company I'd never taken one full day off, and that included the lunch last week I didn't return from. I said I'd already explained about that, that I'd been held up on a job for the Hoffmans, and if he was still annoyed –

I'm not annoyed, Matthew. I'm . . . perturbed. Frankly, you look like death.

I couldn't think how to counter that.

He suggested I took some time off. I said that sounded like a fine idea, and once we were through the madness of Christmas and I'd cleared it with Jonah, I'd head promptly for the beach.

No, Matthew, he said. Take a break now. Recharge. I won't risk my best lieutenant.

Your best Guy Friday?

No . . . Lieutenant.

He swivelled in his chair, then sighed.

You may as well know now. I was sending the memo out later anyway. We're . . . losing the name Guy Friday. We've thought for a long time clients might see it as . . . twee. We felt it was . . . outdated.

I was aghast.

But what do we say on the phone? I said.

He told me he didn't think we should get into this now, and it would all be taken care of by the time I got back.

I said fine, that I'd take tomorrow off.

No, Matthew. Take the rest of the week.

I tried to negotiate, but he proved intractable. The rest of the week it was.

The evening passed in a haze of self-loathing. I'd got it all wrong. Let everyone down. A victim of my own filthy hubris. I thought I was strong enough. I wasn't.

A shame consumed me that I hadn't felt since St Jude Thaddeus. I wasn't even a Guy Friday any more. Just Matthew Viss. I tried to lift, just low, prosaic reps. Even then there was the giddiness. I ran half a mile and broke down. Who knows how long I sat there afterward, staring at nothing?

I reached for my chequebook. Began filling a donation to the little girl. At least this course was still open to me. Money.

Calling the bank to see how much I could spare, I listened to the automated teller, pressed the star key now. Requested a reading of my balance.

The figure made me spin out in my seat. I thought my details must have been stolen, the account pillaged by unseen thieves. I pressed the star key again. Listened harder now as the toneless voice listed my recent transactions. Standing orders, every one.

I guess my salary wasn't as ample as I'd thought. Perhaps I just wasn't that frugal. That was OK. There were steps I could take. Economies that could be introduced. I couldn't think what they might be, but I felt certain they existed. Anyway, I had the credit cards now. No reason to be downcast. It was fine. I finished writing out the cheque, and that gave me enough impetus to run myself a bath.

The way I slept that night and on into the morning a smorgasbord of natural disasters could have laid waste to the city and the first I would have known would be gazing at the wreckage the following lunchtime.

I made the coffee, checked the answerphone. A single message. I heard her draw breath before she spoke. And then it all came back to me. Grace; the opera.

So began my rest cure. She didn't seem angry when I called her back. All the same. I offered to come over, and she said she was busy decorating.

I told her what had happened. About the jewellers, the office. She was sympathetic if non-committal. I guess she thought I might have been lying. She asked if I needed anything, and I told her no, that was fine.

I could tell she was devising a treaty between us. Some tactful compromise to accommodate both her scepticism and the chance I was genuinely ill. She suggested I drop by tomorrow. If I felt up to it.

*

There. You put the aspirin there. The aspirin and the cotton wool, the vaseline and talcum powder, eye drops, mouthwash, nail scissors, moisturiser.

Grace stacks her bathroom cabinet. The new paint dry, but the fumes still hanging. This is the last room. The last to be made hers. Not a refuge, but somewhere to be lived in. Hers by choice. Entered in optimism. She is here, stripped of memory. Purposefully amnesiac. She shuttles the pill bottle back and forth.

The noises she hears from the street outside are louder than her last apartment, the cryptic bawling, car alarms. Yet somehow it doesn't trouble her.

She's getting used to the absence of her tapes. Serving the donors, shopping for groceries. Talking, as she was just now, to Matthew. The smell of the paint filling the air as he made his excuses. Maybe even told the truth. It doesn't matter. Either way, she can sense she's losing him. And she wonders what she's done so wrong. Tracked her own responses while he babbled, trying to find the point at which she said something asinine, laughed inappropriately. Except she didn't. Committed no faux pas. But still he chooses to stand her up, then, when he calls, evade, retreat.

She double-checks the cabinet, the aspirin and the mouthwash. Glances out into the hallway. This is hers now. Every inch of it. And she will be happy here.

The rest of the day was spent in torpor. I paced the apartment, walked round the block. Eventually, I called Jonah. He sounded surprised to hear from me.

I said I was out of the office this week, and he said Mike had already called him. He asked how I was, and I told him fine. He seemed distracted. As if peering at a lost toy discovered under the bed and realising he hadn't much missed it.

I struggled to hold his attention. Assured him there was no reason I couldn't work from here. I knew most of the contractors' details from memory.

He sounded dubious. Said he wouldn't want me to do anything to jeopardise my health. I told him my health was fine. Gingerly asked about the Reilly deal, and he said he really didn't think now was the time to discuss it. That he'd call me tomorrow if he needed me. I found myself thanking him.

He'd almost hung up when I mentioned the pendant.

Oh, he said. I did get Christina something myself. When I didn't hear from you.

Really?

He told me yes. Said he was still capable of doing things for himself. I apologised. Told him I hadn't meant otherwise.

When I mentioned the horticulturists, he said it could wait. The gingko had perked up anyway. He made it sound like this was not unconnected to my own poor health. As if some voodoo trade-off had been made. Said again that he'd call me if he needed me, but that now he had a meeting.

The day sludged on. I went out again. Dallying by the health-food store, it hit me. It was obvious what I had to do next. In truth, it always had been.

I would, for now, cut back on giving blood. Stop, in fact. Just stop. At least til I was over this. What would come instead was different. I'd been thinking of it anyway. Already decided I couldn't just stand by. The rest was simply a question of timing. And what better time than now?

Returning home, I found the number of the little girl's appeal fund. Called and registered as a potential donor, to have a sample and swab taken then examined. To see if I could save her life.

They put me in touch with a clinic in Pelham they said was conducting the tests. The clinic told me they could see me the next morning.

When I got there, the doctor was a few years older than me. She asked about my relationship to the patient.

I don't have one, I said. I just want to help.

She asked if I knew what was involved, should I prove compatible. Even my operation would not be without risk.

If all went well, months of recovery would still await. This isn't something one should do lightly, Mr Viss, she said.

I told her I knew that, and that I was ready. I meant it.

Aside from the blood sample and swab, there were studies of my breathing, chest X-rays, so on. Afterward, they thanked me. Said I'd hear from them as soon as possible. Of course, I hoped – for the sake of the girl – the tests would prove me a suitable candidate.

I guess sometimes you just have to go at the sound of the gun. Do what feels right. Whatever discomfort I would have to endure, a pinprick next to hers.

I barely got through the rest of the week. One day seeping into the next. I slept later every day, sunlight hardly glimpsed.

Gradually, I picked up my exercise regime, restarted my supplements. Lifted more each evening, ran a little faster. Twice, I called Julian. Just to check how he was doing now. There had been no more problems at school. He seemed so much less surly, acerbic. I felt like I was exerting a certain influence. That though we talked of little of any real consequence – TV programmes he enjoyed, teachers he disliked – he valued the perspective of someone outside the callow frontiers of his schoolmates.

As for Grace, I sent flowers. Stargazer lilies, with a box of shortbread. Shortbread had become a motif of ours. One of our private cornerstones. Knowing I had ground to make up, I brought house-warming gifts the first time I visited her place after moving. Told her I thought she'd be pretty excited.

It's the same one I have, I said, as she tore off the wrapping on the espresso machine. She smiled and thanked me. Then I gave her the pendant I'd bought for Christina Hoffman. She seemed delighted. Hung it round her neck there and then.

I stayed with her that night and the one that followed, but though I kept volunteering to help her decorate, she turned me down each time.

I appreciate the thought, she said. But I have to do this on my own. It's important.

Jonah didn't call. When I called him, Bonnie would answer or I'd get his voicemail. Either way, he never rang back. The knowledge I'd disappointed him gnawed at me. I put a lot of stuff down on paper. Ploughed through the books I'd never got round to after moving here, revisited my Eric Handlers.

I would take them all to the signing. I didn't know when I might get another chance. In the years since I'd been introduced to him, he'd become increasingly reclusive. Isolated by his talent. I had no idea why he was doing this now. I just knew I had to be there. The promise of the signing and my test results sustained me.

Then, Monday. I pulled on my cream cotton shirt and fixed my bow tie. Checked the mirror and hoped I looked revived enough for Mike.

On the way out, I collected my mail. Credit-card circulars (even though I'd already signed up for most of them), the blanket appeals from major charities that were now arriving daily. A letter from the hospital. I opened it in the cab to Pearl Street.

Dear Mr Viss, it said. *Re:* (and then the name of the girl)

Unfortunately, our tests indicate that you will not be able to act as a donor for this patient. The patient's family have asked that we pass on their sincere thanks.

I reached the office fifteen minutes early.

Eleanor tugs at the straps of her costume, exits the changing room. Heads out to the pool and walks beside the water. Looks over to the deep end, at the teenage girls along the ledge, the boys pluming, devout men in goggles massing laps like earnest seals, the steady procession to the board.

In the shallows, a bevy of mothers in costumes like hers, children, splashing. Alice is there. Her propulsion somewhere between a paddle and a stroke. Close enough for safety – but sufficiently distant to allow a veneer of freedom – are Tina Karlsson and her daughter.

Eleanor wanders by them, and each beckons in turn. She looks down, catches sight of her toes. They always look dextrous. Fingertoes, Matthew called them. Crouches, sits. Her feet in the water. Then slowly the rest of her. Waits at the pool wall til Alice flurries toward her. Tells her mother to come in further.

As she does, she feels herself holding back. Keeping her muscles in check. She hasn't swum in a year and a half. Another pleasure lost in the shuffle.

Her daughter comes here with the Karlssons weekly. For Eleanor, there's always an obstruction. The return to school, Cale Street's photography class. The novel business of being alone. Til now, cajoled by Tina to accompany them.

Alice floats on her back, a Dead Sea bob. Last night she came into Eleanor's room just as her mother was falling asleep. She was holding her father's newspaper cutting. She had, regrettably, been up early the day it arrived. Found the parcel. Insisted, with the prim self-righteousness she occasionally affects, that as it was addressed to her, then only she should open it. Eleanor knew it meant trouble. And duly, last night, she told her she'd shown it to the other girls at school, and now she wanted to know why he wasn't there when they all had fathers or – Eleanor figured euphemistic – uncles.

She watches her drift on the water, eyes open. Tina Karlsson straightens, stands beside. They smile, remark on how content the girls seem.

I'll watch them, Tina Karlsson says. If you want to swim.

Eleanor tilts her head toward the deep end, feels Tina's fingers play along her hand.

That'd be great, she says. Are you sure?

And Tina nods, and Eleanor turns and kisses Alice's forehead. Kicks out from the shallows. A hesitant crawl becoming certain. Right arm crook then tilling, head lifted into the air. And her legs find their rhythm, beating in turn, carrying her beyond the last of the mothers and children, on toward the deep end, ever faster, more determined, the water breaking to let her pass.

I took my seat. Sipped my coffee, popped a gum. There was a memo waiting, dated from the previous Monday. Sent from Mike and Caroline, it announced that as of tomorrow – last

Tuesday as I read – members of the phone crew were no longer to refer to themselves as Guy or Gal Friday. Instead, when dealing with a client, they should simply use the company's name, followed by their own, and the phrase How may I be of service?

The Greatest Gift, YOUR NAME speaking. How may I be of service?

Any questions, it said, should be addressed to Caroline.

It took me a while to adjust. The first time my phone flashed red, I blurted out, Good morning, The Greatest Gift, Guy Friday Matthew Viss speaking, as naturally as drawing breath. Did the same the next call, and the call after that. Sat with the memo in front of me, trying to translate my absorption into action.

That aside, it felt pretty much like I'd never been away. My cubicle seethed with activity. Over the course of the morning, every person in the phone room stopped by to welcome me back, ask how I was feeling. Mike came past around eleven. Leant on my cubicle wall, nodded at me, fulsomely. I wasn't sure what that meant.

Good to see you, he said. You're looking well.

I asked how the greeting changeover was working out, and he told me smoothly. Then he paused, like something urgent had only just occurred to him.

Good to see you, he said, again, and walked away.

I called Bonnie mid-morning. Told her I was back in the office now, and she said she'd pass that on to Jonah. I realised I was bothering my right-hand ring fingernail.

He didn't call til after lunch. All he wanted was Marlowe's booked for the following evening and a cast iron stovetop grill for Rush Street. I guess he wanted to ease me back in. I knew I couldn't let him down again.

The afternoon was a breeze. I even found time to map out a schedule for the weeks ahead. Left, reluctantly, just after six. Usually, when I was flowing, I'd have stayed til the grave-yard crew arrived. Not today. Today, I had somewhere to be.

I gathered what I needed and made for the door. Walked alone to Eric Handler's signing. I didn't mind that I was on my own. I knew Grace didn't feel the same way about him I did, no matter how she tried. In her old apartment, the copy of 15 Simple Wisdoms I'd given her had sat unread for weeks. I was to have gone with Alison instead, except the morning I returned to work she told me her mother had come into town and expected what she called nursemaiding. She gave me her copy of *Reinventing the Soul,* asked if I could get it signed.

At the bookstore, there were already a hundred people ahead of me, the line snaking to the end of the block. We advanced in halting steps, no one more than six inches from the person in front, shivering in winter coats. Eventually, hands raw, I made it inside the shop. Glanced ahead and behind me. Looked over my fellow enlightened. Most were like me. Same age, colour, drawn from a similar economic bracket, wearing kindred looks of clipped anticipation.

Craning my neck, I could see him. A man in his late forties, small and knotted, sitting cross-legged behind a low table.

The line seemed to be slowing. Now and then a fan would shuffle past in the opposite direction, clutching a bag with the store's name on it, but the intervals were ever longer, more pronounced.

You had to walk by a cash register to reach him. There were maybe forty copies of *Another Soul Rescue* piled to the side. A box of more below. Each person would buy one before they walked on. I didn't know that was how it worked.

When I got there, I dutifully bought another copy. I already had mine with me, but that was OK. I would make the other a gift.

With five people left in front, I got to see him clearly. His face had the accoutrements of healthy middle age, the lustrous hair and even skin, but his eyes were tired, joyless. I realised he'd been using the same author photograph since 15 Simple Wisdoms. My stomach cartwheeled as I counted off the seconds. The woman before me clacked and gabbled.

To Margaritte? I heard him say. Oh, Margaret. OK.

She told him about her sister's biopsy, her own impending divorce, and he pursed his lips and hummed. Said he was just pleased if what he did could help her through this difficult time. Then she asked what he was working on now.

I'd been planning to ask him that.

Oh, he said, it's . . . a progression.

And the woman talked some more, til finally she moved aside. I knew I should take her place. It was just a question of nerve. I breathed, held it. Exhaled.

Hello, he said, as I stepped in front of him.

I bought another copy of the new one, I said. I also have these.

And one by one I passed him the books.

Wow, he said. The whole oeuvre.

He spread them across the table.

So what would you like them to say?

I'd thought of so many possible inscriptions, sage and graceful summaries.

To Matthew?

His writing was fine and slanted. Not dissimilar to mine. He dealt with each book in turn, then passed it back.

Ah, I said, I . . . sent you some . . . of my own stuff.

Wow, he said, returning the last of the books. Sounds great.

It's just that I sent it a while ago. And I haven't had a response.

He frowned, asked me how I'd addressed it. When I told him c/o his publisher, he said in that case it might not have reached him. Or, if it did, his assistant may have mislaid it. If I sent it again, he said, he'd make sure to look out for it.

I could hear a tetchy rumble gathering behind me. So could Eric. He smiled apologetically, turned and locked on to the next in line.

That's OK, I said. I've got another copy here.

I drew it from my bag, pushed it across the table.

Oh . . . Wow.

He promised me he'd read it that night. The restlessness of

the queue was mounting. I leaned forward and shook his hand, its skin dough soft.

I almost forgot, I said.

I brought Alison's *Reinventing the Soul* from the pocket of my winter coat.

This is for a friend. Could it say To Alison?

Sure.

He scrawled across the first page and passed it back. I stood there for a moment, but he was fixed behind me now. I moved aside. Walked back down the line, many of whom glared at me with undisguised antipathy, and out of the store.

I remembered I'd meant to show him my cutting. Now I just felt deflated. I don't know what I'd expected, but it wasn't this.

I had nowhere to be. Grace was putting the finishing touches to her bathroom. So I just walked. Gazed in shop windows at goods I had no interest in, restaurants filled with the full-bellied contentment of couples and families and friends.

Til I reached the hospital.

This time, my course seemed self-evident. I headed straight for the admissions desk. Past the hordes of the minorly injured. Asked the receptionist where the girl with the lung disorder was being treated. No lies or elaborations.

And she told me. Gave me the number of her room. Said I only had thirty minutes' visiting time left. Now, rather than avoiding porters, I simply rode the elevator. Took it to the third floor.

It seemed like mostly private rooms up here. Hers was off a hallway to the left of the main corridor. My brogues whined on the flooring. I hadn't thought of her all day, except to register my surprise at how well I was doing not thinking of her. Her, or the letter. I'd waited for the impact. The sky to fall. It didn't come. At least not how I thought it would.

Do you know what today is, Matthew?

Jonah had asked me this a month or so beforehand. When

237

I'd told him no, he'd said it was the anniversary of Houdini's death.

Very odd, he said. Came through Niagara in a barrel, then expired from a punch to the belly. Testing his strength with a student called Whitehead. And the strange thing is, he didn't die til eight days later. Did you know that, Matthew?

I guess this was how it was for me. A hook to the gut, result pending.

Approaching the room, I saw her father gently close the door and walk away. I lowered my eyes, waited til he passed. Took five more steps and stood outside. Looked in through the window that ran along half the exterior wall.

A tray of uneaten food on a green leatherette chair. Two beds, identical. The mother prone on the one nearest the door. She looked to be asleep. The girl in the other, just lying there. Swaddled in drips and wires, her face barely visible. But I saw she was awake. Staring upward.

I was close enough to the glass for my breath to condense on it. I wiped it off with my sleeve. She must have heard the noise it made, the rattle of the button on my cuff. Inching, she turned her head toward me.

I guess she wasn't used to focusing, or maybe she was just heavily medicated, but it took her a second to meet my eyes. I smiled, and mouthed the single word Hello.

The Cave of Harmony, Charlotte Street. Licensed til three and peaking. This part is his favourite. The moment where everything blends, expands. Julian leans against the wall. A little drunk, a little high. Watches as the silhouettes move past him. The dancefloor an eternal beast. The wonders of a good ID. (Here, he is Ricky Connor of Ogden Ave., a student of Linguistics, twenty-two.)

He still feels thrilled just coming to the city. Here through his own resources, the profits from his loans. His allowance has been severed now. He only spoke with his mother, of course. She told him his father said that was fine, and the money stopped appearing in his bank account. No other comment, reaction.

It doesn't matter. Here, inside this room, he's not the school-boy, callow, needy, hosting parties with suggestible local girls on his father's boat. He could stay here for ever, propped against this wall. Watching some blonde at a private table. (Here, she is Marcia Bowe of Canonbury, studying fashion, twenty-three.) Til Xavier approaches. And Julian knows what's coming next.

Since the beating at the school, both Xavier and Balthus have been in his employment. Their brawn his insurance against a repeat. Now they are – they'll actually refer to themselves this way, without irony – his muscle. And beside their weekly cut, they'll treat his wallet like a kitty, his cab account as communal. He wishes he could disattach them, find another route to safety.

And Xavier walks up to him, glibly announces he's got something going on. Some business, he says. All proceeds toward the company. And to shut him up if nothing else, Julian says Sure, whatever. Pulls himself from the wall and follows.

Balthus next to them, a couple hover by the restrooms. Older, in their twenties even. Boyfriend and girlfriend, or brother and sister. Julian's guessing they're tourists. And Xavier tilts his head and they tag along behind, off toward the fire escape, as Julian asks his friend what is unfolding, but the music drowns the answer and so they keep on walking til they reach the metal doorway that leads down to the stairwell where they know the CC cameras have a blind spot.

Xavier and Balthus still out front, the tourists behind. Julian lagging now, somewhere in between. Through the door and down. On the stairs, the couple smile as he moves aside, stalling on the third step up. And in the well, the four remaining form a circle and Julian hears Xavier say:

Yeah, no problem man . . . we can do that.

And he looks at their expressions as seconds pass and they turn from eager to afraid. As Xavier and Balthus seize the girl by the arm, push their faces into the boy's. And the couple nod again but this time mournful, reaching to unclip the nylon wallets chained to their jeans. Handing the contents to Xavier, watching him split the notes with Balthus. And Julian's friends grin wide at each other and head back up, vaulting two steps at a time.

The boy puts his arm around the girl, then walks toward Julian without meeting his eye. Julian looks down, sees his palm extended. A roll of foreign currency, tied with a hairband. Their emergency money.

This isn't what he wants to be.

And right now, I'm falling harder than I ever have. And I just keep thinking all of this will disappear. That through some quirk of happenstance I'll blink, and when my eyes peel open I'll be inside, at home, with the bath almost overflowing and the television on.

But I haven't blinked yet. And so I'm drawing closer.

Nearer to conclusion.

I can almost feel the street now, the mottled birdshit paving stones.

And now this is a plummeting.

Beyond the third floor.

The woman who lives there is a recruitment consultant. Number four at her company. I know this. She told me personally.

I spoke to her once – brought together by a mix-up with the post – and that was when she mentioned it. And I told her about The Greatest Gift. That I dealt with temps on a regular basis. So it turns out we were in much the same line of work.

But that's not the same at all, she said, as if shocked at my temerity . . . I work in *recruitment*.

And ever since, if I pass her in the lobby, she looks at the ground and pretends she hasn't seen me.

Karen Goodnight skims the page. The CV of the girl who will – should – be in her office in fifteen minutes. Age. Education. Experience. On paper they're all the same. Her role is to screen them. Look past the glib enthusiasm and poke and cross-examine. Ascertain their calibre.

The hard kernel of recruitment. Her perfect job. She could always read people. Assess them with a glance. They say never rush to judgement. That's nonsense.

So much to do. Even without the reunion. The pending reassembly of her final year at school. In three weeks' time, two decades from their graduation. She heads the organising committee. Liaises with the school for contact details. Places the ads in the paper. Always the way. Taking the lead.

Just the names the school sent her had her giggling. The fat boy with his acrid, everlasting body odour. The girl in her sister's hand-me-downs. The retard. Paul something. God. What if no one's changed?

She would, if pressed, admit to frustration with the scant response thus far. She thought people would love the idea. Assumed they'd feel as she does. Be hungry to relive, evoke. Frankly, she finds it difficult to understand. Still, wasn't this always the way? The achievers, dragging along the rest. And always so much to do.

Mike, it seemed, was right. The time off had rejuvenated me. The faintness was gone, and in its place a potent, flaring energy. My kitchen work surface brimmed with supplements. It took me ten minutes just to get through them.

On Reilly's advice – dispensed between his check-ups on the progress of the deal, and my later supplicatory calls to Jonah – I'd started doing andro. The occasional ephedrine chaser. I knocked them back right before assailing the Maximal. And every time I tired, another dart of life pulsed through me.

I stepped up my regime accordingly. Where I'd lifted 9s, I now hauled 12s. Ten miles became fourteen. What previously exhausted me was now merely a warm-up. Hours passed before I faltered, my body locked in an epic cycle of breakage and growth. My arms, veined granite.

We talked about Christmas, Jonah and I. Mulled over presents and holiday arrangements. First, he said, he needed a fitting for a set of handmade golf clubs. Said he was going to treat himself. The rest I had *carte blanche* with: gifts for Christina and Julian, business contacts and relatives, minor Hoffmans from across the country. Then he asked me to book him a lunchtime table at Marlowe's.

He wanted to meet Reilly, face to face. He'd thought the matter over, he said. Thought it might be useful to take things a stage further. I could set it up, he said.

Reilly, of course, was ecstatic. I gave him some pointers on dealing with Jonah. Noted his more pronounced traits. I was just so glad to see fruition. To know I was a part of something.

An hour later, I was making coffee in the Pearl Street kitchen. There was only instant. I set three mugs by the kettle. Alison took hers white; Jon and I black.

I poured on the water. Watched it soak the granules, the steam in my face. Moved to the side, pulled out the cutlery drawer. Scanned the plastic forks and unmatched teaspoons. The only real knife was serrated. A wooden handle with two brass circles inlaid, too small to be useful with bread. Probably designed for meat.

I attended to the coffees. Set the water swirling anti-clockwise. Thought of all the lives I must have saved. The reach of my humanity. Held the index finger of my left hand over the sink, took the knife in my right and dragged the blade across the tip. I was pretty efficient at this by now. I kept the pressure steady, gouged where I needed to. Raised my finger above the mugs.

I gave two drops to Alison, then added milk. When it came to Jon, the second drop ran down the side of the mug. I cleaned it, held my finger vertical. Gave him his customary one sugar.

It wasn't premeditated. I'd just been feeling so alive. Blessed with a vitality I couldn't contain.

It starts at a clinic with a tube in your arm. This is how it ends.

Now I saw how badly I was cut. I needed some form of an alibi. I screamed, til half the phone room came rubbernecking.

It's fine, I said. It's just a nick.

I told them I'd been distractedly hunting for a spoon. Got hold of the knife by mistake. Why should anyone think otherwise?

Elise from Personal said she'd get me bandaged up. I made sure my colleagues took their drinks before I left.

I was all, and I was everyone.

Alison gazes at the postcard tacked above her computer. *Once Emerged From The Grey Of Night*. Sips at her coffee and stares. Waits for the PA to the Acting CEO to call her back. Been waiting for some time.

The Acting CEO of a company that handles other companies' payrolls is entertaining this coming Friday. Alison is managing the catering. There are various dietary issues. A smattering of vegetarians. All she needs are the specifics. Then she can proceed. She wants this done today. Would like an hour to herself this evening.

Unplanned, she went out this lunchtime, bought materials. Things she hasn't had round the place for years. Pads, charcoals, a palette, easel. Could feel an impatient twitch in her fingers as she left.

She thinks the books are helping. She's two-thirds through *Another Soul Rescue*. A book about change, it says. And she can feel it working. Giving her the strength to say: *Enough to the doubts and poisons*.

And perhaps, in time, to hold a brush. Just as soon as the PA to the Acting CEO calls back.

I collected Grace from Mortimer and Upas. Just being around the place had me itchy. I was smack in the middle of my rest period. We were having an early dinner.

At her suggestion, we ate in a fish restaurant that had recently opened ten minutes from Bethune Street. I steered the conversation over fine bones and exotic flesh. She was wearing the pendant from Windmill Street.

I told her there was something that we needed to talk about. It had been on my mind for weeks. She nodded, brow puckering. Reached across the table, laced her fingers through mine. I said if we didn't discuss it now it was going to be too late, and she nodded again, gripped tighter.

It's about Christmas, I said. We have to work out the details.

I told her we should pin down what time we were eating. Who would do what in the kitchen. Whether we should walk in the park before or after lunch.

That's it? she said.

And she pulled her hand from mine. I apologised for not raising the issue sooner. Said what with the fainting and the backlog I'd faced on my return to Pearl Street, I hadn't had the opportunity.

I really wasn't expecting her to look so tepid. I knew it was a major step. The first Christmas together was a watershed for any relationship. I just thought we were ready.

She usually spent it with her family, she said. It was the one time of the year she saw them.

Oh . . . well, you know . . . if you'd rather be with them . . .

She said no. That wasn't what she'd said. God knows, she'd be glad of an alternative. She just hadn't realised that was what I wanted to talk about.

I thought, she said. I don't know. I thought you might want to talk about . . . us.

I do, I said. I was.

And we each looked in different directions as the waiter cleared our table. Quietly agreed we should discuss it another time. I ordered coffee for us both, til she reminded me she'd told me a month before she was giving it up in favour of tea.

I took care of the bill. Put it on one of my credit cards. I didn't get paid til next Friday, so for now I ran on plastic. My economy drive just hadn't panned out. On closer inspection, I simply couldn't see where the fat was. I'd thought about returning the hire car, but I'd need it when I felt OK to give again. Considered paring down my standing orders, rejected that idea in seconds.

I left a healthy tip, made sure the waiter saw me. Then, outside, we stood facing. Grace and I. She told me she wasn't feeling so good. Just wanted to get home to bed. I pressed my hand to her forehead, searching for a temperature that wasn't there. Told her I could take her, but she said she'd rather find a cab.

It's just been a long day, she said. You don't mind, do you?

I told her No, of course not, and after a wordless protraction casting about the empty street I found her a cab.

I'll call you, I said.

I meant it as a statement, but it sounded like a question. We kissed, and she left. I watched the taxi disappear and checked the time. Still early.

The lobby of the hospital was bedlam. A sullen flock of the mangled and panicked. The third floor seemed pastoral by contrast. More like a hotel than a place of sickness.

I strolled by the room, glancing in as if just passing. The girl asleep or something near. Head tilted away from me, hair beginning to mat. Two unwieldy machines set beside her bed now, new since my last time here.

Her parents weren't around. I wavered outside. Thought perhaps I'd sit with her. A watchful presence while she slept. Took a step toward the door. Palm warm on the handle. Heard voices and jumped back. Wary, I moved over to the junction of the corridor. The parents were approaching. Dazed, like they thought they were maybe somewhere else.

I guess they must have been staying here ever since their daughter was admitted. Weeks of beige enamel and vending machines, rest snatched fitfully, never enough, a slow drip of exhaustion. They carried magazines, balanced hot drinks and snackfood. I waited at the corner, then walked up to them.

I hope you don't mind me doing this, I said, but I'm Matthew.

Blearily, they looked up at me.

. . . Matthew Viss.

I told them I'd seen them on TV and in the paper, and they should know that a lot of people's thoughts were with them.

Oh, the mother said. Thank you.

I asked if any progress had been made securing a donor. As one, they said no. I told them if there was anything I could ever do, at any stage –

Then I gave them my card.

Oh, the mother said again. Thank you. And the father smiled at me weakly as they shuffled back into the room.

On my way home, I bought a Christmas tree. An unruly pine, three feet high, shedding maniacally. I kept it in my living room, where it stood, divesting itself in persistent heaps, dwarfed by the weights and fitness equipment around it. I hung it with silver tinsel before it began to depress me.

It was useless make-believing. I knew all the season would mean this year was a pang of absence on the day itself and a titanic increase in my workload.

Beneath the tree at Pearl Street – a luxuriant giant, smothered with baubles and twinkling fairy lights – Mike and Caroline had summoned the phone room for a motivational address.

This, Mike reminded us, was the highpoint of the service industry's calendar. Presents for every taste, budget and purpose must be chosen, purchased, delivered; parties would need to be organised, decorated, catered for. Holidays had to be covered. Flights and trains home demanded research, scheduling, booking. It would permeate our lives in every aspect. Our challenge, to respond with excellence.

The financial imperative remained unspoken. Everyone knew that things were slow. As soon as I returned from my week away I saw the phone crews dawdling, unlit red lights. A busy Christmas could make all the difference.

We returned suitably roused to our cubicles. I sped between regular client calls and procuring Jonah's gifts for friends and family. I wanted them to be perfect.

I braved the major shopping routes, the jostling and hysteria that caught all those who entered it in logjams of bickering inertia, our fingers mauled from the cold and the skinny, unforgiving handles of overfilled plastic bags.

I got each of the Hoffmans a small gift of my own. For Julian, a cabbalistic piece of stereo equipment he once mentioned hankering after. Christina, a brooch in gold and emerald. Jonah, a device called the Infinite Hole used for putting practise that I bought from the company making his clubs.

They each sent me a card. I displayed them with the rest at home. Festive best wishes from clients and colleagues, more ostensibly signed by children from developing nations that I'd sponsored through my standing orders, telling me how well they were doing at school now I'd bought their class some textbooks.

I hadn't heard from Alice. I collated her presents regardless. I'd been preparing the list since October. Whenever I saw something she might like in a store or magazine, in the TV ads that filled every commercial break – the ones where kids tore deliriously through wrapping paper, which made me choke with grief – I'd note it down. Night after night, return with more. Toys of wood and toys of metal, cloth and fun fur, paper, vinyl. The educational and purely frivolous. To be enjoyed outdoors and in the home. Toys that covered the floor, or that fitted inside a child's hand. They massed in my apartment til I drove them to the post office and had them dispatched to the house by courier.

I wrote out a cheque for Eleanor and sent that by regular post. I assumed they'd be with her family this year. Eleanor's family always went big on Christmas. They were sticklers for tradition. Her father insisting on parlour games, mother beseeching him in mock exasperation to help out with the vegetables. Opening one present each before the children's bedtime, the rest the following morning. Like they did last year. And every year. Only this time I wouldn't be with them.

You Better Watch Out, You Better Not Cry

Breakfast tasted good today. Everything tastes good today. The juice, the milk, the lip balm, gum, the very air, it all makes Phillip Reilly purr.

The homeless man who stands outside his building wears a tattered Santa suit. The full regalia. Missing just the beard. A mordant kit of shabby red. He wonders where it could have come from, which skip it was discarded in.

Unless, of course, he is, in fact –

Today of glorious heaven-sent days, Reilly could believe it. He roots inside the pocket of his coat. Finds a note, a shoal of coins. Thrusts them into Santa's hand. And Santa mumbles Thank you, then Merry Christmas.

It's over. The ugly confessionals, eager letters from soulless lawyers. Done. He's back. Now, Reilly tries to name his disposition. Ecstatic, certainly. Vindicated, yes. The hours degraded in that yellow uniform, his slogging recovery at Romane Valley, the harrying phone calls and meetings, now he knows they worked. Justice, he feels, is thriving in his corner of the universe.

Emboldened, he takes another step toward Santa. Throws his arms wide open. And Santa quails and backs away, but Reilly doesn't mind. Today, his goodwill knows no bounds.

Alice's card arrived the day before Christmas Eve. A water-colour of a skating scene. It looked from the paper stock like it came from a multi-pack of the kind I knew Eleanor favoured. Inside it said, pre-printed, With Season's Greetings.

Then, in her own unfinished hand:

Merry Christmas

xxxxxxxxx.

I wept at the sight of it. Wept in the office whenever it crossed my mind. Rushing to the bathroom for dignity's sake, heart shocked from the ephedrine, knowing that when I got back my red light would be burning. With every white box taken care of, the more uptight the call that followed.

This was our last full day of operations. We were leaving our cubicles at lunchtime tomorrow. Not back til the 2nd of January.

Jonah was to be out of contact for the same length of time. He and the family would be at their cottage in Marvendean. His was the morning's first call. He wanted to make sure everything was dealt with.

We ran through the list. Made sure he had each of the presents. That his clubs had arrived – they had, and he expressed his delight at their craftsmanship – that adequate supplies of food and drink were laid on for the journey, that every card received had been reciprocated.

Oh, he said. There was something else.

He said he'd called Phillip Reilly. Told me he thought it only fair to give him his decision before the holidays.

So, he said, I told him yes.

The money was already in Reilly's account. A seeding, Jonah called it. I heard myself exhaling. Said he'd made my day. He told me he was only too glad to help. Then, once I'd reminded him he could reach me at home in case of emergency, we wished each other Happy Christmas, and said we'd speak next year. Laughed. The way you do.

Reilly called within the hour. He said he had fantastic news, and I went with the pretence. Hummed joyously as he repeated the information I'd just been given by Jonah, working up to an exclamation.

Wow, I said. That's just . . . fantastic.

And then he started up again, effusing over his plans for the reception area and the step machines he was buying, and how he could barely keep from screaming.

I was excited too. Even second time around. Filled with the

elation of watching the model boat you spent weekends sweating over sail past the other kids'. A sincere pride. My new little brilliance.

It was just my red light was going crazy, each flash another frantic message clamouring with the rest. I figured eventually he'd wear himself out.

So listen, champ, he said, tonight we're celebrating.

I paused before I spoke. Tonight was our office party. Given our diligence with other people's revelry, our own had rather fallen through the cracks. There were six bottles of champagne to be had in the meeting room. That, essentially, was it.

I told Reilly I'd see him at eight. We would meet in the lobby of the Simonsen Hotel. That was his idea.

Let's do this properly, he said.

The rest of the day was a mushrooming frenzy. The pitch cranked with every call. I could tell Mike was enjoying himself. By early afternoon, the more junior members of staff had been sent out with phones and pagers to comb the stores. In the office, tempers blew. At least one headset flung across the room. Unending white boxes.

Then, by 6.30, it had passed. The calls waning in volume and anxiety. Our party was supposed to have started at six, but those hapless souls cast into the city to fetch and carry were only now filing back.

We had no music. No one had thought to bring any.

Breathing exercises pealed through the room. Mike and Caroline gave up on the new client liaison room, began handing out champagne in plastic cups from beside the water cooler. Me, I was spent. The coffee did nothing but wire my nerves. If I'd shut my eyes I'd have gone, right there.

I got to the Simonsen five minutes late. I'd booked meals and suites here a thousand times. It was just how I always imagined it. The Stilton-veined marble staircase with the deep red carpet and lustrous bannister. The willing bellboys, impeccable guests.

253

Reilly was in the lobby. He wore a sloe-black suit I could tell was designer, but somehow looked all wrong folded round his bulk. Creases where there shouldn't be creases. Weird, obstinate hangs to the fabric. That same blue and salmon neck tie.

His smile was cavernous. A brash display of teeth that suggested mammoth inner faith and the recent attentions of a dental hygienist.

You look all in, champ, he said. C'mon. Let's go.

Into a low-lit oval room with a high wooden bar in one corner, from where the waiting staff dashed gracefully with trays of cocktails, between tables of varying ages bound by implicit but definite wealth. We took a seat and ordered spirits. Had to raise our voices. Toasted his good news. Talked through his plans for the health resort as if that morning's conversation had never finished.

So I just figure we put the J20s in there and see if people go for 'em, he said.

And then we ordered more drinks. I caught him ogling the waitress, and he turned and smirked and asked me how things were with what he called your honey. I told him fine. That Grace and I were spending Christmas together.

And you'll be –

The usual, he said. With the family.

He raised his glass.

To Christmas how we choose to spend it.

Christmas how we choose to spend it, I replied. Then struck his glass with mine and drank. I've never been much of a drinker. Already my concentration was failing. He ordered more. Everyone was getting louder.

So your guy Jonah's quite the brain, huh? he said. Quite the supergenius.

And I said I thought so too, before he delivered a rapt account of how Jonah had told him in minutes – casually, free of vanity – how to guarantee maximum profit and insure against dips in the market, slinging out tips he could have charged millions for with a frightening world-weary nonchalance. Only with every word I could feel myself losing track of the word before, the word before that just a hazy vestige, til the point where what he'd been saying to begin with, the actual gist of his discourse, was gone completely.

So, he said –

And

then

Christ, champ. You ready for naptime already?

It must have only been a fraction of a second, because when my eyes opened everything looked just the same.

I apologised, still woozy. Ran my tongue around the corners of my mouth to check for drool.

How long was I out for?

Relax, he said. A second. Less.

He leant over and grabbed me by the shoulder.

C'mon, champ. You need another drink.

And so we had another drink.

To a regular eight hours, he said.

A regular eight hours, I replied.

He asked after my training. Whether I'd been doing my crunches how he told me. I said I was, that he'd been right. My stomach was like iron now. He sat back and asked about my push-ups. I told him I was doing them just like he'd advised.

One arm, right? he said.

I told him yes, again.

So, let's see.

Here?

Absolutely here. C'mon, champ. Let's see twenty.

I told him I was far too tired and besides, look where we were.

OK. Looks like I'm leading by example.

And he rose, pulling off his jacket. Dropped to the floor. I knew without looking the people around us were staring.

Watch and learn, champ, he said, as he swung into position, right arm bent, hand flat and fingers splayed, left arm thrown behind his back. He got to three before the head barman appeared beside him.

Sir, please. We'd really prefer that you didn't.

And Reilly glanced up from the floor.

No problem, he said, returning to his feet. Just showing off to my friend here. You know how it is.

I understand, sir.

And Reilly asked for two more drinks.

Yes, sir, the barman said, tightly. I'll have them brought over.

To great service, Reilly said when they arrived.

Great service, I replied.

I was starting to feel maudlin. Trying to keep pace with Reilly's banter but growing preoccupied with thoughts of Alice. Eleanor even. Wondering if they'd left for her parents yet. Calling to mind the presents I'd sent and how my wife would always hold my hand as we sat together last thing Christmas Eve.

So, I said, I guess we probably won't see each other again. Now the deal's done.

He told me that was ridiculous. I didn't get rid of him that easily, he said.

To the future.

And I raised my glass with his.

OK, champ. Let's go.

. . . Go?

We're just warming up. Plenty more in store tonight.

The notion was absurd. I was so tired or so drunk, or both, I could barely co-ordinate. My head dropped to my chest. Reilly, conversely, was on his feet and asking for the bill.

Listen, I said, I don't . . . think I can.

It took an age to persuade him. Til finally he said he'd just have to take my share of the fun himself.

We shook hands in the lobby. Wished each other Merry Christmas and said we'd speak next year. Laughed. The way you do. And he left in search of further adventure.

Back at the apartment, I lay on the floor in the living room, wedged between the tree and my weights. Picked up the phone and dialled. Got four digits in before replacing the receiver. The next time, five.

The third time I called, I got as far as the answerphone. Eleanor's voice. It had always been mine when I lived there. I hung up before the tone.

Lay back down, and felt myself exit.

Til the phone rang.

It was inches from my head. I still couldn't make it in time. As soon as my machine clicked on, whoever it was hung up.

Immediately it rang again.

My eyes were open just enough to see it was still dark out. Reflexively, I checked my watch. Just after six as I answered.

Hello? I said.

But there was no reply.

Hello? I said, again.

It's me . . . Phillip . . . Reilly.

He was talking so quietly I thought there was a problem with the line.

I lost it all, he said.

And then again.

I've lost it all.

And in the same confession-box whisper, he told me how he'd gone on to another bar after I went home. Got talking with some guys from out of town. They invited him back to their hotel. There, he had another few drinks.

The hotel was adjacent to a casino. The guys he'd hooked up with said they wanted a hand or two. And he thought, What the hell. He could do this. Be an adult. Just sit at the table for a couple of hands, not play, just watch.

They liked blackjack. The guys from out of town. And he

257

kept seeing their cards and better ways to play them, and they were getting great hand after great hand, doing nothing with the potential, til eventually he thought, Well, what the hell, once more and he got himself a rack of chips, stubby, brightly coloured chips he'd always loved the look of, and he went back to the table, only now he was in the game himself, and the first few hands went south but then the first few always do, til he noticed he was almost out of chips so then he got another rack but that was gone soon too, and that's why he made sure the third rack was full enough to last him, keep him there til his luck changed, and it just felt so amazing, the way it always had, just sitting at the table with the croupier, telling everyone around him how he owned a health resort and they'd have to come down and check the place out, and the hands kept coming and his luck was going to change soon and he realised that the guys from out of town were gone now but that was OK 'cause you just had to wait for your luck to change, just stay at the table, just ride it out, get ready for the big win, 'cause the big win's overdue now, and the big win's what you're here for, and it's coming, you can feel it, you can smell it in the air, know how good it's going to be, and it's coming, going to come for sure, going to come around the corner, and it's coming any holy golden blissful moment now –

And I've lost it all, he said. Everything.

I watched the darkness fade outside my window as he told me of the last few years, the debts, his wife, the store. The meetings he attended. I didn't know what to say to him. What I was meant to express. I think, in the end, I thanked him for letting me know. Said I'd tell Jonah.

And he said he could fix this, that he just needed –

Til I stopped him in mid-sentence, still muzzy.

I have to go now, I said.

I figured I may as well get to the office. I took a bath and dressed. Sat and drank my coffee. And I left my building and walked to Pearl Street in the early daylight, thinking of nothing but the step I was taking and the one I was about to, and all the stores that I passed were already closed for the holidays.

You have to judge it right. When to take the plate, when to have it come to you. It's always overladen. The slightest imbalance could lead to disaster. You pull too fast, they let go too early, either way it ends up in your lap.

Grace watches Matthew as he labours over the bird. Levering the knife into its breast. Steam, rising from the inside. And then he glances up at her. Asks if she could pass her plate.

And Eleanor looks on as Alice does so. Holds it out to her grandfather. Him standing there unblushing in the floral apron he's worn this one day of the year ever since she can remember. She stares out into the garden. Wonders what excuse might allow her to slip out once they've eaten. Here she is, a grown woman, still condemned to sneak into the garden when she thinks no one's looking, starting in fright at any sudden noise before returning inside, frantically chewing on mints.

Alice studies the plate, still in her grandfather's hand. Announces that Belinda Griselda would very much like some more skin.

And Carl tears off another piece. Ruby's always been fond of it. He turns to the potatoes. She has this way of cooking them with onions and cheese. It renders them crisp yet deliciously moist. Beside him are books. The first he's ever owned. The Sully Gomez mystery and a Jack Sloan Western, recommended by the college. She gave them to him this morning. Usually it's cologne or a sweater. After he unwrapped them, she ruffled what's left of his hair and said she was proud of him.

It is 1.51 p.m. She always overestimates. Jonah Hoffman leans across the table, pours the browning over his wife's plate. A small pool by the vegetables, a generous flow over the meat. And there's still so much left over.

It's a little watery, he says.

Christina Hoffman makes sure her glass is full. Sees her

husband opposite, playing lord and patriarch. Thinks of how, for the next half an hour, they will sit through three more courses. Julian ticking off the days before he can go home. Jonah counting the minutes til he can sidle off to practise with his clubs. And she'll keep her glass full til he blithely remarks Still early, Christina.

Careful, he says, it's hot. It is 1.52 p.m.

And Grace says thank you as she lays the plate in front of her. Only he doesn't seem to hear. Just takes his own, and rests it by the bird. He must have said ten words all day. Maybe thirty in total since he got here last night.

He loads up his plate, and they eat.

There are always answers. Remedies and correctives. I could lend him money. Simply give him whatever I could spare. I could talk to Mike about adding his name to our directory of health and fitness contractors, make sure his name was to the fore the next time a Director of Sales and Marketing called us needing their lats firmed or their thighs defined.

I said all this to Reilly when I called him back. Told him nothing was ever irreparable. Told him this in a series of answerphone messages left in the sedated lull between Christmas and New Year. I rang him three, maybe four times daily. His machine picked up every time. He never returned my calls.

I should have talked it through with him as soon as he'd told me. I knew that now. You just never grasp the magnitude of events when they're happening right in front of you. Like the first time in your life that you see a dead thing, and you're peering at it, giggling, waiting for it to play again.

I told him we could solve this, like he'd said. And I believed it as I believed in my own liability, the fear that my actions would bankrupt the Hoffmans.

Then I called Jonah. Despite his instruction not to be bothered til he returned to the office, I felt obliged to let him know immediately. I only ever reached his voicemail. Began with laid-back, non-specific requests for him to get in touch with me. Graduated to pleas. On New Year's Day my resolve deserted me, and I detailed the whole wretched episode. From start to finish.

The next morning, back at my cubicle, he rang. I told him everything, again. Expected a grievous wail, a savage blame.

I see, he said, every now and then, or I understand. As if I were reading out the ingredients on a soup can. When I finally stopped talking, he asked if I'd spoken to Reilly since, and I told him I'd been trying to.

Trying to, he said, without any obvious subtext.

And I asked if he was angry.

Angry? No . . . I'm not angry. It's just . . . unfortunate.

And he said that this wasn't my fault. That the sum involved was not – on a relative scale – significant. He made deals all the time, he said, and some of them worked out, and some of them didn't. That was the nature of his living.

I couldn't do what I do, he said, if I wasn't conversant with loss. The trick is not to lose more than you can afford.

I was filled with admiration. Amazed by his composure. He thanked me for letting him know. Said he'd speak with Reilly as soon as he got back.

Get back? I said. From where?

South Africa, he said, like that was self-evident. The golf holiday . . . The one you booked.

I did?

You did. The 5th til the 11th? . . . You don't remember, do you?

I didn't. I could recall the brand of eyedrops I'd bought him in the first week of our acquaintance. The price of the tyres on his car. But this was gone.

Naturally, your first reaction is to wonder what else you might have forgotten. In my job, a failing memory could be disastrous.

Jonah's holiday, it turns out, consisted of seven nights on the coast of KwaZulu-Natal, in a purpose-built resort where ardent golfers could play in temperate conditions on scenic courses with optional instruction from a former pro.

My declining faculties seemed to amuse him. Took the sting out of the conversation. Somehow, he got on to telling me about the length of Harry Truman's first public address following the bombing of Hiroshima and the brand of pomade he wore while he made it. Til he said he had to go now.

Later, I fruitlessly called Reilly's number and sifted my files for a record of the holiday. There wasn't one. Aside from that, the day was empty. I'd look around the phone room and see (former) Guy and Gal Fridays slumped in their seats, dallying unoccupied. Then realise I was doing the same. There was just nothing for us to do.

I thought business might pick up the following day. I was wrong. By the week's end, I'd carried out five jobs. I mulled over my handling of each as I drove to the Yorkhaven Donor Centre, an hour's ride west of the city. There, I was Grayson Wendell. Now I felt ready to give again. Better attuned to my body's distress signals.

Except this was incidental. Merely a secondary motive. At the franchised bookstore in Yorkhaven's only shopping complex, five blocks from the clinic, Eric Handler was conducting another signing.

I'd still had no response to my outline. He must have read it by now. It wasn't like I expected a contract, or a friendship. In truth, I knew I was free-floating; directionless.

I just wanted his thoughts.

The line at the store was hardly a line at all. Just a five-strong burl of fans inside and a mob of dead-eyed kids skulking at the doorway, staring in at an MDF signing table. No till beside or pile of books. Just Eric and his glass of juice.

When the five ahead of me were done, I stood in front of him. I hadn't brought anything to sign.

Hi, he said.

Hello, I said. How are you?

Great. Glad to be here. And he sat with his marker in his hand, poised for a hardback or audio book.

So? I said. What do you think?

His head tilted, baffled.

What do I think?

262

And then I got it.

He had no idea who I was. Of course he didn't.

I'm sorry, he said. Do I –

And I told him no. He didn't. Not realistically. His expression turned by now through unease to alarm.

It's OK, I said. Thank you.

And I stepped away. Left the store, returned outside.

The wind chill had a vicious zest. A caution you weren't wanted here. The jade green automatic was parked across the street. I headed back to it, jammed on the heating, drank gratefully from my thermos. And while it was my sole intention to leave this place, the ignition somehow remained untouched.

Instead, I sat looking over the objects collected on the dashboard. Old packs of nicotine gum, fruit peel, maps, the Christmas card from Alice. A hire car, parked by an anonymous shopping centre. And all I wanted was an opinion. It's a terrible thing, not even being worth acknowledgement.

When maybe twenty minutes had passed, Eric left the building. I thought he'd have someone with him. An agent, a minder. He walked toward a dark blue saloon, seemed to change his mind halfway, veered instead toward an ATM maybe twenty steps away. A covered booth accessible by swiping your card through a slot beside the door.

I got out and called after him. I guess this time he must have recognised me. He saw me, immediately began to speed-walk. I did the same. He broke into a jog, which then in turn caused me to. I only wanted to talk to him. Couldn't think what he might be afraid of. I saw him swipe his card, and I got to the door right as it shut in my face.

He stood, quaking, behind the glass. I reached for my wallet, pulled out a credit card. That was all you needed to get in. I had the card at the top of the slot when I heard him addressing me, muffled.

I'm calling the police, he said, holding up his phone by way of emphasis. I'm calling the police if you don't get away from the door.

And there we were, held apart by plexiglass and an encrypted magnetic strip. Me with my card, him with his phone. Locked in stand-off.

What do you want from me? he said.

His reaction seemed grossly out of proportion. Then I saw the look on his face. And while I knew he was small, only now did I appreciate to quite what extent. His wrists were dollish, those of a child. The look on his face the same taut dread as Julian's bully.

I explained that I wished him no harm or injury. That nothing could be further from my mind. Slid my card back inside my wallet and told him the truth.

I just . . . wanted to talk some things through with you . . . You're my hero.

He started dialling.

Please, I said –

pressing my hands to the glass.

– I wrote an outline. Just . . . some thoughts . . . stuff I put down on paper. I gave it to you. At a signing. You promised me you'd read it.

The blankness of his expression was not, I still believe now, one of arrogance. He truly had no idea what I was talking about. I noticed he hadn't completed the call.

It's OK, I said, if you haven't.

And his shoulders dropped and the lines by his mouth fell into resignation, and he told me he couldn't read unsolicited material even if he wanted to. There were, he said, issues of copyright. Potential infractions thereof.

And anyway, he said, if you really expect me to be honest with you . . . why would I want to?

I told him I understood. That it was OK. Just as long as he knew I'd meant it – and I said this now fully aware that he would have no recall of me doing so – when I told him he'd always inspired me. And now I was lost, and more so every day.

We stood there til I tucked away my wallet. I was turning to leave when he said:

I don't know what to tell you. I'm fifty-two years old. I've got three ex-wives, none of whom speak to me. Four kids. I hear from them when they need money. I wake a dozen times a night when I can sleep at all, and when I do I think about my death. I have a large collection of vintage cars and I eat alone and manufacture sentences I long since stopped investing any meaning in. And the last time I checked I was twenty-five and life was just rolling out before me.

The wind was picking up, my eyes starting to water.

And I'm happy, he said, if you find comfort in what I do. I'm happy for all of you. But you always want more. So what do I say? Make sure you eat breakfast. Don't lose your temper, but don't bottle up your anger. Take regular holidays and adjust your chair to avoid neck strain. Tell the people you care about you love them. Don't die with regrets. Floss. Carry an umbrella when it rains and sunblock when it's sunny, and try and keep some plants around the house.

When I looked up, he was staring right at me. Pushed open the door and fumbled in his wallet.

You want someone to talk to? . . . Here.

And he leaned out and handed me a business card. An unbleached rectangle on which was printed:

DAVID KUSHMAN

CLINICAL PSYCHOLOGIST

and an address in the city.

When I got back to my apartment, I gathered up the yellow legal pads and the print-outs from the copy shop, and I left them outside in a black plastic rubbish bag. The books by Eric Handler, I took up to the loft.

Of South Africa's many expanses of natural beauty, KwaZulu-Natal is the jewel in the crown. With the coral-fringed azure of the Indian Ocean lilting at its coastline and the Drakensberg mountains providing a majestic border, its marriage of the verdant and rugged will seduce and entrance the walker, extreme sports enthusiast, pony-trekker, golfer or fisherman.

Whether your aim is to learn to paraglide, watch the big game at Hluhluwe-Umfolozi, enjoy a peaceful eighteen holes, or simply breathe the clean, invigorating air of this unspoiled paradise –

It is 12.05 p.m. Jonah stows his in-flight magazine, breathes the plane's phoney cabin air. Gazes from his window down onto the runway. Sees men in orange jumpsuits climb into a buggy, race back toward the terminal.

There is a lump. A nubble in his seat. He shifts his weight one way, then the other. Still feels it. He'll have to move. He presses the button to attract the stewardess, hearing as he does so a message from the cockpit requesting that all cabin staff take their seats and prepare for departure.

The engines jar into life, and the lump disappears. His eyes draw closed. Lowering him inside a foetal nothingness. Watching a figure emerge through the drowse. Himself, standing in the shadow of a mountain, pores open to the heat, handmade driver solid in his grip. And then, again, the wave.

Every single time he sleeps, it's there. Every night this week and every night the week before. In his dreams, it comes to him, imperious.

Last night was the most vivid yet. At his office window once more. Hearing a panic below. And the wave, taller now than ever. Enough to kill the sun. And he stood transfixed as it ripped through the city, a vast grey weapon of unmaking.

A rumble erupts beneath him. His eyes open to the stewardesses, facing him in their seats at the far end of the cabin. Their eyes fixed just past his head. He sets his watch to the time at destination.

It is 4.09 p.m. And his eyes close again into arid paralysis, novocained suspension, mouth drying out, turning gummy. Dropping into half-sleep as the plane rolls faster. Back at the mountain as it bucks and rises.

So January passes as January does, a seven hundred-hour Monday morning. I'd visit the hospital, say hello through glass when I could.

266

Jonah left, and Jonah returned, and in between I called Reilly enough times to lose count. He never got back to me.

Mostly, I didn't even feel like I was there. Slipping like a ghost to the margins as the world sluggishly refound its customs.

I spent whole evenings toiling at the Maximal, breaking only to assail my weights. Running a finger over my pectorals. Savouring the hardness in my calves. Coming home from work thinking I'd just do an hour to get the endorphins flowing, then looking up through the sweat in my eyes and seeing it was after twelve.

I just wanted a respite. Anything not to think.

On a Saturday, I received a letter from Two Cities. I expected another pitch for the Gold Ring Trust, to accompany the messages I still found cluttering my answerphone. Having never enjoyed less than a cordial relationship with the bank I had been with since eighteen, reading it came as a shock.

I had, it said, seriously exceeded the overdraft limit of my current account. In light of this, it went on, Two Cities had been unable to honour three of my standing orders, due to be processed the day before the date above.

The date above was three days ago. Sure enough, there with the rest of my mail was a notice from the Marchmont Gym Warehouse, the company from whom I bought the Maximal IX 450, questioning the absence of this month's payment. Requesting that I contact them.

The letter from Two Cities then informed me I'd been charged for exceeding my overdraft limit, for each day my overdraft limit had been exceeded, and for the cost of sending this letter. I would be unable to use my debit card at either retail outlets or ATMs til the problem was corrected.

Personal Accounts Manager Emily Cainer then suggested that, given the sum held in my savings account, I might consider a transfer between the two. Alternatively, I could arrange a meeting with a loans advisor.

Neither would be necessary. I could juggle the balance of

my credit cards to replenish my account. Live cheap. Hold out til payday.

Not that I felt like I'd earned it. I arrived at Pearl Street each morning ready to fill white boxes, only to be greeted with inertia. The stupor of the week after New Year stubbornly refused to budge. Previously insatiable clients now called sporadically if they called at all. The jobs minor, prosaic. Laundry to be ferried, film developed.

On the first Thursday of February, I took a morning off. Mortimer and Upas had come around again. It was funny. I'd been feeling so detached that I'd almost forgotten. William's hair was in a ponytail.

I lay back, and clenched the ball. Saw the vein rise. Realised I hadn't thought to hide the punctures in my arms.

Afterward, I sat with Grace in the donor's lounge.

We were still seeing each other two or three nights a week. I'd go over to her place after work, and we'd watch TV, eat. Usually, I'd fall asleep on her couch til she'd nudge me awake and we'd slowly troop into her room. A mutual dotage.

I'd tried to tell her about my state of mind on numerous occasions. Whenever she'd talk about her day, I'd wait til she asked after mine. Let the truth bud in my throat before I said:

Oh, you know. The usual.

Now, I kissed her on the cheek as I left. Told her I'd call her that evening. She reminded me she had Carmen the receptionist coming over.

I knew that. It had just escaped me. I said that I'd call her tomorrow and she said to do that and – with my arm stinging from the donation, chest torn by the Maximal – I walked. Cut through the park, indulgently regarding the ducks. Reached the address five minutes early. 10.25.

A handsome white-brick townhouse. Intercom beside the door. Inside, up one flight of stairs, a bland but comfortable anteroom. I looked in vain for a receptionist. Took a seat on a stiff-backed green couch. Apart from that and a reception desk (empty), there was no other furniture. A wall clock hung opposite. I checked my watch against it. They were out of sync. I was two minutes ahead. 10.29, by my time.

I followed the second-hand of each, glancing from one to the other. Til the interior door opened and a guy in his late thirties with thin-framed glasses and a curt scrub of russet hair came out.

Matthew? he said, and I got to my feet and shook his hand. I'm David Kushman. Would you like to come through?

Inside, a desk, two deep armchairs facing, a low square coffee table. A view of the park from the window.

He asked if I'd like coffee, and I told him yes. He walked over to a half-full cafetière on his desk, then handed me a cup, with saucer. Said he hoped it was still warm. His receptionist, he said, had called in sick this morning. As a result, he'd been a little overrun.

The coffee was lukewarm. I drank it anyway. Crossed my legs and returned the smile he now had trained on me.

So, he said. And wordlessly kept the smile on me for one, two, three, four, five, six, seven, eight –

So, I said. And we stayed there, clasped, til I checked my watch again. 10.34.

I didn't check again for another ten minutes. In that time, he smiled at me, and I smiled back. We established that I'd come here on the advice of Eric Handler but that I wasn't a friend of Eric's as such, simply a fan to whom he had passed on Kushman's details. There were a number of long silences, two of which were broken by him asking how my coffee was. Each time I told him it was fine. Then he'd smile at me again, and I'd smile back. 10.44.

And what, he said, would you say you were looking to get out of this?

I don't know, I said. I guess I just wanted someone to talk to.

About what?

I'm . . . not really sure.

He smiled at me.

269

OK. So maybe you could tell me why, after Eric gave you my card, you went ahead and called my office? Eric told you to come and –

He didn't *tell* me . . . He just gave me your card.

Eric gave you my card, and that was why you called me?

Yes.

So what if he'd given you a card for an optician? Or a taxidermist? Would you have called them too?

No . . . I mean . . . is this . . . what is this?

Is what what?

You sit there and trip me up? Make me feel stupid?

I'm not trying to make you feel stupid, Matthew. I'm trying to find out why you're here, and how I might be able to help you.

Pause.

I didn't know where to look, so I lifted my eyes to the window. He stood, walked to his desk and picked up a file. Sat back down and opened it. Mentioned he saw that I'd told his receptionist that I worked as a concierge. I clarified my role at The Greatest Gift, then glanced down at my watch. 10.47.

And you like it? Your work?

Oh, absolutely.

What is it that you like about it?

I like the idea that I'm . . . someone people can rely on . . . It's nice to do work that people appreciate.

It's nice to do it, or it's nice they appreciate it?

Well . . . both.

Hm-hm. And how are things outside of work? You know . . . friends, family . . . hobbies . . . that kind of thing.

Oh, I'm busy . . . I like to exercise . . . I've got a multistation gym at home. Pro weights. It's a good set-up.

And he smiled again.

So how about the rest of it?

The rest of . . .?

You know . . . friends. Family.

Oh. Well . . . I have a girlfriend.

And have you talked with her about coming here?

No.

Can I ask why not?

It just isn't . . . we don't . . . I didn't really want to worry her.

But she must realise something's wrong?

Why?

Well, I'm assuming you might have seemed down recently . . . preoccupied. Difficult to be around.

No, I don't think so . . . I mean, when I'm there . . .

You don't live together?

No . . . We haven't been seeing each other that long . . . I mean . . .

Hm-hm?

I have a wife. And a daughter . . . I mean, an ex-wife . . . It's not . . . like that.

You're divorced?

Separated.

OK . . . And do you still see her? Your wife?

Not since I left.

Since *you* left?

Right.

Pause.

I mean, I've sent money. It's not like I've abandoned them.

Hm-hm . . . And your daughter? Have you seen her?

I told him I was going to call, that I tried to call. That I'd found my own way of keeping in contact. He asked if that contact included my wife, and I told him I doubted she'd be missing me.

Did she tell you she wouldn't? Before you left?

No . . . I mean, that's part of why I left . . . But no, she didn't say that . . . Not in those words. We were married a long time. Certain things don't need . . . articulating.

I crossed my legs. Put my coffee down on the table, then picked it up again. Noticed a ball of fluff on my sleeve. Removed it.

So, what's the other part?

Sorry?

271

You said your wife wouldn't miss you, and that was part of why you left. I wondered what the other part was?

I don't know.

Pause.

All of it, I said, and when he pressed me, I told him it was just hard to be somewhere and know you were a disappointment. To know the people you're with need more than you can give. So you put your stuff into packing cases, and ten months later you're living on Bethune Street.

He smiled.

To make them realise what they were missing?

No. That's . . . I don't know . . . At the time, it seemed self-evident.

And now?

I didn't know the answer, so I chose not to give one. Gazed at the beech tree outside the window for one, two, three, four –

Do you see your family at all, Matthew? Parents? Brothers or sisters?

Oh, I said. You mean, tell me about your mother?

You can tell me about your mother if you like. It's not compulsory. Do you want to talk about your mother? Would that be relevant?

You tell me.

I've no idea. You haven't even told me why you're here.

Pause.

I told him I didn't buy it. That I could see what he was trying to do, and I thought it was hokum. The simple-minded notion that I pour out some childhood melancholia and then it's there, uncovered like a fossil. The source of all my problems.

He kept staring at me, but now he wasn't smiling.

Who said that?

I bit my bottom lip.

Pause.

You know . . . I can barely remember what she looks like.

I close my eyes and I see someone. But the face is hazy . . . indefinite. Like it's in shadow.

Your mother's face?

Pause.

Is this something that you want to discuss?

I tried sipping at the coffee, but it was stone cold by now.

When did you last have contact with your parents, Matthew?

I don't . . . I don't believe in that kind of thing.

In what kind of thing?

They're dead.

I'm sorry.

It was a long time ago. It's not important.

Do you miss them?

No. I don't think I do.

Hm-hm.

And I know what you're thinking. That I'm callous. Unfeeling.

Is that how you see yourself, Matthew?

No . . . I didn't say that . . . I mean . . . I wish they were alive. It's just they were never . . . the people that you take your example from, the people you lean on . . . that wasn't . . . how they were. So I don't miss that. Because I never had it.

When you say that wasn't how they were . . . how were they? Were they hostile toward you? Toward one another?

No . . . There was never any hostility.

Pause.

There was never anything. I . . . just wasn't a priority. I went to school, and I came home from school, and they might ask me how my day had been and they might not, but there was usually a snack for me at just past five, and dinner at seven and they'd say goodnight before I went to bed. And no, they never shouted at me. Beat me. Any of that stuff . . . But I wish they had . . . I wish I'd merited that kind of attention. I wish they felt strongly enough about me to do that.

I knew how that sounded.

That sounds sick, right?

273

I wouldn't say that, Matthew. It's hard to be ignored. Can you remember what they were doing while they ignored you?

Pause.

My mother took pills.

What kind of pills?

Pause.

Tranquillizers. Sedatives. I don't know the names. My father would tell me she was feeling blue. That's what he called it. She'd take to her bed. Then everything would go quiet . . . Some weeks, I wouldn't see her at all. She'd be upstairs, but I wasn't allowed in their room. And I just remember the silence in the house. All three of us there, not a whisper for days. You've never heard a silence like it. A silence like a church bell, ringing right beside you.

And how was your father when this was going on?

He was never much of a conversationalist. His career had kind of . . . disintegrated. I think that had a big effect on him. On his outlook.

What did he do?

He was an accountant.

Hm-hm.

And you know . . . I never did anything of note, so they didn't have to spend a lot of time on me. I was never exceptional either way. My grades were OK. I didn't fight with the other kids or argue with the teachers. I never gave them reason to worry, and I never gave them cause to celebrate. We moved from here to there and . . . they dealt with their . . . situation . . . and I was just there. And it wasn't that they treated me badly. They treated me . . . *politely* . . .

I realised I was crying.

. . . like a lodger who pays their rent on time and always keeps their room in order.

Pause.

But you know . . . like I say . . . I really don't know how . . . relevant this is. Everyone's got their sob stories. You must have heard worse than mine. I know I have.

Different circumstances, he said, affect different people in different ways. It's not my role to judge one person's hardship against another's. Can I ask you when they died?

I'd just started college . . . It was a house fire. I don't know how it started. I was back for a weekend . . . I took the bus home. The stop was at the end of my street. When I got off, I heard sirens. And of course you wonder if it's your house they're coming from. You get that flutter in your gut. But you know it couldn't ever really be your house. So you walk, and you keep not seeing anything outside any of the houses you're passing, and the sirens have stopped but you can make out the lights from the engines instead . . .

Pause.

. . . And then I saw it . . . Just smoke, really. And I kept squinting to check I was right. That it was there. That I was looking on the right side of the road. That I was even on the right road. But it was definitely their house . . . There were maybe half a dozen firemen outside. People, watching . . . Neighbours. I didn't know any of them . . . I wanted to get in. One of the firemen pulled me back. Had me by the shoulder, you know? So I stood there. Watching, with the rest of them . . . Til I saw my father at the bedroom window. I could just about make out it was him through the smoke. He broke the glass. I saw him jump . . . And I just remember thinking he'd be really ticked off about the lawn. You know, with the fire trucks chewing it up. He didn't get excited about much, but he was really protective of the lawn. And now . . .

Pause.

. . . I wanted to get to him. They wouldn't let me . . . The next day, they said he was so badly burned he'd have been dead by the time he hit the ground anyway.

I was crying hard now. Great, authentic saline tears. I tried to recall how long it had been since I'd cried in front of another person.

Kushman was nodding. Like somehow he approved. Wanted more. And the least I could do was give him that.

And ever since then, I said, I've felt useless. Useless to the world. To my wife, my daughter. To everyone. Worse than useless. Like a curse . . . So I never took the money . . . Believe me, it mounted up. My parents were very frugal people. They had savings. Life insurance. But I've never touched it. I keep it in a separate account. It's wrong for me to have it. I did nothing for it. I don't want it and I don't deserve it . . . At first, I didn't know what to do with it. Then there was Alice.

Alice is –

My daughter . . . And I thought it could be hers. That way, it might do some good. So I'm keeping it for her til she's old enough.

OK . . . And you think then she might not see you as useless? . . . Or that you might not see yourself that way?

My words, delivered between sobs.

I don't know . . . I try all this stuff. I try and be a good person. I'm always ready to lend a hand. I don't care what I have to do. If I see someone in pain and I can alleviate it, I will. And I still feel like . . . nothing. Like I could disappear off the face of the earth and it wouldn't make a difference to a living soul. I could just stay locked in my apartment and the sun would still come up and the stores would open and the clients would still get their wake-up calls and tickets for the theatre, and the ducks would swim in the park, and if I was lucky I might get a little white box in the back of the paper, but otherwise . . . who'd remember me? I'm no great loss. I'm just a bystander . . . And I don't want to feel like this any more.

11.23.

By now, I was caked in tears and snot. Kushman turned, reached for a box of tissues from the window sill. The kind with the triple-ply strength and absorbency. He turned back, handed them to me. I guess it was force of habit, but I made sure to wipe my face with my hand before I took them from him. When my palm brushed his, I saw him wince.

OK, he said. Well, I certainly think we're going to have a lot to talk about the next time that we meet.

276

That's that? I said.

Well, he said, I think what we've learned today is we should definitely meet again. And that we've made some pretty substantial progress already.

There were no fresh tears now. Only the residue.

So, how long's this going to take? I said.

How long will what take?

This.

Pause.

It's impossible to say. How long it will take til we've worked through the issues you've talked about today is largely up to you. What I can tell you is that what I do here has come a long way from the type of thing you might see on TV or in films. That's not really an accurate portrayal. We take a much more recovery-based approach these days. A patient endlessly going over the reasons for their depression is perhaps less important than finding ways to combat it.

You think I'm depressed?

Yes, Matthew, I do.

I wiped my eyes a final time, and something in his expression told me what was coming next. And it came. A pale yellow form assigning me tablets with a subtly cheery brand name whose side effects, he told me, might include nausea, hot flushes, headaches and insomnia.

I told him I thought the last one was unlikely and made another appointment. He had to put it in his diary himself, given his temp's non-appearance. Showed me back out to the anteroom, and told me I'd done well.

I thought about what I'd said to him for the rest of the day and longer. Replayed chance snippets. Collected my prescription on my way home from Pearl Street, headed back to the apartment, my weights, my rower, the Maximal. And after that, I made my way to the hospital.

When I arrived, both the girl's parents were leant up by the vending machine on the ground floor. I saw them, ashen, haggard, with an elderly woman I took to be a grandmother.

I checked their features each in turn, panning through a semi-circle, trying to make out which side of the family she might be from. I thought perhaps the mother's.

Then a doctor, sombre and discreet. He whispered in the father's ear. Stepped aside, then beckoned down the hall. The father glanced back, and in a razored moment, I thought I caught his eye. Then all four departed.

I watched them leave. Thought of the girl, three floors up, interred. Surrounded by machines that droned and buzzed. Thought of her there on her own, and I hated it. If she woke now, what would she think? That she'd been abandoned, left here without reason?

Of course, I understood her parents would have to consult with staff in private. But she wouldn't. I guess it was just fortunate I was there.

I took the lift to the third floor. Paced through the beige enamel. Stopped outside the window. I could see that she was sleeping. Face slack and breathing steady.

I scanned the hall for passing orderlies. Approached the door. No creak or scrape as it opened. Subduing every footstep. Terrified I might disturb her.

A tube lodged down her throat, another in each arm. I took a seat on the bed adjacent. A still-warm dent in the blanket. Her hand, limp at her side, hanging down into the air. It struck me I should have brought her something. A gift; a card, at least. This way seemed so thoughtless.

Her eyes flickered beneath their lids. The body chatter of a dream. I inched forward til we were level.

I know this is hard, I said, but you're really a lucky girl. Because there's so many people out there rooting for you.

I listened as she breathed.

And we know that you're going to get better. That you'll be all better very soon.

The thumb of her left hand twitched, then calmed.

And I know that I couldn't give you what you need myself. But I would have. If they'd let me. Please believe that. I'd never have let you down . . . And I don't know why things work out the way they do. Why you got sick. Why I can't help. I guess sometimes you just have to trust that there's a reason.

I stared around the room and, for the briefest pulse in time, I was gone, transported.

A boy of five in another city hospital, watching a patient die.

I was big for my age, but I still only came up as high as the mattress. Had to crane to see her. The strip lights in my eyes.

My sister was eight.

She was eight, and I was five.

Her name was Madeline.

She'd only been ill for two years, so I guess before we must have played together, but I don't remember that at all. Now, I know she had a rare disorder; hereditary. Carried in my father's genes.

Then I just stood there as she wheezed and disappeared. Listening to the sound of breath obstructed. Holding myself perfectly still, checking for a gasp or rattle. There, in a private room, away from the others. The place where nightmares are. The absolute centre.

And every now and then a doctor would appear and my father would usher me outside, and I'd wait in the hallway, pitching a yo-yo or sucking on hard sweets. And I'd come back in when the doctor had gone, and my mother would be crying while my father stood over my sister. Watching her chest rise and fall.

And she took so long to go.

Weeks, then months, through rallies and dashed hopes, my parents looking past me as I gawped beside her, useless. And I hated her. Hated her for doing this. Sometimes prayed that she would heal, at others for me to be struck down too and share in their attentions. I knew envy before I could label it. And when the hospital finally cleared the room, and my parents laid out a black suit on my bed, then I knew guilt too.

Of course, I never talked about her. Never told a living soul. Almost, on occasion. But not quite.

Til I came back to the moment, the girl with the lung disorder asleep beside me. And, in a snap, I realised how long I'd been there with her.

Rising, I lay her hand across her chest.

I have to go now, I said. Then I left. Closed the door as softly as I could.

When the lift returned me to the ground, I got out just in time to see the parents and grandmother come back around the corner. I caught the father's eye, again. Swerved into the admissions room.

It was their time now. I had no wish to distract them.

And I just sat, observing. Thought back over the day. Mortimer and Upas. Kushman, of course. His all-knowing smile. And now I felt rent open. Raw, exhibited. What would I tell Alice I was doing here, were she to appear beside me?

And I asked, out loud, to my shock and embarrassment:

How long will this take?

Squinting Dimly at Your Own Reflection

You can go into space as a tourist now. They'll take you out for a week in a Soyuz. You can even pay in instalments.

Sometimes I wish I had a memento, a hunk of rock or a mission badge. All of that – what little there was – burned up with the house.

And, in the short term, nothing changes. You just go on. Kushman's questions single gunshots released into an echo chamber.

It's nice to do it, or it's nice they appreciate it?

To make them realise what they were missing?

What kind of pills?

Mine were yellow capsules. They could have been for anything. To be taken once daily with food, alongside the vitamins, Provigil, herbs.

I waited for a change in disposition. Waited, kept waiting.

How's the coffee?

The coffee was great. Slapped me into life as I washed and dressed. Ready for the next barren day at Pearl Street.

And so I fall.

Palms open, eyes shut.

Beyond the window of the second floor.

I've never met the woman that lives there. She only moved in a week ago. Took over the place from a couple called Hudson. I barely knew them either. Carl told me her surname was Dean and she'd just moved to the city. Some kind of computer troubleshooter, he thought.

There are countless ways in which the long-term city resident makes obvious their status. The knowledge of where the taxis are at midnight, the nature of certain unmarked premises, an

acrid snobbery or wide-eyed awe over what – to outsiders – are
simply random postal codes. Laurel Dean adds to the list a
practised disregard of the underground map.

She stands in the subway beneath Demotte station, before
the prismatic tangle of lines and dots mounted on the platform
wall. Going to be late for her 12.30. A data retrieval at a car
dealership in Vimont. Wherever that is.

The PA system echoes down the platform. Its exact message
is buried by poor acoustics, leaving only fragments of verbs and
station names. Laurel sighs, baffled by routes she can't follow,
instructions she can't understand. She doesn't know how any
of these places look, outside, above ground, for real.

Try the map again. Take the first train to Beacon Street,
change at Ogden Ave. No, Pelham. Then Ogden Ave. No,
wait, not Pelham. Eastern Market. Definitely Eastern Market.
Or Mohren Street. Or Russian Hill. She recoils at the
strangers' elbows in her ribs, then crouches, easing into the
space between poster hoardings. Her laptop rests beside her.
For safety, she pulls it onto her knees.

Another missive from the public address. Going by the rum-
blings around her, she gleans the next train's been cancelled.
Or delayed. One of the two. An unending stream of people file
onto the platform, wending, barging. Where are they all going to
fit? There's no room as it is.

Stretching out her legs, she closes down the laptop and
holds it to her chest. It's OK. Sitting here, out of sight, dispas-
sion washes over her. Indefinite delays, a voice says adjacent,
exasperated. But that's fine with her. For the moment, she's
happy just sitting here. Just sitting here, almost lost, it's all OK.

Arriving at work, there was a memo. Sent from Mike.
Requesting my attendance in the meeting room. He was at
my cubicle by the time I finished reading it.

Did you get the memo? he said.

I told him I had, and we walked across the office past the
unlit phones. Took our seats. He spoke enthusiastically about

a TV show he'd seen the previous night. I hadn't watched it myself.

Then he hesitated. The way he always did right before he got to whatever it was he actually wanted to talk about.

So . . . Jonah Hoffman called me last night.

And I found myself afraid.

He wanted to run something past me, Mike said. An idea he himself was amenable toward. The idea, he said, was this.

He and Mr Hoffman had discussed my being seconded. There was a project, he said, that Mr Hoffman had asked for my help with. The idea, he said, was that I'd spend some time over at Dutch Street. Just temporarily. Working on the project. He asked me how I felt about that, and I wasn't sure what to say. I couldn't see my answer would have much effect.

I asked him what the project was. Jonah hadn't specified.

But look out there, he said. No one's calling. I thought you'd welcome the chance to get some work done.

I knew I should have been pleased. Cheered by such explicit restoration of Jonah's trust. I was. It was just spiked with regret that Mike was willing to let me go so freely. Everything he said made sense. I imagined Jonah was paying well for my exclusivity. And yes, the phones weren't ringing. All the same.

I was to meet Jonah in two hours. He would be at home, Mike said. Again, something told me this was not a subject for debate.

So I drove north to Jonah's. Reaching the house I saw his car, parked outside the gate. Him in it. Felt my pager vibrate.

Jonah. His message said to roll down my passenger side window. By the time I had, he was standing beside it. Leaning in to address me.

Lovely day, he said.

The sky was clear, it was true. But the cold severe, intransigent.

I thought we might head over to the course, he said. It's just reopened.

And he turned back. Slowed then stopped halfway. Gazed for seconds at his fence. Walked up to it, fractiously rattled its links. Lingered motionless before the security camera. Rattled the links once more. Shook his head and retreated inside the car.

I sat tight, awaiting further instruction. Half expected him to page me again. Finally, he rolled down his own window and gestured at me to follow. And we drove off in tandem, my eyes fixed on the back of his head. Took a right turn after maybe ten minutes. A small sign:

Avelden Country Club

and a wooded approach road, leading to the clubhouse. A spruce colonial facade of smooth white stone and hearty gables. Like Jonah's house cloned four times, lain horizontal. A flag billowing above.

We each pulled in. Parked, he took his clubs from the back. Appeared at my window again. Told me to stay where I was. Disappeared inside, and returned with a laminated guest pass.

We walked round the clubhouse to a paved veranda where trellis tables would surely be in warmer months, looking over a gleaming line of golf carts and the seemingly measureless expanse of the course itself. Three impassive caddies leant up by the wall, waiting to be chartered. Jonah ignored them, directed me to a buggy. Plum, roomier than most family cars.

And so we headed out. Club bag propped between us. The wrinkle of the leather inches from my face. Heads protruding. Graphite orchids. I was still staring at them when we pulled up. He stepped out, grabbed the bag.

Fantastic, he said, aren't they?

The first hole was on an even green. I could see why he liked it so much out here.

Tour brochure pretty. Lush hillocks, aged trees. The pleasures of the country without the undertow of malice and hazard.

He removed a club, thrust the bag toward me.

Would you?

Of course, I said, and I bore it over my shoulder.

He took a ball from a zipped compartment. Placed it on a tee. Splayed his feet and raised his club waist high. Seemed to take an age to settle. After at least a minute, he brought his left knee in at an angle to his right leg. Swung above and behind and took his shot.

I watched the ball tear into the distance, narrowing my eyes against the sun. I had no idea if what he'd just done was good or bad. Monitored his expression for some hint or indication. He just replaced the club.

We were almost at the second hole when he mentioned Reilly. I blanched at his name. He simply asked if I'd heard from him.

I said I'd tried calling a dozen times, but no, I hadn't.

No, he said, Neither have I.

He didn't seem concerned. Just found the situation curious. And again, he brought the cart to a halt, again I held his club bag and again, as he took his shot, I dawdled mute beside.

On the way to the third, we talked about his holiday. He said it had been perfect. Among the best weeks of his life. Everything warm, clean, proficient, attentive, in place, on time, as it should be. He hadn't wanted to come back. Then he paused.

Other than for the family, of course, he said.

Between the third and fourth, I asked after Christina and Julian. Both fine, he said.

And the gingko? I said.

Oh, better now.

And he pulled the buggy over. This time, after his shot, I caught a reaction. A soft whistle. Ambiguous at best.

Approaching the fifth, I realised we were opposite where we'd begun. He sat without dismounting for a moment. Just revelling in the stillness.

So, I said, is the fence OK? . . . At the house?

He looked at me blankly.

You were rattling it. You seemed . . . annoyed.

Which had worried me ever since. I, after all, had hired the firm responsible.

Annoyed, he said, like he'd never heard the word before. No . . . I wouldn't say annoyed. Perplexed. That's what I'd say.

He blinked into the light.

You know what it makes me think of? Shi Huang. The emperor who built the Great Wall. The strange thing is, he was also a book burner. He nurtured lofty goals. Ending local conflicts. The introduction of script. Weights and measures. Coins. And to do this he fought against the plague of introspection. Unproductive thought. And what feeds unproductive thought? Books. In this case, Confucius. So he burned them. And now, because the Confucians, the foot binders, because they seized power after his death, his reputation stinks. So you think, well, maybe the guy's had a raw deal. Because now we sit here two thousand dully introspective years later, and we navel-gaze and scratch ourselves and ponder and babble, and you can't even pay someone, *pay* someone, to build a fence around your house that might stand up in a rainstorm . . . So, like I say, it perplexes me.

And then he stepped out.

Anyway, he said . . . not your fault.

He took his shot, and we moved on.

We were at the tenth when I raised the matter of what I was here for.

So, Mike told me there was a project . . . Something you needed some help with.

Oh, he said, that's right.

And he pulled the buggy over one more time.

OK, he said. It's like this.

The tenth hole was set beside a lake. Trees on one side, water on the other. We stepped onto the grass and, as he reached for his clubs, he told me that like a lot of business people, he was forever receiving pleas for money. Piteous appeals from supposedly – he emphasised supposedly – worthy causes. Begging letters of extraordinary length and harrowing detail.

Of course, he said, if you took them at face value, you'd have nightmares.

They started after his first interview in a finance magazine. When he appeared on the cover, they multiplied. Word gets round, he said. Another teat for suckling.

Anyway, he said, Bonnie files them away til the end of each financial year. Then we look them over. You can't just ignore these people, can you? Not the genuine. Only my funds aren't limitless. There are always those that have to be turned away. The vast majority, in fact. Even then, it's time consuming. Time consuming and . . . draining. So this year –

I understand, I said.

Good, he said. It shouldn't take you long. I'll prepare a budget. You just need to sift through them. Find the most deserving. I'm sure you get the idea.

I told him I did, and he said he didn't trust anyone else to get the job done right. And now, at last, I felt snug again. Esteemed. The aberration of Reilly already consigned to history.

He chose his club, and handed me the bag.

So does that sound like something you might be interested in?

I told him that it was. We shook on it.

His ball was by a thicket of reeds, just yards from the water. I stood back, let him get into position. Heard a clamour from the rushes as soon as he went near them. A steady, guttural moan, til Jonah stepped away. It ebbed into a grumble, then stopped.

Jonah cleared his throat, as if replying. Brought his left foot back around and re-assumed his stance.

And then the noise again. Angrier now, more emphatic. A shrill hiss; bustling disturbance.

Jesus, he said, peering down.

He stabbed his club into the reeds, then reeled back cursing. Fled. Abandoned the club and took to his heels. Through instinct I did likewise, even though I'd yet to see the nature of his fright.

Then I did. A black swan. Three feet, maybe taller. Much of that neck. Wings spread into a reaper's cloak, eyes and bill a matching devil red. Furious and wrathful. It charged from the rushes like a guided missile. Thick grey legs bearing it across the short grass, wings beating frantically. Its hiss a rasping scream.

It made straight for Jonah. Head jabbing at him, bill snapping. And all the time, that scabrous, otherworldly noise.

I suppose it had eggs by the water. Maybe cygnets. And this was simply parental devotion, issued into pure, unyielding rage.

I thought I should intervene. Cowardice dissuaded me. It jutted its neck and champed at Jonah's elbow. He cursed again and scraped away.

It tilted at him. Clamped its bill around his hand a second. His left. Nipping at the flesh, his fingers. And I heard him crying out.

The next few seconds unfolded as a bullfight. Rush and parry. Lunge, rebuff. Jonah trying to escape. The swan obstructing him at every turn. It went for his thigh. Seemed to butt him in the calf as he shielded himself.

And I saw him drop by the water's edge. Reach for his club, take it in his right hand, then scramble to his feet and wait. His face the same mask of earnest absorption that he wore at the tee.

Hands wrapped round the shaft, he lifted it above him. The swan charged once more, and Jonah pitched forward to meet it. He brought the club down as he did so.

Cracked it full might across the bird's head. Just once.

And then I didn't breathe for one, two, three, four, five.

Til, my head turned away, I exhaled. Looked back just far enough to see it. Only from the corner of my eye. On its side, unmoving.

And Jonah stepped away again. Scrutinised his club.

I still couldn't look at the swan. Not directly. But I saw his club was dripping. Fell to my knees as the bile rose in my throat. Stayed there maybe thirty seconds.

Then, Jonah's shoes. I looked up, and he handed me a tissue to wipe my mouth. Threw the club into the buggy. It was another minute before I could stand. Numbly sit beside him.

His left hand bleeding from a gouge between thumb and index.

I think I'm going to call it a day, he said.

And he spun the cart around. Sped back to the clubhouse.

Neither of us spoke. At the fifth, I couldn't help but glance over at the club. Gagged when I did.

At the second, another buggy passed us, trundling leisurely in the other direction. The same as ours but teal. Two old men inside. They waved, but we didn't wave back. We just drove on.

At the clubhouse, he said he'd call me to fix up the letters. I thought I should ask if he needed any help, but he'd run back to the cart by the time it crossed my mind.

I guess he had things to attend to.

And so, in the sanctum of the jade green automatic, I gladly left the Avelden. Ten minutes later, by the roadside, I was sick again.

The rest of the afternoon was mine. Mike wasn't expecting me back at Pearl Street.

What – practically – was there to return for anyway?

I took the appropriate junction, and pointed the car toward Eleanor's.

Half-term, and she's teaching. Scrawling in her notebook. Planning a lesson for that evening's class. The students at Cale Street, they seem to like her. Becoming more receptive.

Eleanor's portfolio lies beside her. She thought of taking it in to show them. Undecided. Wary of their judgement. She leafs through the landscapes, portraiture. Years of effort, technique, experimentation, held beneath plastic. Makes her feel ossified. And like she needs a cigarette.

She can't. She resolves instead to tidy. Keep her mind from craving. Alice is out at the Karlssons. She wanders into her room. Socks wilting from an open drawer. A long disused rocking horse. Yet more glo-stars. Belinda Griselda, propped up on the bed. The second time this week she's left the house without her.

Eleanor changes the sheets. Tucks and flattens. Returns downstairs and opens the windows. Pulls the cigarettes from her bag. Matches. A booklet. Printed with the name of the restaurant from last night. The venue of her date.

The act of a single woman. And she enjoyed it. All the things she'd forgotten the sense of. One kiss at the end of the night, in the car. And past the flare of guilt, it thrilled her. So why should she refuse herself? For what? An unresolved memory? Maybe it's time to formalise this. To call her lawyer.

She tears out a match. A thin black strip with a crimson head. Stares from the living-room window. A car directly opposite, modest, green. Easing away from the kerbside. Her stomach flips at who it is.

She just knows. And upstairs, in her own room now, she searches for the note.

I looked back as I drove away and I was sure I saw a face at the window. A ripple of the curtains, a glimmer of motion. Drove fast, back to the city. I wanted to make it before the stores closed.

Everything turns three-sixty. Alice's birthday was coming up. Her seventh, at last. Her first since I left.

And now I knew how to mark it. How to deliver the most special day of all. I'd reflected on the options over and again, and now my mind was made up.

I was going home. Ending my quarantine. Whatever purpose I'd been serving had either been satisfied or rendered obsolete. I would return.

Grace clean slipped my mind.

I wasn't naive. I knew that Eleanor and I were damaged. Perhaps in time we'd mend. Perhaps we couldn't. Might glimpse a rediscovery of what first tied us. Maybe not. Was it so outlandish to see us being us, again?

There were hurdles, of course. But Alice didn't need to know that. She just needed me. And for that hallowed reason her mother and I would find a way. Come to an arrangement. Sublimate our differences.

There are always answers. And I would make sure that

Alice could believe that. My gift to her. There would, of course, be others. I'd been working on a list since Christmas.

With my account refreshed by payday, I drove up to the toy store. Parked on the corner of Bethune and Sheridan. It was like the homeless had never been there. I walked in with my wallet full. Kept my mind on the task at hand, and only that. No swan, no club. When I got back to my building, weighed down with bags, Carl was in the lobby, reading. I'd never seen him read before.

Hello, Carl.

Hello, Mr Viss.

And he told me there was a package. A fat square in brown paper, couriered that afternoon. I took it from him with the rest of my post. Said I'd open it upstairs.

Inside, I attended to the mail. A second letter from the Marchmont Gym Warehouse, chasing the unreceived payment on the Maximal. I wrote myself a Post-It Note to remind me to take care of it. Stuck it to the fridge.

Then, the parcel.

It held a lavish photographic book. Pictures of the Great Wall. The view from space. A further illustrated section devoted to the Terracotta Army. A card attached. It said, in Jonah's handwriting:

To let you know how glad I am you could come aboard for the project. And my sincere apologies for the earlier unpleasantness – J.

I took a bath, ate. Drank coffee, chewed gum. Swallowed my round of pills. A pair of messages on my answerphone. The first from Two Cities. The same effusive woman who always called, only now even she sounded tired. I skipped past her to the second. Knew who it was before she even spoke.

Hi, she said, it's me . . . Look . . . I'd be grateful if you just send a card. For her sake. Just so she knows that you haven't forgotten.

And her voice rose in pitch and volume.

I don't know what you thought you were doing today. But

I don't want you doing it again. I don't want you creeping round outside like . . . why didn't you just . . .

And she trailed away. I stood there, dumb.

You can't do this, Matthew. You can't just . . . Look. Either be a real father to her, or just send a card. Don't . . . confuse her any more than you have already . . . Please.

I didn't even finish my coffee. Pulled on my jacket, left the apartment. Journeyed again to where I had to. Took the lift to the third floor of the hospital, then walked on to the room. Kept a watchful eye for orderlies.

When I looked inside she wasn't there. Her bed was mussed. Recently slept in. A tray of food uneaten by the window. And she wasn't there.

I rang with fear. Became distraught. Searched for a doctor, orderly, anyone. I ran past scores of private rooms, to the one ward on the floor. A double row of beds and patients. Adult men. Most behind drapes. Few visitors. A nurse, ahead of me.

Can I help you? she said.

And I said I was a relative of the girl with the lung disorder. That I'd come here to see her. Only now she wasn't there. And the nurse took me by the elbow, and told me there'd been a problem. A sudden deterioration. She was in intensive care now. And I asked where that was, and the nurse said the fourth floor, right upstairs, but that I couldn't go up there without any –

I was gone already. Bolting the stairs. The fourth floor, beige enamel. I sprinted down the hallway til it split in two.

Looked left and saw the father, conferring with a doctor. Stood and watched, resourceless, til the doctor absented himself.

I walked swiftly toward the father. Like I was mesmerised. And he glanced up just in time to see me as I threw my arms around him. I ignored the tensing of his shoulders. Carried on the hug. I guess it felt as strange for him as it did for me.

It's going to be OK, I said.

dummy dummy

The first day at Dutch Street, Jonah let me use his private office. Disorienting, the whole experience. Turning left out of my building not right. Getting my coffee from a different franchise, with unfamiliar staff in exotic livery. Seeing the mirrored wall in the elevator rather than Pearl Street's bare metal.

Jonah wasn't there when I arrived. Bonnie let me in. She said he'd be out all day, but he'd told her to tell me I could use his office.

She knew why I was here. Her manner almost kindly. Much of that, I guess, came down to my liberating her from doing this herself. I was still grateful as she showed me through. Waited by the door as I slipped behind the desk. Jonah's face on the magazine covers hanging right above me. The gingko, sure enough, was thriving.

I'll let you get settled in, she said. Before you get started.

And I sat, lost in the view from the fifteenth floor. Tapping out a rhythm on the sleek mahogany. Til she brought in the letters. A brown cardboard document box. Then another.

OK, she said, that's both of them. And she told me I should just call through if I needed anything. I said I would, and she closed the door behind her.

I pulled the first box closer. Removed the lid. Full to the brim with envelopes, 8" x 4", addresses handwritten or sometimes typed. Opened, resealed, and left here. Five hundred, surely, maybe more. I remembered what Jonah had said before allocating my budget.

Weed out the phoney. Locate the most deserving.

And so I picked a letter from the box. Chosen arbitrarily, postmarked from Duvernay. Three pages. Written with a careful hand. I sipped at my coffee and read.

Dear Mr Jonah Hoffman, it began, *I am writing this letter because I hope you can find it within you to help. My name is Wesley Abbott and for the last 3 years it has been my real pleasure to know a man called Joel Meskis.*

And the writer then explained that he was fifteen and a resident of the Shawcross Children's Facility, over in Russian Hill.

I first met Joel Meskis when he came here to do a magic show, Wesley Abbott wrote, *and we all thought it would be terrible. But we still all went to see it.*

Joel Meskis, he went on, was just a few years older than himself. He didn't even have the proper clothes. The top hat or the cape. Except, when they saw him perform, he was incredible. Dazzling feats of illusion, outrageous sleights of hand. All executed in perfect, eerie silence.

Better than anything you will ever see on TV.

And afterward, the boys crowded round him. Slapped his back and cheered. And he would simply nod and smile.

Over the next week, they pestered the warden who had brought them Joel Meskis for information about him. Til finally, he cracked. Told them he'd lived at Shawcross too. That's how he knew him. That's where he'd started his magic. He had, the warden said, been abandoned by his mother, impoverished, unable to speak English. Given up to vicious foster parents, who abused and then rejected him. And then to Shawcross.

And we all knew this story, Wesley Abbott said, *'cause this was our life too.*

At sixteen, he'd left. Alone, cursed with a brutal stammer. He began to sleep rough. Sought comfort in heroin. Now, however, the warden said, he was clean. Living in a hostel. And in the coming months, he returned to Shawcross many times. Each show a new pinnacle of wonder. To the residents there, Joel Meskis was a star.

So they were delighted when the warden told them he'd moved into a halfway house. Was trying, with the warden's help, to find his mother. But, even then, and later once he found a job in the kitchen of a city restaurant, he still performed at Shawcross. And now, when the boys applauded, he'd slowly, bashfully, thank them.

He moved into his first apartment. Had never seemed happier. His act more inspired. The warden told them he'd made contact with his mother. After having to give him up, she'd moved back to her family abroad. Now worked as a secretary. They'd twice talked on the phone.

So no one was surprised or begrudging when the visits tailed off. He had a job now, after all. A home. Even a family.

He had _made it_! Wesley Abbott wrote.

Only that wasn't the reason.

Three months after starting there, the restaurant in the city had closed down. Joel Meskis lost his job. He came to Shawcross afterward, but his performance was confused, haphazard. And when the boys flocked to him, the stammer made him impossible to understand.

Then they learned of a clerical error with his application for benefit. In days, he was homeless again. After that, no one saw him for almost a year. The only exception a boy who – following a supervised trip to the city – swore he'd glimpsed him begging.

We almost forgot about him then, Wesley Abbott said. *Except we didn't. We just couldn't admit it.*

Til one of the boys saw the warden looking mournful. And the warden said he'd seen Joel Meskis. That he'd been attacked by a gang of men who stole his coat and sleeping bag. When he'd tried resisting, they stamped on his hands. Ground his fingers. The warden was going to visit him in hospital. And all at Shawcross signed his cards.

It was six months before Joel Meskis returned. His performance only announced on the day. His hands were bandaged, certain intricacies now out of the question. But he still had it. Could still reduce his audience to gaping veneration.

And afterward they crowded round him, exactly like the first time. And when he'd left, the warden told the oldest boys that Joel Meskis would not be here again. That while he'd been in hospital, the doctors found a problem. A hereditary condition, long since embedded. No one could have known. It probably came from his father.

He had six months. His decline, steep and imminent.

And so, Wesley Abbott wrote, *the reason for this letter is to ask you to please help us to buy an aeroplane ticket for the mother of Joel Meskis so that she can visit him before it is too late. If you worry that I am not an honest person, here is my warden's name and number.*

And then he gave them.

We just want to repay him for the pleasure he brought to us. But we cannot afford the price of the ticket and some of our wardens have said they will have a sponsored run or something like that — but time is short. And if you can help us then all of us here will be forever thankful.

I lay the page to the right of me. First among those I would forward to Jonah. Took another sip of coffee. Picked it up, reread it. Winced. Then cried out. I'd gnawed so hard on my right-hand thumbnail it had ripped and pulled away, exposing the soft pink bedding underneath.

I took a breath and dipped into the box again. Pulling tickets at a raffle. The next, a girl disfigured by her boyfriend. He'd seen her talking with another man. Threw acid in her face.

And so I kept going. Waded through long, imploring missives from and on behalf of sanctuaries for battered wives, those alone in the final months of AIDS who couldn't afford a hospice, families whose homes had been lost to floods or were being repossessed by unforgiving creditors, usually right before the birth of a child. Victims of every conceivable malaise and degenerative illness, besieged with impossible bills. The chronically disabled needing renovations to their house or apartment just to maintain a tolerable life. Medical researchers stripped of their funding after decades of toil, frequently poised on the cusp of a breakthrough. Hardy single parents training as nurses, penniless from child care. Those injured in domestic or shopfloor accidents now unable to work again, or those family members caring for those injured in domestic or shopfloor accidents. Devoutly religious convicts attempting to start over. Elderly couples robbed of their savings by common theft or pension fraud. So many, many kids with cancer.

The worst were the ones with photographs. And they're all smiling. Trying to look optimistic. The older girls made up. Caps on the boys, pulled low to hide their chemo baldness.

And so on through the box. Looking down from the window of Jonah Hoffman's office. Drinking coffee. Gazing out on open sores.

With my head wheeling, I took an early lunch. Every bite more guilty than the last.

And then, begin again. It's like radiation. You don't even notice. And by now they're interchangeable. Funny how our palate never loses its discernment for a million different flavours of bright and spangly, famous, wishful. But the suffering all tastes the same.

Jonah came by around six. I was finishing up as he peered round the door. He asked how I was doing.

Great, I said, ah . . . do you need the office back?

Oh, no . . . Just passing.

He glanced at the papers on his desk.

Good work, he said.

Neither of us mentioned the swan. Then or ever. That night, on the treadmill, I closed my eyes as weary legs hauled me on through stationary miles, saw its red bill champing at my heels. Then joined in its pursuit by others. A chase scene from a silent movie. Grinning children with leukaemia, hounding me in wheelchairs. Joel Meskis, clawing at my back with broken hands.

The next morning, I returned to Dutch Street. Jonah was there all day. I worked in the first office down the hall. Smaller. Old files on creaking shelving units. Bonnie had already moved the letters and boxes.

Every couple of hours, I stepped outside for air. Stood in the place where the sun became a spotlight, warm and vivid. And then I'd return.

By six, there were three piles of letters. The first, the glaringly bogus. Maybe forty per cent of the total. The next, the same mass mail-outs from organised charities that Carl would hand me every day. Possibly a quarter.

Then the rest. The genuine. I immediately knew which ones they were. They were the ones I hoped were fake.

I stared into the box. Still halfway full. The second I hadn't even looked in yet. I could see the job stretching from a fortnight to a month, or longer. And I doubted my capacity for that.

I scooped a handful of letters into my bag. Said goodbye to Bonnie and Jonah. Read them inside the apartment that evening. Read, re-read, re-read again.

Jonah's budget would never be enough. And so, at home, I took over. Wrote one-line notes enclosed with cheques. As many as I could. Til sleep collected me.

Late the next afternoon, the red light flashed in my cubicle at Pearl Street. It was the manager of my apartment. A man I'd spoken to only once before, in the week before I moved here.

At first, I couldn't place him. Remembered as he told me – affably, polite – there'd been a problem with my rent. Specifically, its non-appearance. He was milder than he had to be. Said it often happened around the building. Blamed administrative foul-ups, computer glitches.

And I said Yes, that must be it. Thanked him for letting me know. Told him I'd deal with it first thing tomorrow.

And so it comes to pass.

I vacillated. Of course I did. Struggled with it through the night. Looked on it as treachery. Embraced it as a friend. Even my sleep – my invulnerable sleep – fractured and disturbed.

But it had to be. I knew that. The resolve of years, traduced by morning.

I rang from home, the letters scattered round me. And as I did I told myself:

They're only numbers. Two sets, eight digits each.

I just kept breathing. Spoke to a voice at the bank. Told them what I was calling for. Answered when they asked me for my occupation. Mother's maiden name.

From start to finish, it took less than ninety seconds. The unfelt movement of a certain sum from one illusory place to another.

Only a fraction of what was available. Not a penny more than necessary.

Into my current account. Taken from my savings. My parents' money. The money for Alice. Now chipped away at. Defiled.

But once it was done, it was done. And I had to carry on.

I used it as best I could. Settled my rent. Posted a cheque to Eleanor from the mailbox one block down from Scala. Secured the partial clearance of my overdraft, the debt amassed on my credit cards. And I would make this right. Replace it all. Present it to my child in the form I'd always meant to. Because this was just a stop-gap. A contingency.

Of course, I wrote another cheque to the girl in the hospital. A supplement to my existing standing order. Her condition had stabilised. She would remain in intensive care for the next few days, but the doctors were feeling hopeful.

I'd kept up my visits. Hovered in the corridors. Stayed just long enough to glean the basics, concealed and unnoticed.

I didn't want to distract her parents. For the moment, I would stand aside. Wait til I was needed. By her, or them.

And now, at night, in my living room, I reached for the phone. Made the call I had made so often lately. Listened to the five rings preceding the machine. Prepared to speak, to be recorded. Til a woman answered.

Hello?

I hadn't been expecting this. It took me a second to focus. Reconfigure my message. Translate it into conversation.

Ah . . . hello, I said. Is Phillip Reilly there?

The woman said nothing. And then she told me no. He wasn't.

I waited for more. A scrap of explanation. Til I heard the clatter of a mouth turned dry before she said:

He killed himself last week.

I'd already missed the funeral.

They sounded angry. The Marchmont Gym Warehouse. Downstairs with my mail, I found another letter issued by the company from whom I bought the Maximal. Or, as they tersely pointed out, was still in the process of buying.

Re: The Maximal IX 450

Customer Finance Manager Garry Lerner said, before reminding me the payment I'd missed in January remained outstanding.

According to our records, this is the third time we have contacted you. If payment is not forthcoming, we may be obliged to explore other avenues.

Amid the tumult, it had slipped my mind. I would deal with it. Prioritise. Scrawled GYM on my hand to remind me.

I told no one about Reilly. Told no one about anything. I could have. Right this moment, I should have been with Kushman, fifteen minutes into my second appointment. Except, I wasn't. I'd overslept.

In truth, I think I wanted to.

The phone was already ringing when I got back to the apartment. I made coffee as the machine clicked into life.

Oh . . . Matthew . . . It's David Kushman.

He said maybe I'd forgotten but I was supposed to be at his office. If I wasn't on my way, perhaps I could call to reschedule.

Except, I didn't. I couldn't. Not now. As all around me turned to flame. To walk through the park in the delicate sunshine, then sit pondering Reilly, the swan, the girl in the hospital, Alice's inheritance. My parents. My sister. Watching him smile.

I had the pills. They did nothing, but I took them anyway. I hadn't mentioned them to Grace. If I was spending the night with her, I'd take them before I left. Just like I did that evening.

An early dinner. My established pre-date sacrament. Bath, shave, nicotine gum. Pills, white and green and red.

We ate in the same Chinese restaurant we visited the first time. It struck me how good she looked. I forgot to tell her. In truth, I didn't tell her anything. She'd recount a story from the clinic

– so he's standing there barefoot, and the doctor –

or mention a news item she'd noticed that day

– about half the size of what it was last year –

And I'd hear her. But not really. Right, I'd say, occasionally, and she'd reach across the table. Link her fingers through mine. And I'd look down and see Joel Meskis's knuckles, or a sliver of dirt under Reilly's nails. Then look back up and catch a censored hurt across her face.

She kept trying the whole way through the meal. She'd ask if I was OK, and it was like the words were being held up on cards in front of me. One syllable at a time.

Fine, I said, I'm just a little tired.

And I'd think of how she deserved better. Wonder if she'd already worked that out herself.

Neither of us had dessert.

Just a coffee and the bill, she told the waiter. Then turned to me.

Please. Whatever it is . . . just tell me.

And so I did. About the letters, if nothing else. Jonah's boxes. I itemised their contents. Said I could feel them tainting me. Like washing in raw meat. Then, the waiter. My coffee and the bill. Credit card placed on the table.

You can't do this to yourself, she said. It's going to make you ill.

She suggested I take some time off. That we go to the coast. You know? . . . How we talked about.

And I said nothing.

I know you take what you do seriously. And that's good. But this . . .

And she trailed away. So I asked her what I should do instead.

I just think, she said, it's just . . . too much.

The waiter returned with my credit card. I strained my eyes at the small print of the bill to see if service was included.

Do you know what I mean? she said, squeezing my fingers between hers.

And I told her no. I didn't. That I'd made a commitment. That if someone put their trust in you, they should have that trust repaid.

But Matthew . . . it's as if I can see you . . . dissolving.

I pulled my hand from hers.

So what if, I said, you wake up tomorrow and decide not to go to the clinic? Just . . . not go. Who's going to look after the donors? Who?

Someone else . . . And I wouldn't do that anyway.

Someone else. Right. Someone else'll always do it. But what if they don't?

We were talking no louder than any other diner. I guess people just pick up on the friction. Their glances fell upon us. I put the card back in my wallet. Produced the newspaper cutting.

You see? I said. This *means* something to me.

And outside, we stood facing. My arm extended for a taxi.

I'll show you, I said. I'll show you what it means.

She didn't argue, even when I told the driver where we needed. She just looked sad.

Now, I talked. Through the journey and on into the hospital. About the girl, the nature of her condition. My attempt at becoming her donor. The visits here and money given.

A porter by the elevator.

Sir, he called after me. Sir . . . You can't just . . . Sir!

I took Grace's hand and led her up the stairs, to the third-floor room where I guessed the girl had returned by now. Saw the mother there, asleep in the bed nearest to the door. The girl beside, an oxygen mask over her face now, misting up every time she exhaled.

Do you see? I said. It's all the same. They're all the same. Her, I said (jabbing at the glass), and Jonah. And all of them.

I flung my arms out at the empty corridor.

All of them. Sent blind into the forest. And I know, I *know* what you're going to say. That they're not the same. But I help them both. I'm there for both of them. If Jonah needs me, I'll be there. And the same for her. That's *my* commitment.

Now, my voice was raised.

It's not my role to judge one person's hardship against another's.

Grace just stood there next to me. Then figures, motion. A security guard, burly, deadpan, jogging softly toward us. And the father. With coffee and magazines. The four of us now. The security guard asking did I know what time it was. The same from the father, only louder. Face just inches from mine. Questions peppered with obscenities. Demanding to know what I thought I was doing. The security guard at his side. The mother appearing from the room, shaky and bemused. The five of us now.

You're always here, the father said. We don't even know you and you're always here. So what do you come for?

A nurse running from the other end of the hallway. Doors opening behind her. The six of us now, plus audience. The nurse telling the security guard to fix whatever the hell was going on here. That patients are sleeping. And the father, again:

What did I come for? What did I want here?

And when I tried to explain, he pushed his face into mine and accused me of being a ghoul. Of treating his child as a freak show.

Is that it? he said, nodding at Grace. Take your girlfriend to the freak show?

No, I said, but he just pointed through the window of the room.

That's my daughter. Do you understand?

Grace, crying now.

I tried to calm the situation. Told him I wanted nothing more than to see his child healthy. That I'd volunteered as a donor, albeit fruitlessly. Was helping with the medical bills as best I could. It only made things worse.

So you think you've bought a ticket? he said.

The security guard came between us. Pulling me away by the sleeve. I heard it rip.

I only want to help, I said.

The mother, crying too now.

We don't want your help, the father screamed. And we don't want you here. Then he called me a sick bastard.

I turned, and Grace was halfway back down the corridor. Her shoulders heaving. I followed, guard behind me. The father still bawling.

Grace was in a cab by the time I got downstairs. I watched her leave, the guard watching me. Then escorting me outside. And the traffic keened an elegy as I walked back through the city night.

Connie Soon foresaw it all. All this time, she knew.

Even with the bathroom door closed, Julian can hear them. His friends, across the hall, inside his room, vacantly riotous. He holds the blade under the water, a rich beard of foam over half his face, cheeks and jaw, under his nose. The third time in his life he will do this. Enough fuzz collected to merit the effort. Tonight, he's going out. They're all going out. To the boat.

Another noise, more specific. Something falling, something breaking. Xavier and Balthus, spawning damage.

He should have seen it coming. Their ruin of the money lending. Always too quick to use their fists, too eager to throw punches.

For them, the money was just a bonus. The violence was the point. And yet he didn't stop them. Never raised his voice to protest.

In the wake of his suspension, his parents have done nothing. His mother cried, of course. That's all. His father yet to comment. He expected to be grounded here, confined alone, his profits seized. And still he's going out tonight, with money in his wallet. In time, he's sure, his allowance may be restored.

He draws the blade across his face, down, along his chin. Uncertain of technique. Leans in to his reflection, tries to mimic how he's seen this done in commercials.

A cut. Just small. On the underside of his chin, as it turns into his neck. This has happened – in different places – both times he's previously shaved. Unsurprised, he tends to it. Antiseptic, then a plaster. Another barrage from his room. And Connie Soon predicted this. Divined it all.

Last week Connie Soon, the only daughter of the Hoffman's former neighbours – Julian's best friend from six to eleven – wrote him a letter. She does so twice a year, despite the studied brevity of his replies. This one, like the others, contained no sudden revelations, just simple queries, cheery updates. Receiving it, he found himself devoured by nostalgia. Read each guileless, plain-hearted sentence and thought of himself as Connie knew him, a nervous boy who fed the school pets at lunchtime, was best friends with a girl, enjoyed and excelled at chess and academia.

And he sees that boy in the mirror now, covered in a mask of shaving foam, til his father's pinched features overwhelm his own.

Julian last saw Connie two years ago, the summer after her family moved away. She was visiting the city for an orthodontist appointment. Stayed for a night in a bedroom down the hall. An awkwardness had grown between them. He was, in truth, embarrassed. Anxious at how this – how she – might look to Xavier and Balthus. When he was younger, they bullied him. Now, they were inseparable. He didn't want to risk that. And before she left the next morning, she told him she was glad he'd made new friends, and he heard the caution with which she spoke, and then she said:

You're not like them, Julian. Not really. No matter how you try, you never will be. And I think they're going to bring you trouble.

Then, he ascribed it to envy. Now, he knows she was an oracle. He sluices the last of the foam off his face, the plaster coming loose as he does. Steps back across the hallway, into the bedroom.

There you are, cowboy, Balthus says. Ready for a good time? Then a second til they notice his plaster, hanging from his face now. Shriek with derision. And Julian contracts. I need to make a call, he says. Steps back outside.

I pulled my elbows hard into my ribs, the lactic acid flowing through me. Tucked in position on the natural ash rower, as I had been for an hour. The phone off the hook and curtains drawn.

There are clothes on the floor. A molehill of fabrics over by the laundry basket, abandoned there last night. Grace adds to it now, undressing and leaving the cast-offs at her feet. Never would have done this before. With Jerry watching, beady, finicky. Even in her old apartment, still too nervous for the severance of habit. Here, for now, they can stay where they are.

She stands at the bedroom mirror, her face still blotchy from the tears. Prepares to pluck her eyebrows, as she does once weekly, carried out last thing to allow any redness to fade overnight. Brushes them into shape with her fingers. Holds the tweezers vertical against her nose to check for symmetry, then at 45 degrees to the outer edge. Notes a stray hair, dark and fine.

Anger. She's been trying to figure out quite what she's feeling and now, abruptly, she does. Rage at her own resurgent frailty, her limp paralysis as Matthew dragged her into the hospital and his private theatre. She thinks of the father, his own grand fury, Matthew's carrion pallor as he stood there, inert. Making her complicit. It will not work. She knows this now.

She lifts the tweezers, delicately isolating the single hair at the corner of her brow as if performing surgery on a baby bird. Readies the jaws and pulls so quickly she doesn't even wince. And then it's done.

The water dragging me forward. Bending my back. Chest desperate for release. Trying to make just one more stroke.

Just try and relax it, Naomi says. Imagine it falling into my hand.

Alison lies face down as she cradles her foot. Leg raised behind her from the knee. An understated grip. The way you hold fruit. Naomi asks her again to release the tension. Lets go and replaces the towel. Moves up the table, addresses the shoulders.

As a last-minute favour, she has brought her table to Alison's apartment. Here to attend to a spasm in the back. Still won't take full payment. Now she presses into aching flesh. Solid knots of tissue.

Alison uncoils, drifts into reverie as Naomi rolls clenched fists across her body. Thinks of herself as she was last night, sketching with charcoals in an outsize pad, then returning to the books. She has them all now, piled in the corner, just out of her sight as she lies here. Eric Handler's every published work. Sits in the evenings absorbing them, her sketches laid around her, confidence swelling, self-belief flourishing. She feels Naomi find the very centre of the ache, kneading til her eyes roll up.

And Eric Handler says: *Never underestimate the symbolic in announcing a new beginning. It may be as simple as painting your house, or dyeing your hair. You could feel something more profound is needed. Change your name maybe. Nothing excessive. A single letter might be all it takes. One tiny letter the key to flying free.*

Naomi leans over her. A single finger on each hand pressed hard between the shoulder blades, then tracing a line down Alison's back. Just let it go, she says, hushed but adamant. Just let it go.

*

311

Til my grip gave way and my ams were jelly, and I stepped from the machine. With my arms still exhausted, I stumbled to the bathroom. Sat on the edge of the tub, and reached up for a needle.

A footstep at the bottom of the stairs. Not heard soon enough. A shape in the doorway before Eleanor can react. Why did she have to do this here? Should have had enough resolve to keep it away from the house. She knows there's nothing she can do now. Even if she tries to conceal it, the evidence will remain, hanging in the air. Too late.

She freezes as Alice shuffles into the living room. Awkward, waddling steps that Eleanor wishes she wasn't taking. Each one seems to take an age, til she comes to a halt in front of the couch. Can't sleep, she says. Been trying for hours.

She stops rubbing her eyes, looks up at her mother and says, confounded:

Why are you smoking?

It started as a tickle. A bristling itch in the middle of my throat that I first became aware of right before falling asleep. The cough it spawned woke me, barking and sputtering a full half hour before my alarms. From then, a rattle every time I breathed. Failed expulsions in ten-minute intervals.

I set a water bottle beside my coffee in the office down the hallway at Dutch Street. Jonah looked in on me an hour after I arrived.

Sounds nasty, he said, as I hacked through the pleasantries. Then retreated to his gingko and the view.

I knew I'd have to tell him. He would have to learn the truth; and, for all my misgivings, the truth could only come from me. It was my responsibility.

I waded through the letters in the interim. Made bequests to one in four of those I felt deserving. After writing a cheque to a teenage girl with osteoporosis, I took the dozen steps to Jonah's private office.

Knocked, and waited. A non-specific grunt that I took to be Come in.

He was on the phone. Looked up and held his palm out.

. . . no, I told him I thought that was ridiculous . . . OK . . . Hm-hm . . . That's fine.

And I stood, hands behind my back, tapping my foot til he was done.

Hi, he said, and asked if everything was OK.

I met his eyes and spoke.

It's Reilly. He's dead.

Yes, he said. I know.

Then he told me that Reilly's mother had called him. He'd assumed she'd called me too. He hadn't been able to make it to the funeral, but he'd sent a wreath. Reilly, he said, had hung himself. He'd used a necktie.

It's very unfortunate, he said.

Glanced down at his phone, and then back at me.

Sorry . . . I have to take this.

And he picked up and answered.

Hours later, I was siphoning unread letters into my bag when he put his head around the door.

Busy? he said.

No, I said, my cough erupting.

I'm heading out for a few hours. You'll probably be gone by the time I get back.

Probably . . . if that's OK.

He said that was fine. He just wanted to run something past me. A favour, he said. There was a problem with Julian, he said.

He'd been suspended from school. There'd been another fight, of sorts. Then he explained in detail.

Jonah's son and a group of his friends had been discovered extorting money from younger and more vulnerable students. Violence had been used. Julian apparently the ringleader. Obviously, Jonah said, punitive measures would be taken at home. But he wondered, he said, he and Christina both

313

wondered, in fact, if I could talk to him on their behalf? Find out how such a thing could have happened. Given that the boy seemed to trust me, and to despise them, could he maybe have him call me?

I was under no pressure. It was entirely my decision.

Sure, I said. Of course.

And I thought of Julian in the bathroom of his school, watching me pin a boy his own age by the throat. Showing him the benefit of force. Directing him.

Great, Jonah said. That should put Christina's mind at rest.

He left and then I did. Took the bus home. After my pills, I called Kushman. Now, I wanted to reschedule.

I understood nothing and my heart was breaking.

Three rings in, I got his machine. As my guide rope began to thin and fray, swinging me in cold vacancy. The spaceman's kid, lost among the stars.

And my intercom buzzed. At first, I didn't even know what it was. The sound of visitors. Gingerly, I took the receiver from its mounting and held it to my ear.

It was Carl. He told me, I think, there was a man in the lobby asking for me. I said I couldn't hear him, and he repeated himself.

A policeman, he said. Shall I send him up?

I told him yes. And I waited at my door, staring down the hallway. Mind spitting with reasons for a police officer to come here. Black and fearful all.

Til he stepped from the elevator and walked toward me. Olive complexion, weary curl of the lip.

Mr Viss? he said, training-manual courteous.

He told me his name, what station he was from. Asked if he could come in.

Sure, I said. No bodies under the floorboards here.

He peered at me, scornful, and in he came. Holding my card from The Greatest Gift. Weaved between the weights and toys.

I'll get straight to the point, he said. We've received a complaint. About you. An allegation of harassment.

314

He told me the name of the complainant, and it sounded unfamiliar. Then he mentioned the hospital.

Right, I said.

The father of the girl with the lung disorder.

He asked if I realised the gravity of the situation. That I could also be charged with trespass and disorder. This wasn't, he said, a matter to be treated lightly.

I was listening intently when the phone rang. He paused as the machine clicked on.

Uh, hi . . . this is Julian . . . Hoffman. My mother said –

Sorry, I said. Do you mind if I take this?

And I saw what he saw. A grown man with an apartment full of toys, fixated with a child, summoned by an adolescent. I tried to keep it brief as Julian related the circumstances of his suspension, the series of dire misunderstandings during which in any case he had, of course, simply been a bystander.

Right, I said, glancing over at the policeman in my living room. Listen . . . this isn't the best time.

I asked how long he was out of school for, and he told me a fortnight. I suggested he come into the city one day the following week. We could talk properly then. He sounded like anything would improve on where he was. We agreed on Tuesday. The cop still here.

Sorry, I said. Do you want . . . a coffee?

No, he said. I'm done here.

He told me he didn't intend taking any further action at this stage, but I should see this as a warning. A shot across my bows. The complaint would stay on file, he said. Then he moved toward the door.

The guide rope shredding. Preparing to snap.

For a long time after he went, I couldn't move. As soon as I was able, I took the toys out of harm's way and into the loft. Stayed there with the lights off, soundproofed by concrete.

I coughed as I read through my post. It was getting worse. A hand-addressed envelope in among the junk.

I recognised the writing immediately. The sloping down-stroke of the Ts. Curt finish lines of the Bs.

The letter itself was typed. A message from my wife in clean black print, CC'd to her solicitor. Three lines of text, announcing her intention to divorce me. Explaining I would soon be hearing from her solicitor, named above, to begin the legal closure of our marriage. Signed Eleanor Carlin. Her maiden name.

A supplementary note, handwritten, folded inside. It said she was sorry to have to do this, like this, but she felt she had no choice. Surely it said enough that she'd had to take my address from the sender's details on one of my parcels to Alice.

She had to move on, she said. As I had. She would never, she said, fully comprehend why I left the way I did. Packed a bag on our daughter's birthday, never came back. But in time you adjust. Admit your resignation. And this was hers.

By the time I reached the final lines and their sincere hope we could reach an understanding over my visiting Alice –

assuming you might want to in the future

– I was shaking. Two thousand volts fed into me. I faced the wall. Attacked it with both hands and head.

It must have been five minutes before I stopped. A minor cut above my right eye and a plug socket loose by my feet, kicked out at in rage.

I was due at The Greatest Gift. I tore the letter into pieces.

On my way to Pearl Street, I bought cough mixture. Viscous green syrup that tasted like old mint and paint strip-per. The woman that served me began asking me about other medications I might be currently taking, but I coughed so hard when I tried to speak the other customers backed away, so she just took my money and bagged it.

When I got to the office, Mike took me to one side, unsmiling and panicky. Said he'd had a call from the police yesterday demanding my home address. I told him a relative had been in a workplace accident. Everything was fine, but I'd been down as next of kin, which was sad really as I hardly knew her. He seemed pacified.

OK, he said. Just . . . don't feel like you can't talk to me if there's anything you ever . . . want to talk about.

The phone room seemed busier now. I threw myself into every job available. Claimed any call I saw unanswered. In the spaces between, I had Jonah's letters. I kept no running total. Just gave and gave again.

That night I drove to the North Duke Blood Centre. The night after, the Cavendish Medical Trust. Secreted nail clippings in my colleagues' keyboards, left deposits in the ice buckets at bars.

Kushman returned my call. I didn't get the chance to phone him back. I meant to. Events just overtook me.

And I parked outside Eleanor's house with a card I bought for Alice at a petrol station, drinking green medicine and trying to find a song I knew on the radio.

She can't believe it lasted so long. Never fell apart on her. This worn-out relic that rendered its contents underwater woozy or simply inaudible.

Grace stares at the scuffed metal of her tape recorder. Hasn't used it in months. Just put the machine in a drawer and left it. Felt so easy. Til now. With the machine back in her hand, remembering this morning's untaped exchange with perfect, glacial clarity. Carmen assuring her with daytime talk-show sincerity that she was doing the right thing. That if he made her unhappy she should call it quits. And she agreed. Told Carmen she didn't know if it was her fault. Just knew she had to end it.

And tonight, in her apartment, she waits for his arrival as she has so often. Sometimes he shows, and sometimes he doesn't.

Carmen said that she wasn't going to mention this, but William had told her the last time that your friend (her phrase) came round, his arm looked like he'd been (and then she dropped into a murmur) . . . injecting.

317

He'll be here soon, if he comes at all. Maybe she should tape this, just as a one-off. For reference. See what works and doesn't. Do the job for real next time.

The soup's nearly ready.

She just wants this to be civilised. Free of drama. She asked him over. Told him there was something they needed to discuss. She wrestles down the urge to tape, to practise. Defer. Hears the doorbell, right on cue. Summons her will, throws the recorder back into the drawer. And lets him in. Coughing as he approaches.

She expected sombre. Instead he seems voluble. Kisses her as he passes through the door. Of course, he doesn't even notice the new couch in the living room. Just sits on it and starts to talk. More than he's talked in weeks. And when she can, she says she's glad he could make it. And he says he is too. Says she knows she's got things on her mind, but so has he.

She nods, glad they feel the same. Each sensing the relief of closure.

I've thought about it a lot, he says. I'm getting divorced. And I'm going for custody of Alice.

Her skin chills as she turns off the heat. This isn't what she planned at all.

It's time to move on, he says, as she ladles the soup into bowls.

Are you . . . Have you talked this through with –

There's no need.

She carries the bowls to the table where he sits now. Shouldn't have done this. Shouldn't have cooked. It was a bad idea. Should have just written him a letter. The way you're supposed to.

But look, he says, look, that isn't the important part.

And she lifts her spoon to her mouth. Wishes she knew how to get this back on course. All those hours with her tapes, she realises they only taught her to respond. He catches her eye, the way she thought she'd be catching his.

I've been thinking, he says . . . we should move in together.

She gags on her soup. Feels a drip from her chin, but he just carries on.

I think we're ready now.

And he reaches across the table and takes her hand in his.

It'll be the three of us, he says. Then maybe, in time, one of our own.

And finally, her voice breaks through. Pulls away her hand.

Stop, she says. Just . . . stop. This isn't what I asked you here for. I think . . . we need to step away. From this. From each other. I'm worried about you, Matthew. I have been for a long time. Your moods, your health. The hospital.

Months – no, years – of choked-down anger, pouring clean out of her now.

About, she says, the way you treat me. The missed dates. The silences. Why are you even with me? Do you even like me?

He starts to speak, but for the first time she can remember she says she hasn't finished. Talks straight through him.

You want me to have your child? I've never even seen where you live. Don't you think that's strange, Matthew? Do you think that's normal? . . . I just don't think I'm what you need. You know?

His face, confounded.

And you're not what I need either.

Without a word, he rises from the table. Takes half a dozen steps, then turns. Pulls bank notes from his wallet. Lays them by his bowl. The steam still rising.

This is for the food, he says. Quiet; almost timid.

And she stares ahead til she hears the door close behind him. This is hers. And she will, she knows, be happy here.

I slept in the loft after dinner with Grace. I didn't mean to. I'd just wanted to look at the toys. Must have lost track of how long I'd been up there, hearing nothing but my cough. Faithfully sipping at my medicine. I rocked a little, squatting, arms folded. Curled up and shut my eyes. Woke.

It was still dark. I realised the skylight must have had a tarp thrown over it.

I thought that I'd been out for seconds. Enough light from under me to let me check my watch.

Ten hours and forty minutes.

I was already supposed to be at Jonah's office. The sun greenhousing the apartment as I returned. I left again without bathing, in the last clean shirt I could find. Stopped by Mortimer and Upas.

I don't know exactly what I was there for, but whatever it was I didn't get it. I think Grace was hiding. There was a scene in the donors' lounge when I tried to locate her. William asked me to go. I became confrontational. The cough mixture had me skewed, the caffeine edgy, and between the two I was ragged, unbalanced. Eventually, he bundled me outside. I flung abuse at him – his hair looked like a woman's, and so on – til I started drawing stares from passers-by.

And right now I'm falling.

Neither gaining speed nor losing it.

Gravity = air resistance.

Terminal velocity.

Beyond the first floor.

It's odd. I only ever see the guy that lives there when I'm shot through with tension. I'll walk from the building, and I'll see him – rotund, late thirties – walking in. And he always looks tense too. Seems that kind of guy. Though I guess he must think the same of me. And we'll step around each other and lock eyes and smile, tensely.

Asika Bu lies on her side, the way she has for an hour. Eddie Reece on his knees adjacent, vigilant, prepared.

Asika Bu is six years old. Pure-bred Abyssinian. Til recently a show cat. Escaped through the first-floor window the week before Christmas. Returned the next day, unkempt but safe.

Safe, and pregnant. Taken by some filthy stray. Eddie, inconsolable. His three-time champion, heavy with mongrels.

Today is the second he's taken off work. Eddie works in surveillance. Not so glamorous, he's constantly explaining. Adulterers and con men. Nothing much important. So once Asika went to her queening box, he cleared his diary. Waited as she lay on her side. The way she has for an hour. Til, now, he sees her push.

They're coming. Breaking from her and he wants to help. Soothe her like he does in storms. But he knows he isn't needed really, with his towels and antiseptic.

That's it, honey, he whispers anyway. A fierce contraction, then another. He sees the head, and gasps. Stares in amazement as the body follows. Pinky brown. Wrinkled chamois. Eyes shut tight. A cocktail sausage on ignorant legs. Passing from its mother now.

The most wonderful thing he's ever seen. He clasps his hands in joy. Gets ready for the others.

I arrived at Dutch Street ninety minutes late. I'd never been ninety minutes late in my life. Concocted an excuse for Jonah. He, of course, was fine about it. And I sat in the office down the hallway, continued with the letters til the second box was almost done. Immersed in productivity. One in four my own.

It was late that afternoon when I next saw Jonah. Glancing up, he was at the door. He was supposed to be at a meeting in Canonbury. I mentioned it, and he said he knew. He was running late. But he'd wanted to catch me before he left.

Everything OK? he said.

Great, I said, and coughed so hard I almost strained my neck. He said maybe I should talk to a doctor as he perched on the corner of the desk.

Listen, Matthew, he said. I think we can call off the project.

Oh, don't worry . . . I can finish them tonight. They'll be ready for you tomorrow.

No . . . I mean, call it off. Period.

I tried to fathom what he might be suggesting.

But there's so few left, I said.

I can see that, Matthew. You've done an excellent job.

But you still want me to stop?

He said he did. I could wrap them up now and then, from tomorrow (his phrase), everything would be back to normal.

321

He said something had come to his attention which rendered it unnecessary to continue. I still didn't get it. I told him that, again. He looked at me as if unsure why I might be pushing this.

I'll tell you what's happened, he said.

He'd met with his accountant that afternoon. During their conversation, certain sums became relevant. In essence, he said, there were various situations from this financial year he could write off as a tax loss. Which therefore annulled the need for donations to charity.

It was a tax loss? I said.

And he said he'd assumed I'd known that.

It's very standard, he said, like he was astonished I could be so rustic.

And now you've got a different one? . . . So you're not giving anything to anyone?

He dodged and euphemised. Talked of uncertain climates, sensible approaches.

Is it Reilly? I said, and he tinkered with his shirt cuffs. Is that your tax loss?

One of them, he said. Look, I know you've put a lot of energy into this. But we live in precarious times. You must be aware of that.

I gazed across the letters. Their trauma and despair. The three in four that would go unanswered. A pulse of loathing like air in my bloodstream. I opened my throat. Let the words come.

Did you know before? . . . About the gambling?

He shrugged. Told me naturally he'd had his credit history examined. Had his suspicions as a consequence.

Maybe, he said, it takes one to know one. Though personally I do try not to gamble more than I can lose. I think I may have told you that before.

It was only when I looked at him that I saw the contempt.

You seem very hostile, he said, returning to his feet. And I really can't see why. I didn't take him to a casino. I didn't deal the cards. I didn't even pursue him when he flushed away my money. All I did was give him the means to make something of himself. So what am I being accused of? My accountant deals with the figures. I didn't know they'd stack up like this. If I had, I wouldn't have asked you to start the project. But this is just a contingency. Plan B. Reilly goes up in flames, I salvage something from the wreckage. You're going somewhere hot, you take a jacket in case it gets cold. You're not around, I use the other guy.

And my sense of time and place began to crumble. Drifting into entropy.

What . . . other guy?

The other guy . . . If you're busy or I can't get hold of you, I'll call the other guy. From the other place. Definitive VIP? Something like that. It's not a big deal. My schedule's hell. There's always too much to do. You know this. I must have mentioned him.

No, I said. You never did.

I must have. He's the guy who likes cooking. The one from Rush Street. Actually, he's the one who always chose your bodybuilding stuff.

It isn't bodybuilding, was all I could think of to say. It's general fitness.

Fine, he said. All I'm saying is you have to have a contingency. It's no reflection on you. Just logistics. If you're here, working on the project, then I need someone else to send flowers to Reilly's funeral. You get it? If you flake out and go missing for a week, then I need someone to take your place.

I didn't go missing, I said. I was ill.

Whatever. You see my point.

And he cracked his wrists in turn.

Why are you looking at me like that? he said. You're looking at me like I'm the devil. You think I'm the devil, Matthew?

I just thought . . . I was the one you relied on.

We're not married, he said. You know nothing about me and now I have to justify myself to you? . . . Look, Matthew, you're a very loyal guy. Loyal, and diligent. But you're the biggest baby I ever met. Did you know that? Did you realise that?

He gestured at the letters.

And there's nothing incumbent on me here. I never put a child in a wheelchair. A syringe in a junkie's arm. You need some tacky newspaper column tucked in your wallet to give you absolution, well . . . good luck with that. Personally, I don't use other people's misery to touch up my self-image. I work hard, I provide for my family. Can you say the same?

He shook his head at the sight of me.

The world, in all its pain, turns with or without you, Matthew. Now I've got to get to Canonbury. Go home. I'll call you when I need you.

And then he left.

I waited, then I paced into reception. Told Bonnie I'd just be a few minutes. She looked up just long enough to say that was fine.

Then I walked back, past the office I'd been using. Strode on into Jonah's. I knew where to find what I wanted. Inside his top desk drawer, key hanging from the lock, the royal blue leather document folder that held his company cheques. Pre-printed sheets of eight at a time, with perforated edges and carbon paper beneath. I removed it, carried it back up the hall. Then I sifted through the letters I'd picked out. Found their details. Gave as Jonah Hoffman.

I'd forged his signature so many times on notes to associates and Christmas cards, doing it now was effortless. By the time I'd emptied the folder of cheques, I must have replied to half the most deserving.

Then I wrote to the paper, describing Jonah's generosity. I told them they wouldn't find a better Good Samaritan.

In short order, I replaced the folder in Jonah's drawer, packed my bag with his cheques and the remaining unanswered letters, walked briskly out of Dutch Street. The cheques I posted right around the corner. The letters I brought home. Then I cleared the toys from the loft. Returned them to the apartment. It was almost time now. Alice's birthday was just two days away.

I stepped onto my treadmill. Then straddled the rower.
Broke for coughing fits and medicine.

And this was only yesterday. Back when I was somewhere
else entirely.

He reads it through again. Verifies the gist. It is 10.25 p.m. Jonah
skips through the preface of the letter he received today from the
membership secretary of the Avelden Country Club. Cuts to the
specific. As he thought. That he is, as of now,

barred from using the clubhouse and its facilities, pending
scrutiny of an alleged incident concerning the club's wildlife.

Jesus Christ, he says, aloud. Jesus, Jesus Christ. These people let dangerous animals loose on the course, and then they
have the nerve to . . . Jesus.

He approaches the window. Pulls it open. Looks down across
the city. Screams.

And when he's done, he sees the wave. Taller now than ever.
Closing. Responding to his bellows with vast rapacious industry.
It is 10.27 p.m. He kills the lights as he exits the room.

It wasn't a dream. I know it wasn't that. And at the time, it
seemed perfectly credible. Almost matter of fact.

Come on, champ. Just one hand. For old times' sake.

I heard him speak with my eyes still closed. Then opened
them. In bed, awake. Grimy orange half-light seeping
through the window.

Just one hand, champ. You'll do that for me, won't you?

A shape, six feet or so, outlined against the Maximal.
Nebulous, but there.

You know . . . this really is a great piece of equipment.

Moving slowly round it. Red hair caught in a glimmer.
Then still.

I tried to compose myself. Grasp the scene presented.

How did you get here? I said.

And I looked again, and he was gone.

Reilly? I said, into silence. Are you still –

We'll take the green table, he said, over by my wardrobe now . . . Low stakes. Nothing serious.

And it wasn't a dream. I knew that then, I know it now. All the same, I did what you're supposed to. Pinched my skin and bit my cheek. They just confirmed it. I was awake. And he was as real as me.

You know blackjack, right? he said.

I lifted my upper body, sat straight.

Come on, champ. Play a hand with me and my friend here.

Another figure, hazier yet, standing beside. Reilly's arm thrown around him/her. The sound of clicking fingers.

. . . This is Greg.

We've met, Greg said. I taught him the basics. Didn't I, Matthew?

I started to cough, reached out for the medicine.

Now that's an idea, Greg said. And I heard the chiming of glasses.

A toast, Reilly said. To Matthew.

To Matthew, they said, together. And everything he's done for us.

Til a car alarm howled outside. I turned, and when I turned back, they were gone.

Reilly? . . . Reilly? . . . Are you here? . . . Greg?

Waiting for one or both to reappear. Except they didn't.

I picked up the clock nearest to the bed. Just after four. And it wasn't a dream. It couldn't have been. I was – then as now – awake. And when I'm awake, I never remember my dreams.

I only felt disturbed when I thought of Greg. No one had seen him since he quit The Greatest Gift. His presence a reproach, surely; worse, a premonition.

I lunged out of bed. Found my address book in a kitchen drawer. Greg's number, recorded in the week of my arrival at Pearl Street. I dialled and it just rang out. Fifteen rings. Then twenty.

I rang Mike instead. Six rings in, he answered. I apologised for calling so late, or so early.

What's . . . happened? he said.

And I told him I needed Greg Hopper's address.

A weary intake of breath.

I think he might be in trouble, I said, skirting the nub of my dread. He groaned, and I heard his wife mumble in the background. He said he didn't even know if he had it. Asked if everything was OK.

I told him everything was fine. I just needed the address. After he found it and came back to the phone, he warned me it might be out of date. Greg hadn't been in touch since leaving, he said. Then he gave me the name of a street in Kastallet.

You do know what time it is, don't you, Matthew? he said, but I was already hanging up. Pulling on whatever clothes came to hand. A cream cotton work shirt from the laundry pile and the jeans I never felt comfortable in. My Rockport brogues. And I drove, east. My navigation eccentric. Control of the wheel intermittent. Had the roads not been so empty, there would have been a crash.

I got to Kastallet within an hour. Dense and illogical. Long, generic roads schemelessly hinged off each other. Twenty minutes spent finding the one I needed.

The house was shabby, garden overgrown. Curtains closed. I pressed the buzzer. Nothing moving here but me. Pressed again. Still no response. Held my finger to it, kept it there.

A single bump, then a clattering. Quiet. Then another. Til he opened the door. Stood pig-eyed and waxy in his underwear.

You, he said, like he wasn't even surprised.

You're OK, I said, relieved. You are OK, aren't you?

What time is it?

It's . . . 5.35.

We held our places for a moment, then he slid to the floor.

What are you . . .? he said.

I stepped inside. Helped him to his feet as he cursed, I think at nothing in particular.

You, he said. What do you want?

And he zigzagged back down the hallway.

I followed. Into the murk of his living room. He went for the light switch, missed. Steadied himself and tried again. Bottles, everywhere. A dank smell of many possible origins clinging in the air.

He lay face down on the couch. Sagging on the cushions. A moth, frantic by the ceiling.

I wanted, I said, to make sure you were OK. I . . . saw you.

Waited for a reaction.

. . . I thought maybe something bad had happened. I thought there might be something I could do.

His arm hanging free. Breathing dissolved into a nasal saw. Asleep.

I tried to find something to cover him. The best I could do was a towel, randomly mouldering on the floor. I draped it over his shoulders and left.

Drove west again, the rising sun behind me. Bound to immediate action. Sure of what I had to do once I got back to the city. There was nothing there for me any more. The only reason to return, collection and provision.

Inside the apartment I packed a bag of essentials. Toiletries and pills. Moved the toys downstairs and then to the car. Spread them across the back. More in the trunk. The overspill stacked next to me, high in the passenger seat. And I drove from Bethune Street once more, north this time. A day ahead of schedule. But what would be the point of waiting? I was returning now. To Alice and Eleanor. Coming home the day before my daughter's birthday.

The three of us could visit the park, before spending the evening teasing Alice with the promise of tomorrow. Then wake in my old bed, Eleanor beside me. A new start, a blessed continuance. Everything as it was and should be. The last twelve months a hollow aberration, already struck from our minds.

The sun up now. Driving safely. Ready to collapse into their arms, and to take them in mine.

The seconds pass, and then the weeks, and before you know it, you're there.

I parked up opposite the house. Another life, about to be regained. Baulked at the door, my legs stunned, immobile. Retreated and dallied by the kerbside. Then back to the door no more than a minute later. Failed again. Stepped away. Crept round the side of the house, and edged toward the kitchen window. Peered inside.

Alice sat with her back to me, eating cereal. Her elbow dipping, lifting. Hair past her shoulders. The colour a shade lighter. More like mine. A pale green dress that I didn't remember.

Her mother flitted in and out. She looked to have caught the sun. Her hair had changed too, darker, cut shorter.

Alice finished her cereal. Carried her bowl to the sink. Rinsed it out and placed it on the side. I saw her face just momentarily, and she looked well.

Til she left the room. Just Eleanor remaining. And she looked so happy. Happier than I'd ever seen her.

Then Alice returned, and the two of them walked from the room together, as the sun jutted out behind me and I saw my face reflected in the window. Hair standing on end, unwashed, deep slate pouches beneath my eyes. Skin kabuki sallow, a mottled growth across my cheeks and neck. Their calm replaced with my dishevelment.

What could I bring here? What could I promise but angst and upheaval?

The rest was chaos.

I retrieved the card from the dash of the hire car. Unsigned, now I think of it. Jammed it through the letterbox. Back to the car, again, grabbed as many presents as I could as they spilled from the open door.

And I ran. Just ran. Arms locked over my chest, weighed down with boxes in ribbons and wrapping. Every few steps, I'd drop one. Bend to pick it up, and the others would fall. There was nowhere to stop, reflect.

Eventually, I caught the bus. Despite the throng on board, nobody sat next to me. And as we lurched into the city I saw only one route left open. All others blocked or chimerical. So, to Plan B.

I stopped by the hospital. Didn't care if I was seen. Deposited the toys outside her room. Mouthed the single word, Goodbye.

An orderly ahead of me, jockeying a trolley. A nurse called out from a private room, and he left it unattended. Shorn of fear, I seized the opportunity. Took only what I needed. A pair of transparent baggies and a syringe.

It was coming up for nine when I got back to Bethune Street. Three hours before now. And I was certain. At peace with my design.

Inside the apartment, all my clocks were on their sides, rung out and exhausted.

And I couldn't even remember how this started any more.

But this is how it ends.

Tissue Paper

Lewis Brant pulls the safety belt across himself, adjusts into the driver's seat. The van, of course, unmarked. People see you coming and they're ready. No one's ever pleased to see the repo man.

Everything he needs is beside him. Essentials for the day ahead. Lunchbox stocked with the pulses and fruit teas that he knows he'll grow to like soon. His notices of repossession. Toolbag, boltcutters, Gita.

Of course people say stuff. His family. The guys at work. They call him Harry. Have done since he told them of his budding faith, nascent devotion to Krishna.

He doesn't care. Everyone at the temple, they've been wonderful. These past few months, those things he found so alien at first, the music, the cooking smells, have ceased to phase him. Even the sikhas. He keeps debating whether to have it done. Shave his head bar the ponytail. He's lost so much hair in recent years, he can't see why not. But is he ready for the rest? For the dhoti? The chanting?

He puts the van into gear, pulls out from United Recovery. Slogs through the late-morning thrombosis. Checks the address on the job sheet, the article(s) to be recovered. Maximal IX 450 Home Gymnasium; Name: Viss.

Another caged soul with eyes bigger than his pockets. For now, Lewis is caged too. He checks the map, drives on.

It took me a while to put things in order. Set them how I wanted. Not that this was what I wanted. Just what I was left with.

I exited the building. Visited the supermarket for plastic bags of ice cubes – fourteen-pound sacks that I bore under each arm – then the post office for stamps. The stamps for the letters I'd brought home yesterday. It already seemed such ancient history.

I replied to each one. Yours, Matthew Viss, I wrote at the end of the covering notes, folding the cheques inside the pages.

The last cheque I wrote was for Alice and Eleanor. I made it out to Eleanor Carlin. I thought she'd prefer that. It wasn't quite what I'd expected to leave. Not any more. Still enough to help. Enough to let them know I'd thought of them.

Then I collated the details of every charity I'd given to since coming here. Made myself a list. Each recipient of a standing order or single, instinctive donation. A legion around the country, others from outside. All the places I would never see, but would for ever be a part of.

I calculated how much was left available. Then I called the bank and began the process. The severance.

I'd like to transfer some funds, I told the woman that answered. And then I started. A token, a gift, then another, and on. Down through the list.

She sounded hesitant. Unsure whether this was a joke and, if not, why I might be doing it. I just kept reading out the numbers. Clench. Unclench. Down through the list. Til everything was gone.

Each of my accounts stripped bare.

The woman asked me if this meant I wanted to close my business with Two Cities.

Yes, I said. I suppose it does.

And she started to tell me I'd need to visit a branch in person to do that. There were papers to sign, certain formalities –

But I was already hanging up. Dialling again. Ringing the couriers we used at Pearl Street. I told them I needed a package delivered on The Greatest Gift's account. Picking up from Bethune and Scala. Dropping off at Mortimer and Upas.

They said it'd be with me in thirty minutes. I rose and walked into the kitchen. Looked across the gamut of pills. Many, I remembered, were in the car, discarded. I still had the vitamins, miscellaneous supplements. Calcium, magnesium, selenium, zinc. GinsaMax, soy protein, liver caps, arrowfoot. All of the good things.

I moved along the line, opening the bottles, pouring out a smattering from each. I swallowed them with water, tried not to gag. Fired up the espresso machine. Drank one cup, two cups, three.

The baggies and needles that I'd taken from the hospital I now carried to the bathroom. Sat on the edge of the tub, tied my left arm off with my belt. I drew, then pumped the syringe into the baggie. Repeated til it was full.

My technique was messy, inexact. It held a pint but I may have taken more. A trail of blood at my feet. The second time, I used my right thigh.

And no little brilliance as I sealed each bag, threw the syringe into the trash. Dug out an empty packing case from the wardrobe. Stowed the ice along the bottom and threw the baggies inside. Taped the box shut, wrote To Be Collected on the side.

I almost passed out as I left. I think the door was still open.

I carried the box to the lobby, the letters balanced on top. Swayed beside Carl's empty desk. Called out for him, twice, til he emerged from the utility cupboard opposite. I put down the box and removed the letters.

Hello, Carl, I said. A courier's coming to pick this up. He'll be here any minute.

OK, Mr Viss, he said, turning back to the cupboard.

I stumbled to the end of the block and posted the cheques, then back inside. And when the elevator came, I took it to the ninth floor.

Into the loft.

Stood on a paint can, cracked open the skylight.

As I pushed from underneath, the tarp must have dislodged. The sun, abruptly glaring in my eyes. I drove it open all the way, grabbed the sides and hauled myself out. Til I was on the roof.

For a long time, I just stood there. Nine floors up, and looking down. Standing behind the cinderblock kerb that ran round the perimeter, on the surface that felt like rubber, asphalt, carpet, all at once.

Next, up.

And I let myself teeter, just a little, let my weight take me further, just a touch.

It is 12.15 p.m. At the fifth hole of the Avelden's prize-winning golf course, Jonah Hoffman readies his shot. Throws his left arm across his chest. His day, til now, blighted. Woken by the maid clattering, unable to load the dishwasher. In the study, a message on his voicemail. The girl he booked for this evening, cancelling. Returning to the bedroom, he bent down for his shoes. Held his middle finger to the lining of the right, then felt the heel abruptly split. Italian leather, now destroyed.

Til he decided to simply write off the morning. Face the afternoon anew, recharged. And if some clubhouse flunkey wants to take issue with his presence, then let them. Let them come here and do it to his face.

He wishes he could freeze-dry the moment to come, repeat the scene indefinitely. Each nerve and muscle never more alive.

Then, a snatch of conversation. Colour looms in his peripherals. Holding his stance, he raises his head, turns to the side. A teal buggy cruises past, humming. Teal is for guests. From the interior, two old men wave out, turkey necked and jaunty.

Jesus Christ, Jonah says, lowering his club. Jesus, Jesus Christ.

Inhale. Exhale. Breathe the clean air of the Avelden. The old men drive on. The caddy says nothing. Everything is as it should be. Again, he throws his left arm over.

Except he can't. Without so much as a tingle of notice, a dark wave of pain beams through his shoulder and into his left side, where it sits, lodged and radiating. Then a second. Jesus . . . the caddy must be attacking him. Lost to some hostile snap of psychosis. But no. The caddy stands dutifully off to the right. The pain takes up a level beat. Inhale. Exhale.

Except he can't.

He tries to catch his breath, opening his throat in futile, quickening gasps. Another buggy appears on the fairway. Black. Black is for security. A pair of men, huge and expressionless in military-style sunglasses, speed toward him. Jonah sees them point, then reach down for their walkie-talkies.

Attempts to breathe again, gulping madly like a fish on land, heat in his nerves, dead weight on his chest. Doubling over, he drops his club. The caddy grabs for him as he keels forward, saying something that he can't make out, and his eyes bulge and flicker, the pain gathering to swallow him.

And here, miles from the ocean, face down on the Avelden's splendent grass, the sunlight fades, and Jonah Hoffman's mouth fills with the acrid, primal taste of seawater.

Straightened my back, looked down again. This time it was right there, up close and personal.

You leave a room just to get some air and when you come back everything's wrong. It all looks the same, just how you left it, but the milk's sour inside the fridge, you don't know the language they're using on the radio, and none of your clothes seem to fit any more. Can't tell if the sun's out or it's raining, how either one's supposed to make you feel.

The people in a huddle on the pavement down below, I took their pain, their joy, their absolute indifference, and I plugged right in.

And you start to explain but your tongue gets thick in your mouth and you're just making nonsense sounds with drool running down onto your shirt.

How long will this take?

The arch of my left foot floating in nothing. Then the rest. My right solid. That's quality of grip. The handiwork of children.

I guess after enough disillusion you finally just take the hint. The fated shimmer in the back of your mind that you try and pretend isn't there.

337

I was just so tired. And I gave my acquiescence. A plea for resolution.

You know, right this moment there's eye banks desperate for your corneas. You can help the blind to see.

To not have to struggle into each day and know nothing I could do would ever be enough.

And no angels would come to save me.

My right foot was on tip-toes. I closed my eyes and threw my shoulders forward.

Lewis Brant knocks, and the door glides open. Left ajar, drawn to, that's all.

Mr Viss . . .? Are you there, Mr Viss?

A would-be creep into the apartment, stealth undone by girth, ungainliness. He feels he should announce himself. Loudly declares the name of his company, legal rights of repossession.

His fingers dip into his pocket, anxiously squeeze his japa beads. He yearns for the solace of the temple. Instead, he steps into the bedroom, forehead rumpling at the sight of the Maximal, its smooth black pads and chrome. A shrine to the body. The tool of a narcissist. He refers again to his clipboard, identifies it as the article.

Leaving the bedroom, he checks the apartment again. No tenant hiding, poised to rush him. He returns and crouches at the base of the machine, opens his bag, removes his spanner. Stands, begins to disassemble.

And downstairs Carl hunches inside the utility cupboard, preparing for a test he will sit tonight on the different meanings of similar sounding words. An M, an A. Two Ts, an E and an R. Even now, it takes time for the letters to make sense in one another's company, for words to take shape, those words form sentences. Waiting, staring at the fine black strokes, is seldom less than gruelling. Finally, they come.

Matter. I have an umbrella, it does not matter. Mutter. Please do not mutter, I cannot hear you. Mother. Hello, Father, where is Mother? Motor.

As Julian Hoffman crosses Bethune, and slows at the junction of Scala. This must be it. Where he's meant to come. Arranged last week with the concierge.

He wonders what the apartment's like. How much does a person like that make? Whatever. It can't be worse than home. Maybe he should find a job, move out. A place round here can't cost much.

And a bullish step takes him into Scala, and he looks up just in time to see –

A final swell of memory as I drop past the ground floor.

It's nothing that you think it is. Nothing you expect.

Everything just balled up into one. A blinding glare and shambles like all that's gone before. No dispassionate chronology, just the white skies of a bomb.

A fat Windsor knot on a blue and salmon necktie, the corpse of a swan by a thicket of reeds. An assault in a school bathroom. Burgundy lipstick and a drunk, getting drunker. An outraged father, an unneeded wheelchair, a magician with shattered hands.

A boy of five in a hospital, watching a patient die.

Her name was Madeline.

My father, jumping from the window of a burning house.

And I never gave them reason to worry, and I never gave them cause to celebrate.

They'll tell you that time heals.

I think it rips you open.

It starts with an aperture, so tiny you tell yourself it isn't really there. And all the while it's hollowing inside of you.

And now I know I'm just one among so many stories, fibres bound, inseparable. But the pounding of my heart's noise.

Except it isn't mine alone. Another joins it, deeper, stronger. A sound I knew before, to start with. A dull thump from a perfect blackness. The dark not one of fear but safety.

And I see the grand mechanics now, the shape. The actions that I could have taken, every choice that would have stopped this. Not just in the last damned year, but through them all. A different life. A future.

I see it now with sure precision. The past just that and nothing more.

And it's funny when you notice how simple it is. So funny I could howl with laughter. Laugh til tears come streaming down my face.

All those chances wasted. So ridiculous when she thinks of it. The countless hours devoted to other people's meals and her own drab apprehension. Here it just seems farcical.

Raw Sienna, Yellow Oxide.

Alison called in sick today. Rang The Greatest Gift and told them she'd be back some time next week (once she's through her food poisoning). She can't, of course, remember feeling better. Stands at home before a canvas. An arc of paints laid out at her disposal. Each colour that she's missed with such quiet but ardent frequency.

Prussian Blue, May Green.

Had no proper overalls, so for now she's in her nightshirt. Scanning across the palette, and it all just seems so easy now.

Cadmium Red and Madder.

Brings the knife to purpose, makes a blend. Something bold, a marker. Then reaches out and takes hold of the brush. And on.

Structure White, and Flesh.

Til the last indiscernible beat, and a single frame.

And Alice, and Eleanor.

And I wish I'd left a note. Some means of explanation.

Told my daughter to be great in all the ways I never was, to cling with knuckles white and fierce to everything she has. Everything she is.

I just wanted to be –

It's not important.

Nothing special, none of us.

But this is all we have.

I had so much to say and I talked about figments.
Broken dolls and fallen gods.
Confusion
Anger
Solitude
Regret
Illumination
Sanctity
Retrieval
Completion
Exeunt
As my skin touches ground, like chiffon against gauze.

First, if necessary, you cut the paper down to size. Then, lay the gift in the centre of the sheet. Next, fold the two outer edges of the sheet across the gift, with an overlap of maybe half an inch. Take a strip of tape, nothing more than you might actually use, and attach it over the join, lengthways.

And Eleanor Carlin sits cross-legged on the floor, surrounded by paper and presents. Seven gifts, modest but expertly chosen, to be opened tomorrow on the morning of her daughter's birthday. One for each year.

It's better, she feels, that she does this now. Came home in her lunch break to prepare things. And it's funny, how a notion will just snap into your head. But for every careless act this year and all those that preceded it, she thinks of Matthew now, like he's waving, adjourned in deep slow motion; and for all of that, she hopes that he's OK.

She stares at the wrapping, the bear with the trumpet, and tries not to dwell on anything but what lies inside these boxes.

And I'm sorry.

And Then, Again

It's between my wrist and elbow, inside my right arm, where there isn't any hair. That's where the itch is. And I'm trying to ignore it, but each time that I think it's gone, it comes back.

Obviously, I can't scratch it. If I could scratch it, I wouldn't be feeling it now.

My eyes can only open for a moment at a time. Like someone's filled the lids with concrete. But I see enough to know where I am. A window to the left of me, weather blandly overcast. A rail along the bedside, fitted with a meal tray. Machines adjacent, softly humming.

I've come to twice before now. Fleeting, indistinct. At first, I hardly registered the shock. My presence. Unknown hours later, I heard the doctors talking. To each other, either side of me. Their tone seemed optimistic.

Now I hold on long enough to glance down at my body. An armoured shell of milk-white casts. No pain, but I know it's simply buried under layers of medication. The restfulness synthetic. I bask in it anyway. My only problem in the world this itch.

I try looking to my right. Turn slowly from the neck, roll my eyes as far as they'll go, past the IV stand next to me and on toward the glass partition that separates my room from the corridor outside. Where a doctor stands with Eleanor, but then my lids draw closed to black.

And as soon as I feel able I open them again.

Alice, at my bedside. Peering at me, baffled. And I think for a second that our eyes meet, and in hers I see mercy.

I feel the air leaving me, then entering.

There's flowers on my left, I see, next to the machines.

A hundred wires and petals, in a room off a hospital corridor down which and beyond are always more like me, wounded and afraid. And most of them will live.